7WN513

aka

ISBN 2-913053-04-1 (FRANK, PARIS)
ISBN 1-904893-09-0 (WYNKIN DE WORDE, GALWAY)

A CIP catalogue record for this book is available from the British Library

Acknowledgments

Parts of this work first appeared in *Frank: An International Journal of Contemporary
Writing & Art* and *The Literary Review*. I am grateful to their respective editors and
especially to David Applefield for his interest early on in and the invaluable
support and care that he has brought to the aka project. Thanks also to Roger
Derham for his belief in AKA, and Sylvia Beach Whitman for hosting the book's
first launch.
Special thanks to Eric Koehler for the particular attention he has brought to the
visual aspect of the book. JL

The Publishers wish to thank participating independent bookshops for supporting
this initiative: Shakespeare & Company (Paris), Village Voice Bookshop (Paris),
Elliott Bay Bookshop (Seattle), City Lights (San Francsisco), Kennys (Galway-
www.kennys.ie) and Charlie Byrnes (Galway).

Published simultaneously by Association Frank in France and Wynkin de Worde
in Ireland. Copies 1 through 299 are numbered and signed by the author and can
be reserved at *www.readfrank.com* or www.deworde.com.

The book is published in two jacket formats, one plain the other illustrated. In the
illustrated version the cover art is "She had many faces," 1953, by Juanita
Guccione, oil on canvas, 37 1/2 x 31 1/2 inches. Copyright © 2006 Djelloul
Marbrook, www.juanitaguccione.com and used with permission. Cover Design
coordination: Design Direct, Galway.

aka

Jean Lamore

**Frank
&
Wynkin de Worde**

Paris & Galway
2006

To Maï Da-Zangandu,
her ancestors and her descendants

Other Works by Jean Lamore

Tideworks
L'Homme-Feu
The Kite
Poison Ivy
Sunstorm
Revue Mamba
Diario del Polisario

Contents

Backwater

Should we, like bonobos, mate freely in order to assure enduring social peace, or would it be preferable to fight for sexual possession in the manner of gnus or other feral ungulates, endlessly locking horns to gain control of a harem? A mere contemplator, idly drawing the smoke of fine cut tobacco through a long carbon stem engraved with those mathematical formulas that we have come to consider as the language of the Universe, thus am I engaged in philosophizing while standing aloof on the fringe of a desperate struggle involving a woman and at least three, no less, aggressive males who have almost succeeded in pinning her down. Should I, in turn, engage these other males, in what would surely be an unequal combat, for the possession of an estrous female? Intervening couldn't be a mere question of saving her from rape. Domination would be at stake. Participating in this struggle that's already well engaged could further develop primitive comportment which is daily becoming a growing value. Other solutions are multiple. Even the most cowardly, the most physically handicapped of individuals has a chance to engage in rapid romance, to procreate. The vilest manner of planting one's seed can be taken into consideration. In the present situation, I should remain a spectator, wait until the forfeit has been done, only to become an opportunist by taking my turn. And this is well, for I am of the first sort, psychologically, fearful and devoid of initiative while not far from being of the latter kind physically, recessive genes and centuries of adaptation to chemical pollution having done their work. It is said that man can adapt to anything and I'm a firm believer in this. *Cherchez l'homme!* We shall be flames, but alive, three billion years hence when the sun engulfs Cyana. However, the chance to observe the present spectacle, savour the denouement and then slink off, while taking no more risk than if I had been playing a senso-game,

9

would be my natural penchant. Why penetrate this pocket of micro barbarity that erupts here before me at the turn of the curb, round the street corner? Avoid, circumnavigate! Self-preservation, ease of spirit and a certain notion of civilization, prohibit participation, bind my limbs and anesthetize further cognitive process. And yet this unexpected spectacle exerts upon me an irresistible fascination. I'm drawn to it as was Saint Augustine's companion, Alypius, who couldn't keep from peering through tightly clasped fingers at the bloody spectacle of gladiators eviscerating each other in the arena. No sinner's fall shall this be for me!

Cheer on, break the ranks and leap down myself into this pit! I prefer to take example upon the many minor emperors of the interminable Roman decline, former slaves, barbarians or dwarves, become gods who hesitated not to partake of such sanguinary fare. Revel in it even. Cede to this beckoning. Answer the call, more of a blessing than a damnation be it. To befall, it matters little what fate. Plunge before it's too late.

Four hands should have been mine, a pair to cover the eyes, another to deafen myself with. But then, the scent arising from this event would certainly have sufficed to have bent my will and drawn me in. Perfume of marrow cracked open, lain bare to prying vulture's beaks, he who seeks, requires no guide to reach summits and peaks upon which offerings of flesh, human sacrifices, be they thine own, rest in the purest jest, awaiting to be paid for at the highest prices.

Yünnan is no longer a coastal area, but the highest slope. If you are to ascend, best be armed with plenty hope. Quaff not of this yill. It will make you ill. Wimple-broken water and shattered mirror reflect best the real image you bear. Mountain before you is no hill. Come now, spill blood, till it becomes flood. Say, —I will! She sings to me from beneath the body heap.

In I leap.

Howbeit this is the first of many forthcoming first encounters that I am to have with this woman, echeloned meetings that could form the prehistory of love, and through even, to its future, coming back then again to fill out intermediary phases but never forming a cycle or any manner of circuit, I very nearly withdraw and in so doing, could have passed by. Destined then would I have been to have shared the rest of my remaining lives with relatively inert companions, averting whatever thunders or blinds.

Emerge from backwater and oxbow, head into this swifter current. No longer wade but plunge into the cascade.

I'm wearing chain mail and carrying a mace. There's a strong taste of iron in my mouth. Maybe by some sort of capillarity, molecules from the oxidized ferrous material ride abundant sweat up to the lips. My skin is black, so black that if a spot of it were put on this paper, it would appear to eat a hole through it, this hole leading into abyssal darkness, the illusion created by obscuring matter in the foreground which appears to be a passageway to the depths of infinity.

Should I stop, control myself? A saint awaiting canonization, I must use extreme reserve, never become involved in situations, which could compromise my pending intronization, or unnerve. The ultimate acts of sanctity which I have undertaken? Effacing the images of man from desert regions, where towering Buddhas had been carved into the walls of mountains, bringing down the pyramids, bursting the friezes of Ankor Vat. No artwork shall ever be revered here again! I was a perfectionist, first removing the faces and hands with rockets shot from RPGs. Complete knock-downs were exhilarating, seeing the colossi tumble headlong into the hot sand. But a near-miss would create marvelous patterns, peppering the face with deep holes, chipping off the lip or an eye arcade, an ear even, which would come crashing down. Seek the stone brain. Finally, this massive destruction itself is certainly more of a chore than was the original creation of these blasphemous monoliths. I have become master at destroying these impure images. Talibans were immature amateurs! Rush to Mount Rushmore. Can we, with a single shot, amputate a nose, blow away George Washington's mouth? It's not even a question of being parsimonious with live ordnance. This is art of the highest form. Usurping the work of the wind, the rain and the sun itself. Other effigies, immense ones, must be fashioned in turn from higher mountain peaks, or wrought in the void from within the earth's bowels. Imagine the portraits of Sojourner Truth, Coretta Scott King, Patricia Lumumba (not Patrice), Namdi Azikiwe, Kwame Nkruma, Frantz Fanon or Sister Betty X, dug out from within the deepest shafts of austral mines. Glittering giant caverns forming portraits to be contemplated from within. But first, reclaim diamonds scattered to the winds, sweep through Antwerp and other diamond districts. This glittering reparation, a billion carats, will serve to inscribe the thoughts, biographies and doctrines of these more recent prophets, apostles and their companions upon the inner walls of their portraits.

With no ordinary steam, mouths smoke.

There is no direction here, no time scale, or rather, let's stipulate that we are beyond time scales, before the big bang – which I assure you, never occurred anyway – or after the end of all time. Nothingness then, you say? How very mistaken you can be. In these zones time is torrential, it is churning, bursting in cascades. It devours itself like the serpent engulfing its very own tail; it has already digested a full repast of direction, which it prepares to expulse in cosmic defecation. Geography, what say I, cosmology itself has become tidal. Just now, whole sections of the African continent rise up beneath my feet, slip over the Mediterranean and plow deep into Europe. Kinshasa and Lagos have penetrated Paris, Senetobia Alabama is a suburb of this new hybrid city and all asterisms in the night sky have changed. Los Angeles has gone under, born by the tectonic plate it rides to unsuspected depths where proximity with the core has turned all into fiery purée, an exotic spread with which I'll butter my bread.

New constellations must be invented. "Emancipation," I'll name this one with a man crawling through the coils of a giant snake, the man thinking that he's free just as the serpent strikes his heel, and I'm not really sure whether this section of the Universe hasn't just collapsed.

Perhaps the protagonist loses this fight, or then again, a miracle may spare him. My suit has shred, chainmail links tinkle onto the dirt at my feet, the banner I carry is still intact but splattered with blood. There is confusion between the golden cheetahs and the red background upon which they lie. I kick one of the assailants, the well-polished long pointed shoe reflecting the incoming face in a conical manner, the sole peels back upon impact.

Zanda, for I already know her name for this time, she's beneath them, her dress torn, her blouse rent open revealing the brown skin of her belly with the tight knot of the navel, a wild desperate look in her eyes. Clouds directly above, spiral in baroque columns, distinctly separate from one another, rising to the ionosphere. Am I entering heaven's gates after having taken a painless but lethal blow to the back of the head?

—I perceive things that you are incapable of detecting, blinking red particles streaming through the air, brilliant blue ones too and a green that

I can only describe as being sinople that lazily laces in blinding spirals. Your face, your thought patterns, everything so different from anything I have previously encountered. Something I wish to share with no one.

All of this I realize and utter instantly.

—Madman! Be yee one of they? she asks, gasping.

—I'll gather the sand over which you slip and preserve it preciously, base all of my future science upon just one of the scales which peel from your body as you struggle now. Offerings to thee I shall make during the night when footfall is rare.

The mace rises, comes down with a thud, breaks in two and falls in the mud. It's a sloppy struggle, the awkwardness of desperation which takes hold when death is at hand, is making itself felt. I'm getting dizzy, slowing down, yet I know there is no stopping.

Blunt brick fragment laying on the pavement beneath my face. Someone very heavy is on my back, reaching around my neck with burly forearm. The object on the ground fits perfectly into my hand, has just the right weight. It's not at all a brick but a piece of roofing tile, glazed green and upturned at the end, Chinese style, perhaps Portuguese from Macao.

—Flying eve chip, pagoda piece, I'll wield yee to smash noses and thicker bones.

We rest on a street bench, gasping for breath and incapable of speaking, blood welling from black holes where teeth are missing. Her mouth is very salty when we kiss. The sun comes down hard, drawing the sweat from our tattered clothing and baking our wounds.

—Your skin is so white, stay out of the light, she says, taking what's left of her silk blouse to fashion a turban with which she covers my head.

Looking at the three dead men who lay in odd positions, I realize that one of them, the heavy one, had attempted a classical police arm lock from behind; these, then, were no rival males. They had been after her with specific intent. One has fallen through the display window of a delicatessen, a long glass scimitar traversing his thorax. Smashed oriental pastry drops from the back of his head as I pull him out. His pockets are full of phosphorescent information to be placed directly upon the retina for reading, leaving hands free while in nocturnal operating mode. During the day they are difficult to make out, yellow metaphors. Here's a warrant for repossession of my vital organs with a priority list for the brain classified "abnormal, for research only."

A woman passes, bearing huge quantities of exotic leaves.

Naples has been recently rediscovered, unearthed after having been buried again beneath lava and cinder for centuries. Cargo ships lying on their flanks or keel up, Vespa scooters frozen in time with their riders fused to the seats, cigarette smugglers' long pointed boats loaded with contraband cigarettes, a gladiator's helmet, frescoes with blood red backgrounds, not Pompeian but new ones, depicting rippling green mahdist banners planted square in the hearts of people with no manners. Entire sections of suburban industrial zones are perfectly preserved. This will be of great utility, like Brunelleschi climbing atop the Pantheon of Rome to discover how the Romans had constructed the giant dome, we'll clamber amongst the twisted metal beams, the collapsed walls, to find the correct manner to reconstruct architectural marvels from this lost technology. No copulas, nor arches of stone shall we strive to make. Our quest will be for the understanding of how to construct again, these immense industrial warehouses fashioned from tin, aluminum and plastic materials, surrounded by acres of the flattest cement lots.

Just as we're beginning to mumble to one another, a glass van pulls up in front of us. It's full of body parts, livers, hearts, lungs, hands and heads that slosh. The driver leaps upon me, joined by to passers-by that had appeared totally aloof until this moment. They immobilize me, – the woman, was she then with them? Not the one being aggressed but the one bearing leaves – and amputate my left leg, using a saw-fish's bill taken from the natural history museum.

She's down too, the brown tight naveled-one, by my side.

—I can't stand the pain, take the brain! groan I.

—Not this time. Just reducing your mobility, one grunts, cauterizing the stump with a small blowtorch. A nurse squats over me, filling the reservoir of an electric tattooer's needle with a most brilliant turquoise colored ink.

Follows a brief period without light during which I'm transported, probably in circles. I awake as they dump me into a gutter. It's Senetobia.

—Wherever you go, we shall know.

I lie here for some time, nude except for a witchdoctor's compress covering the stump of my leg. They've finally done the irreparable. In the manner that zoologists used to mark animals for study, implanting computer chips in seal flippers, tagging sharks, painting rhinos, and banding birds, my testicles have been tattooed with the violent blue-green tracer pigment which only castration can remove.

I've lost a limb and this wasn't even Tanzania, Angola, or Cambodia. No minefields here, just crushing debts and ferocious collectors. Or so I think, not yet knowing the full extent of this very serious pursuit/dispossession game.

A phosphine rain comes down mixing with an ammonia mist. I'm wearing Bermuda shorts made of thin cotton, virtually transparent. Did you forget? Helium here is about thirty percent; the rest is mostly hydrogen. Light no cigarettes!

It's only three blocks away but freezing. Certain tropical birds drop dead. I especially regret the death of the song thief, of the migrating species which had accumulated such a vast repertoire of calls from distant lands. His plumage? Hues beyond ultraviolet. Looking through the transparency at the edge of his feathers you could observe the fine loops extending upwards for thousands of kilometers before returning elegantly to the corona of the solar surface.

Wrap myself in a discarded carpet that I bind with electrical wire. Pass harfangs, snowshoe hares and wapitis wandering through deep white drifts.

—Where'll I bury my singing friend?

—In a snowdrift, naturally. Punch a hole, deep tubiform, and insert him beak first. He resembles early interpretations of the bird of paradise when it was supposed that they had no feet.

—A crutch? This iron piping will do.

—Give it a curve and lean upon it, she says from just behind.

—Is the legend of Iron-Crutch Li here to resume? This crippled beggar's body mine again to employ? No Taoist am I!

And so she is not with them in spite of the fact that she growls.

Kneels, feels, heals. Overhead, four immense globular clusters of highly concentrated stars.

—Don't go seeking, I shall bring them to you.

—Those of us who are dead, slumber they? Them, nothing? Do awaken, or are they taken to someplace of forsaken?

She shivers as large leaf under tropical rain. The night falls upon us, the sky having the true depth of the infinite and nothing there trembling. Her orifices, the mouth, the nostrils and the sex are red within, colcothar and cinnabar. Between the faults separating the scales that adorn her body are born flames that emerge with small blue tongues licking. Bring dim light to wrap round us flicking. Love, it is thus.

—If you're unprepared to so suffer this amputation, insufferable mutilation, we can transpose it to some other section of what's being prepared, perhaps the final chapter of the *Book of Fever*.

—Having yet no *nom de guerre*, I would indeed prefer to postpone this *douloureuse* episode.

What's it like living in Senatobia? Would it be purely caricatured to say that fat men drinking beer often leer at you from run down porches where burn pork-oil torches, cotton stuffed into perforated screen doors prevents mosquitoes and flies from penetrating, that while they guzzle there's usually at hand a loaded gun muzzle. That the fan spinning slowly overhead perfectly symbolizes the white supremacy clan of which they are proud, founders and members all, even if they no longer wear pointed caps and white capes? All of them are pale burly apes.

When living here I must open all mail at arm's length while turning away my head, never close the eyes while under the shower, even when soap stings, permit no one to pass behind, not even a small child. The pointed white costumes are now on display in the small town museum and violence is temporarily limited to burning crosses in front of our home, especially when we're out. Sometimes the younger ones paint on the curb before our house, "Black thing, go home!"

Thinking to humiliate us, they cover my car with cocoa powder. A hungry child, pale white thing one of theirs, chews the fender. Lacking the tools necessary to adapt the controls for the comfort of a single legged chauffeur, I ask her to take the wheel. We emerge from this icy zone which normally should have been subtropical and head for interpenetrating cities.

She's much more intelligent than I, driving adroitly and with great velocity through the dense traffic around the loop that circles the heavily polluted city, all the while guiding our conversation in the direction that she desires, receiving calls, putting some on hold, concluding others and taking up with me again, (no advanced technological device for communication, just a small conch-form object).

The low grade alcohol that I'm drinking from completely opaque black jug with a very well rendered pteranodon, wide-spread leathery wings and long fleshy backward swept crest flying over mountain landscape, burns my throat. My head is becoming heavy. I'm incapable of continuing the conversation. I go down, engulfing drugs like a turtle eating salad, slowly, methodically.

We stop. I vomit in a flowerbed by the roadside, the perfect small cone of an ant nest beneath my heaving head. For the ants, it's a momentary cataclysmic deluge that will be followed by a relatively long period of over abundance. An important chapter in the history of this particular colony. A biblical episode. Perhaps they shall haul a child's toy representing a human figure, install it in front of their hill and revere it from here on.

A lawn mower passes very close by and sprays me with grass debris, the strong smell of the freshly cut weeds, she insulting the gardener as I crawl and vomit some more, dragging the leaf-wrapped stump behind me for the simple reason that we haven't yet found the key for transferring out the amputation episode to a more remote part of the story. Reniform yellow ginkgo leaves fall.

Back in the car again.

—Art is finished, she says, —It's become a simple commodity, merchandise, like me filming you vomiting and then selling the images. You simply can't create a work of art all the while thinking of impending remuneration.

Someone screams at her from another vehicle. I'm fully out of sight, knee on the floorboard, my head on her lap. She doesn't even reply, just keeps running her fingers through my hair.

—Let me drive.

—Out of the question!

—Your city driving is too perilous.

—Consider when you almost killed us, looking for the dim Orion nebula instead of keeping your eyes on the way.

—Only once.

This then, cannot be the first encounter; our knowing conversation is proof enough.

—What you just did, vomiting in the flowers, is negation of all social structure, but probably a great step in the direction of a *Real Peoples' History*.

A fur-covered vehicle roars down the lane. Suddenly the door opens, the driver leans out and beneath to examine the undercarriage while speeding at full tilt. Many individuals have become extremely agile, mastering automotive acrobatics. A bus passes with a man squatting over the engine in the open rear hatch, performing a mechanical repair without even stopping.

—Let's drive south now, down to the Riviera, I say.

—But it's all dim, gray and foul, she says.

Seals have returned with welts on their heads. Just across the Mediterranean, no more than a small salty lake, we slash so many throats that all of humanity bears a bloody gash.

—Today I met a remarkable woman, black, very old, hair white smoke. Have been writing chronicles of real history for the past forty years, not the one available to the public, but the kind of history that emerges occasionally from the ground. The opposite end of that with a video camera attached to a missile, beams back to operators. Say the history found in dead soldiers pockets, photos of wife, child, mother or friends playing war before really going there. Private effects snatched with predatory instinct from fallen foe along with recuperated weapons. We can call this clandestine imagery "interrupted love." Decide to destroy the proof of its existence, or momentarily prolong what it had once been before being pressed to pounding heart and taken into zone of abrupt finality. She said that we are all living in perpendicular worlds where our paths can cross once but never twice and therefore the imperative necessity of never letting the one you love slip away, that in truth Africa is and always has been, a much advanced civilization, in harmony with the fifty four galaxies that constitute the local group, especially those members of Leo and Virgo going on into Coma Berenice and Canis Venatici, and that this scale of values is in no way based on economical achievement nor technology; our own Occidental civilization being a nightmare within which she had been momentarily ensnared, something totally alien to the universe itself. I see her often. Her name is VLT (Vera Louise Tubman), a descendant of Harriet Tubman, who beyond her pre-emancipatory deeds, recognized the messianic importance of John Brown's engagement. She's great granddaughter to Typhoon.

We are in the heart of Paris now, more precisely on the deeply embedded Lagos sliver. We eat catfish roasted on small fires down by the river, just beneath the single remaining steeple of Notre Dame cathedral. My teeth hurt terribly, irrevocably wearing down. Not so long ago I myself was a dentist and I shall tell you about it later. Now, man often dies at an early age, usually from tooth infection. But then in these climes longevity has greatly regressed, life expectancy being only forty years of age. There are many new strains of old diseases, malaria, polio, meningitis.

—There was no real profit to be made by the big pharmaceutical laboratories.

—Populations of former tropical zones couldn't afford to acquire expensive cure?

Depriving them of treatment was perhaps the biggest mistake of all medical history. Resistant varieties spread North, returned South greatly fortified.

—Everything here, so much more difficult. Just eating one's daily fare; finding food, water and firewood. It isn't even a question of scarcity. There's abundance all about. But with the heat such effort is required, the sickness and the incessant warfare. It's as if the gravitational force of the Earth, spinning much faster here at the equator, were drawing down upon us, unbridled gamma rays, muons, neutrinos, interstellar gas, supernovae debris and gods know what other curses. You know, science is ignorant of many things yet. It is a groping thing where theory supports theory rather than proving or disproving intuition. Equatorial shift.

Whenever I return during the night I always enter with great precaution wondering if someone isn't already inside, a burglar, a spy, or yet another collector. Keep alert!

Return to this end zone where we now live. Beneath an overpass across which rumbles an endless convoy of train tank cars filled with hazardous chemicals, thieves break down a ttd (time travel device), stealing the vital parts. The area is littered with throw-away from previous operations, piles of time machine scrap: bow-shock shields, olfactory cables, ballast reservoirs containing primal soup, bamboo chassis, old mattresses, crushed baby carriages, furniture fragments.

Together we have three legs and though we hobble our spirits never waver nor wobble.

Who are our neighbors? Just above lives a very frustrated young man, on sick-leave from the police force, couldn't handle the stress, (yes, police forces still exist, though merely symbolic, comprised of individuals who have a nostalgic penchant for wearing uniforms and parading). When we're home he spends most of his time lying down with his ear pressed to the floor just above our toilet waiting in ambush for the sounds of defecation. He tells his impotent mother that he wants a stethoscope for Christmas. She's delighted, thinks he'll make a wonderful physician. Another neighbor lives in a cardboard box in the interior courtyard. There isn't much light down there, but when he meditates, he levitates, rising higher each time. Yesterday he reached the level of the second floor where we live. I observed him intermittently while taking notes from Antonio Gramsci's carceral writings, reading selections of Franco Fortini's *Dogs of the Sinai*, all the while revising Arabian sun and moon syntax. Every time I glimpsed out of the window he was a little bit higher.

Today? Blam! He had risen too high, reached the third floor level where he was shot down by the ex-policeman who couldn't suffer the sight of seeing another human being rising above him.

Also, a girl from Valparaiso, lives just under the rooftops, comes down to use the communal toilet that's out on the landing. The housepainter-plumber-repairman, who's a refugee from Bosnia, lives in the basement.

Urulu is seven now. Shaking together two plastic pterodactyl toys, one large yellow, the other small brown, she explains to me:

—They are performing a nuptial dance.

—Show me.

—It's like this, see. The papa bird walks on his elbows, dips his beak into the water and gives the mama bird a pouch full of prehistoric fish. He lets out shrieks and leaps around her. They are very happy together. The mama bird will make two or three dazzling violet colored eggs that the papa bird will protect against the attacks of predators. These are few because they choose a steep mountainside for the nest, which is made of sharp stones. How did you say we call the eggs, Dad?

— A clutch, my dear.

—Yes, that's it. And I forgot to tell you, the papa has poisoned feathers on his belly that he uses to rub the nest with, so that no other animals will come to steal the eggs. You understand that the pterodactyl chicks will be immune don't you?

—Where did you see all of this? (I'm fearing she merely found the alcohol jug with the well-rendered pteranodon – they're so similar in appearance to the pterodactyls – which I emptied in the car).

—I went there yesterday. Don't worry, I was very careful, just like you and Mom told me to be. I brought along my own drinking water, didn't eat anything that I found looking like a fruit, and I really kept my eyes open for the dangerous ones with big teeth and claws. I came back the way you told me to, not too fast.

—Where's the ttd?

—Down by the river.

—I told you to bring it home. Ours is a hand made model and moss will grow on it in just one day if you leave it by the water's edge.

It is true that even a child can master the skills of space and time travel, especially a girl. Women have proven to be the future of the world. Don't misinterpret. No Amazon civilization is this, but with the accumulating of reduced male longevity over millions of years and precocious female maturity, the outcome was inevitable.

Temporary structures have been added atop buildings by means of bamboo scaffolding, vast plastic tents, huts made of branches and leaves held together with cables. During the storms, which have become much stronger and quite frequent, entire families are blown off of the rooftops, hut and all, landing sometimes far off into neighboring suburbs. We heat ourselves with mox, cheap radioactive sludge produced by throwing together used uranium and plutonium waste, put into a lead box. Horrible burns if improperly manipulated.

Medicine has made great progress. Brain transplants are possible now even if it's true that most cryogenization experiments failed miserably, time having eroded the memory required to conclude research on frozen subjects. At some point, subzero temperatures were not maintained and the candidates to transtemporal reanimation simply rotted away. Some were recycled as pet food others served to raise flies necessary for rare reptile collections. There have been great debates as to the ethic of brain transplant, mostly amongst the creators of garments and shoes, short on creativity, weary of perpetually copying and reinterpreting the models of bygone epochs. Could Michelangelo's brain have been reused, solely dedicated to developing new forms for high heels for example? Yes! Well then, let's find an artist, a genius to be sure, the one who did the complete knock down on the Mount Rushmore heads, cut off *his* head, recuperate the brain, and apply his talent to making heels.

Is this the reason that I've been seeing of late so many headless corpses in the streets, great numbers of freshly decapitated heads bearing a vague resemblance to my own, born by eager ax men?

The building trembles. It is no earthquake. All around, the street is being torn up by an archeological team seeking artifacts. We are obliged to climb out of a small window, crawl over rubble. Oversize banana trees are everywhere. Suburban shuttle trains rumble through deserted stations.

The child through all of this? As only a child could be, she is happy and inventive in the heart of this most dismal of urban wastelands. I must take example on her. Just now she stops to play in the dirt. A passing shower has drawn a worm from the earth without even dampening the dust.

—We're here! Wake up now! Who wants to take a dust bath?

She cuts the worm into segments and rolls them in the dust. It's dehydrating, dying. From an old pan full of twitching mosquito larvae, she pours water over the agonizing worm.

—There, I saved you! she tells the worm with great satisfaction as hungry birds approach.

—You'll be a politician some day, I say.

We head for the Musée de l'Armée at the Invalides where I loot for her Napoleon's small white Arabian horse, stuffed of course, his camp cot, and the little field desk which accompanied him to the battle of Marengo.

—Daddy, did Napoleon kill Henri the First, or did he die of thirst?

—I'm sure he did! Disappear, I mean, for want of potable water, following regular ingestion of small quantities of arsenic.

Take a copy of an old masterpiece into deep space.

On the beach we play with sticks, shells, seaweed and sand fleas. Make little Chinamen using barnacles for their hats. We take long walks together. She places the prettiest shells in my pockets. Sometimes a sticky piece of candy that she's spit out gets mixed in.

I have a dream. Am wearing a well-cut classical suit of fine dark fabric. The tie is green silk with very subtle snake skin pattern. Catches light and holds it. Looking just like one hundred other lawyers employed by the same firm. It owns the entire building, some forty stories, set in the middle of downtown Los Angeles. Lunch break, we all head for different exotic food cafeterias, all set in the foot of the tower.

I awake.

Baby sleeps fitfully on my chest. Are we heading back in time? Was turquoise, is now silver. Scorching hot. Must plunge her repeatedly into cold bath, down to -150^0, try to break the fever.

—Little fire monkey!

An incongruous cinnamon scent coming from her tiny nostrils. Pupils flickering purple. Small green flames in the mouth. Vomerin fangs emerge. She's only teething, but what a scare! Raising space metisse can be problematic.

I make a little rickshaw for her. We go straight into the sunset, glowing trash blowing up all around.

We go past a Laundromat. Glimpse a girl inside reading a book while doing her wash. Whirring noise. Let's push on.

Buy a bottle of wine at Arab grocer. Algerian music.

Past the Laundromat again. It's full of sudsy water. The girl's drowned. Pasted to the window, her book's open to page 10/11, "How to care for Triassic fishes."

Go into a small bistro.

I have my teeth filed to points. Wear a salamander-skin coat. It's said that they can resist fire.

—Shall I cover my head?

—It's not a good day to buy a hat; rather we should go look at a cat.

Straddle a motorcycle with a fresh panther skin seat. Still bloody on the underside.

An old woman at the flea market caresses furniture that once belonged to her. A couple drinking aperitifs discusses vomiting with respect to sailing, the shape of the keel, wave angle.

—Want to rob a bank? All you need are a hat and sunglasses. The video camera's set too high up. Simply jam the door with the publicity panel; hold your chin down and get to work. Garden sheers will do. If you're overly stressed by this first try, go to the hamam, have a fat Moroccan woman massage you from head to foot. Feel her breasts slap against your naked skin. Put on a black garbage bag to sweat. Drink lots of mint tea.

Realize that all that surrounds us is a form of communication. Distrust destruction, it being one of the higher forms. Can we destroy destruction?

Escape by expelling great quantities of air or water and shooting backwards. Leaving behind another *"you"* made of smoke or ink depending on whether you happen to be in the sky, on land, or in the sea. Studying arthropods can help you master this evasion technique. Quickly change colors and surface quality. Instantly grow immense warts to blend with rocky terrain. When living with humans best learn the techniques of elimination, assassination, mass-murder. Go on to genocide; otherwise you've hardly a chance to fit in and go unnoticed.

Overdose anticoagulants to produce hematuria. Injecting saliva subcutaneously can cause abscesses. Complain of pain. Request analgesics. Lie about your medical history. Make these doctors believe almost anything you want. They'll never guess Pseudologia fantastica! Factitious symptomatology. Engage in a cycle of rapid discharge and re-admittance in hospital milieu. To avoid being discovered, change cities, countries when necessary. Can become full-blown Munchausen syndrome.

Drive a really ugly silver BX Citroën from the late seventies. Paint's lost its shine. Window areas are covered with cloudy plastic sheets that hold with ducting tape. Driving's a guessing game. Back seat is filled with broken furniture, tools and books.

Watch for the dip of the needle when approaching magnetic pole. Inversely, when sailing horse latitudes, beware of floating objects. This zone has a history of travelers chucking cargo. Pick some up if you can.

I've added a sports steering wheel and an imitation wooden dashboard. Wires dangle from beneath. Children's toys on top. The ashtray's brimming. Ugly gray seat covers. Hanging from the windshield by means of a suction cup is a notebook. While sitting in the car waiting for Xoma, I make drawings using an ordinary black Bic. Man licking woman's sex, her legs spread wide apart, head thrown back. Clasping hard her thighs, he has an erection. Another sketch: she's on all fours, head turned back over her shoulder looking at him. He's behind her, seen from three-quarters profile, his balls visible between the buttocks, driving erection deep into her. Her breasts hang, well formed. Nipples erect. A third drawing shows their sexes very close together. Penetration is imminent. Finally, the male figure's standing in a phone booth making a call; she's on her knees sucking him. The technique of these drawings is rather awkward, drawn in a state of excitation and with haste. They're certainly of extremely poor taste.

Night air is to be feared. Foul again, just as in medieval times. Dress and act accordingly.

Pawn Shop

It's the most dismal of days, precipitation somewhere between a heavy fog and the finest drizzle. This mist has a taste to it, an odor even; one of illness as if the air were full of particles in suspension blown from the flews of giant beast taken with uncontrollable sneezing fits. Saltiness. Unrefined sodium wrenched from the earth. The crude salinity of salt licks set at the forest's rim to draw elephants out from hiding.

We cling to one another, bearing silk handkerchiefs to our faces. It is said that climatic conditions bear upon the spirit of man, that he can become depressive with the passing of a low pressure system, glum from the lack of light when thick clouds conspire in layers to eliminate all color but gray from the spectrum. I'm certain that all is converging today to bring misery down into the innermost recesses. This rain which isn't one. A violent shower could have washed the skin clean, poured down over the body superficially. But no, this mist penetrates. It digs in with the spiral action of sea-worms attacking the belly of a wooden ship, rendering even the most well contrived structure vulnerable, warping the keel, perforating bottom-planking to penetrate even the futtocks and half-floors.

In bags held tightly beneath threadbare coats, we clutch what last small treasures we possess, the dearest inseparable ones.

—This stone has no worth! Nothing now on Earth. Haven't you heard of the carbon sun they've found? When cooled it'll give the most massive, the purest. These ones are nothing more than gravel. The poorest industrial quality has more sparkle, quips the clerk.

—And the portrait?

—No! Well, maybe. We can offer you only the minimum sum. It's a nude woman you have there. What we're looking for now are tableaux of naked men with H_2O: a river, a lake or seashore in the background. There isn't even a glass of water in your painting. It's a desert!

—Reconsider.

—She has broad shoulders and she's black. That's exotic. But there's no penis, no testicles. No, quite frankly we'd have a difficult time selling this to our clientele.

—I can paint them on! I blurt spontaneously, like certain simple chemical reactions, uncontrollable once they've been sparked.

The clerk slowly withdraws a pair of thick rimmed glasses from his nose, feigns amusement.

K2 takes other jewelry from her pockets, all wrapped in wet envelopes and small paper bags that cling to the gems.

—These need cleaning. And the stones haven't a modern cut, too many facets. They just don't catch the light properly.

She's wearing what's left of her finest dress, hands impeccably manicured. Pilot light glimmering in retina.

Behind the triple thick security window, the clerk rolls the jewelry in his palm.

—Two minutes in the ultrasonic bath will clean them perfectly, I propose.

—Let me see that one, he says, tapping with his finger the thick glass which gives him the greenish hue of tropical fish in an aquarium, —It's an interesting ring that Madame has on her finger.

Two golden monkeys holding an aquamarine.

—Out of the question! withdrawing her hand beneath the counter, — It's my engagement ring.

—I see, says the clerk glancing at me uneasily, trying to understand why there should be any sort of a bond between she and I. —We have another bureau for those who, like yourselves, are in a real pinch and haven't any readily available commodities to offer.

This man has eyelashes beneath his fingernails. The nails are grimy; perhaps his hobby is working on propulsion systems or digging for worms in moist soil during the evening when it's soft from dew.

—I tell you he's a fisherman.

—Only bream then.

—This storm in your head, don't bear it alone, she says blowing her breath upon my brow. —The Bay of Bengal vests its foul humor upon Bangladesh. It's not at all a question of karma, as Buddhists would have you believe. Geography, the lay of the land and the sea. The real protagonist here is exterior to man's soul, alien to his spirit. Maracaibo isn't an oil-rich lake in Venezuela but a zone of thick dust and cold gas, which compress to form young stars. Angola, not the country in Africa but a state prison farm that once existed in Louisiana. Again, be patient.

She speaks in a low voice with soothing vibration, pays no heed to the clerk behind the thick glass, impatiently awaiting a reply.

We've had periods of fasting followed by feasting, ecstasy before extreme pain. Hope and despair. One is nothing without the other.

I remember the feasting and the fasting in that order. Broad shiny leaves upon which were served boiled pangolin, their small nails curled, clutching fruit with purple sap.

Cocoa leaves hacked fine, brittle and scratchy when swallowed that prepare the esophagus for heavier fare. Rare, for once you've consumed your lover, she's no longer there. The bones picked clean can be arranged to form a sculpture. They take on certain patina with time. Rub them with sweat, run them length ways between the legs, beneath the armpits, roll them down your torso. Gently insert them in your anus. Maybe you don't dare do so?

I'm not so sure anymore. Can I pretend to have known periods of real fasting? When in the most appropriate place, the desert within the desert, I nourished myself with the winds.

How say you this be possible? Being enturbaned, my head wrapped in black cloth, the eyes protected with dark glasses?

The wind bore paraboles, pattering upon the turban, sanding down the glasses to opacity, only light traversing. All images were left behind. I couldn't even perceive the masses.

But there were odors and taste. I can't even pretend that they were all that remained. Truly, they must have already been there. An odor of nourishment; a paste; a taste akin to that of flour mixed with water, half baked in earthen ovens and still warm but more certainly related to the primal substance from which life first sprang.

—You're more at ease now, she says. —You see, we're home again. We've returned.

—Indeed we have.

We're in the living room behind the bay window which gives onto the long avenue down which very refined motorcycles zip silently at incalculable speeds towards a right angle turn at the far end of the lane just in front of a high stone wall against which, more often than not, they splatter with their riders like insects on a windshield.

I go into the dining room. On the wall are large beautifully rendered oil paintings of: a handgun; a missile; a mushroom cloud; a canister of anthrax spores. A slave ship named *Esperenza* lying at anchor off of the Calabar coast or is it the bite of Biafra? A very well rendered drawing of her deck plan, the manner in which the slaves were stowed, how at the prow and at the poop they were arranged in a sort of halo, radiating to make use of even the most unaccommodating space.

These art works have no order and are interchangeable. We are discussing deep earth geophysics, the infinite conductivity of the core, the frozen flux limit; again the Chicxulub crater and biosphere changes. The carpet is mammoth pelt, fresh and very thick. It has a musty odor quite like seal skin. The couch is covered with triceratops hide. Welts waxed to gleam reflect all that passes.

I rise, carefully put out a cigarette in a large bronze ashtray with an owl and a baboon facing each other, put on a rust colored trench coat with purple irisations that I had when about twelve, and go into the vestibule where parrots are waiting, twenty three of them, the gray variety with the red tail. I had purchased the lot in Central Africa from a video repairman who kept them in his shop along with a goat upon whose back they rode; feathered cavaliers.

I take four, thrusting them under my coat, and leave. The subway entrance is hardly two strides from the front door. There's still that dust and ozone odor down here. Selling the birds under the coat isn't the easy business it appears to be. They can get excited, angry even, and inflict painful bites. There's a technique to taking them from beneath the coat so as not to arouse them, all the while advantageously presenting the red tail feathers to potential buyers. I manage to sell all four of the parrots in less than twenty minutes. Hardly three shuttles have been through the station.

Emerging into daylight I cross the Pont d'Arcole. A man with his mouth hanging open, loud buzzing noise coming from deep in his throat. Bumblebee caught in a spider's web. He lurches, grasps and clutches on to me. I'm sure he's desperately trying to convey an urgent message but for some reason I'm thinking there's an unsold parrot under my coat that he's going to compress in his panicked haste. I shove him hard and he goes down, cracking his skull on the curbstone. The wind blows sparkling dust around his expressionless face. A newspaper blows up against the back of his neck, wrapping around the head it becomes a hat. There is no blood. One could very easily confuse this limp fellow with a heavy sleeper like myself, the kind who can go to sleep anywhere; even on a busy city street. From his nostril emerges a bumblebee, the deep black variety that promptly takes to the wind. This man is stone dead. I buy a sandwich, take a bite from it and place the remains in the dead man's hand.

—It's much better now. We can do this scene at the pawnshop again. If you're still a little uneasy, we'll just do it quicker this time, she says.

It isn't snow nor rain but mud falling from the sky; cold dirty fistfuls of it splattering on car hoods, blowing down rising steam and making a noise like the thumping hooves of herds on the move in the Serengeti.

—This time there should be sunshine. Unexpected paradox. It will bring the depressive mood out of usual context, at least provide passing atmospheric incongruity.

We have her jewelry, the ring I had made, in a paper bag. Little golden monkeys with emerald eyes clutching an immense aquamarine of Santa Maria quality from Brazil. Cherubins with diamonds and others. The pawnshop is vast, more of a bank this time. Many people are waiting to pawn their valuables. Mostly desperate looking women. They are the ones who usually have the courage to take such decisions while men remain at home masticating salted peanuts and cashews. We have a painting in a plastic bag. The portrait of a tall black man wearing a suit and tie. The clerk calls our number. Crinkling sound of the plastic wrapper coming off of the painting.

—We want paintings of women, preferably naked and if they're set in a landscape there should be no water visible anywhere; an ocean a river or even the least small pond can ruin the value of a work, the clerk says in a very grave manner —and it goes without saying that the woman should be white.

Coming out of the doctor's office we separate, she carrying the child to go buy medicine on the parallel market where outdated drugs are sold by the sack, I heading for the river.

—Wovoko! she yells through the large falling flakes, for there is no sunshine (these things are uncontrollable), and the mud has turned to snow, —No it's alright, we have a little something left to eat.

The doglet is clever, jumping from behind a bush to take two pigeons in her mouth. But then, disoriented, she heads straight into the crowd. Having a sore throat I'm incapable of whistling or even yelling. The dog is lost, our dinner too. Perhaps it will garner someone else's plate. On the ground are two crushed cigarette butts. I shove them into my coat pocket.

Virginia cardinals have migrated to Europe, now perched atop the Tour Saint-Jacques; carmine splashes on the melting sheets of snow that slide from the rooftop.

On the immaculate ground the shadows of the falling snowflakes rise to meet them.

Just ahead there's crimson of another kind. A most dangerous new disease that sunders the victim in two halves. Colloquially referred to as the "splits." It cleaves all that pertains to the human being, beginning with the double helix, the organs and the body itself, with such speed that a man walking down the street can catch the disease, incubate it and suffer the final effects all in the space of a few seconds to collapse in a bloody heap, the body completely torn apart, even the fingers, nails and the hair follicles. In comparison Ebola is nothing more than a common flue. It's not unusual to see someone spurting blood from an eye.

The clerk trembles nervously, running his fingers over a row of zircons in his ear, clicking the chrome ball in his tongue up against front teeth. Instinctively he hates Typhoon.

He passes a card through the slit in the security window.

Outside Godmoney is on the walk again. Not a stride anymore, rather a regular lope.

Real rain now in the rue making the sound of falling spit; each drop separate, viscous and distinct.

—Where's the sun? I ask her.

—Above the clouds, naturally. You love rain anyway.

—And now?

—I'll sell my clothes, she says, as we walk beneath the salivating sky.
—The old Gauthiers, the Alaias. I know some girls who want them. Porscia, Moothun, others too.

31

—But they'll never be able to fit into your clothes!

K2 examines the card. It's very small, about the size of a tube-ticket, made of soft tissue; a deep burgundy color serves as support for an intricate structure embossed in metallic green, dead center.

—What does it say?

—You almost need a microscope to read it, she replies holding it up very close to her eyes.

Institute of Molecular Genetics, (IMG).

Seated in a somber building fashioned from blocks of basalt with natural hexagonal shapes, fit together with great precision. It should have been so. Instead the address, Rue de la Petite Truanderie, corresponds to a pawn shop of the most ordinary appearance, had it been set near the heart of Hollywood or close to the desolate center of any number of big American cities.

The card indicates a research center. What can I possibly find here? It's neither a bank nor even a financial organization of the most marginal kind.

—What are your needs? A two, three year loan?

This man has an unusual goatee, very thinly trimmed that descends black and wraps beneath his chin like the straps of a helmet.

—I'm listening.

—We offer physical mortgage. Consult the list of body parts, which interest us. Should we sign an agreement, we would carry an option on them, just for the period your loan is in effect. In the event that you would, for some reason, become incapable of honoring the calendar that we would have mutually established, default, the designated elements would become our property.

His fingertips are brown from smoking.

—You repossess my body parts?

—In no manner! We didn't sell them to you, therefore we cannot repossess. It's not like that at all. Remember, this is a bilateral agreement. You have come to us and we have offered you a service. A service for which, if I'm not mistaken, you have vainly sought satisfaction with no results as of yet. We can therefore, without pretension, claim that this is an exceptional sort of offer. Of your own free volition, you can choose the amount of money which you need; right here today for example, if you desire to walk out with say three hundred thousand in your pocket, you can. It's within the realm of the possible.

On the desk between us lies an ashtray full to the rim with crushed butts.

—What's the procedure?

—You'll undergo a very simple medical examination and if the results confirm the exceptional qualities detected by our agent...

—What agent?

—The clerk at Mont Pieté Rue des Blancs Manteaux. He calls. It's rare of course. There aren't so many of you.

—So many of us? This is absurd! Who are *we*? As for you, you aren't even an official institution.

—We're private but fully accredited. Our research budget is largely federally funded. But you're in no position to argue. You claim to reside in the heart of Paris but you actually live in the most sordid industrial suburb. The foundations of the house you call home are eroded by chemical fumes. You commute on a broken down train that's open to the four winds and has no security. Mostly out of service forcing you to ride the Seine in a little pirogue that you made with your own hands using an adz. That's all fine but when it's been raining like it has for the past weeks and the current is strong carrying along uprooted trees and so on, it can take you a full four hours to paddle back upstream to your home. Think of your wife and child! I understand that you've also been subject to several burglaries, a hold-up even. That your heart often falters even though you appear to be young.

This fellow is informed, but only superficially so.

How have we arrived at such irrevocable economic plunge she and I? No sudden event. It has come by festoons and cascades, taking us ever lower. The exact reasons I don't really know. The heralding signs were clear though. Trivial things at first, missing buttons, worn cuffs, holes at the knees and elbows, the soles of the shoes; the phone cut off, the television burned out. Household appliances gone un-repaired, everything broken down. Leaks of all types, piping the roof. Dirt sets in. Decline in food quality and quantity.

Rotting and missing teeth are the surest sign, dental care being exceedingly expensive; broken eyeglasses taped together too, betray the fact that we can't afford to pay the oculist.

—Where are we headed?

—I'm no navigator. Were I to sail the Atlantic, inevitably would I become ensnared in the Sargasso Sea, heaving in swells alive with juvenile eels. Sick and lost. If I were to take you to the confines of the universe, it would be much worse.

Our clothing speaks of approaching twilight. Stained with blood, cheap wine, vomit and oil from greasy food. Conversation is no longer one, barely audible incoherent monologues that sometimes, by chance, cross zones of common experience but mostly disperses as if carried off by traversing neutrinos or solar winds. Thoughts blow about like fluffy milkweed seed.

Simple things, buttoning up a shirt or the use of a zipper have become laborious chores. We sometimes wallow in our own excrements, incapable of cleaning up; and even if we had momentarily possessed the volition, the water has long been cut off. There are no cleaning products left, not even an old newspaper to wipe up with. Systole and diastole have become confused, the heart no longer responds to the signals coming from muddled brains.

The document is complex and very difficult to read, fine yellow print on white paper. Body parts are exhaustively listed, from major limbs down to nerve fiber and fluids by length or volume. A milliliter of sperm, a pint of blood, a bundle of hair with roots and all. A finger, the hand (right or left), the full leg with subdivisions: ankle, calf, knee, foot, thigh, hip or whole. Colon, intestine, bladder, liver, lung and heart. Each item has a corresponding value.

—Supposing that I can't meet the deadline, what would the penalty be?

—Penalty? In reality there is none. You simply would make yourself available for an intensive research program oriented around the parts or organs for which the value advanced to you wouldn't have been repaid in time.

I'm thinking: What can I possibly risk? The list of body parts, the order of compensatory restitution exhausted, what would be left to take? Would the brain finally be taken by a conspiratory medical team just before the chief of state was due to have a benign intervention? The Surgeon General transplants my brain into the presidential head. Beyond assassination! This coup-d'etat will be a medical one. The chief of state will be declared insane and destitute of his functions. But certainly these considerations are beneath reality, a perilous underestimation. This is a pawnshop of a new kind, one where people put their ideals, their values, their very souls on the hook; but there's no pact with the devil here, no Faustian undertone, no struggle of a higher ethical order. It's purely a mercantile matter; I'm establishing a mortgage, a benign hypothecation, be it of flesh and spirit. That'll suffice.

I needn't know more. Desperation and the sums of money readily available preclude rationalization.

I sign and leave with a heavy suitcase offered by IMG as membership welcome gift. It's burgundy colored, soft to the touch, the appearance of blood soaked felt. Bulging with cash. The baggage is so heavy that I'm obliged to halt at Pigalle for purchase of little wheels that strap to the underside. Roll easy.

Body Mortgage Calendar.
Sperm will be easy to give. K2 will accompany me. She'll draw greater quantities than I would ever have imagined possible. I'm sure of it.
— Fountain?
— Sir, would you prefer a sexual surrogate? they ask, —At this rate you'll never make the quota. Unsuspected premature aging seems to be responsible for reduced seminal flow.

Following the first blood donation, a massive one from which I still haven't yet fully recovered, I receive a terse communication referring to malarial parasites actively devouring red blood cells in my body which I had failed to specify when seeking membership.
—You'll not give them a single drop of it, she speaks soothingly, takes off my shoes.
—Remember when we first met?
—Was it on the bridge, or beneath the bridge?
—No. The bonobo incident.
—Oh. I wanna go. Accident!

Follows a long period of separation wherein everything that I undertake fails miserably.

I live alone in a cardboard box. In spite of the fact that the box is situated at the heart of an urban zone, no one offers help; not ever. Not even small change is left in the pan placed by the opening of the carton, which I dub "the door." Not that I beg or even expect any manner of alms, yet I can't help thinking: Endzone sub-hero, he who goes unnoticed, nothing will remain of you, even your bones have gone soft, no jewelry do you wear, the fillings of your teeth have fallen out.

Wracked with rheumatism, I'm forced to adopt a prone position, can barely manage to crawl. The garbage bin that's behind a fashionable restaurant seems miles away though it's close enough to smell. Winter sets in hard with ice forming thick crust on my hut. Expensive vehicles are often curbed next to me. I see luxury shoes pass near my face, Espositos and Blahniks that in the fresh snow leave fine-tipped traces. I never glimpse the corresponding faces.

Today I drink heavily. Vomit freezes my mouth to the pavement. I'm really dead this time. Perhaps a less pointless death than the time I died in the very restaurant behind which I just now was hiding. A death which only served to prove that Neanderthal's shorter pharynx (that I now have), though impeding speech, was a definite advantage over Sapiens's elongated one. An evolutionary development which clearly demonstrates in what direction time is actually going. Finally, isn't this precisely what they're really after? The primitive, priceless genes I bear. There. I've just given you the key to this whole affair! Genes desperately sought by a President who doesn't want to get caught choking on a pretzel ever again.

Kids spray-paint my corpse.

I used to have wings. The federal government clipped them off. Claimed that I posed a threat to national security. "Flying Muslim."

At dawn, she carries me off, wraps my body in her fur coat and whispers to me, —Didn't I tell you, didn't I? That it's no use fighting for lost causes: Palestine, Western Sahara, East Timor, democracy itself and many more to come. True, certain animals go against rip tides, torrents and high winds. But invariably they have profiled bodies, bomb shaped heads, tubi-form spirits, tapering to permit penetration. And they never do more than go against flow, only to descend again with it.

—Thaw now! She places me in the backseat of her vehicle, a sports model. Makeup slightly smeared around the eyes, she's obviously returning from a night out in discotheque. The pelt with which I'm enveloped smells of cigarette smoke. Champagne on her breath, she's unusually lively for this hour of the day, probably due to intake of stimulant substance. Confirmed by trace of white powder on the finer hair within the nostrils.

I'll be no winter kill.

She keeps me for a long time in her apartment. Sometimes on the table, often on a shelf where I serve as book end. I hold up several volumes by an obscure author named Castro Soromenho, all written in the original Portuguese versions published by Sa da Costa: "A Chaga" which signifies "the Wound," is the closest one to me, both in position and spirit, directly followed by "Camaxilo" and "Terra Morta." This last one particularly intrigues me. Does it refer to these totally deserted zones of nothingness where I now find myself to be? Utter void where even one's very own bones have been emptied of their marrow, dried and hardened; they readily take flame and burn slowly like the wood of the yew, perfect for long lasting fires. Lands that caravans traverse with the greatest haste, eastern Hamada appropriately named Bled El Chouf or the "Country of Fear."

You thought to find here some respite beneath saplings in small copse? Looking for shade will become recurrent theme. Put to sleep anger, sing gentle lullaby to your hate. Make no great leap, progress by short hops.

Political genesis as interpreted by the Sahrawi strategist Ali Omar Yara: Bearing arms is fundamental to the enterprise of war and the social practice of violence. It is useful to distinguish between the rule of "one citizen = at least one weapon" and an Edict of State which would regulate possession and distribution. True, America had but scarce reservation with respect to the right of citizens to bear arms for self defense or in order to aggress. Not so with nomads who armed themselves only to impose their existence in the face of numerous enemies, not the least of which were formidable European powers attempting to disseminate young African independence by the forced application of democracy upon lands where it would have been the most inappropriate form of government, eradicating ancestral tribal authority, and blowing to the four winds any pre-existing form of social cohesion in order to gain access to mineral wealth and other un-exploited natural resources.

She screws a small hook into my back and suspends me on the wall, much in the manner of an artwork. Flat, brittle and sand colored, I'm in harmony with the interior decoration, mostly in tones of beige.

Incapable of moving or expressing myself in any manner, I observe the way she lives. Often she'll smoke while lounging in front of an entertainment device, a small theatre that reproduces everything, even smell and touch. It makes her laugh. At home she wears casual Prada lingerie, loose full panties, usually purple that she puts on with a deep green silk blouse from India. Striking with her brown skin. I can smell her body. Spend hours just looking at her. She takes great care preparing herself to go out. Knows just what to wear, which perfume will go with her natural smell, enhance it even.

—Stay away from politics, she says, running her fingers over my surface just before walking out.

One day she doesn't return. After several months of her absence, I manage to move what's left of my arms, then the feet. I get myself off of the wall and descend to the floor from which I can rise to explore. This isn't the home that I had known. A long hallway is lined with an incredible shoe collection, thousands of them; "real works of art" she had so often wished for. Her dream had come true. But is she, now too, dead? Hadn't she promised me to return, give head?

In the salon, where I had never before been, there's an immense ceramic image. It's imbedded in the wall, must have taken a full team of specialists to install. The reflection from the shiny broken surface prohibits immediate interpretation. Apparently reassembled from thousands of pieces, none of them quite flush which has the effect of fracturing the image. There's an agreeable smell of plaster and fresh paint in this room, which has a very high ceiling. After a few days time I'm able to place myself at an oblique angle to the image from which point the glare doesn't quite so impair my vision.

Most probably Portuguese of origin, an azulejos technique having served as the base for this work, though colors go beyond the classic choice of blues. Many other hues have been employed giving the richest effect, even gold with final 600° firing that must have come well after the initial 1000° required to fuse the primary cobalt tint.

The universe represented here is incomprehensible. No ordinary surrealism, rather something gone wrong, broken down to shards and fit back together. Dark individuals communicate by throwing long strands of gilded material from their mouths. Would this symbolize the value of man's spoken word, an oral tradition that would have replaced writing for all questions involving higher principles, especially those demanding trust? And here, these structures, palaces of fire, citadels of crystal that stand on end, or spring laterally from mountainside as if gravity had no hold.

This young girl who precedes a horse in the sky, no Pegasus is it, no angel is she, yet they inhabit the air. There are machines that resemble nothing I know and I can't imagine their usage. Some are cube shaped, sitting on edge; they leak brilliant red liquid. Blood or brandy, it is impossible to say. Others seem to be flying knife blades, but the personages don't appear to fear them. Here a spiny contraption that resembles a giant viral structure.

Cascades too, with their torrents, the fall being on the wrong side of the edge. People are represented living in these waters, not only swimming or washing but also making love and sleeping. Some ascend the waterfalls like salmon in rut. It is clear that they have returned to river and ocean where they are perfectly at ease. They have neither fins nor gills. Mermaids or aquatic witchdoctors? Everyone is Black. The only written word of the work is *MariaMag* written in Bold. Is this something I've already told?

We must do simpler things, have children together.

I can't take the hook out of my back, screwed in the middle where it's impossible to reach.

Would it be pretentious to say that there's nothing of random? A predictable sequence? Apply time dispersal. Realize that in this manner, you've succeeded in overcoming two major problems.

Just as I'm unlimbering after the prolonged *accrochage*, a hand-delivered message arrives from Cameroon. It's Michael. He's just arrived in Douala, (still the most humid place in the World, you actually need gills in order to breathe there). He's sent back his house keys with a stewardess who lives in a distant suburb of Paris. Wants me to recuperate them, go to his flat and see if he didn't leave the stove burning. Says he left in too much of a hurry.

The inter-suburban ride's a difficult one, but I owe him this and much more. Heat's unbearable in his flat but surprisingly nothing has caught fire in spite of the flaming oven. See just how he lives, where the delicious dishes come from, cooks them in a closet, washes the dishes in the bathroom sink. Lots of shoes, mostly Italian. Small television. Pretty cramped in here. The neighbors, who occupy luxury flats just above, often complain of the cooking odors coming from dishes they can't comprehend. Too far removed from their idea of a good dinner: pork chops, sausage swimming in much sauce, abundant cream and butter. How can you expect these people to understand the strung up catfish, porcupine and antelope, all turned black from smoking that hang from Michael's window? And isn't he in his own flesh and bone, the incarnation of deep paradox? Speaking German, English, French and a dozen dialects, all languages of Cameroon that reflect a history that these good citizens ignore. Get them to recite, after having learned by heart: "We did, do and will have done, ghastly things." Over and over. White education needs to be totally revised. Ever notice how Black history's mainly written by Whites?

As for what most of us consider as being the future, Whites are always trying to explain things to we who don't really want to know, while they know nothing anyway about things that will have happened.

In my very next life, I'll ride an okapi through the streets of Okazaki. Promise. Tell Tilda to drink down her tiglic before tiglon with teeth as sharp as tines, transpierces thin tin skin of time-sharing body. Fish for timucu in warm western Atlantic waters. Beat timbrels. Don't expect me to charge front, provide perfect target like colonial tirailleurs; I'm more the tip-and-run type. Gulp tisane while waiting for Tirthankara. Listen to tufted titmice. Don't titter when playing tit-tat-toe. Titubation.

But first, me be burglar. Look for jutting ledges and prominent sills; the easiest way to break and enter, and if your home is too smooth, without foothold, I'll still find a way in. So it is with the people I meet. Seek the quickest path to their hearts. Never cruelly, only coolly. And don't go unarmed, repeat I constantly to myself.

Choice of arms:

—Rifle with flamboyant barrel of late eighteenth century design, having a comfortable leather padded cheek cushion on the stock.

—Pistol, little love blaster, with heart shaped grip, "Blast you with love" engraved on the handle.

—Spear/knife with four gun barrels along the haft, tassels, and leather straps forming a diamond pattern along the shaft.

There'll be no habits, and if habits there must, even within habits there shall be none.

Don't hesitate to employ the tokodynamometer; take uterus pressure before labor begins. There's no tolerance limit. Smarm this?

So many of us are penniless. Would God be a simple slumlord?

Spider 2

As a dentist I'm obliged to enter enormous maws, pry them open with scaffolding, and direct workers to build dams round bottomless cavities to be filled with kegs of mortar. It is epic labor, like building palaces in the most remote hinterland. I mission midgets and when these small people aren't available, Pygmies are substituted to wriggle between tightly packed molars the size of trucks. Bulwarks are to be fashioned from essences akin to eucalyptus and cedar, strongly scented wood with antiseptic properties. No nails, bolts or screws of any type are to be employed. Only wooden pegs in order to avoid electrolysis reaction with the gold already present in the mouth.

The framework goes up, spreading the jaws apart wide. In I stride, accompanied by my retinue of Babinga tribesmen. They carry nets underarm that could be useful for catching any game that may still be hiding between the gaps in the dentition, small crossbows for the same purpose; broad phrynium leaves, supple branches, werat vines and ntchami moss, winking with fireflies caught within, taken down during the night from the crowns of the loftiest jungle trees. These materials can serve to fabricate small huts within the maw, be we forced to spend the night in this hot damp place. And besides, it is said that the moss brings money. It can also serve to make compresses to plug bleeding craters in the gums where teeth have been pulled.

But I'm no buccal Schweitzer. There's no humanitarian penchant in me.

Someone has preceded me here. A good practitioner for sure. The fillings are mostly of high quality gold, enormous quantities of it. An electric current is running between the different grades of gold that have been employed to cap certain fangs. Impurities that create sparks arching through blue saliva. I help myself, digging out the sleeping bullion, replacing it with lead. This beast is too strong to be affected by saturnism.

Palatal, vestibular.

This particular head is huge, possibly a branchiosaur amphibian, shaped like a blunt projectile for thrusting through warm mud. Skull templates fit together rather imperfectly, giving the object an armored appearance in spite of slippery skin. Only a head, albeit three stories high, with no body, no limbs. Bumps on the surface can be interpreted as adhesive organs, perhaps conferring to this massive structure a very primitive type of mobility, at least permitting the cranium to hold to objects that it may encounter. An oro-nasal groove leads with gentle curve to nasal pit. Bone plates: dermosupraoccipital, jugal, lacrimal, parasphenoid, pterygoid, squamosal and tabular are easily identifiable.

The development of horns to either angle of the head tends to indicate that we could be dealing with Nectridia straight out of the Permo-Carboniferus. Retention of certain reptilian features, separate coracoid and possible fifth finger could have given clues had there been a body. Cannot be considered ancestral to modern amphibians. The skull structure is too specialized. Considering whether or not this creature arose at the time that Embolomeri were evolving into higher labyrinthodonts or even reptiles, mustn't preclude consideration of the potential perils lurking. Pockets of lethal gases may be encountered at any moment, invisible and quite scentless compared to the odors which arise from the festering gums and the deep abscesses. We carry canaries in small cages just like old time miners. Should they cease twittering, fall dead, we would be informed as to what lies ahead. Wounded prey could also ambush us in a final surge of defense.

Ah! There remains at least one vertebra. This lone bone presents well-developed traverse processes. If this is Nectridia, he's very definitely parallel to Phyllospondyli.

—Dig down now! Heave up this row of teeth. Whole sections of jaw elements must be pried up. Coronoids I through III. It is a most complex ten-piece mandible forming the lower mouth part of my host, bearing two rows – what say I? – three, of teeth, here beneath which runs a puzzle of ossified cartilage, pre-articular, splenial and post-splenial. Symphysial bones have developed with premaxillae to close the nostrils. Stapes abut against the otic capsule. Sound waves are, evidently, not transmitted to a fenestra in the ear capsule. Am I dealing with a fish? Be this a hyomandibular? A crude mechanism. Sound waves can only be transmitted to the quadrate from the lower jaw, which must rest upon a semi-conductive surface, say a pond bottom. Mud indeed! No need for salivary glands when one feeds underwater; hence, as in Xenopus, there's no intermaxillary gland.

Condylar surface is bipartite, a striking example of convergence. I'm tempted to explore, see if the inter-orbital walls of the brain case have ossified to form a sphenethmoid to either side. Leaving the Pygmy team to the work of cutting away the infected gum, I pursue my study of possible phylogenetic relations. The metamorphosis of the hyobranchial apparatus will permit me to establish a semblance of ontogeny.

We wear no white robes, no protective masks, no surgical gloves. Quite naked are we, performing this buccal surgery in no delicate manner. Some of us wear a few leaves over the groin. Protection rather than inhibition. I wear the penile sheath that Xoma fashioned for me when I was shot in the head. They gouge away with adzes, hoes and primitive broad axes. Tooth chips are flying.

Suddenly the cathedral of slime heaves up, casting us all down. Staves of cedar snap sending splinters and dental fragments shooting through the air. A lance has struck a nerve. Analgesic has no effect on this creature. Worse, it has somehow become aware of my supra-orthopedic curiosity.

Instinctively, we adopt the "unken" reflex, characterized by distinctive posture: dropping to the ground, flipping the head and legs sharply back over the body, turning up the brightly colored ventral surface, and, immobility with closure of the eyes and reduced respiration. Any member of the reptile or amphibian families will immediately perceive this comportment as a warning attitude, that just as Bombina bombina, the fire-bellied toad, we are capable of secreting our own poison.

How I yearn to return to that palace which was mine, walls covered with tile evoking the pattern of the leopard frog, minarets springing from the far reaches upon which my imam preaches. Library of incunabula, stories engraved upon camel scapula. Antioch and Alexandria. Long ago we butchered Buddha's fat belly, hauled down Christ from his cross, slaughtered Yaweh. This was not the way.

A chosen people? This promise has proven to be misleading curse. The only valid strategy is to accumulate points, like frequent flyers faithful to an airline. Cheik Yassine was closer to the truth than anyone could ever have imagined. Turn yourself into a human bomb! You'll be seated by the prophet's side, partake of the same fare. But beware! The target's not a racial one, nor even the "integrists" on the other side. Go for the god. All else is decoy.

The Pygmies are singing a deep forest lullaby, better than any analgesic. We abandon the "unken" position, rise, unlimber our tetanized muscles, massage one another. The teeth are jacked up, canaries are dropping dead.

—Ventilate before it's too late!

This infection goes deep, purulence wells up dislodging strata of fermented matter. Bones of I know not what creatures, the wreckage of some strange craft or vehicle smashed down and compacted, buildings even; the capital of a Corinthian column, the buttress of a highway cloverleaf. Here are the holds of ships that sailed from the bite of Biafra and the Calabar coast to Pernambucco. Not the keel sections nor even the shackles but what they held. A plug comes loose carrying cinders from Triblenca.

They, the Babinga catch on long before I.

—We're in God's mouth! they yell.

—Yours, the many facetted forest spirit?

—Not ours but the single ones you worshipped.

—Feel free to intervene.

—See yee not what foul things he's been feasting upon? Is this sustenance to he whom you *rever*? Never should we genuflect again!

—It's time we held a meeting, one of them suggests, dropping a small crossbow upon the pterygoid vestige. It rattles, imitates speech. To this language chopped with hatchet I prefer French, not the syrup of today but the tongue of the *coureurs des bois* who, through wood and weed, went their way partaking of calumet, incorporating the vocabulary of leaves crunching underfoot, seed fluff drifting in the air, bison breath blowing down on sweetgrass. No onontamontapae but abstract, elevated notions so hard now to convey.

We wear hoods. Use big serpents for dental floss.

The Babinga know. It's time to horde seal skins, prepare sunglasses made of ivory with slits for squinting through. Avoid tsunami by navigating in coastal areas with small submarines that hug the bottom. My six-year-old daughter told me so.

—Purge not this abyssal abscess! Let it fester. Burst! Send down its poison to the heart.

—There be no heart! Only a head, God's head. One without body.

Here again, we'll absolve God of his sins. Cap these fangs, bleach them white and, anon, beneath intense blue light, kneel in prayer to please him, for he too is an expert tabulator, and you Xoma, I know that you've accumulated enough points to be by his side. It'll be separation of the most definite sort. Being a vagabond of lava beds and fiery fields, this is not my destination.

Degage ourselves from this confessional of flesh. Take all the gold we can hold. Nevertheless, apply the oath of Hypocrites. We install the most intense blue lights, bring in immense hoses to flush out, pumps to drain. All is water vapor, roiling clouds boiling with blood clot and dental powder, splashing water and spray. The water brings along the smell of earth, vegetal matter, mold and fungi that thrive in moist seclusion, for our water is brought up from the Oubangui, the Uèlé and the Congo rivers to which I speak directly in native tongues. It bursts from the hose nozzle in a ruddy geyser, spewing immature crocodiles, binga fish and pumpkin size fresh water mollusks that carry bilharziasis in their soft tissues. Had I promised sterilized H^2O, antiseptic or even cauterization?

—Now that the Babinga and I have performed our task, withdrawn from this glorious mouth, I pray thee my Lord, bring together thy divine jaws, clamp down firmly, clasp, grind together these teeth we have cleansed.

Jaw. Comes up silently. Majestic smooth, sweeping motion. Awe.

—Gnash not, lest the work we have so faithfully performed, cometh undone!

So it is that I, mere amateur stomatologist, command God and retire in all tranquility, taking the time to properly coil the hoses, cleanse and stow the assorted drills and lances without the slightest risk of being ingested. With the Babinga I share cigarettes, cutting each one into three pieces. They wrap small leaves to form cigarette holders. I see by the look in their eyes that they are uneasy, much less pleased than I.

Don't get me wrong, this is no manner of slavery. In reality, it is they who employ me. The Babinga sign the contracts for dental care, they demand fabulous sums. I am at their service, receiving mere pittance, pocket money at best. I prefer working with Twa or Aka Pygmies, who share more generously with their employees, the day's earnings.

We live in sea caverns, round the rims of volcanoes, beneath howling storms. We eat seal flippers, quite good when pickled, hot sulfur and lightning.

Should I tell you just how it was that I came here? I'm a clandestine voyager, an illegal immigrant who dearly paid his trip. A stowaway who must reimburse the passers for the rest of his days. Cruel voyage, obliged to squat abaft the cathead, slumber fitfully with cheek to the inner fluke of a bower or cling to landing gear awaiting deployment. However, I have become a master binder, capable of trussing with art. I shall tie you with the black-wall-hitch, the catspaw, the rose lashing (placing the open loop of the throat seizing directly over the heart), mousing across the elbow from the biceps to the forearm, to be exact, the same behind the knees to join calves and thighs; very liberal use of reef-knots, sheep-shanks, figure of eights, bowline-hitches and racking. Were I ever to go too far in our play, trespass into that territory which lies beyond life and abandon you there all bound, a mariner would they seek, never a mere stowaway.

So you see, in evading mortgage I acquired this new, crushing debt, which in fact will only add its weight to that first debt incurred with IMG that will eventually catch up with me again. I've said it, bondsmen, bailiffs and "recoverers" are seasoned space and time travelers. There's no escaping them. They are inhuman, perfectly adapted to alien worlds. Perhaps if I were to spin violently to the left, then to the right, could I shrug off this thug. Adopt Coriolis effect.

The grin is of primordial importance in this place. It is one that every creature masters immediately upon being born. Just as antelope struggle to there feet within minutes after birth, in the manner that hyena pups kill weaker sibling, like the vulture chick that casts un-hatched eggs from the nest, the question of survival is quickly resolved here. They are practically born with a smile. An immaculate one, the lips drawn up over perfectly aligned teeth. Yet, there are no dentists or so few! Most of them have been devoured by their very patients, creatures with no patience. Others are amputees having left a hand, an arm and sometimes even a leg. Survivors these, continue their practice by using what's left: their mouths, their feet. I have seen practitioners engaged in mouth to mouth oral surgery. Such gain at stake here! The fever of Sutter's mill, the early Klondike that no menace can quell. How to reason these lustful idiots that I have joined? Tell them that yon star contains more gold than any galleon's hold?

Before coming here, I never imagined that my body would be covered with warts. Ultraviolet light radiating from this small sun makes them stand out white. I spend a great deal of time digging them out. Some have surprisingly deep roots going down to, and wrapping around, vital organs. It's hard work. I suck through a straw to remove the blood that continuously wells up. Could use an assistant or grow even more arms. Limb bouquet. But, being a dentist, an oral surgeon even, I can perform these operations upon myself without help. With the proper set of mirrors I can treat my own teeth and not long ago I even succeeded in performing a triple coronary bypass on my own person, using an old medical magazine for sole reference.

Humans are like metal. Depending on how they are charged, they can repulse or attract one another.

I return to an office, a medical cabinet to be sure. In glass presentation cases are intricately carved dentures shaped to fit the most pointed mouths. Beaks with minute, needle teeth. Prosthesis for dwarf pterodactyls. Some of the apparatus are only visible with optical aid. Mostly gold capped. Many drilling devices, all of them are hand powered. Unemployment is unheard of in my entourage. One man turns the turbine producing current, another fans the flames of a small smelter. We're melting aluminum from old engine blocks to make wrenches. This is family! We can make almost anything.

However, no set of medical encyclopedias, no computer programs could ever contain the information concerning the dental arrangements of all of those creatures possessing teeth that live in this neighborhood. They blow in the wind, gnashing at all that passes, the product of some prodigious pollination, each individual different from the other, spontaneous diversification. They erupt from the earth in living fountains, they drop from the sky, all have complex jaw structures harboring dental clusters. All of them are dependent on their teeth. None are predators, no ordinary carnivores. They are businessmen, bankers, lawyers, fellow doctors, magistrates and politicians.

—We're a majority of women, she tells me, this new patient of mine whom I shall shortly introduce. But before, our most recent conversation:

—Are there no artisans left, *plasticiens*, philosophers, creators of any kind? I ask.

—Creature of underdeveloped lower right quadrant, all that has no real importance has long disappeared. Mind you, entertainers thrive, are even a most vital part of commerce; but they must beware that their performance transgresses not the sole function of *divertissement*. No sullen types here, that might bring attention to stray from the vein of economical purity, the universe of business; lead towards other realms of thought. How misguided you are to think that culture of any sort might have had an influence upon the development of higher civilizations. Were it not for the merchant tribes, life forms would most certainly have remained rudimentary. Why do you think Igbo has become the universal language, just as English, Linglala and Sango, the tongue of Yakoma tribesmen, once were the vectors of expanding commercial conquest? The particularly spectacular sunsets, brilliant carmine and the most intense purples laced with the zigzag of fluorescent green, betray the nature of the ashes floating in the stratosphere. Immolation upon a grand scale of all that is superfluous. Business, Godmoney –you were just in his mouth– have purged the world of ancillary material that might lie in the path of progress. Quite naturally of course. There are no coercive forces here, no repressive police, no oppressive army.

We file, we clean, cap and polish, make bridges, the most splendid dentures. I know all of their mouths, maws, jaws, snouts. The smell of their breath, their grunts, squeals and groans are all familiar to me. Those who can communicate, often confide in me. Always stories of conquest. Some possess wings that we must place just so, before they can recline, open wide the mouth parts. This doesn't mean they can fly.

This one, she's in no way (not even remotely) related. On a classical cladogram, her position would be oblique, a separate and very distinct ramification requiring the annexation of another page.

She claims to recognize me, says I figure in several paintings conserved in the National Portrait Gallery. A hero of space conquest, fitted out with a massive glass suit made of thick transparent tubing. Wielding club-like weaponry in the act of fighting off hordes of aliens.

Her name is M'Ba which means to look or to observe in certain Bantu dialects. Claims to be greatly concerned with the half-life of the more virulent radioactive materials. It's not your normal ecological concern for when it might finally be safe to approach these substances but rather the shopper's worry about when a product will no longer be fit for consumption. Neptunium 237 with its 2.1 million year half-life, she considers to be perishable, fragile fruit it's best to consume immediately. This is well. I'm a firm advocate of nuclear therapy. Physically we've evolved. Body chemistry has changed. It is only now that we realize what a blessing massive irradiation really was. It has permitted mankind to advance with great leaps and bounds. Unearth entombed fissile materials! Our heads are cone shaped, some three feet high. Snort plutonium oxide following pyrophoric explosions! Inhale radioactive aerosols.

—That too! she says, speaking around my hand which is before her mouth. —I knew you were the author of that wonderful thesis *Downwinders, post-Pripyatic parameters.* No evolutionary stagnation.

I have little recipes of my own which form the basis of what I call atomic pharmacopae. I'm a nuclear pharmacist. Just as the witchdoctor goes into the bush seeking his medicinal plants, I gather depleted uranium hexafloride around ancient battlegrounds, I study water seapage to find concentrations nearing critical mass from plutonium migration. I even deal in toxic by-products: adding potassium ferrocyanide to precipitate cesium 137 from solutions of lye, water and cesium. These prescriptions have a shelf life longer than all of recorded history, no matter which direction you're looking at it from.

She heard of me from a patient which I had fitted with plutonium lozenges up the nostrils, a nasopharyngal treatment intended to increase cerebral irradiation.

Her voice is a deep vibration almost an infrasound, hardly decipherable. We opt for tactile communication. Physically, all about her is deep blue. She shares with me her knowledge of philosophy, perhaps long forgotten, she says, but most certainly of the future. The precepts of Moi Iiunga by which destruction is the most important force of the universe, to be applied even within ones own being. Nothing of suicidal nor negative but akin to the beauty which is to be found within the heart of a star which consumes itself with ferocious appetite, exploding to spread its flames over neighboring stellar population, dimmer and more modest; condemned to burn out like small candles in forgotten churches upon which vain prayers are lavished leaving only puddles of wax.

—Creation then?

—Its sole purpose is to satisfy destruction. A slavery of sorts.

—The measure of a civilization is not its technological achievement, nor perhaps even its science.

—Penetrate stars. Go in, impervious to heat. Ahead of it. Observe ocean fish, their colors, patterns and behavior. The fairy cod or the silver lookdown, mother of pearl and chrome.

She's very human, beautifully so, in appearance. Her shoulders are strong, wider than mine, the limbs are thick but very soft, the musculature being enveloped with some fat and a very oily skin. The skin itself being quite dark. She is heavy. I can't manage to pick her up but she's in no manner overweight. Must be extremely dense.

—Prepare yourself mentally, physically. Your biology, your chemistry. Technology has nothing to do with it. Sophisticated weaponry will be of no aid. Adopt ancient hunting techniques. Use harpoons, nets and weirs, camouflage, duck calls and whistles. Make fires on the prows of your canoes, lay low behind screens ready to hurl three pronged spears. Wear large leather ears. The lies of Gog is a recurrent theme.

The surprise is all the greater when I open her mouth. There's a windpipe up front beneath the tongue as with certain serpents. The Ambassador of Where had one just like this but they're apparently unrelated. A row of perfect teeth followed by short fang set deeper in. They are mobile and fold back to permit swallowing. When I gently pull them forward, venom pearls down from fine grooves, drips from the tips.

—Where from is she? mumble I.

—The important thing is that I am *she*, she says,—and that we have already known one another. Yes, I made your home, bore your children.

—The venom?

—Most potent of all.

—For what? I ask, slowly withdrawing my fingers from between the fangs. Thinking of the beautiful metallic red and green wasp, Chrysis ignita, anesthetizes a spider with swift sting, drags off to its nest, lays eggs on hapless host; devoured alive by larvae. All true except for the fact that the victim is usually no spider but fellow hymenoptera. The color blue of the most intense sheen can be seen to reflect from the carapace along with the green and red, verging on orange. Dazzling prelude to voluptuous death.

—A cobra possesses enough venom to fell an elephant; hardly ever does it strike one, she replies.

I treat her many times and constantly discover other fangs. Often, a tingling sensation accompanies the act of penetrating her mouth. Heat radiates through my body, warming even parts I had thought missing.

— It is my gift to you, she tells me. — Part blessing, part curse. Immunity to venom, at least mine which is the most lethal. A child lost in the desert is taken in by a serpent family. He returns to his tribe, a grown man bearing the secrets of the desert, lessons learned. How the spider forms frail round cage with joined legs to roll down dune. Snakes in turn shall clasp tails with mouths to form hoops; rise and roll. They will congregate, operate in packs. These times will be terrible. Imagine an army of serpents on the roll, advancing across the land with no need for road. All graduates of the spider school. The boy, now man, will never fall to serpent's bite.

Close to her face, the pupil's a tiny spiral, barred across the middle. Eyelashes long. Small flews flinging flamelettes, her nostrils perfectly formed, send her burning breath over my face. This smile she wears, be it *factice* with no bearing to emotion? Reptile smile. The grin of a creature lacking sudatory glands forced to sweat through the half open mouth to regulate body temperature. This is no ploy. I see there joy. The prehistory of love. Even an embryonic sentiment, hardly decipherable.

In turn, I remember Western Sahara, the smell of the black turban covering my nose and mouth. The sound of the wind-born sand peppering the cloth. In a turquoise colored room, a small quantity of water was suspended in a plastic bag. Mobile black points which I identified as flies, dotted the surface, inspecting the captured light.

I wandered in the perimeter of the camp, finding the jawbone of a goat with dried skin, part of an ear attached to a skull fragment, or was it a camel? The remains of a truck tire worn down to a spiral of black fiber, ominous nest, and finally, a camel scapula upon which I wrote feverishly, using cinder mixed with the water from the suspended plastic pouch which I had burst, though not to drink. Another kind of thirst.

Combatants of freedom who survived there, shared with me this most rare thing which suspended in small quantities, captured light. In this glittering liquid I dipped my pen, a splinter, my pen, a simple shard.

—You need to go through the motions, we know, a mental calligraphy.

I could have pricked my fingertip, drawn blood to write with. But the few drops would hardly have sufficed.

—If blood were your choice, you should have opened your chest, and written with red ocean as they had done, your history seen from the receiving end. No hadith whereby the Prophet recommends purging the body cavity of its organs and washing the heart to obtain a higher level of purity. He performed this act when only four, didn't he?

—It was Gabriel.

The flies had transferred. They clung to my eyes seeking there the only moisture left, for I had emptied the water pouch. I urinated but not a drop reached the ground.

There the wind was master, making of rocks and pebbles, puppets and dolls that clinked and chimed like metal. It carved cliffs to reveal stone bones of creatures gone. Boring caverns, tunnels and great arches that hummed and sang songs telling how I once was this thing with frill wreathing a bony crest from which thrust three horns, each bigger than I now be, then was. With protective plates going down my back, or this other, all teeth each one longer than a saber beneath immense ocular cavities that must have held eyes that beheld zones of obscurity. The dimmest of heavens and, once again, the faintly glowing tails of incoming comets.

How is it that I so intimately know the comportment of dinosaurs? How when the brontosaurus was attacked by a pack of tyrannosaurus, he would eject his tail, frantically thrashing tons of bleeding meat upon which they would all pounce while he escaped hardly scathed. And this tail would be replaced with a fresh new one in no time. That most all of these giant reptiles would blaze with the most violent skin colors when angered. Many were capable of blending with the surrounding environment at will. That they wore the same frozen grin which never changed. Moved rapidly with mechanical flicking action after long periods of immobility. Pumping action on the forelegs as if doing pushups. They built huge nests of vegetal matter. Decay = heat = incubation. Clucking noises from within announce the arrival of the hatchlings. With certainty, I can affirm that the enormous sclerotic ring of certain ischiasaurs not only permitted the apprehension of abyssal prey, but also served the function of a light bucket, gathering the very faintest parcel of light from the deep night sky as these creatures partook of their favorite pastime, basking at the surface and contemplating the cosmos. Why, when running hand down own spine, feel I scutes emerging? First cousin to the saurian! The ability to remain perfectly immobile, absolutely nothing moves, not even the eye which never blinks, glistening black ball; not the trace of a breath. This is an altogether different conception of time. The head can turn extremely rapidly, jerk with the snap of a mechanical puppet. Dull green above with a perfect crest topped by a row of small claw-like cleats, pink pearls along the mouth, violent green undersides. A drape of skin hangs from the throat. There's a new tail, more slender, fused onto the stub of the old one. Shreds of molt cling in tatters to the thighs.

MORE ON REPTILE COMPORTMENT.

With such oversized wings, how does the pterodactyl walk? In the manner of the chimney swift, it hardly ever touches ground. It's always airborne but if by misfortune it should come to the ground it hops awkwardly with its wings spread wide in the fashion of a vulture approaching carrion. Like the bat, it hangs upside down when roosting. And evidently, rising thermal currents are required to get it aloft. Note the way of opening the mouth, licking a stone, cocking the head.

Not a past life nor a parallel one. Perpendicular and always intersecting. At this point, information is brushed off, adheres. It is for this reason that with time one can become acutely sensitive to others. We are all related to one another but also to animals, insects, vegetation, minerals, water, fire, other suns, the cosmos and all therein.

All peoples will have, in time, their own ordeal. If yours are tribulations of the evening, you should prepare for them with the coming of dawn. Learn to, in turn, convey the accumulation of knowledge, especially the gathering of remote information concerning hidden conflicts, secret combats, all venue of things once known but now forgotten, ideals bearing the weight of imposed silence. Let no one tell you that these things are of no importance, that your cause is one that is lost in advance.

I found that death came to perch here, incubating its brood in vast white nests that were first taken to be tabernacles. These zones were the real war grounds of conflicts planned elsewhere. Sacred to industry as the testing grounds for new weaponry, vital to commerce, for here would be the demand, the large scale market, the remote finish line of the arms race.

—Believe you, me to be politically manipulated? It is you who are manipulated! There's a storm. Not warm, safe before some hearth, I'm out in it. Loping beneath cloud with viridian belly, hoping that lightning shall strike directly down this spine with erect bone plate. This be not fate. Capitulate. Sung, accompanied by an orchestration of shattering glass. No frenzied percussion but the rhythm of monster heart in deep hibernation.

I have one foot upon the bottom rung of the flaming ladder which leads to the heart of a sun or to hell, the latter being up. In both cases I shall confront fire. Adopt the chrome skin of the desert ant, walk briskly on high legs, well away from burning sands. Should you stumble here, there shall be no helping hands.

—Think you to be on some distant world? Look out of the window, Citizen.

All is perfectly normal. A well-dressed woman squats curbside, shining the latest design high heel with oily excrement that she scoops up from the street with her open palm. A boy walks his rhinoceros. It takes special skill to avoid a kill. Snap the long lead, stay well to the side. Guide the half-blind bolide of flesh by using smell alone. A man wearing Bermuda shorts, whom I first believe to be doing pushups on the street corner, is actually lapping up vomit. There's a vending machine with human body parts. A bag of salted hands or ears can be purchased with small change and consumed while waiting for the suburban shuttle train. Probably healthier than peanuts or chips.

—We're cannibals. Our coprolites will prove it.

—Walk on water. Seek sanctuaries however circumspect they may be.

I marvel as she engulfs birds, the spectrum reflecting from the feathers all drawn back, shining in her half-closed eyes.

—Civil Man, come by my side.

I fight the urge to pull off her head. Consume it as if eating a grapefruit whole. Perhaps disagreeable, but a necessity. This isn't violence but sustenance.

A fang breaks off, lodges beneath my skin. I discover immediately that there are several levels of infinity.

The house has been divided in two. Bars run down the middle to separate us. We speak through bars, we share food through bars, we make love through bars, have children with beautiful scales and acerated teeth, who, while still young, go freely, slipping through the bars. Night come, we linger near cascades, fishing for salamanders by torchlight.

—There's no refinement in your manners, she reproaches, —The crag lizard, the soa soa has more education.

We watch an old John Woo movie. The plot is Chaucerian. There are advertisements every three minutes during which time Secretary birds bring her smaller reptiles including several varieties of very venomous snakes. Thirsty, I leave the apartment momentarily, choose a young tree across the street and perforate the bark with my incisors to suck the sap. The tree is full of cicadas buzzing. Rattle snakes too, shaking their tails. This is long before serpents learn to form wheels and certainly even much before the advent of the half snake who will have forgotten that he once was a whole snake, the other half having been severed by witless, fearful individuals who would have mistaken it for the head, thinking thus to *prive* me of necessary venom.

A breadline has formed. Young girl comes up in the tail. At first I think she's just joining the poor, taking her turn for food. But she draws an awesome looking revolver from her vest and carefully takes aim at the back of the skull of the last one in the queue, the man right in front of her. What's she waiting for? Trying to align them all? Blam!

—You're dead! says the whipster, as the steel-jacketed bullet slams through the heads of thirty unemployed. Unlike dominos, they collapse every which way. She methodically empties their pockets, prying crowns and caps from teeth with a jackknife.

Then, from a lower jaw from which the top of the head is missing, she takes a wad of still warm chewing gum and plops it into her own mouth.

—Mmmm, mint flavor, she mumbles, and stumbles away.

Should I have shown her how to finish what she had started? Kick them when down, already dead? Separate the entire head.

An apology for violence: Contrarily to all predictions, the moon has drawn in closer. Tides are much stronger. Even inland rivers have roaring tides. The North has become subtropical. Our own vascular activity is affected, blood surging uncontrollably through veins. Males have trouble putting down erections, females are ever receptive. All violence is magnified whether it is verbal, conjugal or full-blown war. Hark back (or ahead) to Hollywood.

Return before the publicity is over, wipe mouth on sleeve.
—I believe that Flame has brought me here. With it, I have slumbered. Recently walked to dwarf companion star.
—Three million years from now, archeologists will unearth a fossilized bus with its load of passengers. They'll call this animal with its belly-full of humans, Rotopod Terribilis, ferocious predator that moved swiftly on circular limbs; diet: homo-asapienza, (the unknowing ones).
Going to the toilet, I find fur clinging to the stool lid. Proof enough that there's been a mammal in here! Grasping a kitchen knife, I frantically search the apartment.
—Warm blooded, milk-giving thing!
It runs low to the floor, drops an attaché case in its haste and finally escapes through the window, showering the room with icicles broken from the super-refrigerated sash.

A folder found in this case, contains one sheet which reads: *Inherent difficulty in establishing clinical judgment. Third party information, necessary for a proper diagnosis of mental disorder, is understandably quite rare. Individual is difficult to follow, extremely mobile. Assumes different heteronyms, disguises. Has frequent recourse to surgery for physical modification and even complete transformation. Criteria are fully met but difficult to prove.*

Today I take what books remain on the shelf, the very last ones, those that I always wanted to keep by my bedside. Spread them out on the sidewalk for sale.
—It's amusing, says a tall thin man, leafing through *Neo-Cosmology, a Glimpse of Deep Space,* —Like the crusades told by us, the Arabs. A different point of view, never heard, or so little. White/Indian relations told by the Indians. African colonization told by the Blacks. Untold. I myself am from Algeria, says he.
I'm carrying the severed head again, can't seem to get rid of it. Every

time I purposefully abandon it somewhere, it pops up again. This time I hold the head before me, at arms length, drop it and punt.

With the money earned from selling the books, I buy fortified beer, add codeine and consume an enormous quantity. My perimeter is a city bench upon which I collapse.

—Iiunga, she calls me, —God has lost a filling, complaining of horrible pain, you must go and treat it.

It is true, I have responsibilities. The fact that I'm the last one to bed in the evening, the first to rise in the morning, doesn't necessarily make me a good father.

Listen now. It's almost midnight and the sky is just beginning to dim. Call it a brilliant twilight. The bird I hear is a thief. He's been stealing songs from all over the world and I suspect that he may have gone even farther than that. An immense repertoire betrays distant nesting grounds: metallic ticking noises of the Pygmy Sunbird, croaking of the Wattle-Eye, feeble piping sounds, small muffled flute, insignificant twittering of the Fire-Finch cut with long melodious wails of a marsh birds, or the characteristic three powerful notes of the Moho. Then come sounds unfit for a bird's beak, no melody, only a shriek. Must increase tetrahydrocannabinol level to reduce stress.

Hyena

I'm wearing a giant dog tag made of slate with my name written in chalk. Aloba. This nominal blackboard also warns people to keep away from me. Saint Jacques' Tower is still standing, though shrouded in a veil. Once again it is our home, but it now stands on a small island, the Seine river having jumped its banks to become much wider than it was the last time that I had lived here. Not yet the width of the Amazon, but certainly that of the Orenoco, it's no longer a safe place to be, the bodies it carries being sufficient enough proof of the danger one runs if he chooses to hug to the banks. Don't think for as much that the environs of Paris have become a swamp, that we be bog men. The dry season comes with surprising swiftness, never when you're expecting its arrival. Quickly, seize a spade, dig up your water tank-frog then, and be off with it, several more if you can. True, mist still rises from the jungle in the morning, often into the early afternoon, but it is a dry fog through which some try running with their mouths open, inhaling only the pink dust and brown smoke of which it is constituted.

Using the frontal sculpting technique whereby one draws the main view on the stone and then proceeds to attack directly, working around as necessary, I've completed a crucifixion, the Christ figure being cross-less but nevertheless evoking the shape of the cross he was crucified upon by the position he's in. I call this piece "The Prophet". Does this mean I've espoused Islam? It is one of my best sculptures, though I never was paid for it, the arms having broken off at the shoulders while being transported over the Alps.

Sweating. Beeswax, small foundry, fine sand from the river bottom, almost a clay, that takes well the shape of what's pressed down upon it. Mostly make metal pots from broken engine parts, always adding a special touch: two hearts and *mbi ye mo* which means quite bluntly, "I want you" in Sango, the central African riverine language.

I also deal in artwork other than my own, being incapable of keeping up with the demand, producing extremely slowly and more often that not, destroying with uncontrollable rage what I have already done. Artwork is illegal, yet highly sought after. Rare contraband, it's almost a drug. I'm a thug, just look at my mug!

A magnificent ancient oaken door with Anglo-Norman plate bronze from the mausoleum of Bohemond de Tarente serves for my model. Copy the incisions, the smooth flat surfaces with depressed areas for the hands and feet. They've been stamped out rather than sculpted.

My back yard is full of pits, vehicle carcasses and scats from passing cats. You think I might be master to a pack of terrier dogs, run a junkyard from which I sell spare parts? Ungainly African carrion-feeding birds turn the soil with their massive beaks. A marabout, a hammerkop. The wrecks are what are left of the numerous time travel devices that I've owned. It took me so long to learn that there's no point in chasing after it; if you're patient enough, time will come your way in a tumble. Choose your direction; don't fumble. As for the cats, they're prehistoric, swarthy and low to the ground, with stocky legs that are more suited to pouncing than running. Lurking for prey they can remain immobile for weeks. Their urine reeks.

I don't know anymore whether this is Africa, Europe or Asia. Definitely not America. There are no clearly definable borders. There's been continental interpenetration, not just the flux and reflux of populations migrating, exile/invasion. Entire sections of land seem to have suddenly shifted but this is no earthquake. It's as if tectonic plates had collided, overlapped, bringing fragments of totally different worlds together in a blink. This isn't at all what has actually happened, yet in a way, it is. Hornbills now nest in the city. Once revered as sacred birds, they've become a nuisance. Females are confined to mud nests plastered to building facades while males attack their own reflections that they mistake for rival males, smashing out with their massive beaks, the mirrored windows of high office buildings. For this and other reasons, nobody wants to rent out office space in the taller buildings. I occupy a full three floors, from the ninety eighth to the one hundred and first (there are no elevators in these tall buildings that people now fear to go into), filled with endoskeletons, mesoskeletons, rolls of manuscripts suspended from the ceiling to save space. All of the voluminous things that wouldn't fit into the Saint Jacques tower, or that K2 refused to let me keep there: "fire hazard" she used to say, "too dusty, causes allergies, stench." The windows are all broken out. Needless to say, there's no air conditioning. The heat can be unbearable. Insects are everywhere, especially at night when I work by the light of oil lamp, which isn't very bright. Moths, mosquitoes and all manners of nocturnal flying things make the atmosphere less than breathable. I'm obliged to constantly fan the air in front of me. Stinging small flies cling to my face. I cough up a lacewing.

The rhinoceros, which are so highly prized as pets, have brought along with them their very own small ecosystems based upon the dung, which they copiously dispense. It is true that the dung beetles attract in turn the hornbills which find here, momentary respite from their fight with their mirror image rivals, and nourishment to continue that combat. Many new bridges have been thrown across the river and its numerous branches, oxbows and run-off basins. Some are monumental. This one in front of me is made of petrified sequoia trunks. It glitters.

The most surprising thing is that much seems unchanged, technology hasn't gone much further; actually, it will have considerably developed only to suffer a great decline before returning to more classical, less sophisticated systems, much of which were already far beyond the scope of my comprehension. But there aren't the flying automobiles, the futuristic transportation devices that you might have expected, nor are there to be found the extremely sophisticated communication modes there will once have been. This has all been abandoned or fallen into oblivion. We communicate by using trained falcons that carry our messages.

Fuel? Cars run on just about anything; discarded wrapping paper mixed with a handful of twigs and dead leaves, crushed beets, corn mash or turnips. Mine runs most often on whatever table scraps are available, sometimes the carcass of a dead cat or even a pigeon will suffice for the day. You thought only fossil fuels would do? The petroleum companies had everyone fooled. If you're really nostalgic about petrol though, all you need is a shovel full of crude oil. Needless to say, dense clouds of pollution hang in the air, tangible objects that can knock you down, just like running into some kind of a dirty wall. I drive an old Honda of the most common type. I've installed Venetian blinds for intimate moments. The dashboard is littered with erotic drawings and pornographic sketches that I elaborate while engaged in the act.

There are hives high up on buildings. City bees produce a very black honey. They gather pollen from toxic urban flowers that grow beneath bridges. A restaurant advertises "Sea food, low metallicity, mercury free" and you can be sure that it isn't.

—Why don't you go get the fly, I say to the jumping spider.

In spite of the danger, some of us now live down by the river, others in it. It has been renamed the Oubangui for obvious reasons. Binga fish abound, their thumb sized razor teeth capable of inflicting serious wounds, even amputating limbs from adult bathers or carrying off unwary children. The sandbars are rife with Nilotic crocodiles, more often than not napping while they digest human fare. It isn't at all rare that they catch those that frequent the banks unaware.

Fishermen's families live atop small islands and upon rocks where they smoke their daily catch. Pirogues incessantly ply the swift muddy waters, carrying produce from one bank to the other, some coming in from the dense jungle surrounding the city. They're loaded down, low to the water, with manioc tubers, taro, igname and plantain bananas. By night they navigate with the stars or by following the odors if it be cloudy or too smoky to see the heavens (though these waterways be no sea, navigation on the ever-changing river and its byways is difficult), carrying contraband, sometimes artwork; more often, stolen cigarettes, petrol or body parts such as kidneys and hearts, just as smugglers always have and for ever will.

Some citizens have elected domicile in the city zoo, entire families live next to the lion cages (note that lions can speak and carry on conversation), splash with otters and penguins, play amongst the seals and fight with them for their meals. Here's a boy carrying off in his mouth, rotten mackerel that he steals.

Giant incinerators belch dioxin.

I know that I've been struck by lightning, shot in the head. I once possessed a beak, had wings and claws, an immense tail was mine, scutes grew upon my back. I was striped, had whiskers that were as stiff as steel wires. At one time, my rib cage was so vast that an adult elephant could easily have taken up quarters within.

I'm small again, perhaps less cunning than I was before but so much more arrogant, ambitious and cruel in the proper manner.

I haven't yet finished with the transformations over which there's no control, no anticipation. On Tuesday, I was mottled. Wretched beyond misery, my skin teaming with insects. Chemical, phosphorescent and evil, emitting fumes and vapors that no living thing could breath, and all within my perimeter immediately fell dead. I finally became fire, licking and curling blue, red and yellow with heat unbearable. No longer did I have a shadow.

Human remains have been found: bones swaddled in half digested shreds of garments mixed with fragments of eyeglasses, shoes and other indigestible materials, much like giant owl pellets. What beast coughs up these remains? Very often they are to be found in the proximity of giant nests that have been constructed with auto fenders, shredded tires, even small cars smashed down and twisted into frass, all of this, perched atop the tallest buildings. No eggs though, and the avian predator, assuming that it has wings, is always out.

Naturally, now that I'm a geriatric, certain people consider me to be an authority on whatever might be odd. My opinion is solicited. One must be careful. It's a difficult period for prophets. When Christ returned, he was immediately recognized and bludgeoned to death. Wasn't given the slightest chance. Perhaps this is also the reason for which Mehdi, the Twelfth Imam, disappeared in 874 and has yet to return. Mohamed is much wiser, staying at a safer distance while waiting for real proof of fidelity. I came, viewed the scene around one of these nests and slipped a hen's egg painted red beneath the head of the one who lay dead.

—Surveillance. Will never hatch. Will hatch with time. Won't.

The exhaust fumes hanging in the air enhance the taste of pistachio nuts. I leave a trail of nutshells behind me. In this manner I rarely get lost in the city. Language is deep thunder.

Ivory is laid out on my kitchen table, including a huge pair of tusks. I'll sculpt them. Not that I'm a poacher. Remember the truck wreck in *Spider 1*? It wasn't far from here. The tusks had gone right through the cab, killing the driver. I pulled one of the best tips from his skull, which it had traversed through, and through. Lebanese, heading into Sudan with his load.

Next to the tower I've built an oven to bake bricks, twenty thousand of them. It takes forty-eight hours to bake a load and all the while the fire must be tended. Start it going with dry brush taken in from the bush, logs hauled from the river can be added, even if they're soaked to the core, once the blaze is going. The best firing is during the night when the winds have died down, sometimes I'll add small clay effigies upon which I blow salt through slits in the oven wall. This gives a metallic patina to the surrounding bricks. It's not a church that I'm building but a small mosque with an elegant thin minaret to which I'll attach loud speakers. I don't walk so much any more. When I go down to the water from the heart of my little island, I drive an insular vehicle, a really common Datsun that has no windows left. Looks like a little stock car. Nadjas rear their hoods in the middle of the trail and strike the fenders, thoroughly mean creatures. The Honda is on the other bank.

A German girl, though a good swimmer, is pulled out into the current and sucked over the falls, explodes on the rocks at the bottom. What's left of her is taken away by crocs that keep the body parts in their underwater larders for days before swallowing. On an improvised airstrip, an American strides into the spinning propeller of a small plane waiting to take her away. Guess she just didn't see the blades that were transparent from spinning so fast. Her head disappears. It'll take time before these savages get used to the dregs of the civilization, which they once spawned. Personally, I stay away from planes. They're usually over loaded and the hot, windless air doesn't help getting aloft. I'd rather use my own wings. Though many feathers are missing, I know how to use rising currents over brush fires and cliff sides. Taken individually, the feathers are splendid, each having the metallic reflection that the plumage that certain tropical birds possess. Landing smoothly is an altogether different problem.

Leopards love eating dog. Infidels prefer hog.

They perform a dance here, usually around large fires. If you go too fast, your body disintegrates. It's a question of angular momentum.

Zanda and I were suddenly struck by extreme old age. Instant geriatrics. I've lost an eye, many teeth, most of my memory, and can no longer walk. My skin is covered with splotches of depigmentation and hair grows from unexpected places. I spend most of the day screaming from horrible pain that no morphine could ever calm. She has become extremely unpredictable, violent in her reaction to ordinary situations and refuses to take the medicine which I scavenge for her on the black market. She still sings to me Pygmy lullabies. There's distant thunder; tropical storms seem to be circling the city. But it hasn't rained for so long.

I shed my skin like a serpent. Begins an itching in the back, rub hard against the curb, squeeze myself between the bumpers of tightly parked cars. I pull myself out of the skin, leaving unwanted parasites clinging to this floating transparent self. Tax collectors, duns, mortgagees and the general holders of debts that follow me in compact groups, are momentarily thrown off by this transparent me, upon which they vent their rage, each vying for the noble piece, a hand, the private parts or the entire head which they can now fold and take under arm. Some, to which indemnities are owed, are in the rare Red Eft stage, whereby they can walk freely on land needing only the scantiest morning mist to keep their orange skin moist.

She and me crawl, hiss to converse, and piss uncontrollably. We need diapers again, but our clothing soaks it all up to a certain extent, the overfill just drains out. Follow us. We'll feed you!

Try to go home. At number eight there's only a gate. It leads nowhere. Yet this is where home shall be in distant future and we know it. The iron bars are so corroded by the acid vapors filling the air that parts have been gnarled down to wire thickness.

—Butt our heads up against it, wonder why we can't find the island? I ask her.

—Blow on it and it'll fall apart.

We're more resistant; our lungs are full of scar tissue. Microclimates develop in the heart of the city. Ferns, tropical plants and insects thrive in the dead of winter.

—Tell me what we're doing? How did we get here?

Cooking the meat. Red smoke, like that of a distress flare, rises from the charred skin. The odor burns the nose, chokes. How can they take it? The deck is now covered with stinking flesh.

I tell myself that this is definitely the dream. Forget the real one that I was hired to dream. The one where I'm working in the high office building.

Two nights have come in only a few hours. This world spins fast. We're much heavier here. When the sky is dark it has a maroon hue. Stars are perfectly clear, never winking. Does this mean that they're all planets? Such quantity. Had this sun over-abundantly spawned in prevision of there being few survivors? They race across the night sky in patterns totally unknown to me.

She unties me. I had been bound with very complicated knots.

—How can you consume the flesh of such a creature?

—Roll in its fluids. See how we cover the deck with this oil. It's already protecting you from the rays of the carbon star. Once you've rubbed it into your skin, no harm can befall you.

It's an early-universe star, probably one thousand times the sun's volume. It'll only last a couple, maybe three million years.

—How can there even be any planets then?

She cooks the smaller fish that had spilled from the bigger one's belly just before we had gone into the suburbs of the city paved with gold where even the sewers shown beneath the dirt. It's being grilled over a blue fire made with copper sulfate crystals. This specimen has little legs.

—Eat! she says, thrusting a chunk my way.

—It'll make me vomit!

—Think of it as being the blowback of western politics.

—There must be land somewhere.

—Vessel over there, says a brother.

I'm changing again, spines growing out. Long danger. Iodine.

—That's what I love about you.

These spines are purple with a tinge of orange at the tips. My eyes become brilliant green, no less intense than a beryllium fed flame.

It's night-time again. We're all topside, starboard, but this is no boat coming along. Between crests we see a sleek thing bobbing. It's a White man, appearing very long in his prone floating position. His head is turned away from us.

Above there's an asterism that resembles Delphinius, only much bigger, spreading over the entire zenith. The man in the liquid rises and attempts to speak but the wind takes away his words. He can't even turn his face toward us.

Sunlight hits the water with a sizzle-causing aerosol to mist. The wind abates.

—Say a prayer to keep him away.

—Shouldn't we bring him in?

—He's a White!

This sun has no life. It's purely mineral. Several outer shells of gas have already burned off. It is of stunning beauty. Eclipsing objects regularly pass in front of it, revealing their companions that fill the sky. From here, I see a cortege of planets that spread into infinity. To think that scientists once questioned whether exo-planets even existed! This one star has at least seven to eight hundred of them that are visible, and certainly countless others strung out beyond.

We are poachers.

—This sun snuffed, what will become of these worlds?

—Just like the meat left behind when men took only the ivory from elephants, the horns from the rhinoceros, the pelts from the bison, scavengers will come in.

—Destruction on an unimaginable scale.

—Diamond!

Never shall I know how they put out the fires of the carbon star, or how they could ever have managed to take it into tow, the future diamond of incommensurable size. I'm very ill; not the exotic deep space malaria that I had often feared but an extremely resistant strain. One that through countless mutations, had acquired a new virulence that's taking hold out here.

Delirious, I grope in my pocket to find a tiny toy frog that glows in the dark.

One thing is certain: I can't keep away from the jungle anymore and shall always return to it, whether from love or obligation.

—There are cycles that are stronger than alternation. Zaïre was Congo, is Zaïre again. Rhodesia was Zimbabwe and likewise, it too is Zimbabwe again. But never will it be Rhodesia again.

On the return leg we cross the path, once more, of the long white floating man. The one who wouldn't show his face.

—Shipwrecked?

—Stay away! He's a Caïman. An evil water divinity. He has the head of a gavial. All teeth.

—Can inflict nasty wounds I suppose.

—Only to the flesh; much less dangerous than the spirit-eaters of your civilization, of which you represent the perfect specimen.

I think of the seven hundred worlds going cold. Can they interact to form a mass heavy enough to ignite? Another system could eventually evolve.

We withdraw to a beach on the edge of a methane sea. I swim straight out, a great distance being that it's an effortless exercise. There isn't any horizon for this is a giant gaseous planet. A fog sets in. I can't see the coast anymore. Zanda makes a fire to guide me back. It has a purple flame. In cliffs just above the beach are to be found small golden mummies.

—This is good for your fever, she says, presenting what appears to be nothing more than a small leaf of bluish paper.

Upon it is written *Onandaga*.

—I want to return to Cyana.

—I understand, she says —It's good for you. I can respect that. But this time, promise me you'll forget about the Cavern King.

In Paris, the asphalt has been ripped up revealing the original cobble stones. Exuberant tropical vegetation has overthrown certain buildings. The Eiffel Tower has been totally taken apart and reconverted into automobile fenders, casseroles and cheap knives that break all too often when you plant them in the belly of a foe. I set up a small street-side shop where I peddle the very last bolts.

Bistros will always exist and it's with certain satisfaction that I take my place at a sidewalk terrace for my morning coffee after having sold a fistful of rusted screws.

Oloman Klanik arrives in somewhat of a panic. He's become huge and in spite of the heat, wears a heavy fur coat.

—Thought you had died! he says.

—I did.

—Of some archaic disease that's been eliminated long ago, like cancer or aids. People usually return with decorative plants, unusual fauna or strange foods. But you! What have you to show? You've changed so much. Look at me. I'm overweight but I still look human. What are these spines coming out of your forehead? You look like a porcupine!

68

He goes on and on, not waiting for an answer to his questions.

—Come over for lunch. I'm living with my concierge now, he continues, —She makes the best petit plats. She's Portuguese. Want some bakalao?

He rises from the table taking my coffee with him.

—They just installed an elevator. He returns to the table. —Death. That's what I wanted to talk to you about. You missed it. A couple of years ago, a city bus jumped the curb, killing every one sitting here. Me, I was downstairs pissing, taking note of the beautiful ceramic design on the toilet walls. There's a study to be made. They're usually underground. Sometimes they go under the terrace and you can catch a distorted image, through glass tiles, of the consumers sitting above you while you urinate. The decor of the stairs leading down, the patterns on the tiles. Do they turn to the right or to the left?

Someone should make a book about little things like that. Things that seem of no importance at all can save your life. Saved mine, didn't it? Take the shape of shit in the street. Just the other day I saw one standing up like a little puppet, another one pasted to the wall. You wonder how dogs do it. It's sculpture. Real art! But that's nothing of course compared to the rhinos. Suburban gardens. There's another subject for you. You can't imagine what exotic plants grow here now.

—That's death in a way.

—I thought that you'd say something like that. But this terrace thing with the bus, it really shook me up. I thought about you, off somewhere again, probably doing something of extremely risky. Maybe already dead and me here safely drinking my coffee. The bus driver was intoxicated. He reeked of garlic, red wine, just like the early Crusaders did. So say the Arab scholars.

A man runs past being pulled by an enormous rhinoceros on leash. Several tons of power, a certain type of beauty and stupidity. All very difficult to bring to a stop.

It gores two citizens waiting for the bus before attacking an automobile, which it overturns with no effort.

Morning prayers echo from the minarets of countless mosques that dot the city.

—I'm sure that this is all new to you. There was only one when you were last here; it was down by the zoo, as if part of the menagerie, no?

—I've always been a soldier of Islam. Remember when I told you to chuck your Talmud, burn your Bible? Only the Crescent and the Star. Learn your *sourats*. Especially "The Elephant" without neglecting "The Cow," "Hud," "Thunder" and "Al-Hijr."

—I know, "Smoke," "The Bees," he says.

—Don't forget "Nûn or Calme," "The Spider" and "The Moon," each containing several levels of interpretation.

—What do you think of my new coat? he says, rising and turning to show all sides. —I just bought it yesterday. By the way, cigarettes no longer exist.

I notice he's carrying twelve pens, that his fingers are brown from smoking. Lying so inveterately, misinforming, constantly changing reality, isn't his fault at all. Oloman used to be a top journalist. This is "vestigial behavior."

—Tell me again about streamlining information.

—A notorious terrorist declares "there'll be no sleep for Americans until there's security in our lands and in Palestine," drop the end and you've got "there'll be no sleep for Americans," which is much more of a pointless threat and justifies any means of elimination, including leveling the mountains he might be hiding in. You can also change the concept: "we made him, we'll kill him" to just "we'll kill him" which is much less ambiguous and leaves no place for useless reflection such as to who's responsible for the formation of this terrorist.

—We'll have to eat together, I say.

—Yes. You'll have to come over. I'm living with my concierge. She's Moroccan. Makes delicious tadjin. I wasn't able to sleep last night. There's no night left, let's say the darkness is gone. It was like daylight! didn't you see?

—No, I arrived at dawn.

—Zanamya 750, it's a mirror that's actually a full 1000 meters wide, in orbit. Lighting up the night like the sun. The equivalent of 800 full moons putting down a luminous footprint of 150/450 kilometers. And it was blinking! You missed the moon too. Publicity seen by every living being on this planet. First and last quarters light up with big letters, any message desired, fueled by solar panels on the light side. Most brilliant commercial idea yet. Where were you arriving from? Africa again?

—There and beyond.

—They're so rich now. I've heard that Europeans have been migrating there. Ready to do almost anything: street sweepers, dishwashers, shoeshiners.

—Prostitutes and pushers too.

—Indeed, African scientists have been coming here more and more often to study our cultural folklore, our primitive art, our simple fishing and agricultural techniques. Anthropologists too, measuring our craniums, the length of our legs compared to theirs.

—Lend me the crossbow, will you?

He pulls the small handmade, hunting device from beneath his coat and slides it across the tabletop. Disagreeable scraping noise on the Formica. I give him three cigarettes in exchange, (actually only half of one cut into three pieces).

—You only need it for this afternoon? he asks.

I add another two, making five.

—Keep it for the night, tomorrow noon even, if you want. By the way, where did you find these?

—Paid for them at the counter.

—How is Zanda?

—There's a scent about her. Overpowering. It leaves a burning sensation when inhaled. From the nostrils, the throat and deep down into the chest, radiating from the lungs to the heart and throughout the vascular system.

—Can you not speak clearly?

—I'm mythology. Wherever I go, reality warps. I devour truth, leaving behind the peelings, the bones picked clean. The lies that I leave in my wake will be history for your children. Truth is in my belly and I take it off with me. It is something they'll never know.

—Today we are hyenas!

—It's your choice.

Once, I saw two at the airport. Held on tight leashes, the owner intent on showing off what he thought to be black Guishas, right? They were long, lanky, very dark. Eyes so wild, speaking of beautiful violence growing within. Time bombs. I'm sure they devoured the man, finishing off right down to the last scrap of him, even cracking the bones open to accede to the marrow, and so much the better.

There's nothing of constant or reassuring about them, not the kind of women you'd want beneath your roof if you aspire to a secure and tranquil existence. You'll never be able to retire. You have to be some kind of predator yourself to live with one of these. They destroy all notions of romance, of classical love. Whether your story begins in the silence of the sands of Sudan or with the blasting music of a nightclub, nothing will ever, ever be the same for you again. Another type of music is omnipresent, like the triple throb on the planet Qwob where three suns in tight orbit play powerful magnetic games with passing puppet worlds. Percussion regulates the life of all things beneath.

I'm home just in time. We have a conversation, the little one and I.
—Finish your lunch, I say.
—I want to see Babar.
—He'll wait for you. What's most important now is that you eat properly.
—What's that? she asks, pointing at doglet. —An elephant, a baboon, a moray eel, a hyena, a rattlesnake?
—No, they lived only in America, in the Oval Office to be precise.
—A seal then?
—Yes. It's a midget seal. It lurks off ice banks, gulping down any fish that pass by, while trying to avoid ending up just a skin in an igloo.
We say that we are orcas, sheep and dinosaurs. No ordinary tyrannosaurus but archaeopteryx; we've got to be able to fly and pterodactyls have been ruled out.
—Show me your eyes, I say.
She comes in close.
—What do you see Daddy?
Holding her small face between my hands, —forest honey, the deep dark variety, the light of a sun which perhaps isn't ours but one very far away, the ocean deep down where fish have little lanterns on their heads, jungle...
—With cobra snakes?
—Caterpillars are falling from high branches. There are so many of them dropping to the ground that it sounds like heavy rainfall.
—Frogs too?
—At nighttime, there are so many of them croaking together, down by where the two rivers meet, that we hear thunder.

—Daddy, you remember New York?

—The strange parlor where Mamma had her nails done by Chinese girls. They said she had beautiful claws, didn't they?

Smoke.

Here it is. The music is discreet during the day, hardly noticeable, the throb of an overgrown heart at the most, yet already having an effect on coronary activity. With nightfall, it grows. It's no simple tam- tam that might well up from the jungle. It takes hold of everything. There's no escaping. Down to the deep metal core of the planet and back up through the crust sending tremors through the biggest buildings, shaking dew from broad banana tree leaves, casting down sleeping creatures from precarious perches, boiling the sperm in men's testicles and vibrating the eggs deep in women's bellies.

Songs of incomparable beauty arise. Listening carefully, you can guess the shape of the lips, the form of the tongue, the depth of the throat from which they come. It is a land where one never sleeps; there's no rest. Fitful naps at best.

It is here that she will watch over you, keeping vigil so that you may pretend slumber. But beware, he who deceives her!

I know of one man who thought to be her keeper. She told him that her name was Ruth. This satisfied him. Hadn't missionaries preceded him? She was civilized, no? Just before killing him, she revealed her family name: Less.

We're printing many small political newspapers, some of them just a folded sheet. There's more truth in them, more freedom of expression, than was ever available on CNN.

On the bridge.

The sun is blazing; all on the bridge has come to a halt. Beneath the stone arches, the water itself has lost its mobility as if lingering in the shadows to escape the heat. No longer purling, but slick and motionless like the surface of a chocolate custard, it swallows up the stone I throw without even a splash.

A bird is struggling to gain height after having taken a fish that was gulping for oxygen near the surface. Heavy wing beats that hardly pull it away from the inert liquid. Incapable of gaining altitude it slams into the bank where less bold but much fiercer birds ravish the catch.

A Dravidian runs straight for the edge of the bridge, lurches over the parapet and jerks up a bulging plastic sack from the shadows. The contents appear in transparency through the bag: a face pealed clean from some head, a hand, a few organs; oranges too, with cloves imbedded for flavor and fennel leaves. He takes it all beneath the bridge and in the relative coolness of the shadows, prepares a feast.

Just then, an upright stick slips past along the water surface, at last giving motion to the river; indicating speed, direction of the current which today is contrary to where it came from yesterday. Reversal. Wouldn't this be a hollow reed beneath which swims someone leaving the city in the most discreet manner? Perhaps even one of the leading citizens attempting timely escape. Hadn't kings fled in much the same manner?

I repress the desire to lob a lance into the murky opacity, pump bullets around the snorkel in circular patterns.

The girl pulls at my sleeve, draws me down so that my ear is next to her mouth. There's still a milk odor about her and chocolate round the lips.

—I want to tell you secret stories, the whisper hardly audible, a small breath to which modulation has been imposed by her hourly growing will, —turtles savagely attack tigers, rhinos and even giraffes.

She asks me for the tobacco, wants me to renounce.

—Take this stone, I say, picking up a flat one —throw it sideways across the water. Watch it bounce.

A man sidles up, a fat one.

I'm thinking of the Angel. The last years of incessant coughing before the lungs began filling with fluid. Everything was brown: her fingers, saliva and the wallpaper. Widow of a famous painter, she had been obliged to take from the wall the last small paintings which she so loved.

—You can't lick them to survive, she had always said.

Leaving immaculate squares and rectangles on the wallpaper where they had been. Patterns of virgin wall where the smoke hadn't filtered. When the paintings were cleaned, surprising fauve landscapes and portraits of unbearable color came to light from beneath the brown patina. This is how the descendants of celebrities very often live out their lives.

The fat man smells of jasmine. He's overly attentive to the child while pretending to ignore me.

Many new forms of taxes have been levied; thousands of collectors have been recruited. They work on a commission basis. Some are free lance, while others are mandated; all are expected to help themselves. None have scruples.

Smoke from the human-parts roast, blows up over the bridge.

—It could have been anyone's head, hand, they're roasting down there; a magistrate's, a politician's, a student's or even a tax collector's, I say to him.

He nods and goes away, understanding that his disguise is most inappropriate today.

—Don't think that the game's over! he threatens me while retreating as cowards usually do. Unfortunately, they often return when you're the least prepared.

Would I be getting brave?

This is Paris, shortly after the Third French Revolution, the splendid one that has finally put everyone on equal footing. Not just peasants with kings.

K2 emerges from shimmering at bridge end. She's wearing a blond, shoulder-length wig that contrasts strikingly with her dark skin. Lipstick is clearly purple today. Her dress is torn just beneath the arm, the yellow fabric with black spot pattern, revealing the sweating crease just beneath the breasts.

Will the child have a sudden nap? I have pressing urge, wanting to perform right here on the bridge, take the mother on this worn public bench with carved graffiti on the wooden rails. There's a phone number carved out with a penknife. It has no prefix, which means it must be very ancient. Body fluids penetrating the wood over the years have conferred a dark patina to the bench. Sweat, urine, blood, saliva and diarrhea. Overhead, clouds form and undo very swiftly as if filmed by a camera that has been greatly accelerated. How long have I been waiting on this bridge? It's the very one that I met her on, the one that I've been waiting beneath all along.

—Mamma, we waited for you for so long! the girl is angry, and yet she's only been waiting for a few hours; I've been here the time it took for three suns to live out their lives, countless civilizations to emerge and disappear, planets to replace one another, some totally lifeless others teaming with the most dangerous creatures with whom I was forced to compose. All of these things shifted about just as swiftly as the clouds just did. I suppose it's all relative to the child. The proportion of her wait compared to her life span presenting a similar ratio to my wait/life span.

—There weren't even any passing boats to count, she complains.

There's an incident at the foot of the bridge, near the Justice Palace where K2 has just come from. She pays no heed, slowly pulling off the wig and slipping it beneath the bench. Her hair is dark, tangled and wet, clinging to the forehead. Fine curls running down along the temples retain pearls of sweat that throb with the beat of her heart, the extremely slow rhythm of a mammal in hibernation.

If this were winter to her, she would be at home in Furnace, would she not? Be she from there?

— I'm cold, she whispers.

I put my gabardine over her shivering body like a blanket. With the heat, the smell of fermented sperm comes up through her dress.

A group of mounted policemen gallop across the bridge riding splendid gold-shod horses. Grenadiers lacking brass chest plates. It's no throwback. Cavaliers are swifter in dense traffic. They can hurdle over vehicles and most any other obstacle, dismount in a flash. Some wear turbans, others conical caps. All are dressed in a new form of urban camouflage that includes rubble and dust on the shoulders, smeared blood and small smoking fires; a fashion that I introduced long ago.

One's yelling: She's blonde, about 175, panther dress! the voice broken by the clatter-stride of his mount. He's hoarse. I remember the morning, the way she laid on her back, drawing up her knees tight to her chest, offering up to my open mouth everything from the tailbone to the navel.

We go, the three of us, across the bridge. I pushing the stroller with the baby girl, K2 hanging onto my arm.

—She's big. At least 180 tall, maybe 200, Negro with blonde hair, tiger pattern dress! Probably a Brazilian transvestite goes the yelling from one horse to another, as the mounted troops continue thundering over the bridge.

We sit at a sidewalk cafe. They'll always exist here.

I'll never know what she did in those offices. Though the bridge shook following an explosion, there was no sound, no smoke. Never ask.

—I hate bureaucracy, she mutters, drinking deeply from a mint filled glass that turns the world green before her eyes.

Chaos leads to development of an informal but vigorous economy. Thimblefuls of fuel are sold by the roadside in tiny flasks. Cigarettes taken from the package are sold individually, sometimes even cut into three or four pieces.

There are constant coups, assassinations and border conflicts. Nations change of name overnight on a weekly basis. Cartographers are ever printing new maps. We wear panther hats. Solutions are plentiful: succeed in putting aside some money to corrupt officials with; become an official yourself; revert to prostitution; set up a black market booth; move it about.

—Today I pissed on a princess! declares Twelve.

—Really?

—Not quite, he admits. —Had been reading in the toilette, a magazine with a princess' portrait on the cover. Dropped it on the floor to go answer the doorbell. Much later, in the middle of the night while half asleep, I missed the stool while urinating. It went all over her face making a pattering noise.

She and I communicate by using words from languages lost or classified as being depraved. The smell of rain, the sound of dry leaves crunching underfoot are words unto themselves, God's water being the designation for rain and this for at least two valid reasons: in the not so remote past, the arrival of the rainy season meant that slave caravans could no longer pass over trails gone slimy. This is also a time when the earth lives again. Brush fires cease, seeds sprout, toads emerge from the ground and fill the air with their song. For these reasons it is worth reiterating, even if I've already informed you.

There are fewer acts of treason during these seasons when the spoken word replaces what's written. If you have such high fever, perhaps it's because your hand's been bitten. Not by some wild creature whose path you fell across, but by the one you keep and feed. Is this some unspeakable ill deed, or mere warning, which you should heed?

Of no utility to the progress of mankind are these tongues! Waist no longer your breath. Bring poisoned air down into your lungs. In the beginning there's always death. Seek to ascend ladders without rungs.

Very quickly now, two events involving a vehicle: I attack a mobile bank; a trailer stationed in a vacant lot. The plan, instantly conceived with the sudden onset of heavy precipitation, is to hitch up and simply drive away with it while everyone stays out of the storm. But the rains have also turned the ground into muck. My car gets stuck. I steal a truck. Surely it'll be big enough to pull out the car and trailer together. Bad luck! Here rises before me, the statue of a software mogul. The problem being that no one despises heroes more than I. Momentarily forgetting the waiting bank, I ram the monument with the stolen vehicle. It collapses on the cab pinning me down inside. I'm face to face with the giant bronze visage, vertical stripes streaming down its face from years of serving as pigeon roost.

At the Tribunal the prosecutor says of me: Put him in a boat and he rows, give him a pen and he writes. Impulsive opportunist. An amateur.
—If then there's a scale of crime, I incarnating the lowest form, this implies that there are summits.

It's a big house, ours, that's been set adrift in the river. No towers on this listing ruin, our old home from the industrial suburb. Low-hanging acidic fogs had finally eaten through the foundations, permitting rising waters to take it off. We hastily make anchors from refrigerator, oven, a television, big obsolete computers and cast them all overboard. They'll hold awhile. Cormorants flock, roosting on the cables.

The chart of a hyena skeleton (Crocuta crocuta) is on the living room wall. High bones form a crest along the upper spine. The hind legs are shorter than the front ones. It has powerful molars and catlike feet. I believe that it is much closer to the cat than to the dog. We in turn adopt hyenine comportment, develop hyenoid features.
—There's nothing of civilized about you, no culture, no education, she tells me after I burn the dinner.
—Are not pests and weeds more adapted to this world than garden plants with their fragile seeds and house pets that nobody really needs?
—Talibans had a beautiful flag, forbade the cultivation of poppy, understood how women's bodies were employed to sell everything from bubble gum to vehicles.

Hyenodons, prehistoric striped dog, somewhere between the Tasmanian wolf and the hyena, run free in the house. They chase entelodons, the ancestor (or the descendant), of the wart hog – depends on which way you're heading – knocking down delicately carved and splendidly gilden Louis Seize furniture. To control them, I'm obliged to throw Manufacture de Sevres vases and plates at them. The noise of the shattering porcelain finery seems to be the only thing they'll respond to. Has the peculiarly crystalline crack of thunder falling during the Oligocen period from which they originate. How will the proboscidians fare? Can they swim in this thundering current, make it to the banks? A shame to have saved the Moeritherium, Phiomia, and Paleomastodon from glaciation, only for them to drown now. Death indeed a senseless thing? The gomphotherium, brutally separated from the refrigerated hut, will have difficulty adapting to the tropical climate if he makes it to the riverbank.

Fear not for us. If worse comes to worse, if the house were to capsize, the water to turn to brine, we would fuse together to form a single stalked barnacle, cling to the first rock with sturdy peduncle, use our cement gland to adhere correctly. The *I* part of this new *us* will still have a penis, testis, an esophagus and an anus. Of what importance be it that we now possess a supra esophageal ganglion, a mid-gut and a digestive cecum? They all function, and sexually, we're totally self sufficient, since we also have a female gonopore and oviduct. Don't tamper with our adductor muscle! Could it be that, like the worm, we have a cerebral ganglion? Fused together in this manner, we can lay in wait for an undetermined period of time, before re-emerging. Much longer than all of history if necessary.

Such isn't the case.

A convey of trucks rumbles slowly past on the Rive Droite. The trailers are piled high with cinnamon colored soil taken from an African tectonic plate that has plowed into the southern edge of Paris. Where are these truckloads of beautiful red dirt headed for? Who has ordered this haul?

Finally, the atelier part of the house breaks away and sunders, spilling stone and bronze sculptures into the riverbed, releasing wooden pieces, wax models, paintings and drawings into the whirlpools.

—Summon sacred serpents to lick afflicted areas. (Quick panting).

—How is it we're suddenly so old?

—It's the beginning. If you pay attention, you'll find that's the direction of things.

—Smell, I say, presenting her with small bottles.

—Prodigious!

Basic essences: from the scent glands of early beast, the sap of a primitive plant that had no flower, an odor that had the power to lure dinosaurs northward to their death.

Hold a rort. Serve rotgut. Blast guests with our roskos. Rooz each other for being such good marksmen. We're no rubes! Eat roasted rutabaga. Let me look at your phiz. Follow this runaway star now that sister's gone supernova.

You'll need no fuel. Engage in ghost love.

Cobras Coiled

I'm gulping hot soda from a half empty can found in the bottom of a garbage bin, the bubbles are gone. All about seems just as lifeless, be it not for ants teaming in the syrup. How to separate from this foul enough drink, that which only brings more fire to my throat? It would've been of no avail had I possessed filter or mesh, the remaining ale is so thick now that it couldn't traverse even the coarsest sieve. An amber in the making with its clutch of future fossils moving ever slower. How often have I marveled at the chrome armor of the western Sahara variety which seems mercury splattered when scattering on the sand, or the Amazon ant capable of turning its enemies upon one another by simply releasing its Judas pheromone. The unbearable sweetness draws salty fluids from my salivary glands.

Vagina, hers; I miss it so. I had crushed my armpits, my torso, rubbed my thighs and waist into the slipperiness. I had buried my tongue, opened wide my mouth, felt the weight of her entire body pressing down upon my face as I pulled her against me with all of my strength.

It hadn't always been like this. We had hated each other at first.

Who is this fellow blown up by the winds that now lies across my path? Brittle and dry; a mummy un-swaddled and propped up across the curbstone, awaiting the final blow that will return the remains to dust. The hand holds a sandwich from which a crescent shaped bite has been taken. A fatal one to be sure. Be it laced with the most lethal of poisons or was he merely in too much of a gluttonous haste, unable to taste this snack which providence now offers?

Such waste!

Nibbling the remains of soggy sandwich taken from my dead man's hand. Around his head is wrapped in the form of a hat, last week's newspaper. I'll read it after breakfast.

Few things bear here their proper name. Nomenclature is a complex, perverted affair. Today my name is General Barthelemy Orinthal Giap. Pseudonyms, heteronyms or acronyms devoid of even the slightest humor. Neither accumulated titles of nobility nor the multiplicity of Fernando Pessoa, but names borrowed, sometimes third hand; mine chosen in memory of a Congo rebel, general Jean Marie Tassoua who upon overrunning Brazzaville with a handful of mercenaries from Angola wearing long blonde wigs, purple nail polish, a small monkey very often perched on the shoulder, had in his turn usurped the name of the military *lumiere* of Indochina. Barthelemy being Boganda, an obscure Centralafrican president, one of the first, to have been eliminated by European powers for having installed democracy which proved to be incompatible with the remaining economical colonial structure.

Orinthal? The first black man to ever have profited from the derision of American justice.

But here again, when reference is made to Angola, I'm not necessarily speaking of that nation whose capital be named Huambo after having been transferred from Luanda following Dr. Jose Malheiro Savimbi's surprising victory some thirty years after his own death, but rather the state prison farm so named in Louisiana.

Tomorrow I shall be Saddam Hussein, once again, not in direct memory of the Iraqi leader but rather in homage to Kongulu Mobutu who had first chosen this nom de guerre. Son of Mobutu Sese Seko and chief of the redoubtable Dragons, he could easily have written the epilogue to the chapters Shaba I and II of Zaïrian history, had not precocious death come his way.

I remember the color of her blood, the same as the green ink of a pen that I had possessed as a child. One with which I drew arboreal serpents, the broad leaves of tropical plants and emeralds glinting with the same light as that falling now upon this, our other world.

Esmeraldo Orbis Est.

Today I no longer know how to fight, I hardly even think; it is a strain for my brain to maintain vital functions. Anything else would be vain.

On the brink of the great alcohol cloud. I have been living from forced begging for how long now, I no longer know. It's a "go slow" day; all the tow-cars are jammed to a halt. At this rate, I'll never make it to Alaba, see if the merchandise has arrived from the port of Apapa. I could have bought some tokunbo today. Have to develop my very own Junkspace. Run circles round Oshodi, return to Kaduna. People dashing in and out of the traffic selling rotten fruits and 150-grade alcohol, the pitch-black variety made from fermented squid ink. Gold gleaming in beads from scarifications on his lanky arms, a young man vaults over car hoods and walks up the windshields to the searing metal roofs, his big heels rust colored from the dust; shabby socks of red powder halfway up his black ankles.

He's in a hurry, cutting short. The bird's path.

Today I must reap enough to pay for her toys and milk, the opaline fluid she so likes, my serpents and her mother's silk.

Come to an ambassador's car bearing two and seven, long Bakelite black all buffed down with bee's wax. Flame flying from the front, a purple Y, actually a snake's tongue. There's a platinum pangolin on the hood, remarkably well done, all of the scales are articulated; tiny ruby eyes. Even the tongue made of Corsican coral, functions, flickering out impudently.

—Ambassador from where? say I, jumping into the back seat and caning the chauffeur in the head, the occipital lobe precisely.

27' s cold inside, icicles on the windows, frost on the paws. The diplomat wears a heavy coat of whipcord with fur collar, tiny dark glasses. He's listening to steam music from Spiny Park Passes.

—Shut off this noise!

Someone's walking over the rooftop now, the limousine gently rocking under the footsteps. Is it the gold-studded man?

A most beautiful girl presses her lips to the window, only her face visible through the frost.

—My lips are a wound, she says, hanging upside down.

I remember her from a dinner deep in the inner city.

—She dances with the sinister Minister of Finances, the diplomat sputters in falsetto.

The girl scratches the ice from the window with her long nails and whispers, —I'm at odds with the gods.

It had been one of those evenings with cross talk. She had come ever closer through a background conversation about a Holy Land conflict. Slowly she had spoken through that which she now calls a wound.

—I wanted to meet you so long ago, your manifesto with the weapon and text. You're so violent and yet so controlled, she had said.

—How can you talk to me about that girl? I'm here for you! I continue, addressing the ambassador.

—I have lots of money, jewelry too. Here! terrified, he cries out, frantically emptying his pockets onto the eel skin seat.

No doubloons or small currency but large slippery discs bearing the effigy of forgotten deities are spilling out along with cabochons and uncut gems.

A vessel in the offing, "Hootch," is certainly his. It's a glass blower's masterpiece all of one piece blown. Unpolished glass. Absorbing all light when loaded with the black alcohol, it doesn't even glint.

If only I had known.

The ship's anchor's cock-billed, hanging beneath the cathead, ready to drop. Perfectly immobile in geostationary orbit, it resembles a dark oblong moon. Other vessels are nearby. One resembles the underside of a dog's paw; another looks like the blade of a knife.

Music: in low octaves with deep booming percussion. It's an extremely slow rhythm, the heartbeat of an athlete at rest. There is punctuation, fractures that interrupt the flow with the sound of shattering glass.

—Ambassador from where? I repeat.

—I'm from Where also known as Nambucco. I'm here to purchase alcohol, a great quantity of the deep blue variety. Now eager to befriend me, perhaps even save his skin, he begins to babble incomprehensibly.

I know the lieu he speaks of. It's near the outer reaches of the very ancient NGC catalogue, actually part of it. An abduction/subduction system.

—Enormous quantity for what?

—To keep the slaves happy.

—Don't fratch with me.

On the radio, an advertisement for a used vehicle. The high-pitched voice of a fortune teller, —Young man, Scorpio, beware of dominant older women.

My weapon gleams on the seat where my leg should be, only a stump there now. Halfway between us I push it, giving him the opportunity to seize. This completely terrifies him.

—Give me your coat, the tobacco too!

He wriggles on the seat, undressing in a clumsy frenzy, popping off tektite buttons and shredding the silk.

I slap him for this, smashing his glasses, —Slowly...these are my cloths now! You mustn't damage them in your haste.

He takes off the lacquered porcupine quill shoes. —For you! presenting them to me.

I pick one up and strike him across the mouth with it, —I've only got one foot! shoving it deep into his throat, the quills folding back as they go in. It would be impossible to pull out, but he can still breathe, having a windpipe up front like certain reptiles.

I remember the years spent as a dentist, cleaning and drilling fangs, venom pouring everywhere. Easy to treat, could brace open their mouths with a tennis ball, they breathed from the tip hole. Was a perpendicular world as well, totally reptile but nothing like those from Cyana. They were big, beautiful, all female, constantly coiling and uncoiling with pleasure. They had a smell about them: squashed ant when angry, hot amber when hungry or in love. Mine had studied Cyana. She called herself Eve's friend. Female complicity, she said.

I try on the other shoe. Too big. My foot floats inside. Pull it apart to form a strange flat design resembling a fat hand or catcher's mitt.

Space chameleons.

So beautiful were they. Emerald scales surrounding the pink of the mouth. Eyes of topaz that were said to be expressionless. And yet within, beyond the reflective surface, lay one of the keys to the Universe.

Venom that would pearl from the fang tips. It was a dark brown color like the strongest coffee or tobacco juice. Their bodies ever-shining as if wet. She would wrap herself around my fever.

I marveling as she would engulf birds, the feathers folding to enter her open maw and furry creatures.

My client is now totally naked. I leave him shivering in the cold car and mingle with the mob, just another thief.

A dead man's lying up against the curb just as I have said. Thieves have taken everything and fled, even the papers that had blown around his head, the odd hat that I now read. Only the headlines, the child still has to be fed.

Hop over him, stuffing the ambassador's wallet and jewels into my hip pocket. The limousine would have been worth taking but it's stuck in the jam. An hour later it'll still be there but abandoned. I'll return with a chisel and pry the platinum pangolin from the hood. Some scavengers beneath, taking apart the motor, indeed a marvelous piece of craftsmanship, maybe three thousand years old, each component was signed by hand.

Night here is ultra-violet, close to the spider nebula, all that's white glows. Dust, sand, powder and paper blowing in the streets form immaculate cyclones. Teeth shine yellow, the white of the eyes too. The pearl handle of my old pistol is radiant. There are no stars, only those immense arms of vapor and glowing gas that spread into infinity. Perhaps the most beautiful night sky of any world that I have known. Beneath it, all about, treachery and misery vying for the incredible fortunes that are to be made. If you've always dreamt of becoming rich and famous, this is where you'll end up.

My first glimpse of this world? Tiny brindled and brown like a small ape. Evil was its code name. I should have listened.

I walk across the brittle grass, crinkling shards, to hang a mirror on a basalt shaft thrusting from the ground. "Tree" I call it, caressing what could have been a trunk.

Older yet only foolishness in those eyes that should by now hold some wisdom. Unshaven, the white bristle is fluorescent. I'm black, totally black. Not invisible but drawing in the purple light, drinking it up. Just before dawn, heaven for an instant flashes green, serpents shudder and the sun pup shoots above the horizon announcing the arrival of its dull master.

Throb.

It's a rhythm of heat and light, a deep searing pulsation affecting all. A tight binary star.

Implacable is the heat in this end zone of biology, the brink of chemistry.

Don't believe for a moment that this is some sort of remote outpost, a barbaric wilderness devoid of those refinements which civilization can offer. Most magnificent vintage and collector wardrobes are presented in exclusive boutiques. Small palaces where can be purchased dresses from the Mario Fortuni collection, early Balenciaga or the latest diamond nipple-caps and the finest small triangle of gold chain mail with a slit down the center to be delicately worn over the erogenous zone. I cloth here Zanda, the child's mother. Sometimes with fistfuls of gems that I dump on the counter, most frequently at gun point.

I sleep away the morning, curled up in the cool clay of a badger cavern beneath the workshop. Running overhead, the baby's feet, the girl lightly stumbling, out of time.

She's playing with the pangolin, gently kissing it on the snout. She has for it an unusual affection and doesn't break it. Respect, more than a toy. As I fall asleep I hear her calling, —Dadee, dadee...

Kalk-Hutta

It's no easy thing walking the broken back of the buckled bridge. My crutches slip on the bolts where the aluminum coating has pealed. Immense, collapsed in a moldering heap it spreads across the bay, crumpled by a terrific quake, they tell rare visitors here. Just decay. To traverse, it is the only way.

Midway across, a crew appears to be welding or performing some sort of repair; but, in verity, cutting away metal which they shall fashion into knives, daggers and swords. Soon whole sections will roll over and sound, crushing pink porpoises as they sink. Arriving on the opposite bank I unwrap the rubber from my forehead, blinding once again the preventors. Migraines forever is my offering to them.

A most interpolative woman rushes to my encounter, as ever, desperately striving to strike up a conversation. The weather here, as on Cyana were she had so often accosted me, is her subject of predilection. Where had I first seen her? Saskatoon or Coonabarabran? It matters little, for when I confront her, she runs.

Upon this western bank are palm trees and lush tropical plants, hazy beneath an eternal mist that envelopes the residential district. Certain little palaces have a colonial architecture, columns made of nickel and magnesium, glittering mica shingles and malachite arches.

Selecting a most resplendent one, covered with porphyry plating, I stride through the monumental entrance upon which is sculpted the giant winged foot of mercury, the merchant's patron.

The slavers' den

Walk in, just. An excessive opulence. The crutch thumping on the copper flagstones spins their heads all about.

87

—Continue eating, I say, pressing the pearl handled firearm against the foot of the host, (that's where the brain is located). My Gindous enter and immediately proceed to strip the wiring from the walls, making fine coils of the archaic system. They take the air conditioner from the ceiling, piping too. Making a clean sweep of the table they empty and carefully wipe down the plates with napkins before dumping all into bundles fashioned from the tablecloth. Silverware and the crystal glasses are individually wrapped in greasy napkins. These are real professionals.

—Everyone molt!

Snake skins, *renard* pelage, coarse silk drawn from bulky spinnerets, fold gold, and carbon tunics all fall to the floor.

The Gindous are meticulous, carefully shaking off the crumbs and folding the clothes, wrapping the porcelain pitchers with art, tableware from an ancient ship wreck that had been salvaged off the coast of the Hybrides.

The guests are all bankers, brokers, ship chandlers, politicians claiming to be investors; slavers for sure. The sort of gentlemen who would have nothing less than solid silver bits for their horses to champ down upon and ebony calashes for these beasts to haul about brocade covered mistresses.

The packing finished, I sit down with my naked hosts. The heat is setting in fast since the air conditioning has been ripped out. Our feet bathe in water from the ruptured plumbing. Such a soothing manner in which to contemplate the oil portraits that the master of the house has had made of himself. They hang in rows upon the walls, a curious mixture of old Flemish finesse and Venetian exuberance. Detail had been put down with the finest brush, the brush itself confectioned by a master's hand; two hairs, perhaps four from the sable's pelt, no more, to render in turn, a lock of hair, the pattern of the iris with something beyond veracity. No perseverance nor tenacity could convey the fables felt when one views these masterpieces.

—Shall we cut them from the chassis, 'n role? The painted surface facing outwards of course.

—Burn them!

We take the windows too, they being of the much sought after ancient variety of glass that catches passing light, making it undulate and flicker as if rippling water were the substance being traversed.

—All of you be cursed!

From a pot that remains on the table, I lick honey, a synthetic variety with pearls of rotenone in suspension, intense but nothing like venom. To think that it had been put forward like a trap! Tainted bait for those who marvel at painted hate.

Pesticides? I'm no ant!

Speaking of which, insects are coming in through the broken windows, clustering on the naked diners, they slapping away. The six-legged ones leave me alone, some even display signs of affection, perhaps they know.

We withdraw.

Consider that:

1) We are unique. No other humanoids anywhere else in the entire Universe.

2) Humanoids abound. Can be found almost anywhere throughout the Universe.

Now, let's develop the second hypothesis. Skim the surface, no more! Approach it from a temporal aspect. Humans are scattered throughout infinity. It's a fact; I can assure you. From all periods and all walks of life, there they are, living in totally alien, often hostile environments. For example, here's a former President of the United States shoveling (day-in, day-out) high arsenic content coal, his shirt sleeves rolled up, necktie tucked in under the belt. Surroundings seem replication of Bangladesh. A banker, down on his knees with a torn cardboard sheet in front of him, upon which he's scribbled "just for a little food." A few strange coins attest to the fact someone's understood his message. And this bondsman, all tied up like a sausage, waiting to be shipped off somewhere else, hadn't he come after me before? Shouldn't ever get personal about this though. Could rapidly lose credibility. Don't make the mistake of always looking inwards. Do speak with the mouth within your mouth.

How to learn many languages? Easy! Pick up a space parrot. Very old, having had many masters. They speak countless tongues. Cover vast sections of space just seeking seeds.

—I've been a doctor from early on in. You had understood this when you saw how I blew my nose, hadn't you? No handkerchief, simple device (called a *mouche-bébé* in French, or a "baby-blower"), a tube with a small valve that sucks the snot from your nose with vacuum action. It's made of transparent plastic. Quite repulsive but very effective. Studying for millions of years, my science was great enough to heal planets and their stars. Such sorrow was mine when I realized that mankind must be eliminated if Earth were to survive. There are several levels of infinity. All buzz like rattlesnake tails.

The man speaking is small and blue. Often distorted, his head can expand to reach a diameter of thirty leagues. Through the transparent skull can be perceived clouds of sparkling needles. His body is almost microscopic but radiant as an arc welder's torch. Impossible to look at directly. He claims to be the narrator of inner adventure.

—Each shall have his own, he's fond of repeating, —Keep it personal, private, intimate, he says, —It's a secret!

I've become a practical man. After eating snake I use the fangs for toothpicks, the vertebrae will be my belt.

K2 is washing herself on the bidet, talking to me about investments in Lagos. My sperm pours through her tangled pubic hair hanging in curled locks; wet astrakhan. Almost yellow brown, it slips over the immaculate porcelain and goes down the drain.

—I can get them to forward maybe two million, she says, passing a green oval soap between the pink of her palms and then down under between her thighs. It's from Damascus, made from the purest olive oil, cut in big cakes and shipped in crates. I love to feel it, close my eyes and smell.

—There's gold now, just lying all over the property. A young Muslim prospector came to see my father last week to ask him if he could dig on our land. He had found a nugget the size of a potato. Remember, that's where you can pull up young trees and shake rough diamonds out of the roots. They fall like gravel into your hat! she continues.

—Listen to me. Forget the funds; just give me another month to finish.

—No, Lagos. We need investors for remote imagery and so many other preliminary steps. But first, the hunt. We'll be poachers.

Stentorianly I declare this to be a stelliferous sky. Squill will help you spit when sick. Squinny and slip beneath the squinch. If set upon, squush and stab. Don't get yourself into a snit. Eat kidneywart, squaw waterweed and squirrel fish. These'll squirt and squish. Have a splore slurping down slippery spoom. Avoid other spongers. Drink yourself a snootful. Sozzled. Slowly soom. Be a snool.

War: Are not superior beings already amongst us? Invisible, conquering ones, implacably applying to all of humanity the dictum "divide and conquer," (which some of us have thought to make our own, not realizing that it comes from elsewhere). Wouldn't this merely tend to discharge man of his ultimate responsibility?

Or would war be a living thing? A creature which is born, nourishes itself, breeds, has offspring and dies. But always sows its seed before expiring.

Finally, there has been severe cloisonement of society. This has led to *speciation* within humanity itself. Bankers haven't the same morphology as warriors; lawyers are slightly different from judges and criminals strongly resemble policemen. As with ants.

Time? Four seasons are compressed into a single day, an hour, a minute. Why not some measure of time infinitely smaller than anything measurable by nanometry? Direction! In what will have been billions of years as we conceive them to be, perhaps four, maybe more, meteorites will slam into shallow seas sending geysers of animal foam skyward, bringing along desire. To walk, to fly, to swim. Thought will somehow make its way into this mire. Though often associated with doom, it is the action of the spade turning over soil. A necessary aeration. Service will no longer be held in cathedrals. Crowded with infidels making images of each other, posing in front of ancient marble crucifixes all turned black, ironically just as Xt. (Christ) really had been. You contest this melanism? Don't worry about sinning, losing immortality for all of humanity. You're not Yima.

However, always remember that it is in your best interest to proceed in the proper order when pawning: personal belongings, body parts, the spirit. Always hang on to this last item, preserving it as long as possible, and if you must relinquish it, make sure that you can get it back.

You'll see that with time I shall say to you, "I told you so." There'll also be a ship named "Tar Baby." Immaculate, without a spot. Another christened "Bite."

From not so far away a machine is analyzing our conversation. For obvious reasons, it picks up on key words, Hizbollah or Silkworm, (spoken in Arabic or Chinese even).

—I see them. He is telling her. —They steal our thoughts with total impunity. We live in a tent in the forest. There are magnificent birdcalls.

—What was there before the Big Bang?

—An older odor!

Parenthetically, we live on a street corner in Calcutta. I sell rat poison. My wife is beautiful African *metisse*, passes for Indian, sub-cast beauty. During the monsoon our many children stuff rags in sewer drains. Creates further flooding. Vehicles stall in the high water. The little urchin army way-lays drivers momentarily stuck in artificial small flood. Dry season revenues come from repairing watches, painting movie posters, making paper maché sculptures of divinities for religious festivities. Sometimes I'm a ship-breaker, cutting up old time machines. This is messy work, aging fuel tanks often contain dangerous residue. Countless carcasses line the shoreline. Not necessarily ships, just the best place to let them leak their pollutants. Pink dolphins die. I can make a mummy. Strap skeleton to wood frame, wrap with ropes and vegetal matter to give flesh forms, make a clay mask (rendering of face and hands is important; I can paint them), use pelican skin to cover flesh areas. All things considered, we're pretty rich. Still living in a tent though. This episode lasts a good thirty years.

It's Africa now. Not the one you know but an altogether different place. It has been transplanted, the entire continent. Perhaps the leftovers of an intensive re-colonization? Great heaps of moldering, military equipment lie all about. The stinking spoor of western civilization.

Cobras coiled tight in the canon barrels, slithering between the metallic pilot's seat, shattered gauges and rusted control sticks.

Lions are no more. Or: a few have been mechanized. They are of no interest; their manes have disappeared or grown thin from wear. The females have become extremely cunning killers, having accumulated an eternity of knowledge beneath their tattered hides.

Rhinos and giraffes were all shipped off to Cyana where they are in great demand, the most expensive pets.

The wind moans in the muzzles of the different caliber weapons, all heavenward turned, several octaves of the most haunting melody. Emblems are still visible on half-buried shattered wings and tails of aircraft emerging from the red sand. Here the herald of the Moroccan crown, shot down by the Polisario Front that finally won its guerilla war against all that the Occident could throw its way.

Bones have been strapped together and packed, some polished. A commodity. Certain choice pieces have been carved into long thin sculptures, some quite intricate. There are portraits of ancient deities, the beverage god, the arms merchant and God Money always at the top, adorning little altars.

—Your bones! Remember the contract? she said.

Other bones, damaged or attacked by termites, are sold for firewood, by the chord, or ground into animal feed. It's a good business this one. Neither tooth nor knucklebone is to be lost. They're sold in little sacks for children's games, to be gathered and tossed.

The merchant is frail but much more alive than his ware. Speaking through the hole in a spoon that he places before his mouth. A strange little face has been carved onto the backside and it is through this mouth that his words come:

—Put doon yre guinza thar oone myne spar! he crackles pointing to a capstan whelp chock wrapped with rat-line that serves as a table. Shipwreck fragments here in the heartland.

His skin is pulled tight over his own bones, the eyes drawn deep back within cavernous sockets. This talking skull sells silent ones. He's ancient, Caucasian. After having sold weapons from an office, he was obliged to vend them in-situ; no arms left to peddle, he now sells the bones of the dead which his weaponry killed.

—Slake thee, bade he, addressing himself.

Taking posture close to earth, he slips an arm into a narrow hole, withdrawing a gravid female serpent, which he holds aloft by the head, squeezing down on her with wrapped bony fingers. Snake eggs spurt into an enamel pan where they glisten. I see her small yellow eye, there in the sky; unblinking it can vie with the most brilliant of stars. Listen.

I think as I do oft of that land where venom was coughed.

—Take three.

—Too wee.

I hear our conversation; something to rehearse, terse. Hardly the time to reply, it's subliminal as if we had been through it till only a code remains. Susurration. Even that, a burden.

This is the last time!

She is so sublime.

Held high, her head is immobile, the pattern of the ventral scales undulating and almost forming a keel like certain sea serpents. She seeks contact, a desire to climb, to bury her fangs and empty the poison glands.

Finally she wriggles free and sheds her skin, discarding the filth which hands have deposed upon her; the most complete cleansing, like casting away contaminated surgical gloves after having inverted them.

—Suffer, smooth speaking smoodge!

It's finished. She goes over the sand beneath the bone pile, silently as a wave of light.

The scapula peddler, his hand still high, holds the wind. How had he known that the serpent and I?

Of the final exchange which she had cut short, I was never to know the ultimate retort.

The poison is taking hold. I lay him down on the wreckage of wars gone by.

—You should know certain things, you should know serpent stings, I tell him as he lying, dying whispers, —Two would glow, one with wings.

Stuff my sinus with sneesh, only powdered sneezewort.

Watch your snash! Navigate aboard a sneak box.

—Winze! I wis! They've succeeded now in wire-tapping conversations tween angels and the Lord. Know all that's afoot.

A witch moth flutters by. Have my manners betrayed the fact that I'm a wolf-child? Wisdom's a wodge caught in ignorance's throat.

Blown by withywind, traveler's joy, watch that you don't become a w.o.b. When wonky, chew woad till your tongue's blue. Keep wowsers away. Wroth, I'll wrick my head to the side.

We live in a wurley. Huddle beneath writhen branches. Wyverns guard the entrance.

—Want to search us? Show me your wrnt.

While waiting, wear xanthic cloaks. All's been transferred to Xalostoc. But we're no xanthrocroids. To come here, we sailed aboard a xebec. I have extra X chromosomes. Raise xats all around. Sniff xenon when living amongst xenophobes. I'll treat your xenoderma with my saliva. Xerophilious plants grow around where we dwell. You have xerothalmia? I'll suck on your eyeballs as well. Even though you're ill-tempered, you're no Xantippe. Employ my XL tongue. Give you lots of vitamin A. Promise we'll cry together again?

Speak Xhosa. Go South. Navigate the upper reaches of the Xingu. Don't worry about predicted famine. We're xylophagous. Can even eat the xoanons I carved. Keep Xns away. They'll attempt to x-rate our life.

—Come to me, sister sub-adult.

Sudden recrudescence of green fluorescence coming from incandescent, fine crescent. Instant fossilization. There'll be no jubilation! I've just suffered excommunication. Fornication, assassination, germination.

—Storm-beaten cretin, at least pretend to defend yourself against this Lord who thinks you offend! Need no introspection to understand this rejection. Trod on God!

—Poor *poupée*, let's have our *petit dejeuner*! It's all just a *mauvaise plaisanterie*. Don't you agree? (designating Heaven with a graceful sweep of the hand).

Let's defecate together. Brown can be elegantly described, even if referring to an excrement pile: sepia, sienna, pablo, umber, tenne, marron. Would this then be a bill of fare, carte, menu that I present to you? Calumniate?

—Avaunt!

The seas are no longer blue. They have a green hue that makes one feel unusually serene. Closer look reveals floating islands of decomposing fish and cakes of nuclear waste. People live on these new lands. Pockets of radioactive carbon monoxide belching up from the bottoms make the sea boil all around. These are new nations with citizens much stronger, more resistant than we ever dreamed of being. They have beautiful flags that fly high. A naked man with nine ravens on emerald field. A fanion with fangs, one hundred of them, all aligned in rows. They drive cars with dogfaces, some with all teeth out. Entire flotillas of ghost ships endlessly circumnavigate the deserted seas until they finally rust apart or sink during mega- typhoons.

Rain is walking now. We leave, listening, the woman and I, for the laugh of the only remaining predator.

Hyena.

A pack of them, mottled, foul maws agape are downwind.

She strides into the forest wearing the most elegant dress, high heels, her hair impeccably brushed. It is a vast stretch of primal jungle, untouched by man's hand. Yet it is here that entire herds of elephants have been fitted with indestructible motor parts, iridium hearts.

Sweat begins to pearl beneath her makeup. A dark stain runs down the middle of her back, down the gray silk Prada all the way between her buttocks. With each step the needle heels she's wearing penetrate deep into the tender humus of the forest floor. These are not walking shoes, yet she advances, never glances, takes her chances.

Ahead, the little Aka scout crouches, running the jungle rot through his fingers.

—Papa! screams he.

Returns an echo or a reply, —Citizen! very far off though. Certainly a Babinga cousin in this jungle zone where the territories of these two Pygmy tribes overlap.

Drone's wings cling to his thumbs as he turns his head up towards the high canopy. A hive up there. He doesn't need the voice of the green crested honey guide to know. The Judas bird. Even she needs him when hunting doom, the one with the shocked quartz heart, the part that keeps him afoot for so many centuries. It's not the big variety like those the eternal prisoner and his keepers ride, the ones with the purple hide.

I'm abreast of her now, wearing suit and tie, my shoes well polished. It's a beautiful pair with white and black whorls; not zebra but Orcinus orca, the killer whale.

This elephant is small and mean, sporting straight pink tusks drawn in tight to penetrate the dense vegetation. It hasn't the broad sweeping white ivory of the extinct savanna herds.

—Kinshasa is the world capital, buildings that make Bodys Isek Kingelez's projects look like the painted toy models they were. These towers, green and blue, are plated with malachite. They soar, do not merely flirt with the sky as western skyscrapers once did, but penetrate it. There are no subways here. We ride pirogues on wild rivers that churn beneath the city. Soon I will take you there. But for now, keep alert as we draw near this animal which knows no fear.

We come across a tunnel gouged out of the vegetation, sap still running blue from shattered trunks. Mukulungu trees rain caterpillars. No wamba.

Steam lingers ahead, just rolled of the elephant's hide along with fleas the size of prune pits.

For the second time she abruptly covers my mouth with her hand. The scent of expensive cosmetics. Danger is near.

—They don't need snell when sniggling for us, she says, speaking of gods sneaking past.

She slaughters this creature in the strangest manner and with the greatest of ease. There's nothing of ecological about this act. We are predators, super-poachers. Putting huge quantities of wasted flesh to rot, pink ivory to burn, iridium and shocked quartz to discard. It's the gastroliths we're after. Deep into the bowels we plunge, gurgling in the still hot blood, coming up for air at the four-minute limit. I have it, the lumpy convoluted thing!

Together we marvel at the glistening object.

—Shall we eschew?

—Yes, but first we must consult the oracle.

She gathers twigs of different size and essence, lays them in front of the burrow of large nocturnal spider. Returning at dawn, she finds that hairy-legged one has arranged the sticks in specific manner. Our path has been traced with great precision.

Wovoko

It comes down to the river at four a.m., approaching cautiously, then ever more boldly towards the morning mist rising.

Very close now, I can see that pieces are missing. A woman it is, with half a face, a quarter face. Neither amputation nor anatomical imperfection. The vacuity is moving, jumping and shifting over the body; now a leg gone like my own, then an entire section of the torso. The leg comes back perfectly. The effect of a migraine mirage that punches swirling holes into vision but here I know that I'm striving to see what isn't there anymore.

During the interminable wait I've remained perfectly immobile, ticks, leaches and other small hematophagous creatures patiently make their way up my body to gorge themselves and swell in silence.

She laps up the river water like a dog, furtively turning her head to either side as she drinks. She sees things I have never seen before. Structures and beings that surely lie between us, rising from the river, bearing perfume and murmur but invisible to me.

Goes on drinking, her body momentarily intact, kneeling in the mud.

When I advance the entire body vanishes, leaving only the trace of her genuflection in this place.

And yet there is a scent here as if she had left behind lingerie with her odor lingering, into which I could bury my face smelling all of her. Know where it was she had come from, what she has eaten and that which she drank, the trace of her sweat bears the message of extreme effort.

I am sure now wherefrom she comes, together we once were there and partook of the same fare, our arms enlaced, strange brew drank we down.

Rhythmic clanging comes from across the river. The iron thieves wielding their small hammers to the melody of Rhinegold niebuling. They've taken now all but the feet of the Eiffel Tower that thrust stumpily into the air.

Alone I hop in the mud.

Thud, my single foot goes deep with each leap. I am naked, turquoise testicles swinging freely to one side before slapping against the only remaining thigh as I climb the bank.

There is no measure of time, no way of knowing when last she came to drink, nor when again she will return. Only space, such a vast quantity of it. The position that the planet was in then, where it now lies and where it will be when she returns. Perhaps not yet an entire revolution around the galaxy but certainly a broad arc half about.

Will she sense that we crossed paths?

—I have seen parts of her again! It is. These are. Fragments that I shall..., I mutter in the morning air, steam rolling from my nostrils.

Without them the study of life's end becomes an imperious necessity. Intensive care unit in broken down hospital where life timidly trembles upon artificially sustained meat; dusty wards echoing with the complaints and groans of the dying.

Ruby dragon flies arise with the sun, their blazing thoraxes winking in the dawn while dog-birds bark as they pass over the river with heavy wing beat blowing mist into slowly spiraling columns.

Scrape the parasites from my skin and put on the cloths I had left by the cold torch and empty hypodermic. No satin pajamas but a crude outfit made of blue dyed jute that makes me itch.

There is time again and I'm very late. A rubber car awaits me where I had left an equian mount, the interior littered with incomprehensible notes, the delicate bones of some kind of fowl, gnarled clean and a thermos of fermented cuttlefish ink.

I gulp black.

—Don't look back! says a voice coming from behind.

Turning around, nothing there I find. A flash of heat in my mind?

Light within is dim, coming through thick glass ports of reduced diameter, capable of resisting the deepest ocean pressure, imbedded in the heavy rubber body, grayish and flaky on the surface from aging and UV exposure. Rubbing in oil with soft cloth is recommended, especially before immersion.

Massive, squat and almost perfectly round it has long whiskers. Speedy and very silent in progression were it not for the sound of constant collision, plowing over banana tree trunks and fichus roots that obstruct the streets. This is rue de Rivoli. Sometimes fluid from something of living splatters the small windows. It is a brutal ride.

Suddenly a mouth is next to me, only this, hanging in the air. The lips are so well formed, the teeth and tongue too. It can only be hers. But my vision now blurs.

How many things it had said to me, this buccal chef-d'œuvre? Merely the timbre of her voice would send tremors surging through me. No need to comprehend the meaning of what she was saying. Whether she spoke to me of emerald snakes pushing through high grass or the darker hue of a new lipstick, it was all the same. Verbal viagra.

How often had I crushed my own lips against these? How many times had I been into the mouth? The touch, taste and scent of it.

Zanda!

—For once listen to the meaning of what I say! Don't just hear but try to understand, comes the voice through the lips perfectly parting over the teeth.

—I need a cigarette, she continues.

—They no longer exist...

—That, if nothing else, is reason enough to leave this place!

—Is it you who laps water from the river?

—It's only the second time I have returned since this part of the sky has turned halfway around. The atmosphere, the air you breathe, light itself will never be the same again. You can sense this change when you look at old photos. There's a different glint in people's eyes; the glow of light on reflective surfaces is far more radiant. It forms halos.

—You're speaking of technical tricks photographers used to make their work appear more luminous...

—You've been misled. Light was altogether different back then. The way it fell on objects, enveloping them; we paid attention to it, remember all of the chrome, how vehicles were angular and always shining, not like this blistered black mess you now drive.

The mouth, with its perfection, is making me uneasy. It's clear to me that she no longer remembers. I shall begin all over again.

—Why here? I could have missed you. The first time I didn't even realize that it was you down by the river.

—The bridge that lies there in a heap, it once rose over the river and that's exactly where I threw down a cigarette, the one you picked up and put to your mouth. The Pont d'Arcole which you crossed daily, bringing me food when I was heavy with Urulu, your daughter.

Be it then she knows who I am?

—I like the feel of the mud, the silence of the city asleep.

—Don't leave!

The streets are slimy, they smell of mint.

—About anything. You must speak!

I know it's the only way to keep her with me momentarily. Perchance she will begin to remember; other parts will then join the mouth.

—On war then. They had, and this in itself is a paradox, been right when they claimed that there would no longer be any great world wars. Only limited conflicts of the Rwanda, Congo or Kosovo type.

But there had been so many of these local wars, cumulating and finally concomitant, that the effect was globally more devastating than any full blown world war ever would have been.

And at last, had not the nuclear arsenal which never served directly, proven infinitely more dangerous when abandoned, releasing its lethal contamination at a time when man's memory no longer retained? (Here I clearly see she has been absent during protracted nuclear conflict, but fundamentally, she's right).

—But you, tell me of friends we knew.

—Hubert? Remember him digging in the sand to hide his wallet on the beach? The long walks we then took together across the tide flats, seaweed and fish skeletons popping beneath our feet. The perils of his homosexuality in Africa, going from one administrative job to another, constantly changing countries. Falling into the same dangerous traps wherever he was. First in Bangui he befriends a young boy, really falls in love with him only to be blackmailed by his protector, a taxi driver, thoroughly mean type that makes his life impossible with constant menaces. You're the one who had warned him against these situations you knew so well.

An ear develops, small and finely formed, just behind the mouth. Hers without a doubt.

—The protector threatens to go to the French embassy and divulge everything. Hubert pays up. He's in love, oblivious to the danger or rather he quite revels in it.

The ambassador summons him, tells him that he must leave. There's too much at risk. He moves to Abidjan where he quickly falls in love with another boy. This time it's the police chief who blackmails him for an altogether different sum. Things are a lot more evolved here. A wealthy French coiffeur, the young boy's last lover, just died in prison while being held on the grounds of a rumor. A well-known journalist, another acquaintance, was thrown out of the window of his twelfth floor flat. "Yes we have high enough buildings here!" the television announced. The police chief confiscated all of his belongings.

Hubert never really realized the danger he was in. One day his family in Britain received a neat little package, his testicles wrapped in manioc leaves, confirming the deep racism that they had always felt towards those of the dark continent and the loathing of their son's sexual life.

—A White man who attempts to penetrate African society inevitably encounters peril; only the degree is variable.

—When you first saw me...

—Everyone told me to beware of you. "He'll do White things to you. Force you to make love with his dog."

The mouth and ear very dark.

—I had no dog.

—Just the same they had warned me that you would spend all of your time licking and eating me as Whites are known to do.

—This has proven to be true.

—Now I remember you. Together we left footprints faraway. Beyond the horizon where I remain, only returning when thirst brings me here.

I scream in the car, utterly alone. To be robbed of one's dreams is perhaps worse than suffering the amputation of a limb.

An insect the size of a coconut splatters on the window, reducing visibility to nil. Now that she's gone there's no more thrill.

—On the banks I shall pray to thee. Forever, there I'll wait.

Erect a small altar with offerings, cigarettes that I somehow find, little bananas, the ones from the West Indies that she loves, the latest image of Urulu that I have always kept by my heart. It's a small fly-through in the blue hues.

Water. Again and again at the river's edge.

I have a well-developed crest on my head. It isn't blunt or primitive looking but high and fine, like the keel of a racing schooner only inverted. It gives me a fierce look. A noble hallmark! Yet I must beware lest a sudden gust catch this small sail and twist my neck. However, and because of it, I have become keenly aware of wind direction. This in turn has developed my sense of scent, greatly improving my hunting capabilities.

No longer are there street lights or publicity panels to illuminate the night. It is black and those who venture out are assassins, running naked through clouds of mosquitoes.

None bear those scarifications of light that are mine. Blazing poison put there by the daughter of the solar flare. A toxin best not share.

Some, they rare, smear luciferin and firefly purée upon their skin to mime those patterns of light that are mine.

Clinical observations: Dull flickering flames occasionally seen to erupt along the forearms, more rarely on the forehead well above the eyebrows, close to the receding hairline. We suspect that the subject pours slender trails of tar over his body and then proceeds to set them on fire. Thin spirals of thick smoke tend to confirm the use of unrefined petroleum products. Subject sustains considerable damage to cutaneous tissues, confined to overlapping bands in the aforementioned regions. The display of scarifications is symptomatic of pervasive pattern of grandiosity.

Yon a glimmer wan.
'Tis the lamp I had thought?
Scales beneath the moon full shining?
Merely some damp thing caught.
Rather a predator here dining
A vapor, a carrion feeder's breath, scent of beast gorged on things foul.

In the black deep unfurls the necklace of heaven's pearls.

So dark is the night that those keen-eyed can clearly see the great nebula, the one that's face-on in Triangulum. Yes, here from the heart of the city.

—Where does it lie? Easy! Find Cassiope, an M or a W depending on whether you run on your hands or use your feet, its shape hasn't that much changed, only broader.

Midway between there and Mirach spreads the brilliant swath of M31 which has drawn much closer, coming in on a straight tangent towards us. Some claim that a bridge of gas already joins us. This is mating, not collision. Now down to the left, just as far again, you can see M33, it too growing much larger. Easy to find, I told you.

A woman runs past bearing a torch. She pitches it blazing into the water, hides beneath a porch, raising the fringe of her skirt. High up her thigh, she plants a needle.

Her bottom half is bare. I cannot help but stare. It's all that's visible as if it had been abandoned there. I am sure that with practice she has learned to plant the needle directly into the femoral artery. Perhaps she was a doctor with considerable experience in performing angiography.

Deep pain in my chest. Plugged coronaries. Sleep, rain are the best. Just the preliminaries before the obituaries.

This river has many tributaries.

Should I have hugged her, slugged her? At least covered her with a vest, lest others in quest, reap what is jest.

These assassins do not fear you.

They will come in very near you.

Quickly now, it is day. A Negro-faced fire finch grazes the water, its flight composed of flickers and festoons.

Culex and anopheles bring fierce new diseases that make malaria merely seem a passing indisposition.

It is here that, striding lightly, I best favor contemplating the sky, captured an instant by the very water it has vomited down upon the land. Deep pools form slick sheets, perfect mirrors surrounded by the baroque frames of ripple brown water. Delicate bamboo bridges have been put up overnight, spanning the river like the work of some great nocturnal spider.

The air is laced with long tongues of electricity knocking down dead, from their perches, clutches of roosting birds. Steeples have fallen; hardly a spire remains standing on the churches.

Storms dump oceans of water that crush buildings and gouge broad craters into the ground. Nature is much stronger than it was, once again taking claim to that which man had thought to tame.

Vegetal palaces.

Elephants and rhinos once kept as pets have bred to form small herds that wander through the steaming wreckage. Some still have keepers. At the break of day they come to drink.

The river is at its lowest, hardly more than a sluggish current in the mainstream that carries along slowly spinning rafts of drifting water lotus. Most all of the city's twelve bridges have collapsed except for the Pont Neuf which is said to be the oldest, built when stone cutters knew well there trade. It stands alone in the middle of the river, useless to those who wish to cross. The waters have washed away the banks to either side leaving the structure stranded in the torrents, strange monument awash with the debris of past floods. Other bridges have formed heaps in the river that with time have become islands covered with reeds and rushes where crocodiles pile vegetal matter to incubate their eggs.

But the Seine no longer is the docile thing it once was. Upriver, dams have long burst leaving it free to suddenly rage with the tropical storms which are frequent even during the dry season. Brown walls of water roar down its bed sweeping away fishermen's shacks and dugouts, drowning entire families caught slumbering or smoking the day's catch along the banks.

Whirlpools then develop, sucking down wreckage with ferocious appetite, spitting up debris with such force that it emerges from water like breaching whale.

Alone I fish amongst the rocks, turning them over when I can or slipping my hands beneath the bigger ones, fingers churning the murky mud beneath. On the bank I lay my catch, spreading it over a plastic sheet. Coins bearing the effigy of a flaming head, the remains of a refrigerator, a motorcycle frame, here a statuette, much older, perhaps roman. Hadn't I done this very same thing along the Tiber? But then I had been much more adroit, never soiling the fine clothes that I wore.

—Wovoko! yells a woman from the opposite bank. She's Chinese3, one of the ten I keep.

—That Russian man, Illitch. He wants you to start his car again.

This is my latest temporary profession, starting the vehicles of those whose lives are really threatened. If bomb there were, it would be for me. I am incapable of being philosophical about it; each time I shut my eyes while I turn the key, sweating and convulsing so hard that the muscles tetanize.

—He shall have to wait.

M'boulou, the dry season, is upon the land. In the early hours the jungle surrounding the city belches thick fog that mixes with smoke rising from wood fires and floating red dust to form dense orange cover that masks the sun. The thicker the *matinal* veil, the hotter it shall be as the day goes on. It's the greenhouse effect that once prevailed on Venus. I refuse to work before the sun has burned through. If I am to die, it shall be a double blaze.

My home is a high arch of long curved branches covered with broad phrynium and banana leaves that so well repel the downpours. Within, one feels as if he were in a vast green tunnel. It has the shape and dimension of the Azande palaces that were once to be found between the Uèlé and the Mbomou rivers, tributaries of the Oubangui. The women tend small fires upon which they smoke pangolin and little monkeys, the night's catch. The vegetal palace is set in what used to be a neighborhood park next to the Saint-Jacques Tower which shows you clearly how the Seine has nibbled its banks over the centuries. The tower still stands, its base partially covered by the green walls of my home.

When besieged by packs of feral dogs or the more dangerous lycaons and hyenas that roam the city, I withdraw to the top of the tower where a peaceful gray light filters through the original glass windows bathing those objects which I treasure the most. These are not artifacts hauled up from the river. They are things which inexplicably fell from the sky one day, landing in front of the main entrance of my lodge. Huge polished bones, a stuffed blue polar bear and a most masterful painting depicting a landscape which nowhere below exists, yet somehow in memory persists. It is a world of flame, akin to early attempts to portray the sun's coronal bursts; extraordinary form where one can let fancy run wildly. The colors are subdued, deep reds and purples with the most transparent of blues. It is the work of someone who had spent much time contemplating fire, knew it intimately. There are no garish hues. Only a suspicion of brilliancy, yet heat is keenly felt by whomever lays eyes on this painting. The word Gogodola appears, barely decipherable along the upper edge. I am convinced that it has nothing to do with a signature.

Had come with these things, a monkey whistle, nets made of vines and a small hand-confectioned crossbow. These implements I use regularly to call the owl-faced mangabey from the lair he affections high up on the Haussmanian rooftops from which I knock him off with darts fashioned from rolled tins. With the nets I catch the little forest pigs that invade the city at nightfall.

Their flesh is excellent, the carcass is separated, basted with the black city honey, wrapped in broad leaves of certain tropical plants that have become indigenous, and buried upon a bed of hot stones. Once cooked, the meat can be preserved for weeks by placing it atop a small frame over a smoking fire. The ceiling being low in the apartments where I personally take in charge the preparation of the pig, I'm obliged to walk on all fours. Wearing kneepads is a necessity.

—Very well, I can accept this transformation, I mumble to myself as I fumble with the ignition wires which have been pulled from the dashboard and stripped so as to expose any pirate circuitry that might have been connected to an explosive charge.

At the same instant I notice my reflection in the rear view mirror. I have drastically changed and these words I have just uttered seem to be most appropriate. I now have a definite weight problem, having lost perhaps fifty percent of my body volume almost instantaneously; the physical appearance of a terminally ill patient, the last stages of aids or anorexia.

The skull is perfectly visible, the lips no longer have enough flesh to properly cover the teeth, they mostly gone, leaving convenient passages for expelling seeds should I consume watermelon, grenadine or papaya. Papaw is out of season and the pits are too big.

It is perhaps an arsine intake related relapse that so strikes me, but the side effects are unexpectedly beneficial: I will be able to slip beneath the vehicle to inspect the chassis for a cleverly placed bomb; this is a blessing, the mirror that I usually pass under the car for inspection being fractured. Secondly, no comedian will ever be able to interpret my role. This is important in that I detest cinema adaptations of real-life situations. Getting this thin just to play the part would bring on death. Had I taken on weight, even dramatically so, the metamorphosis would have been more accessible to an actor. Stuffing of the nasal septum, even one perforated by excessive intranasal cocaine consumption, or filling the jowls with cotton wadding, are well known tricks, that along with a high protein diet, can give the illusion of sudden obesity.

But this skeletal appearance? Impossible!

I remember the laboratory tests that IMG had run on me, revealing traces of benzoylecgonine, a cocaine metabolite, down-regulation of dopamine receptors, EEG changes and alterations in the prolactin secretional patterns.

Illitch keeps a certain distance, nervously yelling inquiry.

—Do you see anything under there? Take your time! Be thorough as you always are, he screams with his Estonian accent. —Have you checked the glove box, the trunk, for remote control devices?

—Of course, I reply.

—Then take the car for a ride, just to make sure.

This is not for me. I'm sweating profusely, so much so that my eyes are blurred, the vision of an amphibian emerging from its mire. Illitch takes no heed of my deplorable physical condition. It is of no matter to him, the bones could perforate the skin, I could collapse on the wheel; he would only bring me vodka, the one with no label, a flask in which marinate 7.3 mm bullets that would, according to him, give the alcohol a special smoky flavor. He always carries it in the hip pocket of his full length green astrakhan coat.

I suppose that this is the kind of thing that legends are made of, not mine for sure, but those emanating from just this sort of individual.

The ride is bumpy and I no longer know whether it is me or the car which rattles the most. Thinking it well to accompany me and not realizing the danger they share, two of the Chinese women have taken seat in the nondescript sedan. Perhaps they believe me to be in the throws of a bout with malaria. Wanting to sooth me, they rub my neck with wet towels. K2 would have thrown me out of the car. She would have flung the keys in Illitch's face.

This vehicle has seen much use. All of the working parts of the doors have disappeared. The handles have been replaced with ropes, the window frames have been welded in several places. An old newspaper folded in four is jammed between the steering column and the dashboard which is split in two and collapsing.

In an instant, we may disappear in a sheet of purple flame, our limbs erupting into the sky with blown glittering glass particles, the softer tissues, cerebral matter and the contents of the abdominal cavity flecking the walls of surrounding buildings. Organic geyser. An explosion would inevitably take a heavy toll on the passing crowd.

I'm becoming acutely aware of the growing number of children pouring into the streets.

—Is school out?

—There is no school here you fool! (Be this thought for all you educated little waggernaps who take such things for granted).

Illitch snatches the keys from my hand. They are very worn down from decades of use. A shiny lump in the middle betrays a weld. He's in the greatest hurry now that he knows the car to be safe.

—Permit me... I say reaching over the steering wheel to retrieve the green velvet cloth embroidered with golden Arabic calligraphy which I always place there before starting the car up.

—You and your useless Koranic prayers! impatiantly mutters Illitch before roaring off.

All has fallen suddenly silent. The children, inexplicably, have disappeared from the streets.

—Have they gone home for their after school snack?

—I just told you that there is no such thing as school here and in addition, most of the children you see have no homes and even less of a snack, sighs China9 in exasperation.

There's a terrific explosion, ten times the required quantity of explosive. The surprise being that the flame isn't at all purple as I had imagined, but green, very pale green like the abdomen of the lacewing, bearing upon an orange crest the microscopic remains of Illitch.

They will be looking for me, the financial partners of Illitch. It would be better if they imagined me gone with their friend, physically dispersed in the sky by the same deflagration. Alerted by the detonation, they're on the way. The search will be a merciless one. Relentlessly they will go through this area where the buildings have massive walls and hardly any roofing, plastic sheets, sheepskins sewn together or broad overlapping leaves, the surest sign that explosives are either stored or manufactured in considerable quantities.

Today I invert myself. I begin with the colon, pulling it out through the anus; gently at first, hand over hand. These are fragile tissues. It's a long and delicate procedure, being that in turn, the colon brings along a good fifteen feet of intestines followed by the stomach on through to the esophagus and windpipe which ties up to each lung and they in turn pulling down the heart, not to forget the tongue. My interior is now on the exterior, plainly visible to whomever may come looking for me or merely cross my path. You may wonder how this is possible with the bones and all? At a certain point they become flexible, almost gelatinous before hardening again. All that which was on the outside now lies deep within me: skin, hair and lashes. The danger being that this cutaneous material, folded as it is deep within me, is now subject to molding while the newly exposed entrails and organs, the brain even, run the risk of dehydration. I'm obliged to continuously vaporize myself. I glisten! The heart palpitates, the intestines squirm.

This is no internal cleansing, the major jihad whereby, at age four, the archangel Gabriel opened up his very own chest (or was it Mohamed's?) and removed the heart for spiritual cleansing. The very first open-heart surgery according to certain scholars.

Gnats and tse tse flies are never far off. There are other disadvantages as well, not the least of which is the constant presence of small jackals and even larger hyenas coming in ever closer.

Advantages: A whole new spectrum of sensations has become perceptible to me. Hitherto unsuspected phenomenae. Perpendicular worlds are palpable. I'm inundated with incoming signals. Confirmation of holistic intuition. Also the repulsive physical aspect keeps undesirable solicitors at large. Invasive, overbearing friends no longer dare approach me. They think me to be only remains, a heap of meat hardly fit for the lurking scavengers. I take note that not one proposes even a summary burial.

It's a camouflage of sorts; I can hide in the butcher's stall or mingle with the wounded and dying on the battlefield. The most appropriate appearance. Illitch's companions are repulsed.

—How do you know it's Wovoko and not Illitch?

—Look at the teeth! See how they're filed down to sharp points like Pygmy teeth. A mouthful of canines. That's Wovoko.

—But where then is Illitch?

—Spattered along the rooftops, say the ten Chinese women, pointing in unison to the dark splotches flecking facades of overhanging buildings.

—Illitch must have been sitting in the back then. The bomb was in the trunk.

—There's nothing here for science to recuperate. These body parts are wasted.

Once again, they're mistaken. Each organ, each vital part, presents the most interesting anomaly.

I must put on weight. My new occupation demands a certain degree of buoyancy. Swimming shark infested waters of the English Channel, a zone that was once clear of such predators but which, with warming waters, now teams with all types of sharks. A landowner, proprietor of seaboard lots, has commissioned me to swim back and forth along the coast while he hosts potential investors. These waters must appear placid, beckoning even.

But first I eat huge quantities of feculents: bread, noodles, rice and manioc. Lipids: butter, pig fat, sausage. Sweets: candies composed of animal jelly and over-refined sugar, cookies, sodas and syrups with artificial coloring, sometimes green, other times purple. No natural flavor.

—What if?

—Go on...

—I was pulled apart by finned predators beneath the eyes of the very people you try to convince of pelagic tranquility.

—Imbecility.

—There is only one sea of tranquility; not here but on the moon.

—Here too now! Bathe I tell you! he screams, jerking a short arm in the direction of fin fraught sea.

I know well the story of this land. It once belonged to a writer who had been forced to sell it after having lost a plagiarism trial against a major cinema company. They now own the property and want to turn it into a theme park based on the very story which they had stolen from him and turned into a hit movie. A story of a flooded world following nuclear war.

I'm naturally afraid of water but this is nothing short of suicide. Warm expanses are cut by the iciest currents that surprise you when you least expect it. Zones of utter murkiness and then crystal clear water permitting me to see fathoms below. The cold waters are swift, never wide but long and slender channels, they can curl around serpentine, clasping.

Beneath are teaming shoals of sharks. Here schools of hammerheads, there the small blue variety from the deep sea that have ventured in close to shore. On the ocean floor, carpet sharks of course. Sawfish as well. Inoffensive to man? Don't be fooled. They've radically changed their feeding habits.

It's a veritable banquet that's being served up in the dunes.

Eating dog: very savory but disagreeably gelatinous if cooked in a wok. Recommended to deep fry in palm oil. Serve wrapped with coco leaves, (leaf of the coconut palm cut extremely fine, gives body and filandrous quality to otherwise overly gooey dishes). Spice generously.

The smoke blows down over the beach, across heaps of rotting seaweed thrown up by the last storm, over fish and crab remains, oil stains, rusted hooks and torn nets. A ship carcass too, half buried in the sand, that stinks of urine.

My ventricles flutter as I go in. Gently, gracefully advancing in the chill murkiness. Can I, as Daniel once did with great felines, converse with these shag-toothed slippery ones of the deep? That they may lie at my feet in a heap! Perverse? Should I pass for one of them, there would be no salvation for they maul one another with equal glee. To flee would bring them upon me with even greater haste. I curse. The terse fellow up in the dunes, will he remunerate me with the toxic materials that I request?

High concentrations of foreground stars can mask beautiful things. Galaxies mating in deep space or clouds of super heated hydrogen gas.

I swim and I swim looking for something far beyond. I think: No longer do I see the sharks and no longer do they see me.

This is only wistful.

Something glimmers then shines brightly from the sea floor, blinking beneath the passing predators. Ever gently I plunge deeper, pushing aside the fins as they glide by. Down here there are coins strewn amongst the rocks. Surface with a fistful.

—Yoweri! from the dunes a woman is calling me.

Clutching the gold I leave the water and walk up the beach. She's coming down dressed in pink and sky blue tatters sewn together with large chrome laces. The smoke blowing off of the barbecued dog stings my eyes. Someone is cursing up in the dunes. I can hardly see their faces.

—You're freezing, she whispers, then much louder while shaking the gold from my hand, —What's it you hold? Stealing this man's gold! I caught you.

From the dune banquet they come tumbling at the mention of bullion. The terse one is the first.

—Where?

She points to the water. They all splash in, fully dressed, dog fat clinging to whiskers and gleaming on full silicone lips. The foam turns red. They're all dead.

—It's me, Xoma, she says, briskly frictioning my body to get the blood circulating again. —Yoweri, Yoweri, what has happened to you? That was your dog up there they were feasting upon. Look at yourself! It's no wonder the sharks didn't attack. You look like an old shoe or drift wood spit up by the sea. But so fat. I can hardly see your eyes.

—Benthic, I reply shuddering.

—Hush. Stop stutttering.

Together we go over the dunes, up narrow Norman lanes darkening with twilight. Apples have fallen from hedgerows. They lie rotting, half-brown with holes torn into them by yellow jackets and slugs. An acidic odor arises. Early fall. When fire salamanders fray, display yellow mottled skin and lay cordons of glistening eggs in steaming bogs before withdrawing beneath rotting logs.

—Seasons have returned then?

The golden spots roam free beneath the torch we bear. It's a moonless night.

Here's a house abandoned, the roof gone, only the walls remain flanked by an empty tower from which the stone steps have long crumbled. In front there is a small pond fed by a hot spring.

—We shall sleep in these waters, companions to eels, she says lowering herself into the steaming dark liquid.

—Do I know this place?

—You should. We once took it apart entirely and then put it back together again, stone by stone. In these chimneys you made great blazing fires for me. You knew then, how to make fire from even the wettest wood. It was cold. Nettles grew, brambles too. Fog rolled up the lane coming from the sea, always stopping just short of that tree.

A huge banana tree with trunk the girth of most ancient oak but more supple. This one flexes with the winds of powerful storms, its immense leaves provide shelter from deluge.

—Remember when you heated this house to tropical temperatures, ran naked with exotic animals?

—Recall now how you refrigerated this home to arctic degrees, wore polar bear fur, slept with Waddell seals and emperor penguins?

—Time is abyssal.

The ape peddlers' haven.

Contrarily to medical reports, the origin of flames appearing on my body is definitely subcutaneous, in no manner self-induced.

Morning come, we roll from the water. Surprisingly, my skin is brittle and dry like Dead sea cavern scroll. This water most probably comes from seepage: forgotten underground stockpiles of solid low-level and transuranic waste. No danger here, it's just a warm paste.

—Perhaps it's time we spoke frankly on the question of pollution, and here I include alcohol intake, excessive tobacco consumption, the abusive use of substances, chemical contamination and irradiation, all held to be life endangering.

I'm speaking from first hand knowledge, (holding out my hands that are maroon from smoking). What's more, my mucous is dark brown, much like the juice that oozes from the grasshopper's mouth parts when crushed.

—Fear of things nuclear? We thrive on them, filling our homes with pitchblende and uranium ore. A necessity. Natural reactors, such as the one first discovered in Gabon, are much sought after. Entire cities spring up around them! Consider the side effects of heating yourself by burning mox in the living room hearth. True, we don't necessarily die anymore from this type of direct massive exposure to high levels of radiation. Nor is mutation the common lot. No nose at all or set too far over to the side, eyes where the ears should have been, stunted small legs and so on. Tolerance and in certain cases, an addiction to the most violent radioactivity. But then, is this not evolution? Are we not on the verge of becoming something else, certainly closer to the thermonuclear heart of the very cosmos? This is the only possible preparation for most remote future. There shall be three of us. We will be alive four and a half billion years from now. The sun will by then have become enormous, expanding to engulf all planets to, and including, Jupiter. The gas shell of Saturn will have been blown off, gone the rings, leaving only a metallic core revealing surprising concealed cavities where had thriven a strange civilization, driven out by the blaze. Not so with us. We would have been capable of aiding them had we known of their existence. As for us, we won't have died off as could have been expected. We will have had sufficient time to evolve. Our metabolism, already drastically altered due to increasing industrial pollution and mounting radiation over millions of centuries, will have adapted to the intense heat. We will be living within the immense sun. Home *helios*.

I build a crude but very effective scaffolding from hazel shrub staffs permitting me to attain the upper level of the house from which the flooring has fallen. Here I punch a large round window through the wall.

—Why?

—Literary and religious nostalgia. Nemo's Nautilus had just such an opening and so did certain cathedrals. I shall call it a rosette.

—But then again, why?

—Hoping to catch a glimpse of giant squids or saints.

—It is time to return to Paris, she declares, wrapping with wet white chiffon, two bottles drawn up from pond bottom. —We can't open them now. Too much pressure from the heat. Evaporation from the cloth will cool them off. An old desert dweller's technique.

—I have lost certain bones, others have fused. Most of them are hollow now and much lighter.

—You can fly then?

—No, not yet. But I can glide like chrysopelea, ptychozoom or rachophorus.

—But that means you have to climb trees each time. You might just as well brachiate from limb to limb.

—This time we'll walk.

Along the way we're assailed by poachers peddling gorilla fat and ligaments, hands, feet and skulls; panther skins, (only black ones, we're not far from the deepest jungle surrounding Paris); elephant tusks, feet and tails. The stiff bristles make wonderful bracelets.

We come to the inevitable roadblock, the one that always displaces itself to be across your path wherever that may be. No uniformed customs agents here. A single individual endlessly controls our papers, going through our belongings, seeking animal hides, bones.

—Important people, ministers of war and secretaries of state, consume gorilla flesh. It conveys to them the very special power to which they are entitled. However, the acquisition of bi-products, teeth, hides and appendages, by individuals such as yourselves is strictly forbidden.

This man first appears to be Slavic, his skin as pale as the veil swaddling our two bottles which he covets.

Closer examination reveals a perforated throat and eleven fingers on each hand. I suspect a notochord and tube feet. Absence of leaves on surrounding vegetation and the utter emptiness of the perimeter suggests that he filters food directly from the surrounding air by creating concentrated vacuum at will. This is the type of individual that I had always suspected to exist, soft-bodied, leaving no fossil record when dead, capable of lying dormant in unique sort of sedimentation with very low ambient oxygen.

—I have here two persons, one male Caucasian age fifty five, one female Negroid age forty six, going respectively by the names of Mohamed Xeg and K2.

—Repeat, crackles a faint voice, hidden somewhere nearby.

—K2 as in part of quantum superposition leading to anti-K zero.

—Quaff not this ale which has surely soured with age! blurt I as he reaches for the flacons. —Rather examine these, see if they please, offering instead a finely sculpted wax jaw set with needle golden teeth, stomatic souvenir which I keep upon my person at all times.

Boom. The cork explodes from the bottle taking off half of his head. It's not a clean decapitation.

— Storm bottled brew, she marvels, picking up the remaining flask. —Shame we haven't a whole cask.

—New moon execution, I muse turning over a multi-fingered hand in my own hands which suddenly seem strangely under equipped. — Were we to include him on a cladogram along with ourselves and other tetrapods, what do you suppose his position would be?

—Much closer to you than you could ever imagine. Breathing in your ear!

—Carefully study preexisting taxonomies. Then invent your own. Chances are, with time, it will be just as valid.

Goatsuckers with deeply cleft fissirostral beaks emerge from the underbrush and begin a litany of ventilation noises. Clutching the surviving bottle, I join Xoma in the treetops. Together we brachiate, not the dis-articulated, jerking leaps of adolescent gibbons that often as not end up crashing to the jungle floor after having missed a branch, but the long clean sweeps of an adult primate. At this rate, we'll soon be in Paris again. What news has there for me Oloman Klanik? Xoma. Will I be able to find for her to wear ancient shoes by Manolo Blahnik? These things are most uncertain.

Spider 1

She has a dorsal fin. I bite it savagely, taking out large chunks. In the animal world, numerous are the species among which the male pins down the female while mating, all the while inflicting severe bites. No sooner am I asleep than I dream of her again. She's naked lying beneath my face, nipple, navel smeared with excrement. My hands are bound behind my back. The only way to cleanse her is with my tongue. This act must be performed quickly for three reasons:

1. Those features which so draw me to her will quickly become grotesque. She'll become a sexual caricature, the overdeveloped lips, if nothing else, will swell upward touching the nose which shall inevitably push down as noses always do with age.

2. Typhoon's near. Her timeless beauty won't tolerate this infidelity. In these climes destruction stalks depredation.

3. If I don't hurry the excrement will thicken, envelop the entire body, and licking it away will become an impossible task. *Igthe* as the Osage Indians call it.

This woman is a body bearing only predator desire. Pure pheromone. She's off-stage. I'm the male moth drawn in by sexual scent. I shall not succumb.

I take an automobile, vast, the yellow color that I hate. Shiny metallic spheres with engraved patterns of eels serve the function of wheels. I have by my side Awa, a young Azande girl. Her hair, very short, clings tightly to her head from which long stems thrust outward like the antennae of sputnik. The content, thought patterns, dreams and desires, is explosive.

Each jolt of the vehicle could set it off.

We traverse fens where animals lay their flesh to rest forever. They'll decompose, mix with rotting plants and become oil or perhaps stone to be exposed in a museum several million years hence. Of course museums will still exist!

She tells me oonopids can change the color of their eyes, certain fish too, that upon their heads they have hackled threads. Males have bumps and turrets. Dwarf spiders always possess unusual bulges and depressions in the head area. The automobile pushes through reed mace and rushes. There are strange cries in the air. Jackals are calling and once again I wonder at how they so sound like coyotes. Ferns form giant brushes.

—Heat, she stutters, shivering.

The heart of a meteorite, the tongue of a solar flare, or the first millisecond of nuclear deflagration. Establish a scale of comparative combustive values and you shall find that all of these are cold with respect to the fire which burns within her.

—Heat? I repeat.

The innermost core of a giant star, say Betelgeuse or Rigel. One is blue, the other red. Intensity and pulsation are forms of measure. R.R. Lyrae, W Virginis, X Ophiuchi, R.V. Tauri, Z Camelopardalis, Wolf-Rayet and Shott all serve this purpose.

—You'll make love to my granddaughter, she continues.

—I shall be dead!

—Role up the window, I'm freezing.

—What's in your head?

—You're master to none. Accept that first.

She takes my hand with her palm almost as pale as mine. It's searing. Fever I'm fearing. Withdraw my own.

—It's not such a bad thing for you to catch, Grinn and Wozek both created their best works while down with enteric fever.

I look at her, eyes rolling back close to coma. Remember the photo; she naked on all fours, her eyes rolled up just so, probably intoxicated. The photographer's shoes and someone else's hedging the edge of the frame. There was something of obscene about it. What had they done to her? What had she done to them? Who were they? Colonial history was surmised in this one small image.

We are deep in the jungle now. This car is much too big; the patterns have eroded from the spheres long ago. It's not a primal jungle with trees of incommensurable height, but a low brooding one with thick underbrush whipping the windshield, snapping off half rotten purple drupes that spill through the open windows. Insects too. Ones that I've never seen before. Broad wings bearing patterns of an illuminated sky atlas. Ruby eyes flash with laser intensity. Chemical odors. The powder from their wings burns my skin. Spider with a spiny hard carapace shaped like a matador's hat crawls up my arm.

Thorn.

I should have listened when she told me to raise the window. Now it's jammed open.

Radio Kinshasa: "Change the country's name back to Zaïre again!" followed by the flow of all-night music, the kind you hear playing in the little nightclubs that never close down. When do these people ever sleep?

—That's the serpent's mother! she gasps horrified as a mantis-like insect, totally white, takes a threatening stance on the dashboard.

—Nonsense, I say smashing it with my sandal. Pale worm forms wriggle from a gash in the belly. Strange how all things white symbolize evil in these zones.

She's in the back seat now.

—Never, never harm the snake's mother! she's hoarse, unable to raise her voice. There's incredible beauty in the raspy sound coming from the depths of her throat, somehow forming speech.

I'm alone in the front, fighting the wheel while trying to push away the pale serpent brood which is all over the seat and floor board. Cobras just out of the egg are as potent as their mother. Freshly hatched crocs will bite off your fingers or any other cusp imprudently left in front of their snouts. Once again, I marvel at reptile versatility. Why is it they're not yet masters of this world? We once had a pet turtle. Crashing through the kitchen after whisky, I crushed its head. It made the sound of a nutshell imploding beneath the sole of my shoe. There was blood and soft tissue everywhere. Turtle survived, even though blind, and outlived me by thirty-five years.

A village. Like an old western town with battered storefronts along a main street, that's all. Gulleys and ridges of deep red dirt. Laterite. Dead, in a pothole there's a dog.

The radio again with a quiz show, "Harlemite. The correct answer wins a trip to Inga Falls."

Replies come crackling: "Harlemite is a dark gemstone; a meteorite; an inhabitant of Harlem..."

She takes me to a small bar with a wooden terrace falling onto the street. We eat roasted goat cut in thin slivers. Next to us, drinking Mocaf beer with elephants' heads on the labels are three very overdressed men. Black leather jackets bulging with concealed weapons seem a continuation of their skin. The red dust has set into the folds. It streaks down their faces with profusely running sweat.

On the table is a greasy and very used AK-47, brass nails forming patterns on the stock, tassels with pearls and monkey tails tied to the muzzle. It serves as a paperweight to hold down a map, edges blowing up over the weapon like wrapping paper around a gift just opened.

—What are you doing here? bluntly asks one of the three, wearing military camouflage.

—Finishing an unfinished life.

—With her? quips the owner of the monkey-tail AK 47.

—She, part of it, I reply just as bluntly.

—Let's see your papers, says the man with the big leaf-shaped spots on his trousers.

She rises and walks straight over to their table.

—Leave alone a mother of the nation returning home with husband of her granddaughter to come, she hisses, her tourmaline eyes changing color as she speaks, (always purple/green in a fifty-fifty ratio).

—And who's daughter be you?

—I'm Azande and that's enough for you to know, little forest man.

From under the porch, the wind brings an odor of deep jungle mold, the breath of carnivores digesting full bellies of broken prey and the pollen of toxic flowers. This is M'Baiki. Not far down the carmine road is Barthelemy Boganda's grave, a small white chapel turned pink by the dust of rare passing truck.

—What size shoe do you wear?

—Not yours, I say.

—Don't speak to him, she snaps at me.

—Let me take care of this.

—Like you did with the serpent's mother?

—Precisely!

—What's in the car? demands the camouflaged one.

The map blows away as he picks up the gun. Together we go down to the car. Central Africa turns in the sky.

The big one is still looking at my shoes.

—Open the trunk! yells he, the beer in his mouth green.

A rhinoceros hornbill flies over, awkwardness casting a purple shadow on the red dirt. Mosquito larvae team in the ruts. No vehicle has passed here for months. There used to be a night club in Harlem called Ubangui.

Forgetting my shoes he cries out, —I love yellow! Give me the keys.

I'm wearing an old Yoggi Yamamoto suit, late twentieth century of the finest Japanese fabric, European cut.

I am happy. Two problems have been resolved. The yellow I so disliked is gone and with it the belligerents.

The serpents I regret, somehow knowing their venom to be treasure. Could other colors bring or take? Purple for example, holding for an instant the shape of the passing hornbill. The variable colors of Awa's eyes. Vector bearing with each hue facets of the spirit.

Peeling new bills from a bulky roll in my shirt I pay the ale purveyor for the goat. Money fresh from the mint bearing the effigy of Lumumba, the prisoner awaiting death in the acid vat of a Katanga copper mine. Will there someday be currency with the image of Malcolm X?

—US postal stamps have already been printed but that's all.

—It's a first step, but are they stickers or do you have to lick them?

—Stickers.

—Too bad. I was just beginning to imagine a majority of the population to which this image is offensive, being obliged to put their tongue to the ass of Shabaz.

It's then that I notice a fresco on the wall inside of the bar. At first I think it's just patterns of blistered paint. The darkness in here, away from the sun, makes it difficult to see. A scene has been adroitly laid down on this surface by the master hand of a forest witch doctor. A man runs on this dark wall, carrying beneath his arm something bundled. He is glancing back over his shoulder with an expression of glee as he begins to flee. In front, unseen to him, teeth lay in rows on the ground as if the earth itself were snarling, opening up its maw. The hyenas' grave yard. Overhead is a tongue which takes up the entire sky. Behind, nothing.

—You wonder what it is? asks old woman behind the bar.

—No, say I in a hurry to leave.

—It's you! The tongue licks you like a stamp. You were thinking of stamps just now, weren't you? Pastes you to a missive to be sent to the other end of the sky. What's under the arm? All that which you once thought to be priceless but which has no value. What are you running from? The past which you don't have. The teeth in the ground? A hyena died there, your pet and you didn't even know it. As for the artist who painted this...

—No, I simply must go. I can't wait.

—You will. He's the man who just requisitioned your vehicle. He used to be an artist even though you assumed he was just a thug. He created two or three marvelous things, among which a play in four acts entitled "Let's be God, the Christian one." He was brilliant. Had a wardrobe of seventy-five costumes that he took everywhere with him. He spoke twelve African languages and seventeen others. But he performed only this one play. Killing hope was the theme. First he would kindle it, bringing it to be a thing which the spectators could believe in, an entity, tangible right there before them. Something for which they would yearn for, it never quite materializing.

—What did it look like, hope?

—A very beautiful thing, always. But there was something flawed about it each time.

—Blemish?

—Not at all! she says wiping down glasses with a dirty rag. The skin of her hands are luminous, oiled with something that leaks from trees.

—When you speak, she continues, it's always affected by the thinking of those men who shaped the civilization that you come from. Men like Pascal, Diderot or Descartes. Ideas that brought a semblance of deeper thinking, scruples and even the gloss of morality. Finally, democracy which is merely a refined tool for conquest. But that's not for me. When these things all break down, what have you left? Just a smell.

Iiunga was all knowing, she says, — all seeing. He would take this notion of hope and turn it into an animal like a pet or an object, something right there on the shelf that you thought you could pick up and walk away with.

— And the flaw, what was it?

—There wasn't one.

—You said there was always a flaw.

—But that's the flaw, you see, the very fact that there wasn't one. And then, just as you were beginning to really believe in this perfect thing, this hope thing, he would kill it. It was the cruelest sacrifice. A real thrust to the heart!

—And the sculpture?

—A totally different thing, that. Few people ever saw it. In the forest, deep in the forest, at least a two-day walk from here. He heaped dirt to form a big mound long and high that went between the roots of the trees. It became a woman, slumbering but sometimes awake. There was nothing of ritual about it, no deeper meaning, or so we thought at first. When she was awake her eyes would just look up at those patches of sky barely visible through the treetops. The rest of the time she was in a deep dream of which we had no part.

I saw her once, incomparable beauty...with a flaw. She was lying on her side which was surprising because my brother had told me that she had been lying on her back.

—The flaw?

—Her breath; when you passed by her nose, perfectly formed, as big as my arm, it smelled of poison. The sort you put into a man's food to kill him.

—What happened to her?

—The last time she was seen, she was lying on her stomach and groaning. The kind of groans that Arabs say comes from the heart of sand dunes in the desert. It had a rhythm, was a beautiful thing to hear. And then she was gone. Back into the ground probably, although Iiunga said she had risen and simply walked off through the jungle.

—And the song?

—I just told you about the song. You Whites don't listen. Always in a hurry to be somewhere else.

—You said nothing about a song.

—The groan, with rhythm. Jungle honey.

—And this man Iiunga?

—He became a politician, said it was the highest form of art. He promised to build money factories in the forest, make everyone rich. Go to Mars. He made good use of democracy you see. All voted for him.

—And now?

—He's just a bandit! You saw him didn't you? He would've taken the shoes you walk with and even have killed you for them. Don't think he forgot.

—That too can be an art.

—What? she asks just as truck loaded with freshly poached ivory roars by.

—Being a bandit, I answer as the roar grows fainter.

It is ivory from the forest elephant, the solitary one with the darker skin, tusks drawn in tight for penetrating the vegetal mass. Pink ivory. These elephants are much more cunning than the long gone savannah variety. This passing load, maybe the last, is the fruit of a ruthless hunt.

Another woman is shaking caterpillars in a broad aluminum basin held over a fire. The heads crinkle in the bottom like gravel. She uses a swirling shaking motion as if she were panning for gold. The toxic hairs crackle and go up in smoke.

Now they're ready. We feast on them. Warm in the mouth.

—Your ignorance is exotic, Awa laughs.

A hunter comes in from the forest, a smoky mangabey slung over the shoulder. The tail appears to be tied around the neck to form a perfect sling. The skin has been slit at the tip to create an opening through which the head was thrust. Fresh blood flecks the fur. Vermilion dew.

She tells me of the Judas bird, the one that follows the monkeys through the trees picking amongst their excrements to find undigested seeds. This bird's scream is the sure sign that monkeys are to be found nearby.

She wraps cool leaves around my feet and we go down endless small paths. A turacoa bursts from a thicket and desperately flies away. The forest becomes silent, strangely so.

Several things happen quickly now:

We discover an immense skeleton. She strikes the rib cage with the femur bone – which takes two hands to hold – playing it like a xylophone. We turn the skull, cleaved in half, into the resonance box of an instrument, stringing it with panther whiskers tied end to end. Boring holes into it, the thighbone becomes a woodwind.

She asks, —Upon discovering exo-civilizations, can we make profit, expand our commerce? Will they consume soft drinks, junk food, and mass entertainment...and offer in exchange, riches?

I grow nephelia spiders for their huge webs. Make tunics from their silk.

Urulu is with me.

—What shall we eat Daddy? Dugong, kinkajou or wombat? We are egg thieves.

—*Renards* you mean?

—No the dinosaurs that steal eggs. Oviraptors!

She leaves a centipede and a seahorse for me, taking in exchange two old photos of a comet. The one that had come so close as to cause tides to turn, pelts and hides to burn, before finally dividing into four and continuing on its way.

Beneath my vest, I put on a coat of chain mail. Not the tunic made of fine iron rings that Norman kings favored, but an ugly apron made of carbon chips that covers my chest and hips. The kind that butchers wore to protect their bellies from sharp flying bone fragments or bouncing blades and hatchet strokes.

I see the hall of the Cavern King, just a glimpse. He's pale of course, all damp and powdery, gypsum from the heart of the earth.

Here are blind salamanders, fish and shrimp that have never seen the day. No eyes or just minute red pin pricks at the most.

Niter and mold, this place is cold. Down here there's nothing of bold. It's a kingdom of silence, one of patience.

The king has a single eyespot to one side of his head, pale skin drawn tightly over a degenerate eye. His body's lined with segmental slime glands and he has around the maw, soft barbles covered with taste and touch receptors, a pharyngocutaneous duct for expelling ingested debris and subcutaneous sinus between skin and muscles.

I develop a jungle honey export business. Small attractive bottles with the images of animals on the labels, okapis, anteaters and pangolins. Strict sanitation laws put an end to my efforts when chunks of wild hives and bees are found in my pots.

—This is dead calm, she says in the midst of the wildest chaos. —Violence is yet to come. All that you know, earthquake, tsunami, volcano, war, and bold impact are nothing.

Deciphering dreams has become an industry. I'm paid to dream for those who cannot. No reverie but deep, rational and concrete images hauled from zones close to coma.

It's a fossil world. A stone trilobite embedded in shale awaiting the rock hammer's blow.

There is an immense incongruity between human civilization and the natural universe. We intrude upon it. Parasites giving nothing in return. Seek a symbiotic relationship.

We smoke constantly. The odor of tobacco is ever present. We live in small hotels where the curtains, carpets, pillowcases and blankets smell of dust. We also drink heavily. The liquor bill is usually much higher than that of the food. Empty bottles litter the floor. When we're hungry, I rip open bulky bags of dog food and scatter the dry grains amongst the empty containers strewn on the floor. We eat on all fours. When we feed the room is filled with crunching and clinking noises. Though nothing's really esculent.

Escheat. More than land. Her body too.

Episodic epistaxis. Real blood flood. Ergonovine could be indicated. But then, this nose is no uterus, and certainly not one having just suffered an abortion.

I make roofing using equitant foliage. Ere now I learned how. Remember with what vigor mountains thrust up during the Neogene. Erumpent times.

Revert to eschatology. Change the story of our lives as often as I wish. Heed no estoppel. ETD: 25hrs. Control esurience till then. Bite back of hands if necessary, can provoke scars and calluses on dorsum.

Fine downing hair on the trunk?

Lanugo!

I wear fearnought overcoat. Fit iron collars to galley slaves.

A child comes to me bearing half of a letter, part of a medal and other mutilated personal belongings, all bearing intricate cuts down the middle; realize that there's a perfectly matching half out there somewhere. No matter where or when I'll run across this child, we must both return to the eighteenth century in Paris. The proprietor of the missing pieces will know who the child is.

—Damn you, look at me! You're what I was. I'm what you'll be! I scream at a young man.

Very quickly, I'm a kite maker, a fish vendor.

All that I have just mentioned, happens, happened or will have happened, but not necessarily in that order. Some of the incidents briefly described here are lengthy episodes. They may appear to be unrelated. They are not. Capillarity. A few of them shall be recurrent.

We leave the forest which remains strangely silent. She takes me to a city. The streets are paved with gold. A surprising blinding glitter reverberates from beneath our feet. Many other things are covered with gold: dust bins and garbage trucks, piping, even the sewers buried three feet down where they'll never be seen, she tells me. But these are only the suburbs! The dirt is red here. Deep red, like the soil of Georgia or Arkansas if blood or oil were dumped upon it.

—What fabulous mine have these people found? A mother load that surpasses dreams of Cibola! Shafts going to the Earth's center?

—No. They've snuffed a star. One that had a 90% gold core. A bold whore had shown the way. They took hold before it had gone cold and brought it back here for all to behold.

—What technology is it they master? How to prepare such an expedition? This is science fiction!

—I despise science fiction!

—By what means then?

—Firstly the ship there beneath the shed.

Jutting out, the poop of a small vessel. It's a shipwreck on dryland. Rust streaks down old boards, meanders over flaking paint. The lines are smooth, the language of a naval architect, yet hardly the kind of craft that could fly or even float, especially to some place so remote. The doghouse is made of cardboard and plastic riveted together and pleated.

—Adventure never to be repeated?

—Just now they depart for a sun made of carbon. When cooled, it will be diamond.

—They travel with mast down and sail furled? mockingly I query.

—Unfurl your spirit! she replies tersely.

—This ship can't even sail the most placid of seas.

—An inner one!

My feet are bloody from having stumbled over cacti, brambles and sharp stones. Just before leaving the forest we had been ambushed by Iiunga. He had taken my shoes, size 46 Shannon. Awa tells me I'm confused, have been wearing socks made of brambles.

—Come with me, she beckons, boarding the small ship.

We are below decks, the rising heat of the morning draws the scent of weathered wood from the futtocks. The crew passes round a gourd of strong palm wine; tickles the throat with an exquisite gurgling acidity. She speaks with them a language composed of rare vowels and many consonants. I understand. They are her family.

The alcohol is taking hold and I know this ship's going nowhere; even the tires of the rusted trailer upon which it rests are flat and peeled. I pass out; enter a deep sleep in which I'm dreaming again about the office with an urban view: Wearing a gray suit and reviewing a law case that's due to go to court immediately. There are over 500 pages of introduction that must be rationally organized. This will lead to where I plead. I'm the last one remaining in the gigantic office building, probably downtown Los Angeles. A sports car is in the underground parking fourteen floors down. It's not anywhere near being paid for. Neither is my house, an hour's drive away in San Marino or Pasadena, I can't remember, only a stone's throw from the Huntington Library botanical gardens where spiny plants thrive. In this dream, I hardly think of the woman sleeping in the house. She's totally Caucasian. Then I consider the baby that I have, not with her but with the girl down in South Central, the one I love. This part of the dream poses a serious problem, threatens to lower the commercial value or even render it unsellable. This I'm actually thinking while dreaming. Have I, in spite of myself, succeeded in introducing a higher level of rational reasoning into these dreams that I've been commissioned to dream? Beyond the established bounds of elementary rationale so sought after by my potential clients? The ultimate perversion. Or is this simply the proof that, contrarily to what I have come to accept, the apparent innocuity of my commerce is becoming much too invasive; that it would be preferable to side step. Falling unconscious due to massive alcohol intake is no escape but rather a folding together of what should be kept in separate chambers. Divide these, lest they strike up a truce. I can't work on this dossier anymore. Classify and take the lift. Perhaps I can just open a door, climb through an aperture. The lift falls.

The sickening dropping feeling is reality. I wake up. We're plunging into a funnel of yellow water. Hit the bottom and slam back up a foaming crest. It's a sea. The wildest vertical one. You can only fall off.

There's a strong smell of mud, vegetal debris and fish. China, I think, but it's not Asia at all.

The crew are all afoot and braced against the bulwarks. The alcohol has had no effect on them. Many things I hadn't noticed when I had first climbed aboard back in the shed: sculling oars, thole pins, a capstan whelp chock.

—Orzo todo! Hard lee!

Awa's the one yelling in the heart of the yellow gale. It is she who gives the orders here.

—Let go the main!

A dead calm, suddenly and inexplicably falls.

—Alee! Put the helm alee!

We are beneaped. The ship is spinning apparently out of control.

—What are we doing? I scream.

—Fishing.

They haul something of huge aboard. It flounders. Black, very shiny, covered with lights on fleshy stems. Surely an abyssal species. In unison they straddle the creature from the deep and rhythmically massage its underside. Oily magenta row abundantly spurts from the belly. Loaded down with this cumbersome catch we head back into Lubumbashi, obliged to drag the boat behind us over rough rocky terrain.

—The suburbs where traitors once wore neck ties made of flaming tires!

We halt at a small train station where two ancient passenger wagons await on rusted tracks. The crew loads the quartered fish aboard the wagons, clambers all over the roof, spreading out to dry beneath the sun, sections of blubber, gleaming black skin, and yellow flesh all the while smearing the the eggs and oily secretions over the worn steel. Protective coating, lubrication, or merely food preparation?

—Are we never to enter the heart of this city?

Oblivious to my presence, Awa is preparing some sort of a brazero in the corner of one of the wagons. A shiny tin box by the side of which she squats. Passengers mill about aimlessly as if anticipating imminent departure. None of them carry baggage other than a few small animals bound by the legs; jungle rodents, a large turtle tressed with straw to form a handle on its back. A small boy has a mouse on a leash and a sling-shot around his neck. Two young girls carry with them a juvenile forest antelope which is near death, the skin having been stripped from the forelegs, probably in an early morning attempt to struggle free from a jungle trap. Blood diluted with saliva forms pale pink bubbles that pearl from its nostrils with each breath. It's unbearibly hot in here.

—Heat, mutters Awa as I approach her from behind. An elf owl is perched on her shoulder like a common parrot.

—How much longer must I endure this comedy? You said that we were to travel great distance in a snap, capture a distant star even. We hardly left the outskirts of the city aboard the shipwreck! And now we're on a train with no engine.

—Things have names here, she says without standing, large drops of sweat dropping from her forehead and resonating in the bottom of the tin box, —Yeti is the name of the vessel you call a shipwreck, named after a fishing boat that went down off the coast of Normandy with all hands aboard. They had caught something too heavy to bring aboard and it ended up pulling them all under. It was also the pet name of the abominable snowman before being that of a long suburban train that used to shuttle between Paris and the much poorer outskirts. Yes, the snowman was first.

—What can we possibly be doing on this train?

—Propulsion units, plasma rockets, and all other forms of launching devices with which I'm sure you were at one time familiar, all had stages, at least three of them, in order to escape the simple forces of attraction. Had they not? Consider Yeti to be a first stage. This train, call it 1066, will be the second.

—All of these people will be coming along with us?

—In no way. They've just brought us a few necessities which we'll accept as offerings. As I lean from the open door I see an ancient diesel locomotive rounding a distant curve, approaching through the shimmering air. In a moment It'll give us a jolt as it couples up.

It's olive colored with little round portholes and red hoses emerging from the cowling which has been welded over countless times. Brown fumes belch from the smoke stacks, the engine roars in typical diesel fashion and a horn blows, a deep forlorn moan that carries over the sultry city-scape into the heart of the capital and out over the surrounding jungle.

The locomotive passes by on a sidetrack. It's close enough to touch. I can see the engineers through the portholes. The interior is deep blue, icicles hang from the ceiling. No, these are stalactites! This implies a fossil process, infiltration of water, a much longer time sequence. They wear polar jackets with wolverine fur around the hoods, huge mittens and the darkest sunglasses.

—Don't let it get away! I scream.

My companions pay no heed. They're busy catching locusts and fitting them into Awa's tin container where they stomp them into purée.

—What are you doing? Are you all demented?

—You who eructate with erubescent eruciform tongue! yells a man carrying under arm an Alaskan fur cap. —Fool, this is fuel!

—Make yourself at home, You'll have this entire wagon to yourself. A long journey, suggests Awa.

I install nephelia spiders. In no time their webs divide the interior with sheets of the strongest silk drawn across the compartment at unexpected angles. They possess the most elegant palps; translucid amber femur, patella and tibia joined by opaque, black articulations. Adult specimens are already capturing large insects that they roll between their mandibles before storing in the peripheral zones of their webs. I'll soon have enough silk to fashion tunics and pants for the entire expedition. Our uniforms shall be brilliant, silvery with a slightly rugose surface, covering all; even the eyes and nostrils.

Serpents hang in perfect limp coils over branches like carefully stowed garden hoses. Giant geckos are pasted flat across the smooth surfaces of those windows which haven't been opened. The loose skin of their bellies forms pale suction cups against the glass.

Bring aboard cartons full of old whiskey and soda bottles filled anew with a palid fluid.

—More palm wine?

—Carnivore milk with the highest protein content: hyena.

Indeed, someone has gone to the pain of pasting to the bottles, beautifully rendered labels bearing the effigy of the mottled scavenger.

I'm down on the tracks now, restlessly walking in circles. Yeti is off to the side, workers beating copper plates to the keel and strapping on lead ballast. A fannion has been unfurled atop one of the wagons where it flutters above the drying fish carcass. Two cheetahs on a red background. The tip of the flag so tattered by winds of yore that the animals no longer have tails nor hindquarters. Paws, only four. The wagons jolt.

—Bolt! Awa yells to me, holding out her arm in my direction. —Leap aboard gracefully now. The time will soon come when you'll be too old to jump turnstiles, forced to crawl under.

The pilot's porthole is nothing more than a peephole with graffitti of a woman's anus and vagina roughly drawn round it. The image has been elaborated with legs spreading to either side and hanging tits. Squinting through the aperture I glimpse a real woman swimming in a clear blue pool.

She invites me to a restaurant. Like an ogre, I throw myself on the plates of other diners. She tells me that Africans have been reduced to bands of survivors confined to reservations, following a second deeper colonisation. The world's all white. A bechamel sauce. I suddenly leave the table, kneel in the middle of the street, clutching my head as if it were a large fragile egg. Full of dreams being consumed by parasites. Traffic swerves around me. Run down little vehicles and people yelling. I withdraw to the safety of the gutter. Lay down in the soothing water. Can see the moon and the brightest stars. Comes she with spoon. Wants to fight against cars.

The automobiles are o.k. but the tags just don't make any sense. A disheveled blonde is in the back seat of this one. I'd seen her on a poster pinned to a locker door in a factory near Brescia. Bent over peering backwards between her legs, sticking out her tongue.

Antiquarians are buying up furniture and techno-gadgets which we haven't even dreamed of yet, as if they were the rarest ancient treasure.

Stand beneath a mare while reading through a pile of horse-racing journals. Licks your bald head. Scribble some notes in the margins. Which one's the best bet? "Treasure Chest," "Distant Lover," or "Tongue'n Cheek?" Outsiders. Take off your shoes and let hyena bitch lick between your toes. Sublime creole wife comes in wearing blonde wig. Drop pants for total lick down. Paralysed by pleasure, there's little chance you'll make it to the races. Why go to other places? Avoid useless chases.

Leave me be! This is how I think best.

We do the restaurant scene again. I'm eating a dish of gnocci. Zanda's screaming at me, smashing plates. She cuts me severely across the chest with a table knife before finally walking out. I continue eating with my own blood for sauce.

Observe what's to either side of us. Being in between provides a good point of view. But that which is perceived as being infinitely smaller or vastly larger, constitutes in itself yet another in between, both smaller and vaster on another scale.

Vomit green spaghetti.

She returns. While gently swabbing my blood she tells me a story about the Duke of Glouscester. How when on a safari in Africa, he slipped away from camp to relieve himself. Hunting companion emerging from tent, seeing bush move, shot him fearing there was a lion in the bush.

This is happening in the belly of a giant metallic dog which is their idea of how a stage should look. Off-stage, there's another woman. She's always present. Never used to look at me before. One of those types who thinks that just because I'm with an African woman, I must have an immense scrotum and an oversized prick. Can't possibly be anything else between the two of us she thinks.

Zanda leads me from the restaurant scene. We enter fields. Walk through high grass that wets us up to the waist. All the night through, (nights can last for three billion years here).

Concerning American history and Harper's Ferry, I realise that John Brown was right. Shouldn't coins bear his effigy rather than Abraham Lincoln's? Many things are boiling. Africa and the Middle East. Who has sown these meadows? Who will reap them? Will there be a broader application of territorial reclamation inspired by the truely clever Abandoned Arab lands Appropriation Law? Certainly, being that refugees hardly ever return. You don't think that this has anything to do with American history?

Knowing the time it takes for seeds to germinate, the sunlight and water they need. What whiff they give when freshly cut, the sound of the scythe blade against the whetstone. How what grows down by the river is much heavier. Where it is that serpents lay in wait, where wasps make their paper nests.

Evil pilot lights glimmer.

Briefly, we live in the ruins of a slavers house, though no mansion. The structure has collapsed leaving tent-like areas where remaining walls hold what's left of roofing material at accomodating angles. Sleep within these recesses. There are traces of pale blue paint on the worn wood. Just off to the side, where vines and brush have grown over mango, cacao and coffee plantation, there's the sculpture of a Madonna. Erosion has taken away the land at her feet leaving the virgin at the edge of a steep cliff. Nightly, offerings are brought to her and candles are burned for her; by whom, we'll never know. No one has ever seen the night visitor and this place is greatly feared. Occasionally, spirits are seen rapidly displacing themselves in the airs. An intense, flitting red light, about the size of a firefly. These soukounians only appear to children and sometimes they even speak with small charming voices, inviting them to come along for a fantastic trip from which there may be no return.

Direct descendants of the former slaves live all about. As to who they are, there is no doubt. They know exactly which ancestor slept with what master family member and who now carries within themselves the blood of that union. No need to shout. Whites have been absorbed. Would not this be a form of victory, an internal one. (If you're uneasy about this, ruby-throated humming birds will come in close enough to fan your sweating face with their invisible wing beat). We drink great quantities of rhum and contemplate the stars, but also the dark areas where there are none. New patterns appear every night and this has nothing to do with passing cloud formation. During the day, immense white ships cruise offshore with their loads of moderately wealthy tourists. They always keep at a safe distance. It is said that Americans especially fear the unpredictable reactions of French West Indian Blacks, "prompt to riot" they claim. More probably afraid of being absorbed in turn.

Just beyond this valley, which is already jungle, lives the "dog-man". Used to liberally lapidate all curs that passed his way. Now he's one too. Dispenser of vital knowledge, it's best you see him quickly even if it means flying in the eagle's talons to meet him. He has more political experience than all Western Chiefs of State put together; can tell you exactly why shouldn't have been assassinated Raed Karmi and Sheikh salah Shehada.

Imagine it blue, my erection and believe firmly that if I were to wear bermuda shorts, it would pass down along my leg to drag in the street gathering gravel. Convince yourself that I seek accomodating vulva. (This is spoken as an apparent encouragement to the ever patient off-stage woman).

Having run out of wood, termites have become lithophagic.

Near a hill named Monster Heart. Night person. Tongue. Fingers. Isolated Earth clan. I'll warn you. Emotional ties must be limited to tiny speck of land, intimate family (exclude even first cousins), and a very circumspect temporal zone covering not more than two or three generations at the most, either way, (both future and past). Call me Heart Stays if you so wish. Realize that if I give other names, this is no rogues gallery. Help me hunt the seven-eyed panther. Only by night. It's white with blue spots. Has brilliant yellow eyes with small flames around the edges.

I assure you that it's possible. The French government won't even notice. The country's too busy with naval manoeuvres off the coasts. No one's paying any attention to what's going on inland. They've just put to sea a fabulous new fleet with massive baroque figureheads on the prows and beautiful gilden sculptures around the missile ramps. Louis the twenty-fourth!

It'll be a sacred death. The air is full of immature spiders taking to the wind.

Paws

—The door was open, says Twelve.

I know it not to be.

—Can we talk? I'm living in your neighborhood now, just a temporary sort of place. I would like for you to write me up a character reference stressing my qualities, the uniqueness of my work, the vibrant color fields and audio-sculptural concept. Mention my British-Jamaican metissage too. This room here is really perfect for me, he says, glancing around the living room. —I could live here if you'd let me. I wouldn't get in your way ...Ever.

I'm thinking about paw prints.

—It's not possible right now. You know, my African family is arriving tomorrow. They'll be sleeping here in this room, all six of them. Why not seven? After all, you're welcome to stay here with them if you want.

—No. I work nights now, editing a film that I just recuperated; the one that I did in the Tcheky Ak 47 factory some years back. The photo lab in Prague had kept it since I hadn't the money to pay for developing the negatives. So I'm doing that now, all night long in front of these little screens, reviewing, splicing and throwing away. Whenever I stand up it makes me vomit. (Is brilliant; will reinvent cinema).

—Tell me, where is the footprint expert?

Fresh cement has been poured into the deep pawprints turning them darker than the sidewalk surface.

—This would tend to prove that emerging is episodical unless we are dealing with stragglers. As for the cement filling, that's purely political. If you see any more of these traces, alert me before someone effaces.

Together we depart, the pawprints, black stars beneath the street light.

—I'll accompany you to your metro line.

—Number nine.

—You've seen this before?

—Twelve tells me you have long absences but this is incredible! You actually don't know? It's true that they all want to forget it now as if it never happened. Wiping out the paw marks with cement is ample proof of that.

He sweats profusely, the curve between his nose and the upper lip, the deep furrows of the forehead retain sweat. Shivering beneath a worn gray gabardine and a filthy turtleneck sweater of the same color. His skinny white ankles plunge into shapeless cracked leather shoes that have been repaired with ducting tape; probably wears no pants nor even underwear beneath the coat.

The train windows are so covered with diamond-cut tags and other graffitti that they appear frosted. Only steel frames for seats. It's not the Nine line at all but a double decker suburb shuttle dangerously leaning from a snapped suspension system.

The listing train rumbles over a high viaduct from which crumbles stone and masonry with each passing convoy. Gruff Paws mumbles. His real name isn't at all Jerome. It's Oloman Klanic. Beneath, a string of little islands are aglow on the Marne river. This one is called the Ile aux Loups; big fires burning under marsh trees and entire tribes spilling from old mansions with punched open walls, tents spreading down to the river banks. They run over carpets of willow leaves.

There, barges lie low on the water.

—"Tarantula," "Nightmare," "Brown Dwarf" and "Black Hole." It is he who tells me the names; —I walk my rhinoceros along the river. It charges the barges.

—Tell me more about the pawprints.

—I don't know where you possibly could have been in order to have missed what happened. Unless you were recumbant, in a coma or something of the sort.

—Very ill.

His fingers, brown from tobacco, run spidery through synthetic implant hair.

—Pendolino; Italian technology traded with France after Euromerge. This train leans into curves, the suspension system permitting it to crouch with counter leverage to attain frightening speed.

Two screaming youths dash across the central alley and plunge into the night through a breach in the wagon wall, splashing tiny white circles in the filthy river far below.

Professor Gruff Paws tells me that he lives in a geodesic structure made of organic matter only.

—Those boys who just jumped off, their faces pressed down in Marne sediment...

—Will make striking fossils to be discovered several million years from now. Anthropologists will conjecture: a feeding accident, mired while gorging on algae. They will take measurements of the massive body structure. Present records will of course have totally vanished by then. They may hold these specimens to be examples of early craniates.

The green fumes from the mixture of leaves he smokes, slips back over left ear and whips out into the night through the hole the boys had taken. The aroma of kinik-kinik and smoldering sweet grass that once grew on northern plains. Flat cedar leaves mixed with tobacco.

Elderly and very young with no in between, fill the wagon. Suddenly an old woman draws a spearhead from a Tati bag and pushes the tip against the jugular vein of a teenage boy busy talking with friends. It is an ugly weapon with backwards turned spiral barbs all along the head. The kind of tip used by Aka pygmies when they slip beneath the belly of an elephant to thrust a lance overhead, burying the tip deep in the gut where it twists and cuts.

She wants everything they have. The beautiful silk T-shirts with fly-through imagery of Godzilla's open maw, the crocodile skin running shoes, the sleep-man compact dream player they were sharing. It is a perilous situation, she hardly having the strength to push the lance tip into the neck flesh, her hand so shaky that she cuts a zig zag line into the boy's skin. Blood pearls.

It is then I first notice an old man leaking poison from all pores. Spits flame, burning the overhead plastic paneling. They are together. He's so white that the veins appear green beneath his skin.

I have seen before this mixed couple as they are called. Their lack of vigor is more than compensated by the sum of danger that they bear between the two of them. Her skin is the color of a chestnut husk, smooth and brilliant with a deep red hue beneath the brown. Striking contrast with the white of her hair.

—When?
—Irrefutable invalidation of the zoo hypothesis.

—Earth's spin had slowed, then come to a halt, proof that a large invisible mass had approached and now remained stationary somewhere very near. Scientists were able to pinpoint the exact position, oceans having heaved up and staying so at an angle perpendicular to the sun. Even the Earth's crust rose as if yearning for mating.

But there was nothing, absolutely nothing there at his point in space that had been designated by astrophysicians as being the precise place where a mass three times that of the moon was supposed to have been lurking.

Then, just as gently as it had approached, it slowly withdrew or rather the pull which it had exerted upon Earth, abated, laying land and water to rest. The moon, which had also come to a halt, now resumed its cycles revolving as before, effortlessly, around the planet which bore no trace of the unexplained visit other than deep footprints that had appeared, pushing down crisply through rock and cement. In several places paths had been formed. Tracks joined indicating migration or some sort of pilgrimage. Physical obstacles, whether natural or man made, had been traversed through and through. These cutouts where light and air freely passed, had different shapes that were all classified as being zooanthropomorphic in that they reunited both human and animal form to varying degree.

—Converging on what?
—Further study has proven that they were, in fact, emerging and fanning out.

—In other words they had been here all of the time?
—Evidently long dormant. While the dark matter was in the offing, they arose, travelling at speeds calculable but stunning to attain various points from which they vanished.

—They!
—Formidable effort was invested into trying to discover what it was that had been keeping us company for so long while we, oblivious, had insatiably waged war and hardly accomplished anything else.

Mainly mesurements. Something of very dense, having either an extremely high body temperature permitting it to cut through stone or an exoskeleton hard enough to traverse any obstacle lying in its path.

—Any other traces? Witnesses?

—No molten material, no pyroclastic evidence, and certainly no witnesses even though several of the foot print trails cut through highly populated urban zones. Even the exact time of passage remains a mystery. In one case, the form had cut straight through the walls and vaults of a federal reserve bank without setting off alarms or even leaving a trace on video records.

—Striding over a carpet of bullion and freshly minted currency, leaving the treasure totally undisturbed. Definitely inhuman!

—Years of research only deepen the mystery which becomes utter with passing time. A sense of vacuity sets in. We had thought to be alone, at least here on Earth; all the while we were not. Now we are, irremediably so. Mankind altogether is remorseful. Pessimists evoke the possibility that we had been unwitting hosts to a parasite which had sucked away our spirituality before, gorged with it, departing. This theory naturally correlated with abruptly diminishing global faith.

—Or simply a cycle of nature, albeit one on a vaster scale than those which we know; like the cicada lying dormant beneath the earth for seventeen years before emerging to fly off. Perhaps, here too, there will be a point of return.

He's finished talking to me?

I'm thinking of my girl. She leaves her toys on my desk; a small vulture who stoops to peck at plastic carrion, a Roswell that glows in the dark, a polar bear that's too fat and stiff to do anything but stand straight up and the spine and rib-cage from an anatomy kit. On the floor lie little planes and a helicopter, grounded among wrinkled papers. They can growl and flash when batteries are provided.

His home is a dome; slender willow wands covered with transparent tarp. Not far downriver is berthed the "Nightmare."

—My real name is Jerome, he says, his finger pointing to the void in Bootes where, inexplicably, the sky is empty for as far as any instrument can see. —Here be dragons. This'll be our motto, inscribed over the coat of arms for the ship which lies right there.

—The Nightmare? What premice is this?

—We'll rechristen her! Carve the most beautiful cats-head, paint the hull red, she'll have black sails. Look at her line, no barge is she, rather a Class-J of today!

No sooner do I think schooner, than Oloman's voice crackles, broken tuner.

—She'll be a late bloomer, we'll find a harpooner!

—A whaler?

—We shan't spear things dear, only those that bring fear.

—A crusade?

—Of sorts. But we'll avoid major ports. Track down the Zanoobia eternally sailing with her chemical cargo, board mobile prisons, steer clear of Key Largo, brave the Cuban embargo, behave like the crew of the Argo. With no skeletons shall we duel, ours'll be a struggle much more cruel, over the seas of suffering, hope will be our fuel. Load her carefully, that she be neither too tender nor too stiff.

—What'll be the golden fleece, beyond oceans of fire and fury? Cold 'n peace.

—Idealists' dream realists' theme.

—Lure gone in a blur.

—No sailors are we.

—No worthy ship's she.

—There lies our worry, fortunately we're in no hurry, the hold's crawling with furry, pink-tailed things that scurry.

—Why apply nautical terms to an inert thing whose timbers are full of worms, wallowing wreck unfit for tinder? No water will run down those limbers. Has she legs, drawn in beneath her hull, feet or even wings, fit tight out of sight, ready to deploy? Annoy me no more with this moldering decoy, coming from her main-topgallant you'll never here "Ahoy." No Harmattan will ever fill her sails with hot dry desert breath. She's foul with barnacles and grass, all soft within. Touchwood. Lest some combustion, unknown fuel, be stowed 'neath decks, never will she advance. But then, what formidable force would it require to get her higher than this swampy dock?

—Look not so far ahead. Acquire something to turn back the clock. Fit her with paws. We'll not head for fiddler's green. Have us a fête champêtre. Feed on fever root.

An impressive rogue asteroid is passing overhead, seems motionless as the moon, abrupt angles give this one a man-made appearence.

—Consider monumental tasks, like none ever undertaken by man before, ones that would require the coordinated effort of all humanity.

Bore a hole straight down into the earth, traverse the core and continue on out through the other side. Many things would change, there would be a more direct route to the other side of the world, gravity would certainly be affected, climate too.

—Could be the death of us all. Sucked through and spit out. Butterflies riding winds of fire.

—Religious books are full of such things.

A very long period now beginning, when all that I have just described suddenly turns brittle, bakes. Curiously, the change happens overnight. An intense heat, evaporation of water, the river is dry by morning. Many children have died, some elderly have become young. I too, died sometime between midnight and four. By seven I'm eleven. We raise sheep and goats in the city. Camels of the shaggy Mongolian variety are used to carry merchandise. There are broad expanses of desert in the heart of the city. I usually arise around three to wander alone over sand and stone. Tents made of animal skins, usually giraffe, have been set up. They are so numerous that I sometimes have difficulty finding my way if the night sky is covered. Polaris Umi is no longer the northern star. The Earth's axis now passes through the center of a straight long star chain in western Camelopardalis.

At midday it is not uncommon that the entire city will shift, the population taking down their tents and setting them up elsewhere. Perpetual urban nomadism. These are a restless people. They have the memory of wanderers, yet they are confined to a certain perimeter, however vast it may be.

It is a time of no friendship. By day, I lead a blind man. We're tethered together by a stick which isn't nearly long enough. He smells of dried sweat gone sour, accumulated over the years. I'm his guide in a land where I myself am a stranger. We two, work the streets for small change. Coins that have no weight, stamped with impala head. Money that has been devaluated over and again.

Ablook is the stinky blind one's name. With the stick, he pushes me in the direction of noise or smell which attract him. The sound of a crowd, the odor of cooking, especially well spiced dishes, the whiff of money he says.

He has things living in his ears, parasites of a special kind. Small organisms that create an itching sensation and then proceed to gratify the host by scratching but never enough to irritate the skin. And this is well, for he has no hands, only paws that are unsuitable for scratching the inner ear. Sometimes they shift, he tells me, but usually they are very still, listening for him. When he falls asleep, just before he begins snoring, which is a tremendous noise, I can hear them. The faintest squeels, the sound of gnats brushing up against whiskers. They play an important role, interpret and translate. Warning of danger is another of their vital services. I suspect that they go as far as interfering with his thinking and maybe even do they give orders that pass for suggestions.

When the snoring begins, they no longer hear and I can untie the bonds that join us by my end of the short stick. It is then that I slip from the tent, emerge into the night wearing a coat that I dug up out of the desert sands, a simple tailored black winter coat with a knitted collar, Dolce& Gabbana written on the inside. I wander until four at which time I join a Coranic school where I practice writing using a stiff twig that I dip into cinder mixed with a little water. A smooth small board serves as support for the texts. Then we pray together, the other children and I, the ones of us who have managed to escape, and the other ones who are lucky enough to have family. Our imam is a young woman. No veil covers her face. Her name is Aïsha and she wears the sacred hand of Fatima around her neck. She tells us that we must go to Paris, a most splendid city where there are hundreds of magnificent mosques with fine high minarets, where the air resounds with prayer sung at all hours of the day. Sometimes the crescent moon is in the sky just above her when she leads us in song. She has the most beautiful voice that needs no instruments to accompany it.

Ablook is angry with the things in his ears. They gave him no warning of my departure.

Intrude with me into this world beyond life. It can be a mere parenthesis, you can qualify your visit as being a dream, for me it is endless and has no beginning. How I wish to expire in a definitive manner, obtain eternal rest, become nothing, disappear forever!

Cruelty has proven to be of great help, a natural defensive system, like hindgut enzymes permitting the digestion of potentially harmful foreign antigens, particularly helpful early in life when one is unaware of what's really out there; later too, compensating for diminishing defensive awareness and enroaching sentimentality. Key to survival whether that of a nation or of an individual.

—Israel has become a super-state, K2 will have told me in a conversation that I shall have had with her when emerging from a finish situation in Mufta Missouri, somehow slipping back here. It will go something like this: —It's the most powerful nation in the world, covering a geographical expanse that stretches from former Lybia to Russia and encompasses large parts of what used to be India as well. Technique of pin-point targetting popular Tanzim leaders, with no concern for civilian population, led to a full-blown techno-revolution that permitted the fulfilment of Eretz dream and much further development.

—And the Arabs in all of this?

—No, Arabs have not been wiped from the face of the Earth. The "Arab Question" simply hasn't been dealt with yet.

—Fully realise that this information confutes the notion generally exposed throughout the *Book of Fever* whereby Islam would have conquered the world; didn't I just affirm that Paris is home to countless mosques?

—You'll just have to deal with this dilemma on an individual basis. Decide for yourself which version you prefer. No in betweens! No international mediators, no pacifists will ever have been permitted to weigh on this intra-Semitic conflict. Nevertheless, you must take into consideration the fact that fashion restaurants in Tel Aviv now serve up estouffade, quenelle and rémoulade of Philistine, (which is no longer the pejorative term it had for so long been, but now simply connotes a person of Palestinian origin as it once did and always should have) proving that Palestine has indeed been totally cannibalized. True, a few Berbers will have been spared, mainly to tend sheep or perform domestic chores, but they'll hardly be more than gnawed bones afoot, sometimes summoned to provide music for a wedding. The exotic touch, what!

—This is an obsolete worse-case scenario isn't it, peace having been found, quarrels having been settled and new national boundaries defined for a Palestinian state, (however microscopic it may eventually prove to be)?

—Don't believe that this will have conduced to stability. The rubble of Gaza and Jenine shall prove to be the most fertile top-soil for exponential martyrdom candidature.

—Would it have had to have been this way?

I'm stumbling through the debri of a house fire, charred belongings heaped in the street beneath burned out windows. Childrens toys half devoured by the flames, books, bedding, arm chairs, household appliances, burnt wicker baskets with the remains of dirty laundry, plates with the stains of an unfinished repast, melted candles, intriguing broken statuettes, forgotten love-letters come to light again, singed photos. All is damp from water having been poured over to put out the fire and this is proof enough that I've returned to more temperate zones where water can be found.

Sitting in the pile, I go through the correspondence and images. One by one they reveal that this is tricky terrain where guilt pushes its way, a living thing struggling to remain an ever prevalent theme. Will it be transmitted or will it momentarily dissipate only to settle back down like the fine black ash of this ruined abode waiting to cling to the searching hands of some curious wanderer passing through? Fears, hopes and fantasies, some deep-rooted others acquired along the way. For I have the certitude that these charred ruins are those of the home where my parents waited my return, the ruins of the place where my daughter will have expected me to come visiting or perhaps even the place in between where I myself endlessly shall wait by the window, drawing to the side lace curtains decorated with the patterns of time machines and rockets, expecting every minute that she will come to me. Communication devices and mail of course being things of the past and future. Dilemmas for which there'll be no empathy.

Needing some time for reflection, introspection, I set up a tent in the street. Neighbors in turn draw back their curtains to peek at me. Having professed fidelity beyond reproach, I suddenly become a sexual opportunist (but this scene is situated long before, as with the classical fifth filming situation of a movie which is actually destined to be the first episode, even if created much later); without warning slipping into the garage of a woman warming her car before she goes to work. It's hardly dawn. She's wearing a coat but I get through all of her clothing with surprising ease, finally pulling the panties to the side and taking her up against the garage wall (making oil cans fall), on the vehicle, and finally in it. The windows are fogged, there's sperm everywhere. She's not that pretty, at least fifty-five, false blond with a hard face, never smiles, gasps continuously, grasps my sex with vigor and actually pushes it in as far as she can, passing her hand around behind and ramming me in by the balls as if she had been fantasizing for much too long about just this type of situation. Her clothing is a mess but she's still in dress, needs to wipe down, is wearing silk beneath the coat and skirt, has an animal-like quality which she shared with me, empties the ashtray, smells of beauty salon powders, around the mouth's a smear of dirt.

In the tent again, I eat pig and drink excessive quantities of cheap alcohol. I love no one, not even myself, and no one loves me.

The charred contents of the burned out home gradually disappear. Scavengers take some items, most disintegrate beneath heavy rains and float away. And this is well for I seek no means of exculpation and there is no philosophical elegance to be drawn from what belongs to the underlying themes of the *Book of Fever*. Though morally complex it will remain an inconclusive story based on subjects to be avoided in our conversation.

No epiphanies are to be found here. My fingernails are black and broken, I defecate in the middle of the street, swearing loudly as I relieve myself. I become the subject of conversation to the inhabitants of this neighborhood. They give me the epithet of "John-without-pants." Though they hardly have the means to epistolize, there being no postal service, trained pigeons bearing cryptic messages frequently emerge from the buildings, proving that they are sending news to others about my unwanted presence.

Winter sets in hard. I burn tyres to warm myself, chant loudly in broken but full voice, songs that underequiped revolutionaries sang when striding into heavy fire, hymns sung by the factory worker and peasant in field, all unpleasant to those dining on hot pheasant behind closed shutter. Seeing me barefoot, some of them offer me worn shoes. Naturally, I refuse. Don't utter words of sympathy. Bring me butter. Content living in the gutter? Needn't any empathy.

Would you be one to explore my heart? It is darker than the thick smoke that rises from the burning rubber. No penetrating intelligence. No psyche. Somewhere within what appears to be glummer than anything you've yet considered, there could be more than a shimmer, the palest glimmer to which all of this blackness would be protective swaddling.

I'm not fascinated by utopian societies, nor powerful overbearing nations. My interest goes towards those that challenge them, sometimes succeeding in bringing them down. Would not this be like virus bringing about the evolution of the host, being the real progress factor.

Roast these seeds, only these and no other ones. If you haven't any charcoal, place them on the center plate of a gas burner or even in the palm of your hand until the flame burns through to the bone. But be careful that the seeds don't burn! Then grind them down using the stone you brought back from Cameroon... to powder, with which you'll mix more common onions and garlic along with deep forest herbs. Place your fish, the long-whiskered one that you caught by hand, in the boiling oil. Let it fry till the skin is crusty; add the prepared sauce and let simmer. Eat this way often and you'll be much slimmer.

A woman enters the tent. She's slender, her proportions are unusual, surprisingly short legs and long slender arms, well formed breasts. Her mouth is very low on the face, the face being smooth and sweeping up from finely cut nostrils just above the lip, hardly any cheek bone, with eyes set very high and no forehead. Nothing of specifically human. Something of very distant about her and a frightening perfection coming to light with each passing minute. What first appear to be major anomalies prove to be striking improvements. She's from the remote future and it's most uncertain whether she has evolved from mankind. Certain things would tend to prove the contrary.

This then would be validation of the reservoir theory whereby all life forms present on the Earth are potential candidates for the development of diverse civilisations, not only technological ones but other forms even more highly evolved. Would include arthropods, insects and virus. She has with her, a spider of unusual size, one that's capable of waiting by flaming torches. You would think it to be in ambush of some favorite insect prey, the way it will lay with its only seven legs on display, spread out in a mineral pattern way, after having been bundled up all day. Many a moth it lets pass before seizing a fluttering furry bat with sudden flurry. The victim is taken off in no hurry. This spider is no predator. It's a philosopher with eight eyes that doesn't surmise, but rather calculates with little surprise, the time left before you may become its prize. Life's rear guard, a B-team in wait.

She's simply performing some sort of field work, observing my reactions to certain stress situations, sketching and measuring my body parts. My general comportment seems to fascinate her. Like an anthropologist having run across a living Taung child specimen.

Being in her company procures an intense sensation of joy that seems to radiate from deep within the brain, centered in the medullar area or the temporal lobe; zones that control heartbeat, breathing, ejaculation. A feeling that it is hard to do without with once you've experienced it. Accompanied by interrupted flashes of knowing everything, thinking to understand the entire universe, seeing all that has ever transpired, and all that is to come, anywhere; momentarily realizing that certain things will never exist and that you and I are certainly part of these none existant things, that our actions and the reality that we have always thought to interpret as such, are not a part of what is vital. Destruction is the dominating force of the universe and only through war are we even remotely connected to what lies beyond our scope. In decadance we can become palatable to civilisations that inhabit these remote zones, like certain eurasian fruits which only become edible when rotting.

But then this universal knowledge becomes more vague with each attempt to recall, as if the effort of memory were responsable for its dissipation, and finally there is nothing left, and I ask you then, is this not more painful than if I had remained ignorant? Had never glimpsed eternity?

A medieval man huddled by the fire at night, unaware of what might be afoot just beyond the waxed paper covering the small windows of his low-ceilinged stone hovel, while anything abroad could measure, witness movement within; if only shadows passing infront of the illuminated paper panes. Conjecturing: all that is out is necessarily evil and therefore unwilling to press further inquiry.

I swear, knowing that I once knew, is crueler misfortune than never having known anything at all.

Being thrown down into this beggar's skin, rip it off, offer it, these carnal sensations, even the medullary ones just evoked, will beckon you to remain within this garment of flesh.

There will come a day when you will attack your own reflection. And there will be no deception when death disproves all religions bringing utter nothingness to what you once were. With no ear you will not hear when I announce the coming of your worst fear my dear. Now that we're so near, drink this beer, steer away from fish weir. Sear all skin which appears clear.

She decapitates me. Washes my head in a laundromat. I nearly drown.

Fell this last tree, remove pith with handmade adz. Don't neglect decoration, sculpt head on the prow, incise patterns on gunwhales. Fashion paddles from sassafrass wood, embark in the dugout, run upriver along the bank where the current isn't too swift then go out and head downriver crossing ever diagonally, permitting to pass dreaded rapids, slip down along the opposite bank, build fires on the bow, hide behind shield of wapiti skin, lance blinded ducks that drift your way with pronged spear, eat well, there'll be no rest. Ahead, waits a horde aboard forty long ships anchored in midstream. Many small islands dot the river at its largest point, chose one for the night. With perfumed oil annoint her body. Smoke tomba-laced joints? Not that easy. Invasive surgery required to introduce this drug; place it directly on the brain. Trepanation is recommended.

But first: go down to the river and draw water. Carry it on your head in three successively smaller tin basins stacked up atop of each other; walk nimbly on fiery path, balancing load with smooth neck action. Careful for sloshing momentum of water that can develop if you stride awkwardly. Go back after fire wood which you'll pile high on the head again and balance in much the same manner as the water. No worry for counteraction, there's no sloshing here. Now take your wash down to the river, strip down and enter the water, where you can soap yourself down as you do the wash. Go gathering tubers, fruits and leaves which you can use for cooking. These are to be found deeper and deeper in surrounding jungle, the neighboring underwood having long ago been stripped clean of anything that's edible. Take off hunting during the night, track with your own sense of smell and acute hearing. The dogs are just for the company. They're mute anyway. Don't forget to pack extra darts for the little crossbow and mend your nets before nightfall. Struggling game can find tears in the mesh and escape by enlarging the holes.

We raise chickens, no ordinary hens, but pygmy fowel.

She no longer takes notes, registers with her heart, ever attentive, piercing gaze, sometimes I feel uneasy. It is impossible to write her name, not in any known written language do there exist the letters necessary to convey, even with rough phonetic approximation, the sounds that she goes by; and this is the name I will so desperately seek to remember in *Algeria Electric*. I think that it has never been pronounced, somehow my mind is impregnated with this sensation that I know to be her name, and I, in turn, have never uttered the word which could vaguely correspond to what I'll call Fire Music.

There's as much difference between us as there is between a chimpanzee and a human, I being the primate. Sometimes I feel as if she were an anthropologist who would have become overly intimate with her laboratory animal, only I'm not at all a monkey nor is she a scientist. The evolutionary gap separating us is however, just that important, if not greater.

Enroach upon the jungle. Poach. Nevertheless, this is a very sophisticated city. Odors are important. We have developed complex olfactory communication. I've taken to carefully smelling people that pass.

I can tell you just which galaxies are going to interact and how they will react, which ones will just brush by one another, shear off at the last moment, or collide. Many will actually mate and give birth to younger galaxies that will in turn, spin off with their own rotational motion and depart from the parental galaxies contrarily to all laws of astrophysics.

How is she dressed?

She wears no cloths. Her skin looks like shiny blue plastic and it has the smoothness of wind worn objects or those abraded by the incessant action of the sea. Make for her a peignoir from cheetah fur.

I ask her to eat the strongest dishes, the spiciest meats, the most fermented cheeses, to drink the darkest wines and the very most violent alcohols. I impregnate myself with her odors, rubbing myself over her body.

On the wall of our small low-rent flat, there hangs an old group photo of workers proudly posing. Cherbourg Arsenal, 2009. Putting together a nuclear submarine.

Are we ostracized by the inhabitants of the city?

I leaf through a beautifully illustrated scientific book, like the ones on birds, or flowers that you may have been familiar with. This one draws parallels between the topographies of alien worlds and the beings which inhabit them. Razor thin creatures who live on edge, ones with pointed heads, frequenters of peaks. You see camouflage is widespread. But these gaudy ones? Ever see a red chameleon? These ones clearly have no reason to hide. Might they be dangerous? Like certain poisonous insects or frogs that advertise their toxicity by wearing bright colors?

Don't forget that the citizens of this section of the urban concentration are largely of French descent and as with most Frenchmen, they are blasé, oblivious to all but themselves, proud of their history to the highest degree and unimpressed with anything of new that might come their way. Though they can be racist, they have had their hour of glory with colonies spread round the planet and they've always been fairly open to foreigners, even if they've done their share of ethnical cleansing. Seasoned manipulators, they have a certain type of political maturity, contestation is a tradition. Long ago they learned to question authority on all levels rather than blindly following dictates.

I have important piles, obliged to pull down my pants, insert thumb and index, push the mass back up the ass.

This isn't to say that they don't stare at us when we pass, make unobliging remarks behind our backs or even speaking of the waste of a man like myself frequenting an inferior being, hardly an ape, though a blue-skinned one. Highly unbalanced conubiality, they say. But they are too taken with the celebration of political manipulation, thinking still to impose their vision of whom Western Sahara should be alotted to, obviously favoring the Maroccan solution, the French having always been fond of monarchies, secretly regretting their own which they had, nevertheless, so magnificently overthrown. Is this not the apogy of smugness, passing for the champions of human rights while plotting to snuff inter-racial mélange.

Strangely my throat is extremely sore. I feel weak, yet I'm sure it's time to prepare for a war.

But it's a civilization that's on the brink of dispersal. Factions are already preparing the Third Revolution, the deeper one that will overthrow those who have pauperized such vast sections of society after having tantalized them with dreams so well commercialized. They've followed the river into the city, sleep beneath bridges. Live in great filthy camps. No-man's-land where alley cats have become as big as tigers, stray ducks, sparrows and pigeons, mixed with weeds from vacant lots provide daily fare. When they finally launch their offensive, there's no one they'll spare. Time for collective suicide.

Shell immature cockroaches and eat like shrimp. This is most difficult when your limbs terminate with paws, clumsy for decorticating shellfish, stitching a sweater or playing a musical instrument. Practical only for running on all fours, burrowing and begging for food from a standing position with the forepaws gently pawing the mistress's immense towering body, you plunged into delicious drunkeness by her body odors which you so love, come to like the puppy dog that you could be, judging by your paws, sense of smell, cunning for ingratiating yourself when seeking favors. She's my fewterer. Duck the fyreflaught.

We'll invert what's expected. Disguise ourselves as aliens to invade other worlds. Learn their customs to perfection. Just as one of them would be obliged to adopt our own if "*it*" were to properly infiltrate our world: knowing how to eat cheese; the mildest one first, followed by a medium strong cheese and finishing with the strongest. Going form rather bland fresh goat to a mild but fruity comté (*comme avant la Guerre*), before tasting a thoroughly mature camembert or munster. In France of course, not in Asia. Japanese consider it to be rotten milk! How to light your cigar, what wines to choose. The difference between an ordinary paté and foie gras.

Grow a thistly long thin beard that springs from a single big mole on the chin. Speak Chinese. Have extremely long finger nails. Fish with a cormorant. Go deep into jungles to build space industry cities for launching new rockets carrying super-sophisticated satellites. Once again, subdue natives. But this time, pacify them with television entertainment. Keep them happy with lots of over-refined foods and zesty chemical beverages. Organize absurd ceremonies, exchange gifts of model rockets, good-luck Japanese lanterns. Give interminable speaches.

When in other worlds, stay in a night club, beware of unusual comportment. Someone partying at your table who might put out what seems to be a cigarette in your ashtray. Don't hesitate, draw your knife and stab them. Let yourself go. Hold three Saudian princes at gun point (you've already killed their body guard for flirting in a vulgar manner with your wife); take all they've got on them. Chances are, it's more than you'd earn in a life time of ship-breaking or selling rat poison. Break their arms. This is a very peaceful place. You must control yourself to properly blend in. Have no regret, if you hadn't acted in this manner, they would have forced you to dance and perform other humiliating acts; could even have brought your towers down.

Savor the smell of third class travel. Dust, old plastic, cigarette butts. The air is very dry. Your nose stings, often bleeds. Don't hurry. A storm will come bringing mood change. Gloom, but humidity too. Along the way, sex has taken unexpected turn. Women tackle men in the streets, masturbate them, make frothy milkshakes which they sip before injecting into the vagina, the strongest sperm vying for the single egg. Men are fearful.

As usual, returning's a bit rough. A little before dawn, install yourself in small bistro near Place de Stalingrad in the still squalid nineteenth arrondissement of Paris. You'll recognize the strange mosaic in the w.c., the techno music (there's some Rai too), the dirty white poodle that belongs to the owner who's a retired prostitute. The bar's called "le Petit Valentin." The poodle's a bitch wearing a black plastic culotte because she's in heat. The street's carpeted with empty syringes and used rubbers. Slippery going.

Realize that you've arrived just in time to participate in the annual Easter egg hunt, the grandiose one in the Buttes Chaumont park. And even if Oloman's not here to welcome you back you're in luck.

But first, quickly readapt to local customs. Handle handguns, even small derringers will do, with the greatest of ease. Think of firearms being very ordinary and employ them accordingly. Like reading the morning paper, chewing gum or drinking coffee. Killing too. Very simple act. Shoot the dog, his mistress, empty the cash register, go behind the counter and help yourself to more coffee. Shoot anyone who might come in at this point. Make sure plenty of ammunition in pockets. Don't let the old cough drops, lint or small sea shells that might still be in there, get in the way or mix with the bullets. This could prove fatal. Check that Zanda's got adequate firepower too. Practice shooting at each other if no one comes in. Most of all, don't ever forget, this is America spreading it's culture. Of course, there's that old European flavor to it.

—Why'd you kill the alewife?

The sky is simply glorious. The trace of superluminal traffic has left a tic-tac-toe pattern that reaches deep. Emerald with opaline trails.

Hear the horn? Time to go to the gates.

Knife vendor selling bloody blades screams —Cut your throats, kill each other! But don't rob me, I'm a robber myself.

Don't think there are no rules. Solid gold eggs, each weighing fifteen pounds, have been hidden in the Park. Now, if you remember the lay-out of the Buttes Chaumont, you'll understand that anything's possible: hiding eggs in the little pagoda crowning an artificial pinnacle, beneath the suspended bridge, on the lake bottom, behind cascades, or why not in the bushes? The hunt is open to all who can pay the one thousand dollar entrance fee or equivalent value. Weapons are permitted. It goes without saying that on the eave of the hunt, organizers have already introduced many guilded lead replicas, taking home the originals. Counterfeit maps are for sale. Around the entrance are the traces of a stampede where a crowd wielding ghurka knives, baseball bats fit with long ten inch carpentar's nails, and metal detectors of home fabrication had pushed there way in. It's clear, there's been much pre-dawn killing. The gates having given away before sunrise, the sounding of the horn was purely symbolic.

We go in. The hunt is almost over. Some valid maps had led the fortunate possessors to real eggs, while others still sweep vacant sectors with obsolete mine detectors, totally inappropriate. A burly man with an elaborate world map tatooed on his back holds aloft a lead egg. Spindly lithe youth jumps astradle and sticks long thin blade in China. False egg dumps into pond, women and men fight with oversized carp for the pseudo-prize. Lots of pink foam. The fish get there food any way. There's some mortar fire. Grenades go off here and there. Clever couple, archbishop and altarboy, with sled head for opposite gate, smoothly sliding over the dead. Nobody'll harm this pair, the prelate has survived two revolutions, countless executions. Descendant of both blue blood and white nobiltiy, he's respected in a nostalgic sort of way by the French crowd.

—We'll have a big cage full of mangabeys. Cathedrals will be off limits to tourists. There will be a proper dress code, women will have to cover their heads, men will wear suits and ties. I tell Zanda as we follow the two through the blood and smoke.

—Respect my allergies! Space parrot proved impossible companion. Digging into the walls with his strong beak to find electrical wiring which he ripped out, provoking flash fires. Monkeys at home can be even trickier.

The crowd cheers the clergyman.

—Ecclesiastic troll! scream I, —You, I'll never extoll!

Immediately, he jerks glove from ordaned hand and throws it at my feet in the purest tradition of chivalresque encounter. Instead of picking it up, I drop my pants, remove my filthy underwear, fling them in his face. The crowd jeers me.

— Such a tiny shrivelled prick! laughs someone.

—For you, it would become a big stiff one? ask I.

The grievance-bearing holy one, naturally prefers fleuret. Having no experience in this aristocratic passtime, I very acrobatically vault behind, shove grenade in his surprised open mouth.

Poof! No dud, extremely dense cranial matter stiffles sound. (This musn't pass for heroism nor even an action scene wherein I would be playing a positive role. This ecclesiastic fellow was a push-over. In the vilest manner, I took advantage of the situation).

The sled is ours. The crowd goes for the share of eggs we leave. The altar boy finds a new companion.

I'm still half naked and this is just as well.

Have we had our revenge?

Algeria Electric

"No dogs allowed." I push the door and go in. Listening to Jimmy Oudid. Me wearing T-shirt with the Algerian flag printed on it.

The sushi bar. A Japanese man all in white, only the very finest materials for his jacket, shirt, pants and shoes. He's wearing a fortune in designer's clothes. Gold bracelets, three watches and several heavy rings about his wrists and on his fingers. Sitting at the counter reading the *Azai chin boum*, he snorts occasionally, very discretely. Stock market satisfaction.

He sits directly in front of the refrigerated display window from which a long glass tube throws a dull greenish glow up under his chin and into the eye sockets as if he were swimming over luminous schools of fish in shallow shoals. Here, no slices of raw tuna, salmon or cuttle fish are proposed.

What appears to be a woman's leg, whole from the buttock to the thigh, knee, calf and foot all splendidly formed, lies offered to the diner in the refrigerated case. The toes are delicately curled as if the limb had been severed at the height of extacy. The ruby color of the blood pearling at the upper extremity confirms the quality. Blood remains brilliant only if death occured during orgasm or extreme violence.

The limb is intact, flawless, certainly cleaved from the most perfect body; immaculate as if powdered with kaolin and presented with great refinement.

The Japanese man smokes a cigarette, noisily drawing and expelling the smoke. Slowly he turns the pages of his newspaper. Crinkling noise of the recycled paper.

—Mermaid, he mutters. He looks up at me, the glow in the eye sockets giving way to shadow.—The flipper's clipped to reveal the underlying toes; tastes like dolphin but much more delicate to the palate. Try it!...Hai, he grunts and returns to his financial paper.

My flea phone begins to jump just as the hostess comes to seat me. It's Almaisa calling from Blida in the heart of the Triangle of Death.

—There was an explosion this afternoon, another bomb.

—Are you alright?

—I prefer the bombs to the night raids when they come down out of the forest to butcher women and children with axes and knives.

—How can you live with that?

—It's ok. I suppose that I'm getting used to it. I was reading a book when the bomb went off this afternoon.

—What did you do?

—I stopped reading and just sat still listening, trying to guess where it had gone off. I've gotten pretty good at it; there've been so many bombings these past few months. I can even figure out the direction and the distance from the sound; of course, I have to take into consideration the echoes from the buildings or the wind factor which can be tricky too. This one was in the suburbs I'm sure, no more than a couple of kilometers away: Beni Mered, Ouled Aïssa or Chlef.

—What were you reading?

—Sinbad! What do you expect?

—How is it there now?

—They've got it all wrong!

—I'm sure, but maybe we shouldn't talk about it.

Akihiro Mina background music in the restaurant now. It's a revised version; some of the instrumentals are computerized and a percussion rythm grows from shattering glass, goes crescendo towards total cannibalization of Mina's strange voice.

It comes back wobbly.

—Are you still there?

The line goes out, cut with an overlapping conversation in Arab. A can just make out parts of it, something about a dog. Kelboun.

Atsuro Mori arrives, one of the biggest fortunes in the world. His grandfather was the owner of the Pacific Teal cargo lines, world monopoly on shipping nuclear waste. He had reinvested in the Rokausho Maru atomic waste disposal factories. He sits with the one in white.

The line comes back. I can hear her very clearly now.

—What are you eating?

—Dolphin. But tell me, what has become of the Blida psychiatric hospital?

—It's now called the Frantz Fanon Psychiatric Hospital.

—Are they concentrated on a special field of study? Perhaps in memory of Fanon?

—Yes and no. The speciality is the treatment of survivors of the massacres, mainly children, orphans. It has nothing to do with Fanon.

An entire nation awaiting sacrifice. Isaac beneath Abraham's blade; only these bearded men holding the knives over us are father to none and no god holds back their hand.

I have to go out of the restaurant, there's too much interference with the connection. The waitress sticks her head out to tell me that my order is ready. I waive her off.

What animal could possibly be dense enough to leave deep pawprints in the stone pavement? I follow the tracks for a ways.

Contrarily to the laws of astro physics, three nearby subdwarves go off with a triple dull thud.

It has born down with enormous weight, whatever's responsable for the trail of prints I'm following. Were it quantifiable, the weight of western doctrine, military and commercial conquest applied to the African continent over the centuries would be much heavier. Is it possible to bear down upon entire nations, very young ones, with such force that nothing emerges, no blade of grass, no vine? And if something does sprout, surely the growth will be crooked, hugging the ground and even reentering the soil.

—Keep dying until you finally die.

Wade through rock, stride through tide to reach a place where we can hide. A small cargo anchored in Algiers' bay. Hull no bigger than a felluca, yet we're deep down in. Hollow sounds come up from the bay bottom. The ship's named "Sheba" but she's no African queen. Her hold is empty except for an occasional electric spark that arches through the dark. We put down our carpets on the foredeck, orienting them towards the Mecca, turning them when she swings on her anchor. It is glorious praying here, the city sweeping in a grand white arc round the smooth sheet of sea upon which we float.

We aren't Muslims of a moment, no hasty converts are we. You thought it sufficed to avoid eating pig, drink no wine, say your prayers and respect the ramahdan? The Koran is a pure miracle, but only when read in the Arab language. You say of this sinner who preaches, that the word he teaches, reaches only those who believe in hollow speaches. When you cast stones upon satan, make sure that the Kaba is to your left, and these stones should be small ones, hardly more than pebbles, lest you miss your aim and strike a fellow muslim who by inadvertance could have placed the Kaba to his right and would therefore be dead infront of you. These regrettable accidents do happen, fires sweep through the city of tents, meningitis finds its way into even the purest water bubbling from the spring of Mount Arafat and sometimes we crush one another in a panic prompted by the repression of undue political manifestations. But the illumination that comes from the reunfication of all of these people of different nation, race diversification, together for a moment of sanctification, is a blinding light, perhaps one million times more so than the radiance which swept Saul from his horse on the way to Damascus.

Such events have been overshadowed by man's penchant for pragmatic realism. But in reality are we not already living within the sun's upper atmosphere? Inhabitants of the star who will be drawn in by her, engulfed, elements of a fast dynamo problem which for the moment remains mathematically unsolved. How to mesure the magnetic field decay? Carefully observe the polarity of field lines, learn to discern between that which is like and that which is opposite. We shall reemerge, being drawn into the base of rising plumes guarantees ascension. Convection will go unimpended.

It is a very complex situation. Monks have been slaughtered, journalists and writers, even musicians, many, many women and children, especially babies. It is unsafe for anyone to travel or to sleep. Perhaps at one point true fundamentalists did the killing, but most often it was expatriates, Afghan Algerians, trained in Pakistan by the CIA to fight against the melting Soviet Union in Afghanistan, returned from this conflict it can be assumed that the American government found here the perfect introduction. Destabilize the young revolutionary nation with terrorism, sweep the economic stakes. You thought only talibans had been trained by the CIA?

Put aside provisions for future consumption, a leg hung in a larder, an egg with shell harder, perhaps of stone containing yolk only perceptible in the extreme ultravioilet.

In turn, special forces receiving secret orders from generals, pasted on beards, donned Afghan pants and swept down on isolated villages to roundly slaughter, always careful to spare a witness, while reassuring control posts set up along the roads by men in regular uniforms, were in reality bloody ambushes manned by the real bearded ones, now clean shaven. Seek yee haven?

How to advance in this most perilous zone?

Come evening, it's the stern that swings out, pointing the bow westward. We slip down the anchor chain – it's made of glass – to bathe in the still water. Swifts slice the twilight with their sickle wings, shrill cries becoming fainter as they circus ever higher, finally disappearing amongst the stars. It is said that they never perch nor roost, that they make love in the airs, bear eggs upon their backs and rear the young while flying. When dying they ascend to even greater heights, so that dead, they never return to earth but join the heavens directly.

Other ships lay at anchor. Different angles betray shifting currents. One bellows diesel smoke from winged double stacks. She's charging up her electricity.

In Algiers, the electricity has been cut off. The city is ablaze with torches, the smoke coming off flames that flicker with a rythm as if the entire city were breathing, the heavy breath of agony which precedes healing. The glow hangs low beneath thick smoke that covers the city with clinging mantle leaving the sky above perfectly clear. Stars do not blink. They seem suspended, unwavering attesting to the utter stillness of the night air. Most of them bear Arabic names. The Scorpion hovers, immense above Algiers bay. Acrab, Dschubba, Alnyat, Wei, down to Schaula, the stinger, and, exceptionally, Mars has snuggled in next to Antares. Together they glow red. Just to situate you: overhead, Kifa Borealis is a brilliant emerald in the borealic crown.

Breeze comes from the shore bringing the odors of the city, the smoke, spices and the scent from deeper inland where rocks, sand and dry shrub are cooling.

—Are you afraid? Weary of inhabiting these lands where fallacy and verity so deliciously blend. What is true, what is false?

—I have faith in this land where revolutionary history has defied the law of money in so brilliant a manner.

—But the massacres, fundamentalism, terrorism? How to have faith in a country where women and children have paid such massive tribute? The throat of innocence so often slashed. The earth isn't porous enough to soak up all of the spilled blood. No sponge. Rock.

—See how they have continued, found solutions to the most critical situations, all in dignity. These were trials, of the most evil sort to be sure, brought down upon Algeria by powerful nations jealous of its anti-imperialistic stance. And hadn't she, above all, defended the cause of desert warriors, the very ones who had defied the West.

Hardly a handful they.

We slip in then, I say, not the normal way. Swimming beneath the surface, smoothly with no haste permits to observe the sharks of the bay. Unexpected varieties have congregated here. Have no fear. Squattina skim along the bottom spreading fleshy wings, sand devils too. Angels having no affinity with skates, rays or chimaeras. Tasseled wobbegongs, cat sharks and dwarf dogsharks team just off the beam, There's a school of cigar sharks gorging on green lanternfish come up from fathoms countless. Gogolia. Sicklefin smoothhound, mandarin dogfish and mermaid's purse in the bottom weed. The most luminous of all sharks, Isistiusbrasiliensis, are here too, illuminating the bottom of the bay with the photophores covering their glowing bellies. I stear clear, having hardly yet recovered from a severe case of ciguatera poisoning that I caught while feasting on raw reef shark liver. Yes of course the bull shark, carcharhinus leucas, he who at this time so freely forays deep inland, far up the Amazon, the Zambezi, the Hooghly, the Mississippi or the Atchafalya rivers, regaling himself upon devote Hindous wading in the Ganges, hippos, zebras, children from the Missouri Bootheel or Peruvian Indians.

I've seen him, not so long from now, develop legs that permit terrestrial incursion. It'll be an immediate conversion, not the slow awkward evolution of the lungfish. The aquisition of agility that permits bursts of stunning speed. The ability to run down a horse or tackle bison that will have, by now, returned. But this running bull shark operates only during the night. It's simply a question of humidity, the night air providing the dew necessary to prevent dehydration of the skin. We, by then shall have no feet, ever aloft as the bird of paradise was once thought to do. There we'll mate, raise our young and philosophise. But beware lest you should fall to earth. With no limbs with which to alight, the landing will be a hard one. Rub Moses soul over your body. You needn't be an elasmobranchologist to know about this. Indulge in oophagy.

Long ago, scientists discovered the place where God lives. We've been there, she and I, and much farther yet. It was a very vast sort of place. Here things are more circumspect. All at once, you can take in the evil wrought in his name, the misinterpretation of the written word as well as the very best that he can provide. No need to hide in wait. Stride by my side, abide to certain simple rules that only fools would neglect. Spiritual misery won't be your fate, nor shall you be one to assassinate.

Don't criticize my internal mobility nor attempt to analyse my mental instability. Both are extreme. I slip past four, five and then seven. Just after midnight I arrived from beyond heaven. The landing was smooth, though the immense structure shuddered a lot.

Thought I came in on a ship? Had you fooled! The dissertation on squaloids? I know sharks well, sharing with them (and cats), the same eye structure, the tapetum lucidum, a remarquable adaption which enhances night vision. Female carcharadon carcharias, the great white shark, are philopatric.

I recuperate my baggage, slip home. Coranic prayers begin softly, around three fifteen in the morning. Low, barely perceptible at first, they are progressively amplified by extremely powerful audio sytems. The walls vibrate. I'm sleeping directly beneath the mosque from which wells the most beautiful song. This imam must be an angel. I'm elevated, born in the airs by the prayers. Entire city becomes an instrument, curved wall open to the bay, from which echo the songs sung in different octaves, from near to far, some a mere whisper. Babel Oued gives the refrain, certainly the most beautiful one.

Weeds have grown right up to the windows. A night wind blows them flat. Fluff born seeds ride the hot air, taking hostage parcels of moonlight. Sleep for forty-five minutes before leaving again.

I'm in a distant suburb on the opposite side of the city. I went beneath the zoo. Now I'm racing through Algiers. Armed guards hang from the vehicle, bang pistol butts against the windshields of other vehicles jamming the streets.

—Blida?

—The Frantz Fanon Psychiatric Hospital.

—Why there?

—A lesson of light. Here a black man took up the cause of the Arab, who, in turn, sought emancipation from French colonial occupation. The French never did accept Algerian independence, nor has anyone really understood the moral implications of Fanon's engagements.

Recent events have made of Blida the Triangle of Death. Yet it is here that hope is the strongest. Certain points in time, certain places in space, remain monuments to which it is well to return, especially when returning from farther than far. Semaphore of hope, even if its feet be awash with blood.

—Ebb, purple tide! Don't return! Blood hasn't the abrasive action of certain acids. It'll confer the most beautiful auburn patina.

As we approach the suburbs, I realize that there's been a real building boom here. Lots of drugs are sold at the zoo near Ben Aknoun. Dried up vegetation, restless animals that can no longer sleep, the music being loud and incessant. Sun blazing with never a cloud. A girl found with throat slashed, a thief shot by his victim, a cyclist crushed beneath a truck at Tènes, a shepherd run over by freeway traffic while trying to round up flock at Azazga, a drowning at Azzefoun, another at the mouth of the Chenoua River at the Wilaya Tipaza near Oued Nador. Strong currrents due to west wind and river flowing into the bay. What could have been a peaceful dip just two days ago, proved fatal today. Nature is that way. Tides change too. You could say that this person was killed by the moon. The same day, a ninety-one year old woman named Mira was fatally struck by a train while attempting to cross the tracks at El-Asnam, Daïra of Bechloul. She wanted to catch this train. The train caught her instead.

Just as Perseus was carrying Medusa's severed head when he came to save Andromeda from Cetus, so now am I again lugging the Haitian man's severed head while trying to get my bearings in this immense city which I once knew so well. I could easily be mistaken for a fundamentalist having just perpetrated a massacre, taking along with him the proof of his forfeiture, or a soldier, member of a specialized anti-terrorist unit, working under secret orders, disguised as a fundamentalist.

At Houari Boumedien University, I made a speech, addressing myself to youth from Cuba, Cambodia, Irak, Palestine, Western Sahara. Don't recall what I told them. Probably condemned US long-term foreign politics concerning their respective countries. This was the eleventh day of august in the cyanic year of two thousand and one. At the very moment that I transcribed this information, exactly one month later, airplanes carrying their passengers were transpiercing and sending to the ground the symbols of a political power that had brought death to hundreds of thousands of muslims over the world for decades.

Should I have regret? If you draw back, take broader scope, you'll begin to perceive that in fact there is a form of divine justice, though it may appear to be much crueler than what one might have assumed.

Driving back, I stop along the road to buy half of a cigarette, hot freshly baked bread, an ear of roasted corn. Fruit from the prickly-pear cactus.

—Take out the spines. I'm no turtle!

Today's mistakes will become tomorrow's rules, not only in grammar but also in politics, religion, warfare, and most of all, in love.

I see my reflection in the rear-view mirror. Huge head, completely out of proportion with the atrophied body upon which it rests as if it had been removed by crude decapitation and awkwardly put back in place. Regret. Not mine, but the executioner's. My complexion is very dark. Is this not the Haitian man's severed head which I'm now wearing? Some devilish surgery having taken place while I was absorbed by another chapter of the *Book of Fever*. This is what is to be expected when you work with no plan, advancing like frost forming on a window, all over and nowhere at once, rather than with linear regularity, as from A to Z. Dr. Huey P. Newton suggested going form A to B or even from A to A1/2 rather than from A to Z in order to not disassociate revolutionary momentum from the People without whom any revolution would indeed be nil. This then would be the reason for the decapitated head having stayed by me for so long. It wasn't me that bore it all along, but rather it was the head that clung to me from fear of being separated, waiting for the right moment to take its place atop my shoulders. Then this *I* isn't me anymore. Indeed, I thought not to recall what had happened to the head when I had kicked it into the heavens in a desperate attempt to rid myself of its constant weight. I had thought the unwanted cranium to simply have disappeared, perhaps plucked from the air by some enormous predatory bird, or taken off by a hyena after a hard landing in the bush. Kids had found the round object and engaged in a vigorous match of football, one that would have drawn out into the night, beneath the moon in the dunes while young girls gently beat drums and sang. I remember this well, bouncing over the still warm sand, being propelled into the night sky by small naked feet, gently coming down to land, the song repeated throughout the night, the distant bang of mortar fire. Morning come, they had swaddled me in a turban made from the most brilliant blue silk.

What's it like being Haitian? Naturally you'd expect my head to be heavy with images of Toussaint l'Ouverture atop a rearing horse. I'm more obsessed with disassociating his remains from Fort de Joux in the Doubs where his bones were mixed in with ciment and stone to raise ramparts higher over bleak cold valley through which French feared invasions to come. Geography being the real protaganist again? Most miserable mausoleum following Napoleon's treason, incarceration in this cold damp place and death by pneumonia. I have now, broader vision of the West Indies, know for certain that this zone is one of the deepest spirituality, the highest human values, and blinding light encompassing Carib Indians, the breadfruit tree, Aimé Césaire, Jean-Price Mars, Magloire-Saint-Aude, René Depestre, Métallus, Dany Lafferière and voudou brought along from Benin. No mere caricatural appraisal. To bathe in the waters of sacred cascades deep in the wood; purification, coming clean being born again as with no other baptism.

Being Haitian can also mean overhearing conversation between French tourists visiting New York for first time, realizing that they too can be very racist, (they think I'm black American, don't realize I speak fluent French). This is deep disillusion. Had always dreamed of the land of Droits de l'Homme and early abolition. But no!

Take out this brain! Off with the Haitien head! It's incompatible, too human, beyond cunning. See, this mind's running; has no respect for barriers. I'll have no part of any "Hydra project."

Algiers. There are now twenty-five million souls living here. It's the greatest ocean port of the world, with Lagos being the only serious contender. Marseille, Genoa, Barcelona have all declined, an exception being made for Naples risen from its ashes after new Vesuvian mega-eruption. These have all become ports of exile for miserable northerners attempting clandestine immigration to the southern eldorado, heading for ultimate destinations of unimaginable wealth and social stability:

Kinshasa, Brazzaville and Bangassou along the M'Bomou.

It's so dark down here, my bones ache from the fall, don't know how many are broken. I've fallen into an open manhole, the cover having been removed with malicioius intent. It's a trap that'll be set for me in *Cortez*. I shall have so scrupulously avoided it while there. Forgotten, thought that it would have remained there, but it followed me here. Guilt hasn't pursued me for as much, only this open sewer mouth. And here are the manhole covers, Exhibited on palace walls like great badges, trophies, some are worn about the neck like military decorations. Heroism or merit.

Something hanging round my own neck; sort of giant dog-tag made of slate, a small black board with hand written text in chalk, can be regularly wiped down with moist sponge. Lear at me, jeer.

Caverns are capital to man's development. Were not the prophets Jesus and Mohamed frequenters of caverns? St Jerome, with his lion, Daniel and the lion's den, and the fact that they now speak; these actions can be imagined in grottos. Withdraw to Onandaga caverns, (Qumran dead sea scrolls were found in caverns, also see the importance of small grottos in the Tora Bora area; cave warfare and cavern combing). The desert too, was where Moses (nothing to do with the afore mentionned Moses sole, a flat Red Sea fish whose body fluids repel sharks), met with God, the place in which the prophets meditated, conversed with the devil and discovered themselves. The desert of Zif and the cavern of Ein-Guedi were home to David. John the Baptist was also a man of the sands.

Rushdie was wrong. Khomeni was right. The fatwah against him should have been carried out. Popes had tidied up the church in just such a manner, had they not? See how the Bible has become so easy a target, vulagarisation of the Mass. How much better was the Mass in Latin! Look now at Notre Dame cathedral, crowds of tourists eating, throwing down greasy wrappers, taking photos, laughing, making prayer impossible (see the conversation that I have with this edifice, deep into the night); Islamic revolution, how different from other revolutions!

These sewers lead nowhere. Every ten feet they've been walled up to keep terrorists from circulating underground. Reason for the high death toll during the november 2001 flood that swept through Babel Oued.

The water had nowhere to go.

When I finally manage to extricate myself from the sewer-grotto, a man approaches me, —I've been in a coma for 25 years, says he. —Just woke up. Your initials J.L. stand for "Joy" and "Light."

I want to speak with him but he's engulfed by a crowd rushing to a concert. Taken away. A mountain of crutches left behind, proves that these are all cripples, miraculously cured and running.

I'm speaking with pale, frail man. It appears to be Oloman, fifty pounds thinner and considerably dumber than he ever was. Health care? Dental treatment? Part of the solution to permanent nomadism is bringing along your own doctor. I must have worn him out. Not that they haven't doctors and dentists here. But where I just came from, there were none, and I swore to myself that I'd never travel alone again.

No turbans, djellabas or other exotism here; we're dressed in twenty-first century western attire, though threadbare at the knees and elbows. There is no brilliant conversation between us. We are seated face to face in a little bar which I entered after forging small canyon through the crutch pile and pulling back strings of glass beads hanging from the door of this place. Dirty turquoise colored walls hardly reflect pale blue light coming down from 30 watt fluorescent tube. Two glasses of tea (no alcohol here), so sweet it hurts our teeth, flies incessantly going for the moisture of our eyes. Outside is slaughter, blades being silently drawn across throats again, wind-pipes awash with blood. The victims are wheezing and gurgling. Sweat is pearling on Xoma's upper lip, my shirt is soaked. How much more of this can we bare?

Just across the room:

Other female figure is seated off to the side, behind the emaciated man I'm assuming to be Oloman. Her face is in the gloom, but for the tip of her nose; now the forehead. She rises, turns round facing the opposite way, and bends over showing all, her naked body beneath shawl. I can't help but looking at her. Splendid. Off-stage woman.

—I know when you're looking at another girl, even if it's just from the corner of your eye. Your whole face changes.

—Time is mating, procreating. Eternity is being spawned. For the moment, time is fertile. There will come the death of time.

This is Gog.

—Perhaps we're sages from other ages, enacting here what Chiefs of

State surely must now be doing, each in his own sanctuary across great oceans, at a safe distance from the massacres they've ordered. Just as phantoms return to the places they once lived or criminels come back to the scene of their crimes, so am I a perpetual revenant.

—Giant one. Civilized man. You who think to be timeless, of incommensurable wizeness, master of commerce and technological achievements. He who holds wheat in one hand while balancing napalm in the other palm. No birds will alight to drink from this one. It is said that you've invented the air mine, counterpart of the land mine where you had already excelled in imitating pebbles, seeds, nutshells and other innocent looking husks. Now you've given the world the butterfly mine, the moth, the blowing leaf. From here on in, victims will be mainly children, sometimes kittens and puppy dogs, a rare entomologist here, a curious botonist there. Don't attempt to fool me. I know my camouflage patterns. If I sometimes confuse early Waffen SS "peas" with U.S. Army Desert Storm "chocolate chip" motifs, I can readily descern between Hezbollah suicide pattern with its small five-eyed red faces, Iraqi Baath party design of miniature oasis, Angola MPLA and Burkina Faso, both with splendid flowing swaths of leaves.

Purveyor of kindness, dispenser of humanitarian aid, these times we approach will be difficult for you. You who sought to eliminate the desert man, are you not making a desert of your own land?

But no erg, reg or hamada is this. It'll be a region without bliss.

Was it Ho or Giap who had said that the desert man couldn't wage guerilla warfare in these zones of arid geographical nudity? How mistaken had he been! The Polisario had so brilliantly invalidated the theory. When you'll send your techno troops into these rocky warrens, bulky bio gear will quickly become impossible to wear, the finest grain of sand will take away artificial night vision, cut communications.

For centuries now, nights have been illuminated by enormous quantities of incoming debris, rocket boosters, junk satellites. Old women, though they still live in houses facing the sea, can't bare to look at it anymore, so many of their men has it swallowed up. Only gulls reclaim the bodies that wash ashore between rusted ship hulls. So it is with the sky. This is why they stare at the land, often hanging their heads and looking all day at the dirt beneath their feet.

—This is all trivial. What's important is the realisation that the creaturers of the triassic were mere wimps; before, long before, there were much more formidable monsters of which we haven't the slightest trace. And just as far into the most remote future, there will be new, infinitely more formidable predators whose embryonic DNA we already carry in our own bodies. Impossible you think? The taste of things has already shifted: cows have prune flavor, while small purple drupes have the savor of meat. I myself, am undergoing secondary sexual modifications of the manus. And, haven't our values shifted too?

We're on the outskirts of the city, just beyond the huge urban bulge that sprang from Babel Oued, the old fundamentalist quarter. The moula moula, small black faced desert bird, flicks its white tail indicating the direction. He announces sunrise as surely as the imam's prayer.

The woman who exposed what was beneath her shawl, embraces me, says —Go now, you're free as you've always been with me. Just don't forget to call.

I refer to my notes: Geo-politics have considerably changed. The importance of small guerilla groups, perpetrating terrorist actions, striking and then disappearing within the midst of dense civilian populations where no massive counterattack is possible. Elusive, ever so effective. Putting former great nations down upon their knees. Genuflexion.

Leaving the city, I wonder if this hasn't become the home of a perpendicular civilization that while exporting Islam had also mastered electricity in a totally different manner. Harnessing lightning.

It's the Ordivician. I'm walking through a grove of immense ferns and inverted trees whose roots spread into the sky absorbing ambiant humidity. Hanging upside down from the branches are pterodactyls, sleeping with their immense wings wrapped around their bodies exactly like bats. Urulu will have been right.

Searching for somebody's name, someone I wanted to tell you about, I remember her face, what she did and just why the particular thing she did was so special. But the name? No, it evades. I feel the way my tongue must curl to pronounce her name, but it doesn't come out. Put this search on hold, remember that I must find the name. Later, or before, yes, but find it! Tomorrow I'll remember that there's something that must be found, but what?

Lost treasure: I buried a treasure. Much time passed. I forgot where I had buried the treasure. Then I forgot what this treasure had been. Finally it was as if there had been no treasure at all.

The Sea? Perhaps, in the manner of pirates (am I not just inland from the Barbary Coast?), I hid my trove down by the sea. Quickly, I turn away from the desert.

The sea. Come to it. Today the sea is a sombre brooding thing, full of hag fish and conger eels. I'm sure it's thinking in a very oceanic sort of way, "Come out upon me, you can't keep from sinking." Many things speak now. The sea is one of them.

I'm more and more uncoordinated and absent-minded. Is this precocious aging? The onset of some new disease due to the consumption of unusual wildlife or the immoderate intake of human flesh? While swimming, avoid salps and comb jelly.

Remember that there is now full blown synergy between HIV and malarial infection. Parasitic infections are re-emerging. World warming increases areas of vector survival.

I myself now qualify as a parasite of the biosphere. Must avoid host immune response by continuously changing antigenic coat. Can avoid detection by introducing myself into intracellular site. Survive within the phagolysosomal vacuole. Control pH to avoid drop and check reactive oxygen radicals. Inhibit digestive enzymes. Immunosuppress!

You haven't any fertilizer left for your potted plants? Use night soil! Simply squat and push. It's an inner ecology.

Never enter a free-living environment. Nutrient uptake: If thirsty, seek milk from a lactating bitch. While suckling, beware of transmammar transmission.

Twelve is back. He has taken on a certain assurance, a confidence in one's self that only comes with time, or with rapid success. He's still an opportunist. A very good one. A diabolical scheme has sprung from necessity. He has a new film project. Wants to tell the story of a construction site set on the French Mediterranian coast in the late sixties or the early seventies of the twentieth. Somewhere around Marseille. The extreme tension between the foreman, a racist Frenchman, and his crew of Algerian migrant workers. The connotation in the context? Would be a question of repressing budding consciousness, turned over constantly like wet cement. Taken up by the trowel, it'll hold bricks together.

The problem being that it's impossible to find a virgin coastal area in southern France today; all has been so overrun by real estate. There's not an unbuilt parcel of land left.

—Do the shooting in Algeria, I suggest. The coast is splendid, with just the sort of construction sites you're seeking for the set.

—But the logistics, with the massacres, terrorism and all that?

—I'll present you to Senators, Ministers. Imagine the paradox! Being that: A story of French racism toward ordinary Algerian immigrants, would be filmed right here in Algeria! And when you see the movie, you'll think it's southern France.

—Wouldst you make another movie with me? On the Polisario. And a third one. Pure fiction of course.

—Fundamental.

—Have no fear. Our protection is assured by Flempt, a fierce creature who fears no flame.

—We'll be irretrievable!

Tigers of Glass

Monopod, single legged! Because the collectors have made away with the other, only one remains. It's simple arithmetic: two minus one equals one. Three legs would have been a benediction, a provision rather than an infirmity. Those handicaps and deformations which so repulse, may actually be in certain cases, a great leap forward in the evolutionary process. A leap which we would, by instinct, be unprepared to accept. The irony being that we misinterpret the rejection impulse which wells up in us, thinking it to be a normal reaction when confronted with malformation or debilitation which would risk to compromise the future of humanity if reintroduced into the gene pool, not realizing that this aversion may be an instinctive reaction of defense when confronted with what might, in the long run, prove to be a superior form of life or at least the manifestation of one of those unique adaptations that have permitted the progress of living species over the centuries, leaving those others of us whom are not endowed with it by the wayside.

Perhaps even severe mental handicap could in some manner be considered an evolution in that it brings us closer to perfection, the purity of those mono-cellular organisms that we call primitive even though they are much more in harmony with the universe than we ever shall be.

Slow over the shell grit and slippery algae I go along the beach, the crutches sinking deep with every step. Hardly more than crude canes made of old pipes strapped together with electrical wires. I'm wearing a ridiculously small leather jacket, well oiled and shining where it's drawn tight over the shoulders. My belly, exposed to the sea breeze, spills over old leather pants with voluminous codpiece.

Having developed a tolerance to their venom, I'm obliged to carry two mambas now. Needing a bite every quarter, they hardly have the time to regenerate toxins.

—Seek the more potent blue ringed octopus in the shallows. Hapalochlaena maculosa, even children know this today.

Pass a shipyard where lies a beautiful keel, again the work of some forgotten naval architect. Only the futtocks and the uprights remain. It would be an impossible task of restoration.

Beyond, resting upon bamboo scaffolding, hulls glisten, gulls listen. A group of technos are being repaired, the smugglers dream vehicle, they are finely fissured from incessant exposure to bow shock. Repairs are being made with an alcohol torch; most delicate work, the green flame coming from a microscopic needle.

I pin the little blue-circled arthropod to the bottom and sit down with it in the shallows. It's so difficult to find maculosa this close to shore. The venom, I savor, an electrifying tingling gradually takes hold as I lie in the gently lapping tide, cone shaped clouds passing overhead. The heart falters, skips and takes off with another rhythm.

Dvořák.

There's a golden haze over the bay, an ancient Claude Lorrain portuary scene but perverted and perilous. Children come towards me laughing, a small dog named Chernobyl churning after them and belching a trail of black smoke. They throw it balls which it fails to catch, collapses into an ash pile.

Off in the bay a ship is being cut up. Purple smoke sublimated with powerful lights.

A very adult looking little girl with ferocious ferret features approaches me; insolence has permanently curled her lip.

—Are you a pirate?

I'm unable to respond, the venom having taken a firm grip.

—Why do you only have one leg? she inquires, shamelessly curious as children can be about infirmities.

—I lost the other one.

—Where is...

—Dendroxa.

She draws away in fear.

—My father says its per, perpen...

—dicular, I complete the word still too big for her small mouth to wield.

She runs just as I begin to explain —No, it's just over there, but she's already at the far end of the strand, down by the old fortifications that reek from everyone pissing in them.

I have, in the past, been a dentist just as planned. It is a paradox that this is when I acquired notions of deepest core geophysics.

A vendor comes selling silver velvet drupes with ice pulp.

—Cigarettes?

He has them! Rare luck, the little gray package with the mackled narwhale on the wrapping.

—Keep these for me will you? passing him the crutches, I say.

The sea is at ease, not I. Rolling into the deeper water I'm relieved of my weight and lazily swim. Ships are at anchor on long ceramic chains.

Sea captains carousing in Surinam.

Who could ever have dreamed that they would one day look like this? Higher than galleons, sails of the Chinese junk, black and rust colored, painted with golden hyenas and vermilion rhinoceros. Hulls of teak with tar just as before, yet so different. These ships can go anywhere! It isn't just lore.

High above, a black and white satellite with long whiskers named "Catfish" combs the sky for information. It has nothing on me.

The baby is on my back. —Dadee I want to swim with you, far out where the ocean is cold, deep, dark. Pressure.

I don't bother with taking off my clothes. They balloon out filling with water.

We return with nightfall, slender chrome fish spilling from my shirt. They have snouts like seahorses and eyes big enough to apprehend the dimmest distant star.

The vendor planted my crutches above the high water mark. Baby runs for them and drags them down to the water's edge for me. But she doesn't give them, prefers dragging them over the cobbles with a loud clatter, laughing just out of reach. A woman already.

She goes up into the bushes by the bay boulevard and returns carrying a twelve-foot long cobra. Remember, this is India!

I wrap it around my torso and we go off along the seafront passing little shops, blaring horns and screaming children.

"Double Helix," "Mola," "Ucello" and "Mosca" were the names of the ships we had seen this morning. She is repeating these in a strange litany, hardly audible. Now I know that she can read.

At a snack shop she spills tar soup on her white dress and throws a porcelain bowl at a boy who was laughing at her, hitting him square in the head. It splits in half leaving a black line in the middle of his face which bleeds some.

—Guie, guie...uahh, she utters little guttural animal calls; —Dwai ohah...nwa, she begins nodding while pointing skyward. —That, that that!

—My leg?

She nods vigorously.

—We'll soon go after it, (relic cult has developed around the limb, see notes).

The children have gathered menacingly. Some clench water guns filled with acid in their filthy little hands. She is jumping up and down gleefully as the owner of the shop advances, a syringe full of panther piss at his belt.

—That's what we came for! peeling the bandage from my forehead. The scarifications don't emit the expected flames. Fortunately the cobra wriggles.

Protect my tiddler, conk the cuddies.

She throws crockery and screams with joy. Suddenly tired, she curls up for a nap at my feet.

The fyce over, scoop her up off the floor; it's a mess with broken glass and rusty razorblades, fluid everywhere. Manage to stagger to a stool straight across from a mirror. I see us. She's so small, perfect and beautiful. I broken and old. Getting bald. A thick smoke fills the bar. I realize that small fires are creeping along my skin. They should be smothered. It's impossible to do while holding her. Opaline fluid, I pull her bottle from my pocket. She should be mothered.

The room has cleared now, they have all withdrawn. They didn't know what the combustion meant but had some sort of suspicion. I serve myself from the locker, cave crickets with rock salt, a horseshoe crab that's over cooked and too dry. Two vials of urchin mash.

She awakens and finishes her bottle leaving only glistening gristle. Is angry now and throws down some spoons, stamping her little feet and crying. I take the time to wrap a strip of black rubber around my head.

Outside passes a transparent tiger. Only the stripes are visible, walking, wrapped about the remains of what he has devoured. A half-digested man and an electric fish flashing dimly. In the sky are three Saturns, one green with blue rings, the other two, black. The tiger treads on seaweed and lichens.

—Look! Stripes and circles, she whispers, her breath tickling the inner most reaches of my ear.

We smell him going by.

—Glass tiger pass!

—Along time ago the sun fell on dinosaurs' backs in big splotches of light. The air was crackling, full of lightning and burning chemicals.

—Boom... crack!

—It's Algeria.

—I'll soon be going back there.

—No Dadee. You stay in your office, I'll lock you up, her forehead is perfect and round like a little planet.

Jook.

We hail a taxi. A patch of fur is hanging from the rearview mirror.

—A mouse! she asks excitedly, awake again.

—A tail, explains the driver, —Only half. An Australian fox tail, given to me by a traveler. It was hanging off of his hat. I suppose he thought he was some sort of Davie Crocket. When I asked him what it was, he offered it to me! Generous sort of man. Then I picked up an abandoned dog. He jumped into my cab and immediately snapped it off, gulping down the other half.

—How now it smells of cinder in your cab?

—Just before you, I picked up a fellow with more than one drink of squid ink in his belly. Having frayed my way through the most murderous traffic for more'n hour, hot as yourselves know'd it were. Then he tells me to turn round, he's lost his shoe and wants to go back where we've come from, that's were it is, he's sure it's there. Yelling and reeking, he forces me to go back to this place that stinks as much as he, like fish thrown up too high by the tide that rot in deep piles. Disappears into the night, he does. There's still the fish smell in my cab, so I gets down on all fours in the back and finds his shoe. Burns it, I do! Me so angry! Would you have, belching himself — preferred the chtonian stench?

—Please take us to the Snake Keys.
—Is that by Monkey River?
—You're the driver.
I have horrible gastric pains from ingesting an excessive quantity of leaves difficult to digest. The need for a second stomach like the great nasic monkeys of the Mollucan islands. For now, I'm bent double.
She's talking to me again, not the girl but her mother:
—Let's go back to that so dim area, beyond the methane dwarf.

Evolution. With time snakes have learned to form circles and roll like wheels. I am Bukwas, man of the woods. Engaged in my retinue are drowned people.
Oowekeeno!
—Wawer. Wake up.
I realize that we are again wandering, not through woods but in an immense urban landscape, devoid of any beauty, the only one that I merit. The small one is atop my shoulders, scratching the whiskers of my chin with her tiny fingers.
To either side, gas blows off in giant plumes of blue fire. The street reflects the empty sky upon which we seem to be walking. This is the garden where I was held captive, a brittle most inflammable puppet exuding resin amidst the combustion.
Why is it that I must remember?
Together we play games of her invention. We are Eskimos gathering blocks of ice with which we fashion an igloo. Then we stalk seal, waiting for them to surface from a hole in the icecap.
—Daddy, take the harpoon and don't let them escape! Beware of the polar bear.
Only a child could play in this most devastated landscape. She sits cross-legged in the middle of the desolate street. There's nothing here, only wind blown dust, a few struggling weeds growing between the cracks in the pavement and great dark stains where smugglers have drained used oil from tired engines. She strips the leaves from the weeds;
—Bison fur, the stems will be our lances.
—Arrowheads! she says, gathering gravel. Lumps of tar, —Daddy Indian, these are wild ducks for dinner.
—Yes my papous.

I'm guilt-ridden, so miserably have I failed in my role as the family breadwinner, that we now inhabit the far reaches of the most dismal industrial suburb.

The sky is bacon fat: red yellow and brown strips through which fly fossil planes, 747s that have been extended and over-extended. The welds are shabby, I-beams jut from the bodies. Some are jointed with accordion structures hooking together two or more fuselages. The runways have also been extended, several miles long sometimes running over rough terrain.

Our home is a shack just to the side of the runways. The interior walls are covered with pasted magazine pages that serve for wallpaper. In the garden we grow vegetables. Rows of carrots, Portuguese cabbage, onions and a few sweet potatoes. Peanuts and a little bit of cotton, only enough for personal use though.

I have become obsessed with my facial features which seem to be in constant mutation, the nose swelling, the ears detaching, flesh beneath the eyes sagging, hair falling. I spend a great deal of time each day checking on the progress of these defects, stooping down to see my reflection in the chrome of car bumpers, rearview mirrors, store windows. I also stare at passerbys to see if they are looking at me in an unusual manner. Finally I wear a turban, grow a heavy beard, wear big sunglasses, go abroad only at night and remove all of the mirrors from my shack. I become housebound while awaiting corrective surgery.

The garden needs to be watered, tilled. I must go out in spite of the heat, wrapped in a blanket, a broad hat over the turban, two pairs of sunglasses and a smoking pipe to ward-away gnats attracted by perspiration.

—You who hoe there, we look for Afeworki, Zenawi and Horsechild!

Small cloud of mosquitoes surrounds them. Attracted from under foliage shade by high CO_2 output of intruders foreign to endemic zone.

I'm perspiring heavily, an overextended Boeing is nearing critical velocity behind the purple heads of the cabbage. All is shimmering.

Which weed, what wood grow here? This is: water willow and bladderwort, marsh-monkey flower, foxglove, and snapdragon. This is not: dog bane or milkweed. Here, horehound from which I brew tea. Pipsissewa for making chimaphilin, a diuretic drug, love-in-winter or the so-called king's cure and Indian pipe.

—Might yee be of those whom heedlessly think "never me?", steps squarely in pile of human feces serving as fertilizer, wipes away with hand, and with same hand sweeps sweat from around smile.

—Never me? reply I, mimicking the mien, perfectly erect with arm sweeping the air in an ample arc as if attempting to hark back to the manners of a certain nobility. I cannot control myself. In so doing, other afflictions befall me. Suddenly I'm convinced that my organs have been removed and replaced with alien ones. This then, would be the reason for the scar tissue covering my body? The roar of departing craft is deafening, incessant, there is no escaping. Hush kits no longer exist and there's even stiff competition as to who'll have the loudest engines. Passengers fight to be seated closest to the exhaust ports.

I attempt communicating with the visitors by using the sign language that our family has developed while housing beneath the thundering airstrips. But it doesn't seem to have any efffect on the intruders leering over my fence. Did you know that deaf-mutes living in France cannot communicate with, say deaf-mutes living in England or the geographical zone where Great Britain used to be? And French sign language has no link with spoken French either. These three individuals (they always come in trios, the one performing, accompanied by two legal witnesses in case of trouble) have evidently never gone to the effort of communicating with deaf-mute individuals nor paupers living in thundering habitat, or perhaps they are familiar with these practices but only in a foreign land from which they may be now arriving.

—Gesticulator, weed sprinkler, answer our questions! This one is immense, long gray hair greased back with cod liver oil, the odor is born by a breeze coming my way. This seems very realistic because the aircraft are coming from behind me, taking off into the wind as they should. He has a rather squarish visage marked by a severe case of smallpox or acid thrown in the face. His nose has been broken several times. The suit he wears fits too tightly around the waist while the shoulders seem empty.

The river is just to their backs. Rafts of refuse ride yellow sucking water that smells of yeast.

One fills a jug with river water. Noisily, they slake their thirst.

—You're to come with us, with out making a fuss.

—Play blind hooky? Use your blood money!

Little ones to either side both have thick beards. I suspect that they are mechanical.

Follows a period of relative quiescence. I assume that they've abducted me.

Notes: Subject is obsessed with imagined morphological defects. Could be a case of body dimorphic disorder. When conversation was engaged we witnessed echopraxia and echolalia. Temporary motoric immobility ensued, followed by excessive motor activity.

(Their hands are still filthy, welts along the neck from countless mosquito bites).
—We've heard of your clever dreams.
—I haven't had one for many years.
—Tell us about them, the last one you can remember for example.
—In theory.
I'm being kept in a gigantic mud fortress that's been built in the center of the city. It has the shape of an immense oven but there is no fire for the moment.
The interrogators take a break to munch on sandwiches stuffed with freshly severed human ear and pickles. They drink warm beer that when swallowed fast, tickles.
—Why is it you constantly refer to desert situations?
—"also known as" is a project. Notice how much science fiction is set in desert environment. Immediate, cheap exoticism for several reasons. Firstly the West, where consumer markets are the strongest, is totally ignorant of Arab culture, aside brief interest episodically sparked by trying to comprehend what motivated Arab extremists to target occidental civilization, westerners know nothing of the Orient, the Maghreb, Africa, nor even of Islam in general. This brings an immediate intrigue. The unknown! And, is not filming in desert location cheaper than any other type of decor?
—How did you arrive here?
—I came on a Greyhound bus.
—No horoscaph?
—What better time machine could there have been? I tell you, when

you're in a small Midwestern town, trying to escape a local sheriff with his hastily deputized posse in true western tradition, you'll take the first means of transportation that presents itself, even a public one.

—Even if it means contaminating us with twentieth century sub-humans? says one of the mechanical ones.

—Bring in the illegal aliens, says the big one with several times broken nose.

I recognize a young Black male with scars from gunshot wound on left arm, (small entrance hole on backside and big exit wound on front surface indicate being shot from behind; likely encounter with LAPD), a Mexican migrant worker whose hands are severely excoriated from years of underpaid farm labor, an elderly woman who wears a torn night gown and doesn't know who she is, two youths with glassy eyes still clinging to fortified beers laced with codeine available at pharmacies, all fellow passengers on the bus.

Brutally they throw in the fierce teenage girl who had jumped into the passing convertible that I had been driving.

She lands at my feet.

—You'll find no editor! Your story is fraught with minor political events and worthless, cheap contestation that only serve to pinpoint at what moment in time you where stranded when inventing your tale. There'll be no printing of this rubbish. It's too set in time. A dead give-away! Even a child would know that you were hiding somewhere at the edge of the twentieth and twenty-first century. You're no seasoned time traveler. What we want is more royalty, stories of court intrigue, great naval battles, fleets more splendid than that of Louis Quatorze, gilded armadas pitted against one another in turquoise waters, legs arms being taken off by grape-shot fired from bronze muzzled couleuvrines, eyes ripped from their sockets by hook-handed sweeps, wounded massively falling overboard into shark infested waters, visions of intestines trailing through bloody foam with close-ups of excrement being expulsed and slowly descending, upon which smaller fish feed.

—What we really want, says the second mechanical one, with surprising soprano voice —is rational thinking.

The big one is angry, pushes him back. —Faugh! Much later that you're supposed to say that! he tells the high pitch voiced interrogator. Drops his fecket.

With *Wovoko* it was the well-developed lungs attached to Neanderthal pharynx that they were after. I had lost both arms in *Onandaga*. Sure, they've grown back, several times even, but never like the original ones. Sometimes I have paws, at other moments my limbs are wings, but never, ever have I had normal hands and fingers again, although the sensation lingers. What are they after now? These can only be IMG employees scouring this part of the time collision wreckage zone as they so indelicately call it, beloved home to me where it is possible to come across just about anything that has ever existed or will transpire, at least in a fragmentary manner. Better than nothing, I insist.

—We've copies of the letters you exchanged. Found in the girl's jeans, your shack, he says, and without producing them, he declaims them with accuracy proving that the texts have been well rehearsed:

"My darling. Your last message has an abstract quality to it, which I dislike. You ask only about the children's education (two times six = twelve girls) as if you see in me the guarantor of their upbringing. It's as if, enamoured with a sentiment, you love only your own love of me. You can't see the me that I now am but only the one that you once knew. You've become *irreal* to me; my memory of you is confused. The letters which the birds drop from the heavens all bear distinctive curved incisions with angular tearing and important punctures, often taking out key words that could have proven or disproven the expression of real sentiment. These puncture marks also show that birds of prey with serrated talons and dangerous beaks bear our correspondence. Are there no doves or pigeons? True, violent winds that blow between us, call for strong-winged messangers. Angels have failed here, haven't they?

I wonder, have we not become fantasy for one another, and in being spirits of sorts, so separated by time and distance, hasn't our love become stronger than it ever was? I'll take on any form, become any thing in order to be with you but for a moment. I have been told that your own clothing, the caverns wherein you dwell and the shacks in remote industrial suburbs that you frequent, are filled with my letters, often unopened. It is said that you even use them for wall paper."

—This is actual, it be factual, I say.

—Yours are cryptic, unromantic, devoid of the slightest notion of love: "I would prefer that you forget my very existence. Distant love is impossible. We cannot nurture illusion. Remake your life, I conjure you to banish any memory you may yet have of me. If you must, think of me as being an amputee, obese, dirty, impotent, vulgar, excessively brutal, an alien, a beast of ill omen, reptile with purulent maw, a virus that can only bring death, a perpetrator of genocide, the vilest racist, he who can do no good, so ugly that he's obliged to hide beneath a hood, who never could do what one should. Forsake me, I implore of thee, call me *It*."

—The pitiful reply is written here, he says, unfolding letter found inserted in open wound. It's written on synthetic material, still wet with blood that separates light into chromatic constituents, liquid rainbow pulses through her veins: "All of these things I'll learn to love, knowing now that you may take refuge in these repulsive affubulations."

Would these then be angels in an advanced stage of putrefaction, their wings worm-eaten? Clubfeet and claws give clues, yet no devils are they. Time is such a vast thing that even infinity shows wear; their clothing, I have said it, is thread bare, they no longer have hair. As for faith they have bled it, not a drop of divine elixir remains in their veins.

—You? "I so wish that you could feel the pain that separation draws down deep in the bosom, beneath double erect nipples, the anxiety that grows daily to become roaring fire by nightfall, making sleep an impossible wish, driving me to undertake, from thirst, the most distant pilgrimages whereby I seek out waterholes, kneel down along damp banks, cupping together my hands over black mirrors reflecting infinity. On this smooth surface there are no ripples. Never does my thirst or my desire for you slacken. My heart, wind torn leaf is shaken, waiting to be once again taken. Only by you. No thanks."

—I'll be ready in a brace of shakes. Do whatever it takes!

These fallen angels constantly change hats, switching mortarboards for shakos and, inevitably, one of them must don the white conical hood that has somehow come along from the small town museum. It smells of mothballs. Goldfinnies ply shallow water. This is Europe, confirmed by the appearance of glittering proliferation of cetonia aurata. How's this possible? We were just in Gondwana witnessing the separation of landmasses that were to become Australia, South America and Africa. She wears the gold topaz ring that I had offered her after we had pawned the Santa Maria aquamarine. Milkweed seed float in the air. Coma Berenice is my preferred constellation. In my heart, it has long replaced the starkness of Camelopardalis. Heart become, now that she's here, combustion chamber which no explosion can tear apart.

—Come! I say, reaching down to my feet where she's lying, thrown down by the time-battered divine company.

—She then wrote: "I cannot imagine you as you are today, what you might have become. The memory of the way you were remains with me and certainly forbids reinterpretation. I prefer to stay with that image of you, as you were with half your brain blown away when you so stupidly tried to impress me by venturing openly and in full day light into the no-man's land. You were so delicious when washed down with rum. Would it be impossible to revive Wovoko or the man who came back as Muphta along the banks of the Missouri?"

—I have an urge to squirt sperm in your face (I'm almost yelling this), miss the open mouth, make mascara run, but this is not at all what happens. Undress the bottom half, leaving your upper body entirely clothed, I settle down on you for a slow meal, gently pushing your knees up against the breasts, the entire vaginal area is open, offered up, awaiting my mouth which comes down slowly, deliberately. We have time. Have I told you how you taste stronger with age, how I love the lines around your eyes, at the corner of your mouth, the white hairs that are beginning to appear at your temples, the place where your skull is the thinnest, perhaps the heat of your mind making the color turn ash near the ember? And while I feed noisily on your sex, I want you to relax, smoke a cigarette or even read a paper; my fingers gently run round the contours of the anus, up behind it toward your tail bone, where there's very fine silky hair, back down again to these thicker curls, all wetted down now, over which my mouth slips. I will pursue this repast, ignoring any move you make, refusing to penetrate, even when you pull me in toward you. I'll resist, no matter how firm your grip. Until finally it's strong enough to uproot a young tree. Only then shall I enter. We'll pause. I'll read French authors aloud to you. They're the best for this manner of reading, having written while listening to themselves write. The thought may be unclear, but the sound is always there.

—I'll not listen when you protest, tell me it's impossible all of this. Together let's piss. I hear the gentle hiss.

—How is it that these structures, entire palaces, neighborhoods, the city itself, parcels of the landscape and even continental fragments, could possibly have traversed billions of years virtually intact? Do they suck along in your wake?

—Things that I love, like those that I hate, accompany me in time. Though none be splendid enough to offer you, at least they'll do for decor.

There's been much talk of re-establishing laws, religions, and other abstract notions. Maybe they want more than my thick brow structure, the short pharynx, perhaps they're really after the rational dreams. But only Oloman knew of this! True, he did act as an agent for me and I have made some money selling these visions of office work, of legal procedure in the making, always imperiled by the introduction of political considerations which, seen from here, pass for the most furious fiction.

—My fere, were this building fenestrated you could contemplate becoming a felodese.

—No windows, no festoonery. I say.

—End this fliver and his Flo! Cut them to flitches! say the scruff-faced ones.

Flummox, they'll be fobbed. Increasing enmity. Find there foible. Very near, booms a fog gun. Fools foison in folkmoot.

—Why this foofarraw? Enough footle. Forfeel ye?

Ah, but they have all three, diplomas in forensic psychiatry. Fozy trio smells of foulmart.

Masters of deception, needn't declare, "I bequeath to you!" Riding dust born by a gust, these captors have haptors. Just as the honey bee's infested with tracheal mite, tongue worm lives in lung of snake, fecundity brings enormous risk. Onchocera volvulus will impair their sight. Seek subparietal glands, look for dorsal hook. Constant discharge of lamellae secretion. It's an evasion mechanism. The *tour de force* is the pentastomids' glands secretions which match host's pulmonary surfactant. Uncontrolled helminthes infections and associated diseases, particularly in developing sectors of the universe, due to the turmoil of widespread conquest, thoroughly validate early theories of Stoll and Crompton. Cross infection is inevitable. Horizontal gene transfer. Spacio-temporal scales have been fully invested. Check your orbital fluids! Haven't you been eating raw Carcinus maenas? Nesting throughout the Holarctic? Living with swine in Asia, wading in rice paddies while playing with pye-dogs? Check the skin of your scrotal pouch! Infection foci. Anticipate an explosive onset of Katayama fever. You'll be subject to rectal cancer too. Together, you're both the definitive and intermediate hosts. Taenia solium. My garden's full of it.

A first spasm betrays what I had suspected all along while watching these men feed on raw pig, crunching down on live crab, swigging from jugs of ruby river water. Subclass piroplasmasina. Accidental hosts, sporogony occurs in the tick vector. Cerebral rosetting is already underway.

—Don't ever blunder into this world where blood is the plunder. Fall to backwater fever. Malaria etiology is now infinite and you'll never be able to grasp the full spread of its pathophysiology. Impossible, I tell you, now speaking directly to my future fornicatrix, young Zanda.

Things go very quickly here, or perhaps this just goes to show how long we've been in their custody. They've had time to interrupt normal sylvatic cycles. Eat poorly cooked frog and snake.

Possible control of enteric helminthes parasites? No piperazine, pyrantel, or thiabendazole available here. And even if there were, it's not certain that the side effects wouldn't be lethal to these individuals whose metabolism it's difficult to pin point with any real precision. I'm not for sure if they're even humans at all.

Classic anaphylactic shock and rapid death. This is the Third Universe, a risky zone of late development.

Free, we exit the windowless building and enter the fog. Find for her a classic Chanel jacket, pre-Lagerfeld if at all possible and big sunglasses, (the fog emits intense radiance as if small suns were circulating close to the ground, and this could very well be the case today). Morgenthal Fredericks? Hard to say, the name's partially rubbed away, but in any case, they're very protective, wrapping around the edges of the face.

—Must find our girl. But aren't we heading the wrong way? She must be older than we.

We're riding a scenery wagon. Passengers of the boat truck. Rapidly shifting decor in preparation for the following act.

—Return to caverns. Catch blind cat. Become chthonic. Wear winking cincture.

Entrance obstructed by vehicle. Back seat full of marbles and toy cars.

In the bedroom are shoe models, strewn jewelry. I'll make a double portrait for her birthday (Valentine's Day of course), like Boldini with thinly painted, sweeping strokes, even if I have to grind my own pigments, catch the sable, cut stems from the right trees, harvest cotton and linen, weave the canvas. Crush linseed and poppy seed.

—Wovoko, let's go! But first, Darfur will be our weigh station.

—No, not these eastern wastelands lain bare by Arab slavers! Go deeper, penetrate. The Upper MBomou. Feast on forest turtle, touraco cooked pheasant-style with just a dash of rock salt.

Code Pattern

—How's your patient? Does she play games? Chess for example. It can be very revealing, help us to interpret the pathology which she's suffering from.

—Just how does Maria Magdalene play chess?

By setting up the pawns in a wide arc, holding back a point formed by rooks followed by a shaft of bishops, knights and queens. The kings are off to one side. Black and white are mixed together.

This Portuguese girl, a genius, painted patterns that were keys to the mysteries of the universe. At only ten she was hired by the most reputed azulejos factory of Lisbon for her deftness of hand. She was capable of laying down the most delicate unwavering lines with gradations of cobalt that would turn a deep blue with fire.

How had this come about?

In the beginning:

Maria Magdalene had invented her own reading method; from left to right and upon reaching the end of the line, immediately tying in with the tip of the line beneath and going back from right to left. Continuity rather than stopping and returning. This implied either reading each other line backwards or writing it backwards. She was capable of both. Her teachers were horrified and considered her to be on the verge of insanity. They tried breaking her of this habit. It was then that she began cutting paper in large circles upon which she wrote texts in spirals, spinning the discs to read them. She excelled at mathematics, playing with formulas unknown to her teachers who only saw there confirmation of steadily progressing madness. Maria Magdalene was banned from the school benches.

She began drawing and painting intensely at home. Stupefying images all in lavis of ultramarine blue depicting some kind of epic civilization;

strange buildings set in jungle, beasts unknown, neither monsters nor divinities, all of unnerving brutal beauty. Machines that were intricate and complex, remote by their refinement. The skies divided into abstract zones having no rapport with classical constellations, were covered with unknown scriptures, crisp as if laid down with razor edge or diamond tip.

Her father, Joaquim Seabra, decided it was time she work and took Maria Magdalene to the Vieuva Lamego azulejos factory in what was then, the tranquil countryside surrounding Lisbon.

Her work went smoothly; she completed the apprenticeship in just half the time it took most to simply become familiar with the technique and then she was on her own, repeating the patterns and scenes from models that dated back to the eighteenth century and before.

One day the director, Luis Antonio Negros, arrived furious.

—You've made a horrible mistake...you filled in the faces with cobalt. These people look like blacks now!

The tiles just out of the oven made a barely perceptible tinkling noise as they cooled.

—And so they are intended to be, she replied with the tranquility of one whom confirms that which is evident.

—We'll have none of that here, cut the director, dropping the plate to the floor where it spread like the rays from an exploding star to the far corners of the room, fragments flying beneath the rough shoes of the other young girls employed for the unwavering homogeneity of the patterns they daily copied.

By mutual agreement between shamed father and insulted director, punishment was decided upon. Five palettes of fresh tiles were prepared for Maria Magdalene and laid out on tables. She was locked up alone on a Sunday with order to cover them with the most repetitious floral pattern from the ancient catalogues of the factory archives.

Monday morning, the anatomy of another world, immense and intricate, was waiting. Kings with the darkest skin attended upon by the most ineffably pale slaves, their immaculate tone being that of the porcelain itself, reigned upon a land where all again was as unknown and strangely beautiful as that which she had painted at home after having been banned from school.

Upon these plates, there were not only blues but several other hues, even gold which implied several firings in the great ovens of the factory, from the highest to the lowest temperature; work for a team of stokers over a seven day period, not that of the frail lone girl that had been locked up on the day of the Lord.

—Never should we have obliged her to work on the Sabbath. It's the devil's hand, 'tis his breath hath fired the enamel! cried out Luis Antonio.

—This is neither Angola nor Brazil. Pernambucco gone mad! Signor Negros gesticulating, yelled, addressing all those present.

The employees crowded around; none had ever seen such a marvelous work. Even the fireworkers whose charge it was to start heating the kilns, left their ovens to come in and admire the plates, for it was as well a technical achievement as it was an artistic masterpiece.

The director charged in amidst the employees, ruddy in the cheeks and screaming, —This be not your place, round this infamy, pressing as if it were your milk. Back to your ovens, you bakers of mud! Cleanse those ashes that the firing of this horror has there left. And with that he had it all taken out on a cart pulled by a little donkey and dumped in a pile.

Maria Magdalene came to work late that morning, passing through the long room where the other girls all fell silent, dropping their slip laden brushes and staring. Before the director could even say a word she waved him away as if he were only the most insignificant of apprentices, —No falem me moral..., her voice trailed behind her as she went to gather those personal effects of hers that she kept in a little locker.

At that time, Maria Magdalene, with an obscure Portuguese author named Castro Soromenho, were the only two whites in the world to have cast blacks as protagonists in their creative work. Soromenho had lived in Angola before returning to Lisbon. Upon publication of his work, he was ostracized and forced to exile in Sao Paolo Brazil. As for Maria Magdalene, she was interned.

The pile of fractured tiles bearing the strange world that the young girl had conceived joined a glittering small mountain constituted of all the rejected imperfections from the azulejos factory, those with wavering traits, smudges, cracks and bubbling from improper firing.

Lisbon spreads out and the shiny fragments of the potter's rubbish heap throw up glittering patterns on the bellies of incoming planes. It's a modern archeology. Maria Magdalene's world is on hold. So is Castro's. They've just begun to take on tutorial value.

These things I learn while pursuing possum deep in Missouri woodland. Following the prints that the pink small feet have lain down in bottomland mud, I stumble upon the ruins of an old mansion, which once belonged to Badger. He was a doctor, treating patients with daily bleedings rather than with herbs. South, twenty miles through forest of deciduous trees from which leaves are falling heavily, lies Shanghai. Not the China coast city but the remains of what was once known as the meanest little border town, a place where people were burned or hung while new songs were learned and sung. Here it was best not to be black of skin nor to wear blue uniform.

It is a time when the bison are returning and mithka, the raccoon, is in rut. A season which corresponds to October, to be exact, several millennium hence. Once again, black bear are plentiful and we eat very flavorful purple pumpkins no bigger than nine-pound cannon shot, small and round.

This time, our first meeting occurs on the left bank of the upper Mississippi and it is of no importance that we have already had a child together, an eight year old girl now asking for a harmonica, a book on gothic writing and carnivorous plants that are neither indigenous to these zones nor alive anywhere on Cyana during this period. This is the remote future. Coastal cities have all disappeared; immense urban centers have been built on mountain peaks. Not from fear of rising sea level (we had all been wrong about that), but from fear of what might emerge at any time from waters that hadn't really risen at all. In addition to this, Americans had realized during the war against students in Afghanistan, what a formidable advantage it could be to withdraw into mountainous terrain just as the Talibans had done.

I have size AA antennae. My ship is called "Stray Cat." Notion of time is based on concepts developed by the Aya Baka of the upper Oubangui. Neither lunar nor solar. I can tell you with certainty that immortality is the worst curse. Giants have been a constant in children's mythology. Recent events have obliged me to revise my view, realize that it's true. This mountain refuge, monumental dung heap. Rain is sticky saliva dropping from an oversized maw that hovers in the sky. No dog's but God's. Soon I'll go up there and treat his teeth.

The poor are poorer than they ever were. Only the super wealthy populate these crests. When they've had enough of soaring, they pour to what's their idea of paradise where I sometimes live as best I can, watching them arrive by immaculate waves, waiting for the most opportune moment to help myself to the golden manna which they bring. Sometimes they come accompanied, but usually they go whoring. Our women are still the most beautiful. If this is too boring, go exploring. Pretend to be adoring. No servant, masseur nor shoeshine am I. Forced mendacity is recurrent. But I'm not a beggar. I simply help myself.

Don't think that I haven't any fun while breaking and entering. There's always something of exciting about penetrating into the private world of another, especially when this personal universe is a transposed one, an environment that has been brought along. That which is indispensable, that which he cannot do without. He'll leave the codex of righteousness on the night table, a fascinating book, no bigger than a billiard ball and having the same ivory luster, that tells just how to build a superpower on the foundations of dead Indians and abused Blacks. It'll never be said enough.

But this now is Jamaica. A lieu where Indians and Africans are yet to be found, even if they're thoroughly mixed together and in small numbers. A treasure. Hurry to see them. They won't last forever. Haven't Arabs been eliminated? This I discovered reading a publicity brochure negligently left on the bathroom floor. It melted in my hands like a *hezbollah* web-site being snowed out, to avoid the propagation of certain fundamental truths to be found there.

The codex is a very dense book and I've only been able to read it by fragments, each visitor bringing his own, but never leaving it behind when he departs. There seems to be an inseparable tie between them and the sacred scripture. A small satellite consciousness which replaces the one they no longer possess. Certain chapters are populated by fabulous dangerous creatures that rendered the ascension of the summits a perilous enterprise. Dark ones. No surprise. Believe in these lies? It would be unwise.

Say: "It could have been like this but it wasn't really so. See the Black world on its knees. It hasn't fallen for never did it stand." And, you know, I speak while brushing what's left of my rotten teeth with the tooth brush found in the bathroom, filming myself with the video cam left behind while they've gone down to the beach. I won't steal it. I've made off with all of value that's to be found in their room. Except for the camera.

"Why did the thief leave it?" they'll wonder. The visual recorder is the delayed pleasure model so appreciated, where the viewing is only possible upon returning to the mountaintops.

There, they'll discover me brushing my teeth with the very brush (zoom on my festered gums) they've been daily putting into their own mouths. The theft which had only been a disagreeable vacation experience will take on new traumatic value. To realize that they've been cleaning their teeth with an object that's combed my righteous moss, been in my mouth and up my butt! Filming this anal acrobatics was a difficult operation. No passing indisposition. The thief will have a face, private parts. No ordinary hot man. The memory of pubic hairs caught in the brush, which each one had thought the other to have placed there by jest, will bring perpetual unrest.

Magistrates, judges to the highest court, they'll become depressive, severely damage throat tissues with aggressive mouthwash before reverting to dangerous acids, have their teeth pulled, consume only purées while dentures are being made, avoid looking at each other, tell friends about it, suffer ostracism, become heavily indebted to therapists, in turn consume dangerous drugs. Finally, beggars in their own right, they'll be thrown out, tumble from mountain peaks and live in the lowlands where they'll wish they had beaks to protect themselves from the other freaks that live down here and communicate with shrieks.

Is this, for them, a visit to the demon's den? Maria's porcelain plate kingdom before it broke? Or the shards put back together to form a huge glittering platter. Does it really matter? Down here you'll both be fatter. The diet contains lots of sugar. Chemical rain falls with a patter. You've become just another bugger. Sorry if the good dream's come to shatter. A nightmare? Shouldn't have gone to Jamaica. Think I might care. You'd rather be awake, ah?

Join me, we'll feed on hatchling birds fallen from the nest. Incapable of flight, it's when their bones are soft that they're the best. Then we'll be lungfish, crossing desert expanse, seeking the smallest mire while struggling not to expire.

I have rational dreams for hire. One's where you can join me in an office, accomplish secretarial tasks while I prepare more important affairs. We can be very serious, work overtime, organize and attend conferences, develop knew long range policies, propose budgetary cuts. I'll show you how to create a filing system. We'll have access to oceans of information, punch cards, reel-to-reel tapes, CDs and much newer material. Learn how to harness thunderclap electricity in order to use a recorder. There'll be great order.

There are Gabon vipers underfoot. Thick as a man's arm, loaded with venom and so well camouflaged. Each one is the protector of a forest divinity that is at home between the fangs. Peddlers run briskly, hawking bags of high quality human livers and hearts. Certified clone origin but usually taken from the homeless. Barbecue vital parts.

Oloman's down here with me. Friendship, I think, but he's only after my rational dreams. A wealthy client up there wants to purchase these office worker visions. Rival micro factions compete, raising the value. IMG has gotten wind of this, reclassified my brain. Have their own client; a winning political candidate with perfect presentation but lacking rational thinking. Considering brain transplant. Will I be obliged to go after my own brain after having in turn borrowed someone else's, K2's, Twelve's, (Eleven's), or even Oloman's before he returns to his new heavens? But then, with whose brain shall I replace theirs while waiting? It's only now that I finally realize the real value of the severed head that I've been lugging around with me for so long. To think that I once punted the Haitian's cranium for want of riddance!

Would I be Perseus bearing Medusa's head? Then surely am I soon to meet with Andromeda. (This is the Milky Way speaking).

Disguise myself as a doctor or a dentist to perform a medical Coup d'Etat?

How will I accede to the summits?

Foothill filibuster.

I have learned to live by dodging, to travel by taking the most convoluted path. Near Kiev, Pripipia to be exact, exist vast zones of leopard-skin contamination, patchy maps of death through which it is best to pass swiftly. Avoid pre-Pripipiatic feeding habits. Caverns are the best for lodging. Do not gather wild mushrooms, herbs or fruits, even if they appear mature and tempting. Let game go free. Slay not the wild pig and keep feral dogs at a safe distance. Never wash with or drink well water. If the surroundings turn deep red, pass immediately to a greener world, even if it's only a painted one. No need for an emerald universe; pistachio or even a drab olive color will do. Watch for red. Certain dragonflies will appear. With these you shouldn't attempt to converse. They may have ruby eyes. Beware of bay seeds that may find their way into table pepper, red fruit out of season, irritation around the eyes that can be attributed to crying (never forget that everyone here is emotionally unstable, highly over-sentimental); or blood from superficial wounds. It should be green too! Withdraw to deep forest area. Skin rash, sunburn, measles! All should now be green. If red persists, begins to appear in patches on leaves or in the atmosphere, return to red zone and chances are that you'll perceive everything there to be green by a simple effect of chromatic reversal. You must know by now that what you believe to see is indeed reality. This applies to law, history and just about any abstract notion that exists. If you discover that red really is the dominant color (rust is very often the first warning sign), go back to green. My name is Afeworki but I'm also known as Caleb or Wovoko. Call me Toussaint for the moment.

Realize that if I'm often absent, it's that I'm obliged to go to the Calabar Coast to supervise a launching project for putting into orbit the sculpture of a gigantic female nude. Ultimate homage to an Amazon civilization. It's disassembled and stored in paper-thin segments beneath sheds.

I've given other names and physical appearances. Many are improper. Please now, call me O.O. We haven't time anymore, for giving full names. Speak to me quickly, remember that even if I can resist extremely high temperatures, I still must turn the key in the ignition, get this vehicle going before it melts. The tires are already afire. It's a yellow Dodge SuperBee with black cowling on the hood. I've cut off the roof with a torch to convert it into a roadster. The back is loaded with statuettes looted from Indian graveyards. Not the graveyards of pre-Columbian civilizations, but more recent ones that are to be found within proximity of the reservation sites from which the last remaining American Indians were just eliminated by the legal application of

democratic rules which did away with their tribal structure. The lands
have been returned to the federal government along with the oil wells
which had been mistakenly attributed to the Indians. Prosperous casinos
built by the tribe now belong to the government too.

Don't be put off by my looks. I'm wearing Bermuda shorts that are
too small, squeezing the belly out against the steering wheel. Scars of
countless wars cover my skin? Self inflicted wounds!
It is while driving this vehicle slowly through a small midwestern
town that I cross paths with her for the first time. She's wearing a torn
tee shirt and jeans, barefoot, with hands handcuffed behind her back.
She's being escorted by the local sheriff, going on foot from the county
jail to the courthouse, a distance of about five hundred yards. The
sidewalk is blistering hot. This appears to have no affect on her feet.
Cicadas are making the air buzz.
She runs, jumps into the car with a summersault, and lands in the
passenger seat. We drive through a labyrinth of back alleys that are
often to be found in the immediate vicinity of the city square of small
towns, slipping past the rear entrances of pool halls, bars and run
down boutiques. There's no seeing into these shops, the doors being
closed to permit air conditioning which fills the air with a humming.
We're hungry but the little grocery store that I'm looking for, the one
that smells of fresh bread and sugar smoked ham, no longer exists. I
drive to a shopping mall at the edge of the town. We shop. The
supermarket is teaming with overweight, very white citizens. We fill
the trunk of the car with peanut butter (I'm thinking of George
Washington Carver), soft drinks, cold cuts, factory baked buns,
industrial bakery cakes loaded with frosting whipped into purple curls
and green twirls, several packs of frozen crawdads with spicy sauce,
napkins, paper plates and plastic spoons, catfish too. Lots of beer with
ice on the bottle. We'll picnic along the steep slippery banks of the
Marais des Cygnes River, somewhere between Nevada and Butler
Missouri, the name of the waterway being proof enough that *coureurs
des bois* made it here.
The scene where galaxies revolve very rapidly while approaching to
mate can be done by using models, but just as you would take
precautions with the preparation for the sequence of ships riding out a

tempest or that of a flaming tower, aware that the rendering of water and fire that are intended to be on a vast scale, often miserably fail due to the physical characteristics of wavelets, water droplets and flamelets which can very easily betray the small scale of your project by the timid forms that they assume, great care must be taken to assure the that the effect of tidal tails, the disruption of gas clouds and dust lanes, do convey an impression of incommensurable power at work on a scale that defies the possibilities of any cinema studios.

Equip this vehicle with two reverse gears, one for going backwards, the other for withdrawing from tight situations. Exchange the tires for spheres, which shall be chromed and incised with delicate patterns that are functional while evoking everyone's fears. Seek no code. There is none. Replace transmissions, drive shafts, with hoses that bring fluids to play on the shiny new globes.

Finally, we'll need no sophisticated transportation device to escape. The environs of Kinshasa will come to us, just as will entire portions of the universe. But before that, we'll have ample time to finish our picnic in the woodland while listening to forlorn train whistles and the raspy call of blue jays. Late autumn ants converge upon the leftovers. This is Indian summer. It's all that remains of the Indians other than some Chief's effigy stamped on the nickels in my pocket or perhaps the name of this place. Osceola.

The handcuffs are difficult to remove, being made of an unknown alloy, polished smooth with no hinge or keyhole. I feed her by putting the food into her mouth and raising drink to her lips.

We make love. She uses her mouth and feet with great agility.

—Have you always been bound?

—Soon I'll bind you in similar manner. Then you'll find that nothing's less certain. Your universe is like the smallest dark room with only one high window to which you haven't yet pulled open the curtain. Dusty and stifling in there.

Things will happen, more surprising than a blind man suddenly seeing, the very one whose pockets you regularly emptied while helping him to cross busy streets, a paralytic rising to walk, a dead dog running off, sending into the sky the vultures that had been feeding in his open belly. Things far more stunning will occur, proving irrefutably that nothing is definitive.

AKA

If you still believe that when we first met, it was I who dropped down from a tree on you, think deeper. Remember the feel of the spiny bark covering the limb from which you were waiting to pounce upon me, the tickle of poisonous leaves brushing against your face, the smell of oozing sap and over-ripe fruit that made your eyes sting. For all of these reasons, and many others, you were in tears when I came, walking down the path that passed beneath the tree you had chosen as your hideaway, the most uncomfortable tree of the whole forest.

Crying man who fell upon me. One who could no longer remain in ambush. I wonder if it wasn't a form of martyrdom that had been inflicted upon you? Did you not see the thorns of the tree? How they were covered with dead animals that had been put away there in storage, awaiting future consumption. The larder of some creature that would inspire the butcher bird.

Ah yes. But this was your tree and no one had forced you down into it; down I say because indubitably you were arriving from above when you first came to the forest. Only one freshly emancipated from the small curtained world that was yours, could choose such a perch.

Why is it that you wanted it to be I that would drop from a tree? Is it that I'm Black?

You learned many things with suddenness. Firstly, that generosity runs deeper in Blacks; forgiving seems to be abysmally anchored in our culture. Our souls are oceans, generosity lying between the bathyal and hadal zones. Unlike other peoples, we make not commerce of our suffering but go on to other horizons. Advance! That I know many things and not just concerning life in the forest, in spite of the fact that you had spent an eternity educating yourself in the little closed world that was yours, and that it was you the barbarian, the primitive tree-dweller with predator behavioral patterns which it would be good for scientists of African descent to study.

The wings we now have, were no god-given gift. There have been many miserable failures. Wingless men with beaks, women with bird feet and no feathers. If we are capable of flight today, it is that we have roundly paid the price in unsung suffering.

It's time that you unbound me.

Why am I handcuffed? Simply because I was the only person of color in town, though only passing through like yourself. Here, they honor

198

tradition with a museum that displays white capes and cone shaped hoods. True, the charge makes no mention of my race. This is forbidden. I'm simply the number one suspect in a shooting incident that occurred miles from here and centuries ago. Rules are rigid. Descendants of those who were ever eager to find and burn witches, while forbidding music, having no penchant for clemency.

—Talibans?

—No. Puritans, the founding fathers of America!

—Haven't they evolved?

—Certain things have come to transpire. For one, they no longer perspire but sweat through the mouth like dogs and reptiles.

Don't think these situations only arise in rural areas, there's just as much backward action in greatly developed urban zones where it goes completely unnoticed.

Splendid birds wait to be born aloft by rising air currents.

—Why is it that you pretend to hunt for possum in this woodland? I can?

—It is reputed to be stupid, a very primitive creature which has somehow managed to survive. Close to the very first mammal.

—And for this reason, greatly advanced. Zora Neale Hurston wrote in the chapter "Love" something you might want to reinterpret: "Love is a funny thing; Love is a blossom;/ If you want your finger bit, poke it at a possum."

Important government members hide in these small towns. They are dispersed throughout the Midwest and have no means of immediate communication with each other. Regularly they are secretly flown around the country, to other obscure locations. This is for their own safety. An all-powerful secret service runs the nation. Citizens are constantly given a positive image of their country through highly developed media. Have no notion of the truth. Patriotism is kept alive to the highest degree by periodically permitting foreign terrorists to perpetuate savage inexplicable attacks on innocent citizens. All out retaliation by the use of old war surplus in distant lands keeps public support on a high level. There's always a humanitarian touch with grain or peanut butter being dumped down on civilian populations along with the bombs. Ostracize those who dare criticize. They're no less than traitors. As for the terrorists, let's just convince ourselves that they're jealous of our way of living, of our values.

I prefer nettles, brambles and other undesirable wild weeds to garden plants. Why are they so despised by gardeners? Is it that they sting without even providing roses or fruit in exchange? Rather, wouldn't it be the fact that they can survive without our interference, that they needn't our help to thrive. Don't we prefer fragile specimens that require constant attention, new varieties that would never have seen the day without man's intervention, all the while making abundant use of herbicides against the wild ones.

She tells me that this is civilized point of view, that if I'd been born in the jungle, I might be capable of understanding that the vegetal world needs taming.

Perhaps she's right. Maybe plants really did coalesce to lure dinosaurs into borealic zones where they eventually died off. There would be then, a fundamental struggle opposing flora and fauna, no real symbiotic relationship.

Finally, are not these mutating mosquitoes? Purple sarracenia has become home to mutant mosquito that is immune to the aggressive digestive juices of the carnivorous plant. Genetic modification brought on by global warming spells due to massive pollution has led to new life cycle where winter dormancy is minimal. What began with Wyeomyia smithii has affected anopheles. Blood consumption is on the rise.

No medicine available for treating trypanosomia, the main ingredient, efloritine, having been monopolized for the fabrication of beauty creams sold here, at no modest price, to eliminate superfluous pilosity. May Africa sleep soundly!

This is evidently long before entire geographical sections of the dark continent come plowing into the West.

These long filthy streaks running down my face? Would I now too have musth glands? I wouldn't think of bamboozling you.

Highly infected, we kiss and shiver. Remember when we'll first meet down by the river? Beneath this same bridge, they'll roast your liver!

She's wearing wrap-around sunglasses designed by Christian Roth. In the reflection. That's where I see what's really happening. Small theatre. The image, though tiny, is crisp. The sound? Indirect, comes as an echo from distant hills. Permits me to connect the wisps of smoke I see, to the distant boom.

Slaughter again? No. Actually, beautiful things are being done all around. But it's dangerous to look directly. Can burn the retina, cause permanent blindness.

It's strategic warfare, bombing with more precision than you ever imagined possible. Taking out only the bad ones with no collateral damage whatsoever. Brilliant blasts, concise nuclear mushrooms hardly any bigger than the vapor columns of steam blowing off New York City streets in the winter. Performed by a ballet of minuscule drones, that fills the air like so many toys. And, many toy companies have already massively copied the models in preparation for Christmas sales. That's all that remains of Christianity.

—Don't move. Let's just sit here, hold each other tight.

Many people have turned to salt. Elephants, magnificent parrots, come in from the jungle to lick them.

Are you really disappointed? Had I promised you action in every chapter? How can I drive the idea home? That I'm beneath anything that could come to mind. A sub-anti-hero. The sort of person who'll slink away when challenged, wracked by spasms of uncontrollable fear at the mere thought of responsibility. Ready to divulge any secret at the mere idea of upcoming torture. Betray friends, loved ones; abandon anyone, even his very own children.

She kicks me in the ribs hard. Tells me to rise.

—Don't let yourself go! If you don't move now, you'll die. And this death will be the final one. There'll be no coming back, no modification possible this time. Get up! she screams directly into my ear, turning another light into my eyes, more brilliant than ten trillion suns this one.

Naively, I had thought that I had unlimited credit, that there was some sort of reincarnation ever available, like picking fruit from a tree. But autumn has come. It is a galactic season. One that will last longer than all of cosmic history.

I pull her shoe from my heart. This is no proof of sm. on either part. A hard strike was the only way to get me back on my feet. In love, don't cheat.

—Why do we constantly return here? In spite of the fact that in our wanderings, we've pushed back spacio-temporal limits? Habituation. Nostalgia. Devils reared in Hell will yearn to return there. Bringing along old political considerations. Handfuls brought to the mouth like jellybeans at Easter.

We live in underground parking lots, beneath bridges, along irrigation canals. I'm her pot wrestler, her kitchen mechanic. Do thriving business beneath winking neon lights. Firearms are readily available, have become an integral part of our civilization. Indispensable, like food or entertainment. Don't attempt to disassociate these elements. Communicate by shouts between bouts of splendid shoot-outs. Desert and jungle have both made their way into the city just as the city has encroached upon the desert and invaded the jungle. Down by the river's edge we do our wash, spread it out to dry along the shoulder of congested freeways where exhaust fumes will speed evaporation.

Possum=I can, (Latin). Strive for this from here on in and before.

Yllpo

It sounds like chinaware breaking with crystalline purity upon impact. But what comes down now is organic; carcasses of gnus with huge chunks of rotting vegetal matter, mud slamming into the street with a thud. Dry peat blows up dust.

Debris of God again.

Small altars are hastily set up before even the body parts go cold. Calvaries and oratorios.

Prayers are said.

Others have fled.

Some are dead.

—Remember the black rubber galoshes you wore to protect your feet from icy slush when you were a kid? They had the cleverest metal snaps, patented, that jingled when you wore them ajar.

Cheap with no insulation.

—Feet would freeze.

—That's just it. I'm sure thousands of them could be found to fit the feet of an army of children that would sweep through the country like Kabila's troops driving out corruption. Congo once became Zaïre only to become Congo again, however beautiful the concept of zaïrinization may have been. Zaïre again when?

—Compare what's comparable. This is the Occident. Borealic cunning developed over centuries.

It's only techno gloss, mascara of modernism covering what's Dark Ages once again. Mechanized medieval. The children are all about, waiting and willing.

—Where is Kabila?

She had in her pocket microscopic plastic bones and spider molt in a bottle. Exotikashun!

203

The carcass of God hauled down by the woman in the street. Was this merely what God wanted her to see of him? The reply that her recriminations merited? Or perhaps that is all there really is to him. One thing is certain: there are oversized teeth here, big enough to require scaffolding if you want to examine them.

Piles of rubble block the city arteries and deep pits into which one's eye is drawn are everywhere. Going down to depths never yet attained, water pours from the walls and cables dangle. Former structures are cleaved and sundered leaving cavern like openings, where there had been underground malls and tunnels and great vaults from which wealth once hoarded had been hauled. Pumps gurgle in the bottoms.

—Has the city suffered a bombing, deep and precise, gouging out immense pockets?

—Only real estate promoters. Having total immunity they dig with impunity, laying foundations for towers that will dwarf the decors of even the wildest science fiction films.

Here the deepest one plunging through bedrock with its central shaft bringing up heat from magmatic zones; this then would be the central spire, there those six pits cast about like ejecta circling a deep impact site, are the foundations for flying buttresses.

Something the size of a small bear but agile and most uncub-like, has been following me all day, remaining just at the limit of my peripheral vision. It has been grunting.

The buttresses will cast down passing night upon the city.

—Mirrors!

—On the north side?

—Do you remember the last Znamya projects? Lunar mirrors alternate with publicity, blinking down upon Cyana (if Earth has already been called Cyana, we'll opt then for Thalo) fragments of day into the night.

—Think.

—Tharae Klinfra.

There is a stench about the rubble mounds. Great moldering heaps, entire city blocks, whole neighborhoods smashed down and pushed into piles by mammoth earthmovers.

—Komatsu?

Furniture fragments, toys, shredded curtains sometimes blowing in the breeze between broken blocks of cemented bricks and splintered boards. But mostly a paste, everything pulverized and melted together. Indiscernible, man and building as one. It smells of dust here. Not the kind which comes down with sedimentary action, but rather the fine powder of time released with destruction.

—Hadn't they moved out the former occupants?

—The smell, you understand they're part of the rubble now. It would have taken far too much time to relocate them. History shows they are eminently recalcitrant, hanging on to habit and memory. There's no time lost this way.

—Thou shall not slow God-Money's stride.

—Chalk it off to terrorism, will you.

A green thing, the size and shape of a willow leaf, swirls in stool water. An expelled liver fluke of a new type.

With the snow, wolverines have come, digging into the rubble they hoard body parts and ferociously defend their dens from intruders. Looters seeking jewelry and gold teeth often suffer severe bites that infect rapidly.

Some of the mounds will be planted. Their natural shapes will make wonderful botanical gardens. The rest will go for landfill along the waterfront. Create sacred land? A great hatred can.

Build bayside marinas.

—Were not these then, the remains of collapsed towers following terrorist attacks?

—Assuming it would be so, these would be no looters but good Americans still trying to understand some two hundred years later, "Why us? We're supposed to be the good guys!"

Why have we come to Kroy Wen? Paw paws are ripe in Missouri.

We lie down together in a small room that gives onto the street. The child sleeps at our feet. The steam pipes that draw deep core heat through the building are impossible to regulate; control valves have been welded wide open.

I open the windows.

Jays call from somewhere.

There must be trees, or they have adapted just as pigeons once did to nesting in the anfractuosities of buildings.

The incessant roar of dump trucks makes it impossible to find sleep. Rhinoceros and elephants are every where in the streets; some are being washed, others are defecating. They are revered and left to roam freely just as cows once were in India. Sometimes there is a goring or a trampling but this is accepted.

Finally it comes. Sleep.

No longer in the office, I now organize entertainment. As I sit aloof in the corner of a vast bar, a middle-aged man with prematurely white hair comes straight to me. I know him from where? He sports a vest, silver diamond cross pattern finely sewn of silk with an elegant fleur de lys tie. It reminds me of when the French royalists hired me to sue Marks and Spencer for having printed the royal emblem on hygienic paper.

—Don't you recognize me? The necktie reunions that you used to organize...

Comes to me a young couple seeking a place to hold a fête galante. I take them beneath the flat keels of dry-docked barges.

—There! I tell them, —Between the steel scaffolding, in lapping seawater.

—We'll get cold, wet!

—But you're all set. There's a sense of intimacy here. We'll work on the lighting; you can do anything with lights. Think of how the reflections from the water's surface will send luminous snakes wriggling overhead.

Man with tie still with me. He's Haitian now. No hesitation, collapses in the street. He steps out of himself and helps me load his own body into my car. It's an old FireBird convertible with tattered top down, which greatly facilitates throwing in the lifeless body. There's only one seat in the rear to make room for the engine, which is to one side like with a Vespa scooter, making balance precarious around curves.

—You're not a lawyer anymore?

—Yes, still. But I have two jobs now. There's hardly anything left to defend. On the other hand, everyone wants to organize parties, society events in exotic *lieux*. Like your necktie thing. Only too bad it finished in such a sordid manner, all of that bondage and strangulation.

The car overturns in a curve ejecting the Haitian. Castro Soromenho had written a book on fate in Angola, bearing the title *Viragem*, which in Portuguese means the curve and much more. The turning point in one's life; just this sort of situation.

Oum Kalthoum faintly sings from within the wreckage as I *degage* myself from blowing steam, blood on paws.

The Haitian has gone through a display window; the body, headless, lies in a pile of Versace dresses turning the white fabric pink. It's just now I realize that he merely copied Courege on this model. But he used green on that short coat. Clever.

The trunk of the auto is jammed shut and the files for the case I'm going to plead are stuck inside.

—Dai mi un colpi di mano! I yell at a passing boy from little Italy.

—Verse yourself upon Giacomo Leopardi's Elogy to Birds, he replies. The silk vest fellow is gone.

I try to pry the trunk open with the arm of a mannequin from the *vitrine*, but it snaps at the elbow being a replicate of those models from an era when anorexia was fashionable. Finally, using a leg, I succeed. Inside is the Haitian's head but the dossiers are gone. The head would have eaten them? No matter. It shall be exhibit A. Imagine the sensation it will provoke when I plop it down in front of the Congressional Subcommittee.

—Ladies and gentlemen we have decapitated our Black community! Civil rights legislation has proven to be so much slumbering paper while over the years the government slaughtered rebels and encouraged drug addiction to guarantee that revolutionaries, never again would there be.

It's time we gave Alabama, Georgia, Louisiana and Florida in reparation.

—Traitor to your race! Are you no longer White?

My demeanor is grave. Not a fleck of blood from the severed head has stained the impeccable gray flannel suit that I wear.

She shakes me, awakes me.

—You know the places we could have crossed paths before?

—The Kamiokande neutrino detector or data from the Subaru 8.2 after refitting with infrared detectors; Voyager I beyond the solar system.

—Chances are you wouldn't have known what you were looking at.
—Nor you.

The predicted tropical storm has come; ripping high overhead it leaves all beneath unscathed. From the green clouds come the muffled cry of squealing pigs. Immediate mugginess sets in, thawing body parts that the wolverines had been hoarding.

Imprudent insects venture from their cocoons to partake of precocious spring while off the coast, waterspouts churn the pallid sea skyward.

One touches down on land. It's a full-blown funnel, sucking stuffed blue polar bear, dinosaur rib cage and Pygmy paranphalia out of the Natural History Museum before skipping across the Park to empty the Met, from Tiepolo to Gogodala.

In much the same manner that a tornado had once dumped bison down upon a besieged Mandan village saving them from starvation, these treasures will in their turn rain upon a starved people somewhere else tomorrow or yesterday.

—You can't eat paintings!
—Nor fossil bones or Babinga nets and whistles.

Workers started the construction of the flying buttresses before even that of the main structure.

Together we hold the girl upside down, strapping winking small red skates to her feet. Across the only remaining smooth surface she takes tiny crouching steps.

I'm reading *Sassou One Year After*.

Remembering the trees I had left there, in the Congo I mean. Cut at the base they release bubinga wine, the red fermented sap that spurts from the stump like blood from a severed head. Men and women would come bringing jugs and cans from the jungle to fill, drinking themselves ill, incapable of wielding chain saws. Always, I would be the first to slake my thirst. Drinking till my bladder would burst, I cursed.

Heat. Yet, wasn't I able to fell over a hundred trees (really big ones) a day?

Toads down by the bank are barking like dogs, their croaking grows to thunder with evening. A big boned girl turns the screws of a video cassette player with the tip of a bowie knife. She holds it firmly between the slippery black skin of her long legs.

There are three rivers here. The Kadeï and the Mambere join to form the Sangha which in turn flows down to the Congo just beyond its junction with the Oubangui.

Then we're near the Sangha reserve?

Just above it. But here there's no conservation here. You have only one bullet that cost you 100 francs CFA. You can use it to shoot a cephalope, hardly big enough to feed three, or a gorilla with plenty of meat for all. The decision is yours to take but make it a quick one before this black furry fellow slips away.

We study Whites. Two Italians came here twenty years ago. One opened a shop in the village, selling tins of double-concentrated tomato paste, black Asepso soap and other things. He married a local girl. His compatriot set up a repair shop to fix tractors and trucks for the Romanian logging camp. He married the sister of the other man's wife. Then these two Italians who had come thousands of miles to this jungle, couldn't find anything better to do than to cuckold one another, each thinking to be the only one to do so.

The entire village followed the clumsy tricks that each one deployed while coveting the other's wife. It was thought to be a European ritual. So evident was it to us what was afoot that no other explanation seemed plausible. The grocer would ask the mechanic to go fetch his truck that had broken down on the jungle trail. The mechanic would wait for the shopkeeper to go drinking with the Romanian loggers.

On the day of mutual discovery the grocer barricaded himself in his shop, firing with a rifle upon his rival who promptly returned, riding a Caterpillar which he drove through the shop. The grocer took refuge in the surrounding jungle, sniping from the bush for weeks during which no one was safe walking about, before finally disappearing forever. It had been a little Sarajevo, only greener and hot.

Probably devoured by a Black Panther. The biggest ones left on the African continent live right here and they have a very real talent for catching stray Whites. More silent than any other predator, the odor of stale milk, garlic and wine which exudes from the skin of a white man attracts them more than anything else, even more so than the scent of dog which passes for their favorite treat, right after pig.

There was a giant Ukrainian who had deserted the French foreign legion. No one knows why he had come here except that maybe it was just the farthest place away from that which he was trying to escape from. Whenever he was drunk he would go into the jungle and rape a Pygmy woman. They caught him in a raffia net like the wild pigs they hunt. Parts, his thighs, torso and arms, turned up on a market just across the border in oriental Cameroon, Yakadouma precisely. Very neatly presented, smoked and wrapped in broad banana leaves.

Others had come to place tiny black and blue plastic traps high up in the treetops to catch tse tse flies for medical studies.

On the high plateau lies Belemboke just between Nola and Salo; a Jesuit missionary has set up a medical dispensary. The furrows going to the pharmacy are understandably deeper than those leading to the chapel. We are often ill and up there, the air is better. You can see the stars at night, Tucana 47, and even begin to guess the configuration of the land, the hills, the direction of valleys and the rivers that drive through them. It is here that you sense, keenly so, and I have said it before, that the very land is a protagonist.

Europeans can dream of Switzerland or Normandy, forgetting the heat for a moment unless they too are taken by fever.

The Romanians have long gone, leaving behind all of the heavy machinery of the industrial saw mill. Impossible to take out even bolts which we could have beaten into knife blades. Two caterpillars brooding yellow masses are abandoned deep within the warehouse. Another one's in the riverbed where it had been left along with the sunken steam ferry.

Elephants come down to the river once again, not only for the morning drink but to bathe in the heat of the day.

In the middle of the river lies an island covered with the thickest vegetation, leaves virtually black, smoke rising from little fires where smugglers burn fur from the monkeys they prepare to eat. Chestnut colobes and cercopitheque are the best, ascagnus being more difficult to find. The District Governor resides here with his wife in a brick house abandoned by the French colonial administration. The Whites think he's a witch doctor. They bear him offerings, diesel fuel to run his air conditioner.

It's so cold in his house that you can leave game out on the tabletops. Beer bottles frost over. People come here for important affairs.

Pick your nose with an icicle.

You can find anything on this island. Viagra for the Whites who want to rival with the natives. Mortars and RPGs for rebel groups heading into either of the two Congos they wish. Contraband diamonds, uncut but any man's guess as to what's inside. Hard drugs arriving from Amsterdam or the Americas. The latest hyper-computer? Place your order!

We wear sealskin coats inside. White with gray spots and whiskers drawn back near the eyeholes. My wife's a beautiful woman from northern Angola. Lunda. Her father's village is Unita sanctuary countless centuries after Savimbi's untimely death.

We call this island of danger and abundance, Manhattan.

Chocolate water sucks around it, gurgling incessantly. It carries the perfume of the jungle: mold, rotting fruits, the piss of big cats and other things bold.

Upriver to either side, Bandas dig for diamonds along the banks, by hand with no more than picks. Tailings have formed little mounds over the years, just above the high water mark. But it is the Muslims who have always had control of the diamond trade here.

In Salo they're building a new mosque of cement. It has a beautiful little minaret. We'll bring blue tiles from Portugal.

Permit me to show you the way to my modest pilch. It isn't Orion that's straight overhead tonight, but a much brighter star, distant companion to the sun which has finally drawn in close. It'll serve to illuminate the path, throwing down more light than the full moon. At the zenith, Eridianus is no longer the river of pearls it once was, that led so nonchalantly to Canopus. The jungle belches clouds of hot vapor stored up during the day, momentarily engulfing the stars.

Crux rises just over a strange little mountain that's very close to the village. Something screams from the crest, utterly alone, bringing no echo or reply from the sleeping trees beneath. A pygmy dog has joined me, trembling against my leg.

Dairu sleeps with his long staff by his side. No one knows the path that leads to the mountain top. It's a forbidden subject. The entire world has been explored thrice over but no one has ever been up this little hill, for that's all it really is.

I strike out over the field that serves as landing strip for the rare craft that ever make it here. The pygmy dog follows. Day's warmth still rising from strewn stones between which serpents slip.

At first, low vegetation hardly waist high gradually growing thicker, then high brambles covering me entirely. Here, an abandoned house. Just walls and empty windows through which push young trees, yet this building can hardly be more than a few years old.

A path behind the recent ruin leads up through thorny trees from which hang pieces of meat. The butcherbird sleeps as I push through its larder. The going gets much harder.

Versailles! Indeed, at the top there spreads that vast palace which once adorned Paris's western side; taken down brick by brick, the entire chateau has been rebuilt along the crest of this small jungle mountain (And why not? Did not Napoleon bring back Egyptian monuments to the French soil? The Place de la Concorde's obelisk for example), the gardens with the fountains, gilded sculptures made of lead with intricate ancient plumbing systems. What splendid effect this ruddy water spewing forth from Triton's mouths! Just now, workers are employed at putting up the mirrors in *la Salle des Glaces* while in the surrounding park a young princess, hardly six, vaults well trimmed hedges of boxelder, riding a nervous Arabian stallion and pitches long lances through huge hyenas. These are no ordinary scavengers, but giant cavern variety brought back from periods of glaciation. Saber-toothed tiger and woolly rhinoceros also figure on the *tableau de chasse*. Tonight we're giving a Grand Charity Ball for the orphans of America, incessant ethnic wars having taken a heavy toll there. Endeared by the images of underfed little Caucasoids, we will give generously,

What was I doing erring in these junglelands, like a sleepwalker still clad in pjs, blundering through thick vegetation, scraping fire ants from my satin pants? Hadn't I obtained my diplomas from the University of the Ubangui? Wasn't I a state-employed schoolteacher, an administrator; a public employee living on a system, a caricature of the administration installed by the French in their colony. Bird droppings left behind by the colonizers after the independence. A much sought after, secure position, which, in theory, guaranteed regular income.

Things had gone well right from the start, the first president who was assassinated, had in common with the third one, that they were cousins from a western tribe of the Lobaye region that makes its home in the lowlands of the Ngoto forest, but especially the fact that the colonial authorities had publicly beaten to death both of their parents; altogether, four family members, for having dared to defy the newly imposed colonial tax laws. Women and children were rounded up in the villages and deported if the men had chosen to hide in the jungle to avoid paying the quota. A fatal deportation where they would usually die of pneumonia, tuberculosis or other respiratory ailments in damp poorly ventilated cells. And this third one, hadn't he been incorporated into the French army, fought a war for that country, become the president of his own newly independent Central Africa Republic where the French president loved to come on grandiose safaris returning to the land of camembert, Colbert and the Grand Robert with his pockets, satchels and valises brimming with diamonds. Hadn't the French especially encouraged this third one to follow in the footsteps of Napoleon, become an emperor in his own right? France had furnished the imperial carriage, the crown, the throne and seen to the entire ceremony making sure that it was truly a memorable one for the Centralafricans. This event was an amusement to the French, in the pure tradition of *singerie* paintings. Finally when the truth about the diamonds, the safaris and general carousing in the hinterlands made it to the ears of Parisians, it was decided that this emperor had to go, that he must have been a sinister ogre all along. Conveniently, he suddenly became a cannibal, children's bones where discovered in his refrigerator, he was put on trial, destituted and locked up while the French installed yet another president, this one a fearful little man who had briefly held office between the first and third ones; but the return of this second one was short-lived, an inconclusive experiment, he being so afraid of absolutely everything (and one can easily understand why), unwillingly thrust into this space so appropriately called the "parenthesis of death" by his fellow countrymen, he was incapable of taking the slightest decision. He left in a hurry, ceding his place to yet another president, this one also chosen by the French and injected to save the country. After ten full years by which time it became clear that there would be no promised democratic elections, the French had his witch doctor assassinated; in these zones, presidents have a way of cumulating power, often being clergymen of western formation with ties to the Vatican, abbots or bishops, as well as high-graded military officers trained in the school of war of the former

mother country (Saint Cyr for example) and invariably invested with
ancestral power that takes its roots in sorcery. The reunification of these
three forms of power serves to form a unique political concept. However,
kill the witch doctor and you've destabilized the ensemble.

Why this political discourse?
Atomic audit has proven that downwinders weren't alone.
Contamination was global, reaching even the deepest jungle sanctuaries.

The tobacco is a harsh one, coffee is *robusta* and the lion that frequents
the bushland of this area is of the meanest sort, I have said it before, the
most cunning hunter's hunter and with that, its tattered short mane
makes for the most pitiful trophy, (bring on severe case of ailurophobia).
The land is rife with diseases long eradicated in the West: polio,
meningitis, Aids, malaria, a plethora of parasitic ailments. There never
was any profit to be had here for the major pharmaceutical labs. But
then these people had become surprisingly resistant after having paid
the heaviest tribute.

Today is Unday. Neither Sunday missing the S nor Monday without
its MO. It's a day undone. A good day to engage informal subsumption
to incorporate what has traditionally been left aside.

How the once wealthy western nations had sown the seeds of their own
demise! I tire myself of telling you death had come from within. Draw no
parallel with the fall of the Roman Empire; or rather yes, I prefer that you
would. Power, hegemony bring on cynicism whereby the civilization, if
indeed we can call it so in the case of America, thinks itself invincible, and
perhaps is so, to a certain degree, materially speaking at least.

Haul off willy-nilly, take a pig in a poke.

As with the Roman Empire, midgets, court jesters, assassins, and
perverts all came to power in America. Never in full view though, they
were disguised, as handsome comedians, dashing politicians, men with
a grip on politics, loud-mouthed and carrying oversized sticks. These
were spiritual dwarves, buffoons and killers.

Expert at the politics of entanglement, self-endowed with the
authority to tread on scorpions and serpents while vaunting their own
bones to be tubes of bronze, these were thoroughly disingenuous types.

While we of the subcontinents, had grown stronger, genocide having had the perverse effect of an unnatural selection, that though laying low untold hundreds of thousands, millions even, had yielded unexpected generations of new finely honed survivors.

Rwanda, Liberia, Somalia, Sierra Leone, were so many laboratories for the Occident.

Think this part of humanity, the darker races, would merely have been shaking the tin cup for a few coins while showing their infirmities?

To resume, rampant illness rendered us resistant to the most virulent strains of disease while the economic hegemony of the West forced us to develop surprising parallel systems which in the long run cannibalized, and devoured the established world order, running through Lagos, Kinshasa, Algiers (it seems a paradox that such enclaves as Cabinda and Bangui proved to be perfect hubs from which to operate out of) tied in with Dubai, Singapore, Paraguay, Hanoi. Other zones that the West had wished to preserve in the spirit of a grand natural reserve, Borneo, Sumatra, Amazonia and Congo are now the center of thriving parallel industry. Hadn't there been a decree that any Africans living within game reserves, near the limits, or even in the surrounding countryside including major cities, should go native? No Western attire permitted! Wear leaves, sarongs made of vegetal fiber. Keep things pure. This is what Westerners want to see of Africa, Amazonia, Borneo too. Let's preserve mankind's natural treasures!

She gets boiling hot. Really angry now. Says that Occidentals had no qualms about burning down their own forests, killing off wildlife, polluting.

—Where are your wolves and bears? Woods and lairs? Spare us your dreams of virgin forest!

Meanwhile, jungle has gone north. Cities like Chicago, Stockholm and Tokyo have been completely swallowed up by tropical vegetation against which even the most powerful herbicides were to no avail, killing off the population rather than the vegetation.

Don't ogle at me so. Did I pledge to provide oodles of soothing blind patriotism? Hadn't I promised recurrent cliche political provocation?

—Haven't I made it perfectly clear that the West's worst fear, the spread of Islam, has come to be? It's a *fait accompli*!

You must simply learn to live with it. Isn't it the one religion that encompasses the others, a synthesis so to say? (this is Oloman speaking). He's here with us in Versailles on the crest, no passing visitor but an artist in residence. Writing a thesis on America's appropriation of the old German Mittlafrika strategy whereby Germany had attempted to cut the continent in two from East to West, joining her colonies of Tanzania and Cameroon in an effort to oppose itself to the North/South axis of Great Britain which ran from Egypt to South Africa. In turn, America adopted and applied this technique, leaving deep footprints in Somalia, Uganda, Rwanda, Zaire, Algeria and Angola, changing horses whenever necessary; for example, first riding with Savimbi's Unita before siding with MPLA and Dos Santos. Simply a question of what party presented the most potential in economic contracts, petrol, diamonds, nothing to do with democracy or human rights.

Teach man to do as he would be done by. Engage in heuristic adumbration. Survivors only prove failure, symptomatic of how short of the goal had fallen the West.

Needn't we deal more massively here, with these ontological problems? Let's take a break.

I'm wearing a large cape made of grass and bast, long tough fibers of the linden tree, over paisley design Roberto Cavali string underwear. If you wish, I can pull them down, peel back my foreskin and let you feed on some sloat:

Take the case of the remarkable Rwanda genocide. Follow the career of the Tutsi Paul Kagame who, momentarily wearing Ugandan uniform, was trained along with his officers in Fort Leavenworth Kansas Special Forces training camp. Mustered along the border of Rwanda they were waiting to intervene when a missile of American fabrication (surplus from the first Afghan conflict, the one against ailing USSR where the U.S. had trained a whole host of Islamic fundamentalists —including Talibans— along with future Algerian Armed Islamic Group terrorists that would later kill some 200,000 Algerian civilians), was fired by unknown troops bringing down the plane aboard which were just arriving from the Dar Essalam crisis summit, Juvénal Habyarimana and Cyprien Ntaryamina, the respective presidents of Rwanda and Burundi.

Let's assume that I'm to be your beadsman, paid to pray for the salvation of your soul. Simple mental deterritorialization. This'll be your cargo cult. One made of nettle and thistle.

Had enough of this Kung Fu fighting in the treetops? Off then to the place he kens of.

From up here, there's a splendid view on another hill, Mount Sinai (remember that nomenclature can be a very tricky thing here) where Von Lettow-Vorbeck's guerrilla troops almost made the junction. It's also Yulu-land, not Zululand, but the dominion of Fulbert Yulu, the Congo priest who could have saved Lumumba, a very fertile sector indeed for political reflection, and if inspiration is long in coming, just lay on your back beneath the night sky, watch the steam rise, masking the heavens, lose your bearings, forget even your own body, ridiculous small appendage attached directly beneath your head. You needn't any time-traveling device, no horoscath, just step into it, walk right into the ticking clock. You're nothing. Leave behind your liver, spleen, and bladder. If upon returning there's only a beggar's body available, infirmity riddled flesh, one crushed by life's woes, again don't hesitate. Try it on. Pretend that you're shopping in the most expensive boutiques along Rodeo Drive, that you've got unlimited credit, can afford the very best. Sure, it'll adhere, look in the mirror! Go live in a cave, misbehave, don't try to save the other *you* who was such a knave, don't even think of digging for him a grave, his bones now pave some cathedral nave. Don't put yourself in a position from which you'll be considered as the one who forgave, (this is whispered).

Her shoes! She too has been shopping again. They're set on high thin heels, the shape is perfect, sublimating the form of her foot, and just as in Cinderella, no other foot could possibly fit. But these slippers aren't made of glass. They're covered with fine fur, encrusted with small chips of ivory (see, elephants still wander here) upon which are incised miniature erotic scenes. Wasn't I entrusted with the concept of chivalry? And not only these. Another fine pair: pale emerald satin covering the most sublime shape, thinnest high heel that elevates the hind part of her foot to the limit of what is supportable, a tassel of diamonds falling from the ankle that gently swing and glitter with each step. Christian LeBoutin of course! In this game I'll be the entrant. Epée drawn, I'll protect my princess from those who cast their Eolithic eyes upon her.

Hush! It's my turn now, to cover your mouth and nose as you once did mine. Listen to the panther pass. You'll here his belly gently gurgle while he digests the remains of Italian immigrants, (it got both of them). The palm I place over your face smells of time stolen from star cradle, borrowed from dying galaxies. Light scooped up in a ladle. Yes, these things have a scent that leave their trace just as smoke does when passed through. Together, we've all been hauled down from there; we're just unaware, having no memory, preferring warfare which though sometimes truly noble, just doesn't compare.

It's not because of the passing feline that I quiet you. Don't criticize this *rapprochement*. You did give me *carte blanche*, didn't you?

She sleeps fitfully, awakes with a migraine. Opens a deep gash in her father's face with clean sweep of kitchen knife. This happens while we're seated at breakfast table. Blood gushes into his coffee. He's not her real father anyway. He tried to molest her when she was ten. Her real father was a French colonial judge doing his apprenticeship in the African colonies. Had lived with her mother for a year before leaving for another colony. This all documented by an ethnologist in a remarkable book, *Un ancien royaume Bandia du Haut-Oubangui*. It's all written there. She's the grand daughter of the most powerful African queen, direct descendant of sultans. But the cut wasn't for that. Reaction to comment on how Africans "just burn down the forest with no consideration for ecology." That's all. Will need a good thirty sutures. She sews him up like the butt of the stuffed guinea hen we ate last night, using thick thread and oversized needle. He doesn't even wince. We finish our coffee, smoke some cigarettes. Agree that he should watch what he says being that he has several *metisse* children of his own.

Morning mail has arrived. Much publicity, pile of bills and other reclamations. Go through it wearing bio-warfare gear.

On the wall are portraits of myself. One is a large photo of me wearing some kind of military uniform with many medals pinned to the chest. Another is a finely painted canvass with massive gold frame. I'm holding an AK-47.

Banish transition. Read Doctor Fagunwa. Frigate birds now fly these skies. Ants carry eggs shaped like tuning-forks.

Go to deeper abyss. Down here, the child can reorganize her bedroom, learn to play with small lights to attract extremely shy fish.

When swimming at the surface, push away bloated cadavers farting from post-mortem fermentation in the intestinal tract.

Live in a fossil world. But don't think that we're secure. Remember, we're no safer than the trilobite awaiting the rock hammer's blow.

When discovered, we'll be forced to do guard duty. Instinctively, know that sentinels are destined to be neutralized. Abandon the post. Shut your ears to screams that arise.

Reality is a blunt obtuse thing thrown across our path like the low stone wall hidden in the field which abruptly halts the journey, shattering the knees. Thought to have been traversing virgin prairie? What's this that crunches underfoot? The bones of countless dead!

—Be this instinct?

—I haven't any.

Yet I possess a certain ability to recognize in a very animal sort of way, scent, sound, varying degrees of darkness, certain kinds of light and to feel humidity and temperature fluctuations.

Reduce communication to a flicker. Yearn for remoteness.

Does suspicion of impending doom seem to be your travelling companion? It's a dismal day, this one. The fault's not yours. Clouds hang immobile sprinkling the land, pearling from leaf tips. Mist rises from trees. Not as smoke which would simply blow away but more like the ink of an octopus refusing to dissipate. Cloud of doubt.

When weather finally clears off (don't worry, it eventually will; this is no giant gaseous planet is it?), wait for nightfall. Leap through Scorpio's claws, Zuben Elschemali, Zuben Elakrab just beneath Zuben Elgenubi.

In the city now. Cinema has become a domestic affair. Implosion. All homes are fitted with cameras in every room, especially washrooms, bedrooms and toilets. Spectators stroll the streets, going from door to door where small screen show what's going on inside.

K2 has new shoes. Low boots cut from two human faces sewn together. Zipper wraps full round twice. Opens through eyes and mouth. "Speak'n look shoes." Talk and see.

Before birth, children have learned to choose their own names. Places of power and beauty. It is said that a river, spring, or creek can influence them even from a great distance; water's never far.

Carceral art has become blue-chip value. Art dealers have invested in works produced by prisoners living in deep mineshafts. No loss. All profit. When they're uninspired they polish little perfume bottles for the couture industry. Prisoners provide the very cheapest labor.

Drink celestial liquor. Carry armor-piercing ammunition. Keep three treasures. Induce sneezing to shake nuts from trees.

Were there to be sudden universal peace, no more war, tragedy or incomprehensible cruelty, would God be simply bored, suffer from severe withdrawal symptoms, or might he even become mortal and die?

Leave all belongings behind. Become a skeleton. Make yourself a cactus costume. Adopt an elf owl.

Winter has come.

I have been having a very special tattoo made. Black now covers my entire body, except for tiny specks of white reserve. This is no attempt at becoming an African. Simply a representation of the night sky, the pale dots standing out like the faintest of stars lost in celestial immensity.

Naked, I sit curbside where passing traffic throws icy slush over me. I munch frozen mint syrup with ice. A female elephant pisses. Urine torrent that turns into sharp ice shards and tinkles while falling. Take them up. Spear anyone who comes too near.

Instant summer sends children climbing into the upper branches of mango trees, beyond the reach of those wielding long poles from the ground. Avoid green mambas that slip from limb to limb. Gather the fruits and let them drop into the shirts that other children hold like open nets beneath the trees. Splat! A child falls, blue stain and twinkling small cloud.

On the methane beach, by big green fire, read to me from "Cane." Scratch harder cunt! Be thy nails blunt?

Someone has been following me for a long time now. Someone of unexpected. A child, a small girl? Physically, she's much more agile than me. Can track me down anywhere. Formidably cunning. Impressive intelligence. What am I to do? How to evade?

Out some distance from the shore is a ship. On the deck lies a swaddled sword sheathed in down. None know it to be a weapon.

No hill is this mound upon which we have transposed the palace. It's an evil hornito, emitting toxic vapors from its sides. If we dwell here too long we'll suffer ham's fate. Move again before it's too late.

Onandaga

The file on me states: *"He comes up out of the street; not through trap doors or sewer plates. He just emerges from the ground. Steps out of it, strikes incessantly at invisible things and blunders into that which is real, things he apparently can't feel, i.e. buildings, cars and other objects, as if he doesn't see them."*

I hear bagpipes playing, which I hate. Must keep moving like the shark drawing water over its gills. Immobility would be fatal to me.

Try to locate a wild dog bitch. They have at least twelve nipples, sometimes fourteen.

The streets are slimy. Atlantic climate dumps rainfall and draws in fog. Great pumps bring up water from the river. Some of them date back to Louis Quatorze with wooden wheels and leather belts hauling up the water from the bottom where the silt is the thickest. It's a damp place. New varieties of bacteria and all sorts of water-born diseases are evolving.

I'm feeling very dense. The entire city has drawn its weight down upon me. Unable to sleep I walk the streets conversing with buildings. My shoes push through the sidewalk. The surface breaks around the soles like thin ice, leaving prints behind.

We no longer have light bulbs but burn tallow fat candles. The plumbing has been ripped out and beaten down into copper ceremonial shields. We are obliged to go down to water holes, balancing basins and buckets, the largest possible, upon our heads.

There are no stars visible from here by night, only large clouds of toxic gas sublimated by the powerful beams of searchlights.

Around the water holes, predators lurk, contemplating patterns of scum that form, swirl and dissipate beneath volutes of thrown off steam.

—Protective suits are of no avail. Remember ghost shirts, the panther costumes of the Anionitas, Vungara vegetal robes, all supposed to protect those so clad.

—Against bullets?
—From Whites.
—Evil be then pallid?
—The theory is valid.

An archeology of light in that all upon which we gaze, remote yet ablaze, is no longer as we see it. Our senses are lost in a haze. Astronomy and astrophysics are sciences of the past.

Were you now to pace that world where a merchant once brought spiders, only their skins would you find there, riding winds so gentle that they remain intact, eternally floating.

—How then to see the present?

—To be close is the approach. Even if separated by this table, an arm's length no more, we don't see each other as we are but as we were nano-seconds ago.

—Together then?

She sits upon me, rubbing hard over my waist, up onto torso and upon chin. Her skin soft and oily. I push into the weight of her body. We are one. Scent is mine, hers mingled.

—You can return to Cyana. It is a weakness I can concede but beware, don't recede.

At the time she speaks these words, a hundred guns are at her service. She dominates the valley from a palace made of fiber, bone and stone.

—The fire you stoke burns green.

These caverns haven't changed. They once had an Indian name. Later, tourists visited them. Now a king reigns down there. He who howls from the wolf's mouth. The bear spares him. Hard to kill, he has valuable knowledge.

I had expected this kingdom to be blind, colorless and cold. I find creatures of great cleverness that are bold. Their sight is keen; eyes are large disks resembling those of certain prehistoric fish, in no way atrophied. They can detect incoming comets years before their arrival. Rise from wells seeking hells, roam between four and five bells. 'Tis the hour of thieves.

One admitted to a night club by chance is elected best disguised of the evening. Glistening stench upon which all marvel trying to guess the secret. How had he done it?

A bath of fermenting hagfish. The rest is easy; phosphorescent powders exist.

Before going back down he slips past the ruins of an observatory, his large eyes blinking at the faint glow of remote pygmy galaxies that astronomers never were able to detect.

There is nothing of human about them though they look much more so than we who have developed tails.

The Cavern King rejects the gifts I bring.

—We have all of this and much more, (voice coming from windpipe).

Everything here is slowly fermenting. Chinquapin husks and toy ducks fashioned from vegetal matter brought down from above. The call of the loon, thing they love, resonates. There is mold but nothing is old. Down here they have grown spontaneously, overnight, as flies once were thought to do.

My tail is pale with gray spots like sealskin.

—What else do you have to offer?

They are disappearing, receding along the cavern walls, withdrawing down great halls.

Escapes King-Clever.

It will be years before I have another chance to capture him. Beneath a rotten log in Sarawak. Be teeth, forgotten fog on the Kamak. From this journey I shall return empty-handed.

Deep in the cavern, sleep falls upon me. I'm in a law firm office with a view on a golf course. Smog has set in, making the greens barely visible. I'm arranging in a great circle around me, dossiers that I must review in preparation for a case which isn't yet anywhere near pleading. This is only the preliminary stage of Discovery.

Just as Samson had with the jawbone of an ass, struck down a thousand Philistines, so shall I with this maw clone made of glass, take myself many brown palace queens.

The impossibility of the deed, the probability that I succeed.

The zoo has been closed; the animals sold off to the owners of small circus and menagerie. Some have been shot and stuffed to replace museum exhibits devoured by mites.

In ocean troughs deep beneath the surface, sperm whales engulf giant squids after stunning them with paralyzing blasts of ultra-sound. We know nothing of them.

—Tell me, what do you think they prey upon? A single sucker is a twelve-inch disc lined with teeth, the cusps of which would pull off your face! What is it that they chase about after in this cold black place? The pressure down here is like that of an enormous planet with dense atmosphere.

—Stomach contents indicate things luminous.

—It's the only one with skin bituminous.

Part of the street is ablaze with sunshine that falls circumspect like a spotlight in an ugly little theatre to illuminate a pile of bright pink vomit. Small mountain with an artificial hue. I'm sick whenever I'm away from you.

It's now recognized the world over that politics and warfare are the highest forms of art. Kakugi Percival Nguamu (aka Iiunga), was a precursor operating out of his jungle sanctuary years go.

Using humanity as primary material like the artist's palette or the sculptor's block of stone, creating with it and then destroying. The formal syntax of war. Civilizations carved in the round alternating with zones left alone. Very sophisticated structures with clever formal devices. An elegant alternation between carved masses with smooth surfaces and areas decorated with simple incised geometric patterns. When studied, war presents all of these aesthetic qualities, rhythmical modulation of volume, tension of line, surprising precision with effects of balance.

When I awake, the cavern is gone. People are in the streets belching flame. It is a new custom, finally fulfilling the desire for possessing fire within one's mouth which smoking cigarettes had only partially satisfied.

Two men seize me.

—Prowler! together they scream, pilot lights glowing dimly in their round open mouths.

They have fur on their hands, purr as my hair stands.

Leave, arms separating from my body at the shoulder joints. A greater sacrifice than the lizard's tail cast away, but just as effective this last day.

Away to that zone where minor planets and stones with craters bear names. She was right in that I shouldn't have receded. Not even for the cavern dwellers. How shall I embrace her without arms to hold? Slither and roll, serpent! Shiva or an arthropod should I have been.

Perhaps, slowly they will grow back. Nothing is less certain.

Amongst asteroids.

I have taken along Lutz D. Schmadel's *Dictionary of Minor Planet Names* but it is of limited assistance to me. Leafing through can only be accomplished by using the tongue. The pages end up sticking together from accumulating saliva. I wear the accompanying CD as a labret.

Limpopo is the name of the first stone upon which I make my home, mostly composed of the silicate so common in this zone; plagioclase feldspar and pyroxene. I'm standing knee-deep in fine-grained regolith! My allergies are acting up. Must quickly change habitat. Transfer to JE_1, Aoki which is quite charming but covered with cutting asperities, Benua then and UQ_{11} before approaching Mariobotta and then going on to Morpurgo. It is a rugged world this one, similar to Gaspra in size but much more abrupt. Ejecta material and space weathering have conferred to her a bluish patina. The girth of certain craters is impressive, gouged out from the metallic surface with clean circular sweeps often leaving enormous empty hemispheres that go down half a mile or more. Rims are steep, thrusting hundreds of meters from the surface. The day that two big strikes hit simultaneously from opposite sides (or even at intervals), there will be a window clean through Morpurgo. That day shall surely come, for coincidence becomes a certainty given enough time.

I begin to appreciate the similarities, dynamic at least, of transneptunian and cisjovian objects. How different they are from those lurking in the Oort belt. Hardly a glimmer comes from these ones that are much dimmer. I walk endlessly, the sheer joy of being able to attain the horizon without it slipping away and once upon it, falling off or actually being jettisoned in some entirely unexpected direction. No need for arms here!

Abrupt edges. The thrill of pitching stones from my mouth and having to dodge them as they hurtle back towards me at terrific speed. Or, better yet, playing catch with myself; using my teeth like a happy dog tossing his bone. No risk of breaking the fine points sharpened by Twa tribesmen. There's no weight here. It's like snapping floating feathers from the air. I'm all-alone!

From here to BU, WK and HA. Glowing green from olivine or sombre with carbon. Onward to others un-catalogued, remote or dark even drinking in light, beyond absorption. I name them now, these newly discovered ones: Ganges, Mekong, Oblate, Cheetah, (obviously yellow, mackled and exceedingly swift). Oatcake (gritty but edible), Darfur, Uèlé (hardly more than a pebble, this one is alive; the nucleus of a tempest moving amongst the others) and Ndouroutérétimo where when you stride forwards, you actually move backwards.

You see that I have chosen the names of rivers that I know well. Also Darfur, that region of western Sudan where the standard-winged nightjar mates, casting down its long feather pennants that litter the dry ground before nesting. When this bird flies it appears to be pursued by two small bats hovering above each wing. Just like the hornbill, it is also attracted to brush fires, lancing with its beak those small animals driven out by the flames. But foremost, Darfur is an empty zone swept clean by slavers and endless small wars.

Ndouroutérétimo means "close to your body" which Zanda would endlessly whisper to me, barely audible low warm and clinging; morning vapor rising from the Sangha river deep in the heart of the Central African Republic.

How had we first met? Perhaps arms shall erupt from my shoulders while I think of our first encounter.

A small transistor propped on my shoulder, I had been crossing the Rue de Rivoli while listening to a Haitian song, *Si ton cœur était mon garde-manger*, when I had had with Zanda this first of our many first encounters. A fine rain was coming down over the city. Most everyone had an umbrella or a raincoat. I was wearing a small plastic grocery bag on my head, the handles hanging down around my ears, giving me a perfectly miserable and ridiculous appearance by European standards, but I had seen Pygmies do this with discarded wrappers left by eco-tourists. Other peoples as well, most of them treasuring from there on, this newly found rain gear. Suddenly she cut in front of me, her head and feet bare. With each step she took I could see that the flamingo-pink soles of her dark feet were leaving perfectly formed hot, dry footprints on the wet pavement. Her shoulders were broad, the skin burning. Even the fabric of her dress was dry from the heat radiating from her body. The drape, the fold, the way the fabric clung to her hips, rising slightly over the thighs with each step, all spoke of fire within. She was volcanic.

Incapable of keeping up with her, I followed the trail of heat that she was putting down until I found her again sitting on a city bench, searching her bag for a cigarette. To each side of her, the freshly fallen rainwater pearled to form little puddles reflecting the sky, gone magenta with the day's end. Lighting the cigarette she rose, smoke rolling down slowly off her half-open lips. Gums azure, teeth fluorescent. Eyes long and oriental drawn to needle curves at the edge. Without a glance for me she departed, leaving a hot patch on the bench. Was it the odd dislocated walk I had? Broken hips.

I knelt. With my face to the trace, I felt.

—Why does he pray there in the rain? a passing pale boy had asked another one with him.

Down by the river I had caught up with her. She spun her head with a fierce glint in her eyes. And then slowly, deliberately, she took the cigarette from her mouth and flipped it at my feet, sparks showering in the gloaming. She didn't turn and walk away but just stared in disdain. Picking it up I put to my lips that which had just been upon hers and drew the deepest draw.

She had shaken her head in disbelief and walked away swinging the long blond hair of the wig she wore, over her dark shoulders.

I remember the taste of that cigarette butt, strong, the flavor of danger.

At that time her name was Zanda. This I wouldn't know until much later. Back then, I would have named her Typhoon I think, or some other name denoting strong turbulence. Thinking her gone forever, I had paced the bridge over the river late into the night. I think that that's when I fell in love with the river and its bridges that lie now all in heaps. Very early in the morning, a tear in the violet clouds over the city had revealed a deep blue patch of sky where a comet's tail drew a curve of phosphorescent green mist. It had later collided with the sun setting off the most violent solar flare, proof enough that it had probably been moon sized, much vaster then any of the asteroids where I now hide.

They are sparse these small worlds. Though apparently clustered when viewed from afar, it is difficult to glimpse another one from in here.

Exile? In no way.

Assessing damage: I still haven't upper limbs, and certainly no wings. This is the perfect place to lick my wounds.

We have taken his arms to the laboratory. Analyzed the sleeves of the jacket and the shirt, sampled dirt from beneath the nails. Examination of the light that poured from the open veins was non-conclusive. Drawn broken fangs from beneath the skin. Some sort of time keeping device beneath the skin of the wrist. All was labeled and stored for future reference:

Unknown substance, organic.

Vomerin teeth.

No reasonable explanation for what appeared to be brilliant light but has since faded dramatically.

Some kind of ceramic tile like that which used to be employed to protect the underside of incoming shuttles.

A strange sort of soil.

This report is signed, countersigned and classified.

She has given me rendezvous in a small Vietnamese restaurant, perfect copy of the one that used to be Rue de la Verrerie. I have disguised myself with prosthesis that look like arms but are not, obliging me to ram the door with my shoulder to enter.

—Bring me drink in shallow cup.

From the street a woman comes leering to the window, her face underlit the same green as the mint syrup that I lap, dog-fashion, from bowl.

Peering in, she examines attentively a display of rigidly plastified food with a fork riding an upward spiral of noodles.

Salivation.

It is then that I realize that this woman is she. Zanda!

Salivation.

Once seated by my side, she speaks not a word but first eats. Raising her lips in a snarl she dips a strip of fish in sauce, noisily sucking but never chewing or swallowing. She breaths heavily, the air here clearly too thin.

Panting, she looks up at me over the debris of her repast, dark sauce having formed around her mouth an explosive pattern that she doesn't wipe away.

—Maybe it's a mistake being seen together, I begin.

—The only mistake is believing that it took four and a half billion years for intelligent life to evolve here while in reality life of a higher form has already developed independently, only to disappear several times over this period, leaving no trace, or so deep down that it will never be found.

—Deep down? You're suggesting that there could be fossil traces deeper than ever suspected? That's absurd!

—Tectonic plates don't merely push each other around, separate or overlap. They can also plunge deep towards the core, sounding and taking with them the traces of entire civilizations.

In the corner of the restaurant there is a red lantern that illuminates a little cavern within which is seated a small Buddha. Our girl would always leave the table to go there.

—Race religion and territory, I suggest.

—Apply the nature, its topography, to the plan of things. What is commonly referred to as destiny. How one valley, a river will bring inland an enemy that would have otherwise continued his way down a coast. Mountain passes, pinnacles and broad open plains all play their role. It is in a way they who command. These are the real protagonists!

—Should we then observe the way galaxies and groups of them fit together? Study more attentively the patterns of their distribution?

—Life here being the smallest parenthesis, she mutters, slowly, deliberately plunging her hand into a bowl of oily hot egg noodles and withdrawing it shining.

—How far out of balance can we get? I saw you looking at the lion, remembering. The lion looking at the gazelle in another cage across the alley, it could have been a valley, yearning. Mandrills eating lettuce and carrots while the cercopithec with brilliant turquoise testicles climbs a cement tree.

—You too have sky blue balls, she whispers in my ear as she passes her slippery hand into my pants.

—Think of medicine, she continues, lubricating me with her fingers which feel like lips and tongue.

Inadvertently I caress a fake plant that is here only for decoration. But this plant is real. Some of its leaves are dying, yellow and brown. Malady a gage of veracity then? Apply this to other beings.

At this point there is an uncontrollable warm inundation.

—I shall adopt a new rhythm of sleep while we are here? Two hours during the night and brief three-minute intervals spread out over the day, I propose.

She leaves the pants unbuttoned with my penis hanging out. It continues to drain on the floor.

I'll be incapable of putting it away without her help. I knew that, without hands, something would be amiss, but not this.

—Look at yourself. You are already incapable of staying awake in this restaurant, your brow is one big wrinkle, your eyes are black with fatigue.

I'm incapable of communicating any longer by means of an evolved language. With no hands, signs are out of the question. Reduced to the use of infrasounds and pheromones.

In my mind I write again the *Book of Fever*, remembering Majabat al-Koubra, those impenetrable dunes in oriental Mauritania.

Suddenly she seizes me by the nose, covering my nostrils with the palm of her other hand, not the oily one. I can hardly breath.

Using infra-sounds I ask her what she is doing. She rumbles back with a very low noise like that which comes from the elephant's belly,

—Keeping you quiet as danger passes close by, so that you won't be heard. They're just behind this wall now.

I remember how Mungo Park on his way to Tinging Tang had clasped his hand over his horse's flews in just such a way, keeping it silent as danger passed close by the thicket were he had taken refuge. It was the narration of this surprising act which had proven to me the veracity of his entire account and in the same way I now know that here lies reality; that my arms have indeed been taken from me and that the world of offices and legal affairs which I enter upon with the coming of sleep, though somehow related, is in fact where the dream is to be found.

The palm of her hand smells of smoked game, earth freshly turned up and crushed pepper of the most violent variety. Odors that I have long associated with Africa, the deepest zones where there pass no visitors, where fish possess heads in the form of projectiles permitting them to point directly into violent torrents. Regions where lakes fall onto the land making it shake. Lightning there has color; violet, green and sometimes the yellow of topaz.

They are so near now that we can hear their scales scrape.

—What name be yours tonight?

—K2.

—Katu?

—No, the letter K and the number 2.

—Like a robot or some sort of techno nomenclature?

—For the most fearsome peak of the Himalayas, the one that makes Everest seem the peaceful country hill.

From beyond the wall comes the call of a seal. It is someone coughing up fluid in the final stages of lung cancer. Pints of pleural liquid. But I'm stuck with the seal image, the sheen and the smell of its oily pelt, something that I know I've felt. Was I once an Inuit?

Odor of a mackerel not so fresh, the brushing of stiff whiskers. Broken chunks of ice mackled with black blood. I knew it!

The cough becomes a desperate fit of choking. The tumor, it must be a really voluminous one, has taken a grip on the aorta, the trachea even. It ruptures filling with blood the lungs and throat of he who lurks beyond the wall. A purple fountain welling up. He sprays the alley with the content of two full lungs before going down. He'll not have my other leg.

It's raining again. The blood washes away bringing bulldog sharks up the muddy brown torrents that sweep through the streets. Few people realize they can come this far inland following rivers for hundreds of miles seeking filth or wading prey. Their attacks are wrongly attributed to binga fish or hippos.

We walk in the rain, face up, mouth open, drinking down all that city poison which the sky has for so long stored in brooding low clouds.

—It is time we returned to the jungle. But first, let me develop formidable spear-like appendages, the unicorn's lance, something that will instill fear at a glance. Horns that spiral and soar, like the kudu's or those of the more elusive bongo that keeps to the deepest forest thickets. The cock of the boar too, a more viral spiral with which I shall ram my sow, planting the grain with such force that never shall it drain.

Resolutely, we head out of the city, following the riverbanks. It's raining hard and all is blue, not a violent light but an eerie hue. Tcherenkov light!

In the suburbs now, the banks are littered with broken micro-theatres, pieces of horoscaphs, countless soiled mattresses. Here someone has diced the foam rubber of a pillow. There lies a carpet, a fine Ismir that's a pale sand color with an exquisitely woven design. Cast away in the mud. Be it a magic carpet? One upon which we could, perhaps, ride?

We nap, curled together in the roots of a willow.

Daybreak. Dogtrot.

It's an industrial zone with small houses nestled between giant crumbling factory chimneys, vegetation reclaiming the land and becoming more and more dense as we advance. Baobabs and fichus thrust through buildings, vines wrap around walls. Cyprus trees vie with iroko for the right to destroy what man's hand has wrought.

Just as certain dreamers used to build ships far from the sea in the quiet of their suburban yards, nurturing the hope of some day circumnavigating the globe, the prow of their project jutting over the garden wall or the poop emerging from the garage, here too now, weekend hobbyists construct from kits, cheap time machines with which they hope to reclaim the time they have invested and much more. Most of these efforts never go beyond the preliminary stage and the hulls lie gathering moss and bird nests if the termites haven't yet eaten through the wooden framework.

Some have in haste, decorated the interiors, covering old automobile seats with sheepskin, anachronistic steering wheels and rearview mirrors with panther pelt, felt and shiny tassels, after having abandoned the propulsion problem. A few have built modest sized particle accelerators, usually favoring a figure-8 configuration rather than the classical circle, even if it meant a life time's effort, hacking through the encroaching jungle, cutting through the neighbor's lot and fighting ensuing feuds all the while unwaveringly pursuing the ultimate goal: time itself which somehow seems to be taking on momentum to escape ever farther just when success is near at hand.

But many have been successful in their efforts, as here a happy family carefully unloading nodosaurus eggs from their well kept ttd (time travel device) which has just returned from a weekend trip to the Cretaceous beaches of the Tethys ocean. The children have sacks full of pocket-sized early mammals destined for pet shops.

Momentary indisposition due to mechanical bowel problems. Intestinal obstruction as result of ingestion of hair balls.

A neighbor has installed immense aquariums in the steamy shaded alley next to his dilapidated wooden shack. Using my forehead to rub the condensation from the glass walls, I can just make out the shapes of perfectly immobile, massive Precambrian stromolites immersed in blue-green water.

Along the river aways, anglers are barbecuing their catch of jawless Ordovician fish and Silurian acanthodians which have been reintroduced into the Seine and its tributaries.

A master craftsman has set up shop in the ruins of a small factory, turning out perfect handcrafted models of different designs for ttd connoisseurs. One is shaped like a polished dolphin skull, another has the form of a teardrop with no visible seams or entry port. None are very big though. These are sports models for the bachelor or a couple accompanied by a small child at the most. They are very swift and difficult to control with any degree of accuracy. You may very well miss your target or even enter abyssal time. Returning to the point of departure is a gamble.

Various propulsion options are stored on benches in the open shop: an ancient Maserati engine (probably taken from a model SM Citroën), containers of metallic hydrogen sampled from Jupiter's core, coal sacks, pouches of deeper fossil fuels, ores and oars next to a jerrycan of activated dark matter.

Behind the shop there's a junkyard of ttd's that have served their time. Mounds of broken carcasses and vegetal matter from which leak an organic soup that forms pools of smoking waste.

Embedded in the fender of one machine is the broken off tusk of a mammoth, another bears the scars of an encounter with carnivorous Devonian whelk, which taken along by returning naive holiday travelers, devoured all within and half of the working parts before the vehicle somehow miraculously crashed into a city park gazebo where surviving musicians of the Spiny Bark Passes group who had been playing neorap, tore the gorged mollusks from their shells and immediately scratched out new melodies on the hollow convoluted husks. The giant gastropods were left to die in the blistering sunlight with no consideration for paleontologists rushing to the scene to examine the hitherto unknown specimens.

"Flagrant example of the growing schism between the scientific and cultural communities," read the headline of newssheets of the day. Someone has partially covered the interior of the wrecked vehicle with the cover story, pasting the pages to the cowling like wallpaper in an anonymous gesture which can be diversely interpreted as the manifestation of deep cynicism or profound respect to the memory of the deceased.

Sweet smoke emanating from clandestine rum distilleries floats in the air as we near fields of unkept sugar cane that surround abandoned high rise towers of ancient low income housing projects.

—We're almost there, so close to the jungle now! Black honey again, agouti and electric fish too!

— It's an obsession. I'm the one from the jungle, not you, replies Zanda, her dark eyes drawn to long thin slits in the blinding sunlight.

—Beware! Rather than dreaming of forest fare we should open our eyes wide, swear that the night bullet will spare we who dare.

—But it's now high noon. Need we fear the firing of this nocturnal ammunition?

—Only three cartridges are nightly provided to the sniper with infrared vision who inhabits these towers. Misses he his mark or be there a paucity of targets in the dark hours, he'll not hesitate to run the risk of permanent amblyopia in order to take out his victim. He'd rather become stone-blind than pass up a shot. For him, it's a necessity.

Indeed, ambulators other than the well-hidden bootleggers, duck low and scurry between protective trees and mechanical debris.

—I'll go first across this open clearing, heroically, I declare — walking slowly, perhaps reading from a book, while you slip along by the sugar fields.

Without giving her a chance to protest I advance into this last barren space separating us from the forest. The cement underfoot glitters with imbedded quartz particles. It's spotless as if swept clean by some janitor's broom. No brown stains of dried blood here. I'm sure there is nothing to fear. From the cane fields comes the singing of artisans engaged in their distillation. These are happy songs, ones of joy, of life, of unlimited hope. Birds seem to accompany them from surrounding trees. There isn't here that ominous silence which so often announces danger.

Awkwardly, I wrench from my hip pocket the *Book of Fever* and open it to chapter nine. It's sticky with sweat. My penis still hangs from the open fly, much smaller now and covered with a saline crust upon which sodium seeking gnats converge.

—Take to the dunes, I read aloud as I slowly advance into the *degaged* zone. —Growl, digest full belly of civilization. Ill, wander. Burn by wells without water, yours will be an ocean. Trod wave. See these stones, how they sinketh not. Be they pumice, meerschaum or some rock brother to gas? Pass! Seek cover. Let the desert antelope be thy master. Most of all, learn that his horn will someday adorn the wall of some great hall. Addax!

Part of my skull rips from the side of my head. It floats for an instant in front of me, visible to the remaining eye that hasn't been taken out with the shot, the sound of which comes seconds later. I see my blood showering the pages of the fever book still held high by the hands to which nervous signals shall no longer flow. A piece of my brain even, about the size of a walnut, is pasted to the paper. But these hands, these arms, are they not of flesh and bone? My own!

Blam, comes the detonation.

Why had I gone after the Cavern King? Onandaga.

I'm thinking fast before it's all finished for me. I'll never survive such an irreparable wound to the head! Even if I did somehow cling to life in the most desperate manner, it would never be the same again. Confined to a bed with tubes through nostrils and throat. This story is surely finished or I shall be obliged to tell it from here on in, by appropriation of the past tense or even the future anterior. Blink it out by using remaining one eye's lid? Someone shall have to transcribe.

Zanda should've buttoned me back up again. Perhaps she'll gather unfinished notes, complete by using the third person. Had I begun by using Latin, the ablative absolute would have served perfectly. *Vita facta.*

I collapse sooner than I had imagined, the artificial leg being useless when no longer assisted by the real one gone limp.

We'll never make it to the jungle. At least not I. I would so have liked to have been buried there. By the side of a little red dirt road. Not far from Barthelemy Boganda's grave or deeper into the bamboo forest of the Ngoto.

I can assure you of one last thing before I die: there are none of those all illuminating radiant spiritual light effects that NDEs tell you about. All is black. There is nothing and you are indubitably a part of this utter nothingness. I have always professed there to be no life after death, no single God, and in these speculations I am not deceived.

Mufta Missouri

Furnace is a cold place. A low one where it is impossible to rise above a kneel. Yet this is no den of prayer. Fantastically flat, a spider is pressed to the ceiling. Observe this one. Perfect geometry of the eight-legged ambush. Thing of crystal, this mineral symmetry? A passing moth draws the spider from its immobility. In a flurry of powder the act is done. A bat that shares this low place with me, interrupts the feast, plucking spider and moth. Love and feel.

How, in turn, shall I prepare this fare? Xoma is a heavy smoker and even when cigarettes no longer existed I always carried for her a package with required combustion. The strangely folded newspaper that I pulled from the dead man's head will do well for cooking this velvet-winged collation. But then, am I never to read the content? The technique is simple, something I learned in prison: fold the newspaper so that the sheets overlap one another diagonally, then wrap into a tight cylinder; light the innermost sheet. Slow flame consumes from within with a gentle spiraling action. A headline ignites and turns brilliant blue before disappearing: "Scientists discover where the Devil lives." A perfect little stove for warming coffee. Across the top, I lay the bat with wings folded. No need for spices or condiments.

—But you, say I to myself, —have royally tricked yourself. This is no sepulcher, merely bolted ferrous materiel, attire from which there is no easier chore than to retire.

Thorn socks have I, blood doth pour from my feet to form clotted trail. I'm naked and semi-devoured by wild beasts. Straightforward to the Yad Vashem, then to the Wall of Lamentations, in that order. A friend, survivor of Oswiecim, too old to travel now, has given me a prayer to insert between the stones of the wall. How to fold it? Which crack to push it into? Shouldn't I be above, at the mosque of Omar, performing my ablutions? Not far away a new sort of martyr, young and very pure, falls beneath well aimed bullets, into his father's helpless arms. Mohammed Doura shall give his name to mosques and universities the world over. These things are not at all incompatible.

A soft-shelled vessel awaits me. It's covered with mush, the insides are lush, can cover great distances in a rush. Christened *Hush*. Here, by the ignition, lies a key chain with stuffed animal. No! A human hand.

Again, circadian cycles have greatly accelerated to become blink.

Someone is whispering in my ear, —Antennae are geniculated, curved or jointed. Nepa rubra, once menaced with extinction, has become dog sized, floats just beneath the surface and breaths through a long tube on the abdomen. Plunges to seize fish, sometimes attacks divers. Its great proliferation has very nearly decimated the fish population of the Seine river.

Something prickly in my hand now. —Hispella atra, needle covered beetle that can speak.

I cannot see anything at this point. Whomever it is who has been mumbling to me, now curls my fingers over the spiny object and raises my hand to my ear.

—Indeed, this small thorny thing talks! I want to exclaim. —Be this language? Grunts rather.

—We are in grave danger, you immobilized, I by your side attempting every sort of sensorial stimulation. We must escape or hide.

Rising pulse is the only possible reply.

—For several blinks now, I've been drinking soapy liquids. I'll pass urine copiously and together we'll blow bubbles into the piss. We shall conceal ourselves in the foam produced by this simple procedure.

All is warm. We're immersed in cuckoo-spit. Froghopper technique.

—Realize that time is a violent turbulence. Constellations and even vaster configurations which far surpass the breadth of asterisms that serve as reference to what is considered immutability, are as ever-changing as the designs drawn by the wings of swifts and swallows chasing after one another in the summer sky. Stars, indeed, entire galaxies and even vast groups of these, blow about in just such a manner. Many burst. Who could have imagined? No one durst.

Herbig-Haro stars have all gone on, acquired corteges of planets, greedily spent up their helium, and swollen to devour their own planets before generally going supernova. Magnetic anomalies of unknown origin remain as mysterious as ever and we have also learned, at our own expense, that lensing masses such as Abell 2218 all have an obverse side from which keen-eyed creatures can observe our local group, picking out galaxies, individual stars and even orbiting planets and their biotope constituents, while we struggle to view even the very brightest QSOs.

The voice is muffled by the foam. I'm acquiring smell.

—Massive particles do not weakly interact nor is missing matter irrevocably non-baryonic. Come together forth.

I open my eye to discover Xoma's lips moving just before me at the distance of two, three or even five finger breadths but no more. The words I have been hearing are coming from her mouth. Vocabulary of penetration. Other sounds as well, so they will, too, though rather more feebly. The foam, if ever there was any, has receded. Butterflies have converged around her eyes seeking saline solution flowing from lacrimary glands.

—When you died I hated you more than I've ever hated anyone before, she says, oblivious to the wing flutter. Catoptric colors reflecting from the butterflies, flash in her black eyes. —You abandoned me, so stupidly; left me alone with nothing but a corpse missing half of its brain, convulsing, and bleeding all over me. There was even diarrhea in your pants, urine everywhere! Was I supposed to have wept over you? Should I have dragged your body off to the side, away from the sniper fire?

I stood over you and kicked you mercilessly, cracking your ribs, making what was left of you, vomit endlessly. I heard a scream, not yours. The sniper had fallen from his high tower, perhaps too taken up by the vision of me demolishing your body, the last thing he would have expected; or perhaps he was just blinded by the daylight and stumbled off of his perch. There remains the hypothesis of ricochet: the same iron brought nigh, so as to cleave. Following your practice, Yoweri, I most appropriately named him M'Gone Fall, for future reference.

Your blood most ruby, you had an erection — eminently visible since your sex had been dangling from your open pants— as it is said that men sometimes do have when theirs is a violent death. A girl came from the cane field and tried to ease herself onto you. I wrenched her away with a violent twisting action. I think that you somehow felt this. Perhaps you were already in her.

—Never was it granted me to feel the effect mentioned.

—Nay, and this is a worthy remark, the opposite part including the heart having been already dead. Yet there is naught so strong as to do away with passion. Where it has once blazed, it may return full force. The blood was clotting, flies were setting in. A percnopter, the Egyptian vulture with white plumage and the long gambodge yellow beak, had come down. I managed to drag you into the cane field. Bootleggers came and we washed you down with rum. Built for you small shelter from cane leaves trussed together.

You lay rigid as I say. Looking south, I put you in my mouth. I planted you deep within me.

Had we really hidden in our own urine, blown to foam? Indubitably, yes! The odor is overpowering. The stench lingers. The smell of low leaves lacquered by passing big cats marking their territory, tunnels and alleys where vagabonds empty bladders of low-grade alcohol.

—You were unusually stiff, big in all, she continues, and we are walking. I'm in no way invalid but the cognitive process is severely disrupted. A cat passes. Comes a tree, barren, bearing no fruit but heavily laden with skulls that are planted on every limb, branch and even tied to the twigs. Then a fish breaching the river scum and just now, and only now, I think cat; the striped alley variety referred to as Soriano. Past the wreck of a time machine, this one made of papier-mâché, a pile of XXL shoes that prove, I believe, beyond any possible conjecture, that there are now big divers beneath the surface, and this in turn explains why the bottom fish are breaching with such vigor. Men carrying fishing weirs upon their backs.

Christmas tree, now I think, the immaculate bone decoration perhaps the most appropriate I have ever seen. The perfect Yule. You'll agree that there must have been a massacre here? Or, were these not trophies, as Xoma not injudiciously remarks.

—The ejaculation was ultra-violet, fringing on deep blue. I made for you a penile sheath.

Indeed a most beautiful work of art, woven from the finest purple and green naturally died wool, golden wires laced throughout, represent beasts to come, incoming bolids and distant galactic configurations.

A tunic too. Somber broadcloth upon which I stitched with vibrant fibers the portraits of prophets: Marcus Garvey, Malik el Shabazz,

Lumumba, Farrakhan even. Brocade rather than *tapisserie*, there being no loom in these fields of doom.

After a while there abode company. A hyena bitch heavy with milk. Where was her whelp? She no pet, an expert at contemplating the carrion you now were. O yet! Desert dweller, wrapped in pink shawl and black turban, wheezed with each breath from years of breathing blown sand. Of the face, only sunglasses were visible, reflecting all that which surrounded him but nothing from within. Carapace of cloth and glass. A lifetime of emerging from sand storms to attack the enemy. With a reed flute he kept the mottled opportunist at bay. There was also a prowler prowling the limit of the cane field; the last barrier before entering the jungle again. A man, rather heavy set, wearing winter clothes. He kept his distance and I never could quite make out his face. I felt as if he were some sort of shepherd trying to turn us away from the forest, head us back into the urban structure. Perhaps it was simply Oloman mourning the fact that this could very well have meant the end to the lucrative rational dream trade you had going with him.

—This shoe pile proves that we are indeed approaching an urban zone. The city once again. Should we not turn about, head out?

—Many things have changed. The jungle has come to the city. A more vigorous vegetation, spores blown from potted Precambrian plants, grafted Tertiary twigs devouring their host, seeds sown with the greatest insouciance in botanical gardens, throve on an atmosphere poor in oxygen, laden with toxic chemical fumes that had replicated primitive conditions. Heaving up even the highest buildings, running roots deep into the vital infrastructure. Parts of the city are cantilevered, shelves suspended over thundering cascades. I'm not speaking of ruins, no ordinary dystopic decor here.

There has been large-scale role reversal. Rabbits gripping cudgels, clubbed to death hunters, broke down shotguns and converted the barrels into the most fashionable grain silos, small but adroitly engraved.

We had both been mistaken as to the intentions off the female hyena. She produces a full gallon of milk daily, the most nutritive of the mammal world. Certainly the reason for my recovery. Far more cunning than the Roman she-wolf lurking in Tiber hills with suckling twin gods at her nipples, this African scavenger knows the glade, the warren, the den as well as the city from which with blade at hand, advance men who are barren. Seek not to decipher the code, but rather the code hidden within the code. Deep pilgrimage.

We pause to refresh ourselves at a tavern near the torrents. Here, a shoe designer buys the thorn socks. The mist rising from the thundering water smells of detergents. There is beauty in this pollution. The air sparkles with broken rainbows, colors that I have never known.

—What is this black containing a feeling of vermilion, that blue which tastes iodine? Tell me now. Invent no language.

—The first color is merely red seen by someone who is dead. The second is the hue of resurrection, taken in by the mouth, and naturally, from beneath the sea.

The hyena is wading.

Ale is served up. We drink from long spiral goblets with no feet. Beaten pewter shaped like koudou horns that oblige us to cradle one another's heads while embracing, the drink held high. Harmless snakes slip beneath the table forcing us to draw up our legs. If only they had venom.

—Many, many things have transpired since you died.

—How many years have passed?

—Billions. Measurable in space rather than time.

I can see the city now, rising through dense forest mist, quite vertically in places, and thrusting out over the river where it is at its wildest.

—Would we now live in high cliffs, emerge like swifts, swallows and bee-eaters, communicate by singing?

—Here too, you must earn your living.

—Where?

—Beyond death. See these street sweepers, four abreast, how they flick their brooms together, pushing along immense piles of garbage. Pick through this mobile heap, an archeology of the future. You'll find there news of events yet to come, discarded packages of the most powerful toxic material – caviar to you – and tickets for games played only in nuclear ocean.

—This death thing, I cannot fathom it.

—An inner chamber, easy to enter. Once within, you must strip off your memory and discard like soiled clothing.

—A molt of sorts?

Loach have come to the surface of small ponds lining the river. Tail up, they make guzzling sounds with the anus through which they are breathing as they often do when oxygen is lacking or when a low-pressure system is moving in. Hence the appellation of weatherfish.

— Memory has measurable weight. If you really insist, it is always possible to remember certain passages. Episodes of exploration, trade for example. Accumulation is paralyzing burden.

—Colonization! I remember now. A massacre beyond those perpetrated by Cortez. We wielding monkey wrenches and primitive clubs. We had come unprepared, with no weapons at hand. Our only desire had been to establish commerce, create a demand for products. They so benign, the urge had been too great. We slaughtered them like baby seals on ice banks. The shear quantity was exhausting. Blood ran purple from bodies that resembled living gold. But no gold here, nor even seal skin. We should have considered learning certain things from them before complete extermination. Most memorable was the utter silence. Only our heavy breathing amplified by the suits we wore.

—Space suits?

—No. Suits and ties, summer dress, light colored and very elegant like what you might wear to go to the races at Longchamps or Chantilly for example, but obviously completely purple by the day's end. And, of course, strange little hoods made of crystal, which permitted breathing the atmosphere. Very little gravity meant that the air was full of floating body parts, decapitated heads, limbs and torsos all leaking fluids that were thick, running in lines like the silk of some massive spider, all a glimmer with dew.

—Heads and limbs, they were humanoid?

—Humanoids abound! They are virtually everywhere in the universe.

More on Death then:

—The chambers are numerous; let's call them way stations. Usually you are alone in them but sometimes they can be occupied by an animal, another human or humanoid who might do his, her or its best to convince you that the universe is a dead place, that no humanoids exist anywhere else, nor even any other form of intelligent or even primitive life forms for that matter, perfectly ignoring the fact that its very presence is the living proof that the universe is a heavily populated place. Then again, when you are convinced that you are experiencing the most extreme form of solitary confinement, look always for a trace; examine the minutest element, even if it appears ambivalent. A scuff mark, a dust particle, the taste of salt even, or the faintest whiff of an odor. All of these must be taken quite seriously.

The hyena comes up from the river, a small albino crocodile in its maw. Found a chtonian cult upon this cousin – what say I? – brother from the river. Tyamba.

I have told you her version of my death, mostly in her own words. It is true that I haven't held the promise of using the ablative, but then is not now Latin, just like myself, a dead concept hardly fit for any other usage than that of scientific nomenclature? There shall be no indication from which or where. There are two other versions of the same event, altogether three, including my own which I shall now relate as best I can for someone having just recently lost an eye and part of his brain:

Before collapsing, my vision of the world was cut in half, the eye that was blown from my head took along with it, by some uncanny miracle, that portion of the brain permitting it to understand what it was seeing and even conferring upon it a semblance of autonomy; hence a fourth version of my own death. It spiraled outward, rendering a dizzying spectacle of myself, that is, the major portion of what was left, standing in the middle of a most desolate little patch of barren landscape. But this eye, this cerebral fragment, in their catapulting liberty, realized for me —and away from me— that I had been over equipped all along. A parcel acting as a satellite, though operating within a very limited cycle, could indeed embrace new concepts of the self and even undertake remarkable physical exploits. Monocular global vision being the first: the extremely rapid rotation permitting a full 360° view of the scene.

Discovering myself from the exterior, albeit from a pulsar's point of view, was a shock and I must warn you, from here on in, that any other version of the successive events should be subject to caution. The man standing there, me, wasn't at all an amputee. He very clearly had three legs. Arms gone? He had at least six of them! Looked more like Shiva than anything else. Down how many a somber path have I already guided you, through this man's vision of things? Had the time of cathartic revision rung, too late; the muffled bell of a ship slipping beneath the waves? Should more credit have been given to police reports, medical records and psychiatric archives concerning this individual? True, his sex *was*, for some reason, hanging from an open fly and the impact of the projectile which wrenched this eye/brain fragment from the head had definitely left a fairly large crater in the head. But to pretend that there had been mutilation would have been a lie.

Free of this *me* for a moment I could have taken in entire sections of the world, recounting what it is like to be the very substance upon which wings take their lift, or even light which now transpierced this ocular globe-*me*, filling this it-*me* with pure luminous glory. But then the eye, the free *I*, fell in turn and landed off to the side, by the river where the land was much too low.

I am swamp, finally realized this independent eye, holding many immature things within sticky clutch, teaming pupae that shall in turn take wing, ferocious larvae, deep-rooted reeds. The last vision was one of ants advancing over a living bridge that they had constructed by hooking together their mandibles in order to reach *me*. It is uncertain whether they will ever make it. They appear to be stricken by parasitic cordyceps sporophore which instantly sends vegetal stems thrusting from their bodies.

Is it so with all body parts that become separated from the individual? Do they generally become small traitors, as was the case with the eye-*I*? If so, the memory of what I were, would greatly suffer, were an anthology to be compiled by these missing limbs. Here would be an ablative tale based on ablation. These dissident versions should be pitilessly eliminated.

It's a time of big solitude. In my absence, I have been given the names of Mufta and Missouri. The first one is for the name of the Koranic school close to which I fell. It is said that the first morning prayer had an effect on me. Xoma says that my own lips began to move as if I were reciting the prayers along with the children whose voices rose beneath a waning crescent moon. I felt great commotion. As if my body were being jerked into the sky and dropped from high, upon the ground, breaking every bone. This sensation went on interminably. It is the first thing of which I have any memory of after having died. Perhaps a deity was attempting to take my soul which was too well anchored in the flesh. I have seen sea gulls and even crows practice this technique with mollusks or nuts; the shell or the husk being too robust, the bird takes it aloft and drops it upon rocks in order to shatter the protective cuticle and release the tender prize held within.

The second name being for the river which was no longer the Seine, but rather the Missouri in its upper reaches where – and when – raftsmen bucked the torrents, riding logs strapped together with bison gut upon which they had very often heaped far too many beaver pelts. Many drowned. Others were raft-wrecked, married squaws and thus assured that their descendants would share the suffering which the oncoming American colonists were to so un-parsimoniously vest upon the Indians over the centuries to come before the return of the bison. However, this river not being that one, it still runs through the city of Paris and it could just as well have been renamed the Oubangui for that matter, in which event I would have been named Mufta Oubangui.

This is beyond death. Many things have happened during an immense quantity of time which I can only qualify as an absence. It is said that the great galaxy of Andromeda and our own Milky Way have drawn together. First there was the formation of a tidal bridge much like the land bridge which once joined Russia and the American continent. Then the two galaxies drew together to mate. But this was mere flirting, Contrarily to all predictions, the result was not a much larger elliptical, but a dense, compact spheroidal, almost a dwarf, where stars were much closer together than ever imagined. But now then, had not another, much vaster eventuality, begun to loom from the horizon, we as a galaxy, albeit a compact one, advancing toward what had always been known as the Great Attractor and which now came clearly into view with each new galactic revolution. A lensing mass of unimaginable density, the core of this portion of the universe. Had there ever been here what was once referred to as a black hole, it would have been full to the brim, the singularity would have been effaced, awash with overflow, disgorging rather than taking in.

All of this seems incompatible with my presence, the existence of the city or even these stones down upon which small gods have cast me. They should have turned to sand, melted down and formed again. The galaxy itself has had the time to procreate, die and resurrect thricefold, fertilizing along the way the void in its swath. This is certainly what has happened. New worlds are now a stone's throw away. All forms of life exist, not only humanoids, which seemingly have sprung up and disappeared again, almost everywhere, but also every other manner of life. Long ago, the equation was formulated, not by any brilliant astrophysician but by an unknown contemplator: $T+M=I$, *Time+Matter= Intelligence*, perhaps not the form of intelligence which we can easily grasp, but certainly, in most cases, an intelligence most appropriate for survival. Can barren rock of the most mineral purity or flame burning clean of the slightest organic materiel, give then venue to life? Given enough time, the most forlorn stone, the purest inorganic vapor, the hottest fire and even the deepest void shall all contribute to the coming of an intelligence. Life, however, is an altogether different matter, though not an unrelated question.

—I prefer big solitude, being utterly alone in a stark universe, the only living entity, the only thought.

—You ought to be pleased then.

—Hardly, if it so teams.

—The truth being, and we shall shortly define truth, that there is absolutely nothing out there.

These people that I once knew, still here just as I had left them? Concerning Xoma, there is no problem. It's a question of female patience. The billion-year calendar that she evoked would then be plausible. I do not believe in cycles. I cannot conceive parallel worlds intersecting, or irreality preying upon reality, yet time and space are here, somehow overlapping. Perpendicular worlds, yes! No tommyrot, this.

We halt, smoke a calumet with red rock bowl sculpted to form assassination. Our tobacco is labeled Black Magic, from la Concha, a New York tobacconist. Still has plenty flavor. Other substances have been mixed in but this is no blend. Albatross are low over the river now, proving to what extent this body of water has spread beyond the banks. They have become resistant to metal and can indeed digest whatever hooks they ingest when feeding on the baited lines that fishermen trawl behind long pirogues manned by fifty furiously churning paddlers. Fish too, have developed a tolerance to the plastic refuse they swallow, even a taste for it. There are no edible fishes left. We eat those that are unfit.

It is known that terrestrial erosion effaces the traces of craters provoked by incoming comets and meteorites. But they are falling with such regularity now that the landscape is dotted with cavities, some of which are still smoking.

We are in the city again. Paris or Miami, I'm not sure. Great sections of Kinshasa also imbedded within. Certain overtones of New York, for example, rue Lulli. I've promised you another version of my death and we are heading to with. I'm a man of the roads and by-ways, a caravan dweller. Passing before a mirror on the facade of a candy shop (Russell Stover's always had purple tinted mirrors that would convey to any contemplator the aura of spiritual elevation that may have been wanting), I pull back with white long fingers what black oily hair I have left. Though the crown is totally bald, my remaining hair is nine feet long and I'm obliged to spend hours oiling it with bison tallow as Blackfeet and Crow once did, before rolling it into baskets. My shirt is wide open, down to the belly and many votive pendants of massive gold hang from chains across my hairy chest and even down to the huge belly which is mine. I'm wearing a wide-collared, laced white shirt and ridiculously tight pants, fuchsia hued, over komodo hide boots died an almond paste green. Looking brawly. Just a well dressed cullion. Take me for a dwola? Keep your ear to the ground.

I can sing, marvelously so.

A gypsy disguise, an inappropriate parody, you might surmise. Rather, deep felt homage to urban nomadism and to those whom along with Jews, dwarves, twins and homosexuals paid such heavy tribute to early experimentation in technological genocide. But these are mental badlands upon which we shall do well not to dwell.

—Gaetan, Xoma calls to me, waving her dark arm in the air as she recedes into the city crowd, —Down by the river..., It is a dance, this gesture performed by the hand before the face. No adieu, rather bid to convene in another lieu.

She whom I think of as being the prehistory of love, its future that will come and come again, and moreover, its present which I forever carry with me – even beyond death – my *helios*, my helium, my lithium and when necessary, my valium, withdraws as even the most flamboyant Greek goddesses do at one point, from tragedy in the making. This, however, is reality and no heavy velvet curtain shall drop upon the scene. It will go on immutably, no matter how dense the obscuring dark matter, how blinding the photon flow, darkening or illuminating the actors. The playwright, the director in all this? Is there no control? Have they no word to say, no grip on the events to come? Hardly. We are not orphan actors out on our own. We are assassins – I have furnished ample proof of this all along – cannibals devouring the very boards beneath our feet with appetite so sharpened that we lay to waste the future before it arrives. Indeed, the future becomes recession, a thing already consumed. But then, can we not conceive that to go backwards would be to progress? In an absolute sense are not primitive organisms most in harmony with the universe? And if the future is to be maintained as a serious consideration, should we not apply to this temporal notion, grammatical rules of the most elementary sort? The future anterior would do well. Not only does it offer several options, a splaying of reality which permits playing with our very existence. Hesitation, regret even, acquire here their titles of nobility. No longer do "I could have been" or "She would have had" merely convey a sense of supposition, they become alternates in their own right. They transpire, passing from supposition to hypothesis, on to theory and finally lead to an altogether new form of reality. Ambivalent and shifting. A zone beyond the future, back from where one must step ever so nimbly, and always, just off to the side. A peripheral area, an unobtainable land of lingering, into which it is most difficult to penetrate. By gentle shuffle, advance pace by pace to the middle place. There, I shall say that I should have, when I will have had.

Here too, epistemology is reversed. Fallacy, disinformation and erroneous notion become values that dethrone verity which in turn becomes a shameful thing, – what say I? – no longer exists! Is this not delicious new reality? But then, had not western civilization been precursory? History itself, based on the most blatant lies. The United States, for example, with its Constitution declaring freedom and equality while the architecture of the nation, indeed the very foundations, were based on the most savage, abject sort of slavery. The events to follow, merely the history of Whites' struggle to maintain the position to which they had with such barbarism heaved themselves atop the economical pyramid. What is real, what is not, I ask you? A civilization based on written dogma alone? A shadow nation? Should we have so shunned oral tradition? I better understand those creatures so fond of snacking on our abstract notions, religion, law which they skewer and eat raw. Highly fermented, the foulest of tastes they say, procuring tingling sensation in the palatal region, on down to the esophagus and beyond, sometimes even provoking uncontrollable diarrhea akin to cholera.

It is in this land that I now stroll. Njate Wooto.

—You were thunderstruck my friend, a most spectacular event!

It is Oloman Klanic, sitting at the same sidewalk terrace over which one hundred buses have plowed in the past, killing all except him; for he was always absent when such accidents took place, gone to urinate, buy cigarettes, acquire chewing gum or cough drops, ask for matches, purchase a newspaper, or pay for the bill. Never was he even slightly scathed. Not a splinter, not a glass fragment ever came his way. Not even a projected drop of blood to stain his vest. Calmly, he would delectate himself with the spectacle.

—A terrifying bolt, with no direction. Vertical, but no one could tell whether it fell from the sky or rose from your head, which was probably negatively charged at the time. It was a brilliant green, went through and through your body, blowing off your shoes and melting your eyeglasses. Your body was smoking. We all took you to be stone dead.

—I was shot, I tell you.

—Well then, you've been killed at least twice! Look here, he says touching with his fingers my eyebrows, —the lashes, the brows and even your hair have all but burned away. There's scarification too.

As for myself, I've just had a complete medical check-up; am in the most perfect shape. I spent a full week at the hospital undergoing every imaginable test. You, however, look terrible. Want me to get a rendezvous for you with the medical team?

—What's in that suitcase? Going on a trip?

—You know I never travel, but just this once I must go to Portugal for a few weeks. With Conceicao, you know. She so insists.

I, in turn, insist on paying the bill and go inside. An enormous noise comes from the terrace. A bus has crashed through. Oloman is dead. He will have had only one death. The bus passed directly over him, taking out all of the viscera most cleanly, like an autopsy. The head is flattened leaving his profile pasted to the pavement. The brain has spattered all along the surrounding walls, drawing a design of rather fanciful sweeping arcs from which little clumps of cortex slide down leaving straight lines, pink of course, which are strikingly perpendicular to the curves.

The suitcase is unscathed. It looms next to what's left of Oloman. I realize now that it's immense, constructed of the most rigid gray plastic. Taking it in hand is almost impossible. The shear weight nearly wrenches my shoulder from its socket; the handle digs into the palm. What can possibly be inside? I'll manage somehow to drag it to my warren, a third class hotel that I share with Algerian immigrants who work mostly night shifts in nearby time machine factories. It's the least I can do in Oloman's memory.

Just off of Place du Colonel Fabien, about thirty meters up the Boulevard de la Villette, going towards Place de Stalingrad, an exotic flag made of pink and turquoise lingerie hangs from the window along with plastic sacks containing victuals. The lacework of a mint colored brassiere rivals with the extravagant beauty of the sky. In my room, a masterpiece: A suit made of thick, perfectly clear glass segments with transparent silicone joints. It's a rather heavy attire but protects so well from the high pressure geysers of sulfuric acid which erupt from the thorax of Buthidae, not the scorpion but an individual about the size of a seven year old child that levitates and glows under black light in much the same manner, – tubercle beneath the stinger and slender graceful hands – when lanced through the exoskeleton. Not at all monstrous but rather angelic in appearance.

The suitcase is impossible to open; the combination lock resists the sturdiest knifepoint.

Comes a rapping at my door.

—Bko Kra, I'm Oloman's son. I've come to take his things.

He's a young man, black hair brushed straight up, highly agitated as if having just taken near lethal dose of stimulants.

—What things?

— The suitcase! he screams, pointing at the glass costume, an armchair, before finally designating the baggage lying on the floor.

Oloman had never spoken to me of having had a son or any children at all for that matter. And he and Conciecao did have many pets, though mostly reptiles, as if to compensate for a dry bed.

—I must have it. It's the only thing that's left of my father, (suddenly calm).

K2 is doing her hair, much shorter now, in a bathroom across the small courtyard. She uses a brush of her own invention: a slender brass tube filled with cedar embers, the shaft covered with porcupine quill. Perfumed smoke blows out through the window. Down in the courtyard, Urulu is squatting and spitting on something. —Drowning an ant, she yells up to me.

The boy takes the suitcase. It bumps heavily on each narrow step in his wake. With growing momentum, the suitcase pushes him down the steep stairwell until he falls and breaks his neck. The impact opens the lid wide. Conciecao is inside, neatly divided up into morsels that have been vacuum packed in transparent plastic.

How do I know that this meat is she? The aquamarine ring, the one the pawnshop had refused; Oloman had bought it, saving us from malnutrition at the time, and offered it to Conciecao. I dig it out from the package.

—Santa Maria is back! yell I, across the courtyard to K2 as I wave the ring from the open window.

The shower announced by the weatherfish has arrived and washes clean the ring.

I return to the landing. Where is the boy? The suitcase with the packaged meat? Lycaons and other feral dogs have dragged him off. Neighbors are quick. They're already preparing providence over roadside grills.

—What is this weight upon my shoulders, this sloshing noise coming from behind?

— Have you no memory? It's hapalochlaena maculosa in a seawater tank strapped to your back. A portable aquarium of sorts, permitting you to keep at hand these small octopae from austral sea, whose bite be so potent. The blue-ringed ones that are a mere three centimeters long.

Walking is awkward, must find the cadence to be in rhythm with the slosh. We are out in the streets again, arm under arm, the little one running ahead. Don't ever say you'd rather be dead.

After an easy holdup (I'm an opportunist), not even a holdup, just a rip off, I try to find a vehicle.

Hush awaits, stuffed human hand in the ignition.

Monkey's Muzzle

—How shall we progress in this jungle?

—Walk through the treetops, naturally like the great primates of Sumatra or Borneo. No swinging or leaping; we'll just stride through the branches that sway from crown to crown. The most supple of walkways. The cat's path.

Above flow resplendent clouds, much higher than they should be. In the troposphere an aurora tropicalus. As we cross the crowns it throws down a green glow on our upward turned faces. These lands are called Southward Burned Places.

Orientation beneath the night sky is difficult. I make myself a small sky atlas. Alien uranometria. Find the pole here, the zenith and the nadir. The ecliptical is crowded, the most fertile of suns having spawned a brood of planets that form an uninterrupted chain. The abundant progenitor of a spider or fish row. But does not this super-abundance indicate the order of things to come?

A high price shall be paid to predators. This profusion of planets, this exuberance, is no sign for rejoicing but rather heralds impending decimation. Never forget numerous offspring means that the toll will be heavy. Sheer quantity is the only hope that there will remain a few survivors.

From what quarter shall I strike?

The complexity of this sky. Constant retrograding causes confusion. Precession occurs often. All is dim here, but for a few furiously variable suns and the cortege of brilliant planets. For the rest, broad bands of the faintest stars blend together to form chords. The black pockets of uttermost void are the more readily recognizable points of reference. As was Edward Emerson Barnard's, my sky atlas shall be one of darkness.

I am virus. I have ridden the foulest accretions of stone, mineral and gas having no name. Bound frozen filth from zones unknown, beyond the Oort belt, perpendicular to it, from whence nothing ever before has come.

Disintegrating high in the ionosphere to be drawn down as a fine rain upon equatorial lands where the Earth's pull is at its strongest. Brooding then for long years in the womb of undisturbed sea or forest.

Sometimes spalling off the backside of incoming meteors that slam into desert sand or ice cap. Always far away from the eyes of my future host.

—You hadn't heard? She was having lunch with her friend. 3QZ rose from the table smiling and collapsed. *Rupture d'anevrisme.* An hour later she was dead.

—So young! We saw her just three weeks ago at Gabriel Henri's birthday party. Remember how she and Mouthun were talking about swallowing, or not, sperm?

She was wearing an animal skin with great gray patches and had said that it was the most disgusting of substances, something which she preferred to spit out. Mouthun had told her that she should just gulp it down whatever her inhibitions might be.

—She had always complained of severe headaches. We all thought it was just migraine, the price to pay for all of those nights out.

On the table lie a perfectly presented spine, coccyx, L1 all of the way to the upper cervical with ribs, intact, forming a basket. They have a pinkish appearance with shards of meat clinging to the bone here and there, the vertebrae still enveloped in their iridescent membrane, defracting light into separate hues, purples and greens with the blues of oil slick welling up.

Fresh organs gently lain into the rib basket; an oversized liver, a heart with its crown of yellow fat.

Our host is Roog. His grandfather was the first to harvest methane cake from the Gulf bottom. This led to the discovery of endo-civilization vestiges compressed in pockets of organic fluids mixed with crude oil. What little was identifiable proved indigenous and far more advanced than we shall ever be.

—Contrary to all concepts concerning time necessary for the development of higher intelligence. Trash callograms, junk evolutionary theories!

—What is it that was found?

—Beneath the iridium blanket, under the shocked quartz layers, far below Precambrian; when the world was all marsh and fen. Artifact fragments. The first of which were lost when brought up having property akin to that of liquid sodium, exploding when it comes into contact with air and dissipating forever.

Others like old wine turning to powder when uncorked.

One slab was preserved. It's over there in that caisson imbedded in the wall.

Dye your hair blue.

Better for you.

—You need no special device to see that these are the remains of some sort of being, pressed up against the glass. Only remotely anthropomorphic. The skull, though crushed flat by the pressure, clearly shows a well-developed crest. Rows of tiny pointed teeth. Eye-sockets are mere pinpricks. They circle the skull. This creature had hindsight!

—A carnivore in the vegetal realm? Was there, then, an intense light for the eyes to be so small?

—Crinoids and other primitive vegetal forms were extremely tough. Such dentition would have helped to break down the fiber. But it also possessed the endless intestine necessary to digest that which was indigestible. And yes, as for the light, expelled methane was often ablaze in the sky giving off the brightest sheen.

—An altogether amazing resistance to decomposition, high temperatures and the incredible pressure that turned all else into petroleum and gas.

—The remains contain great quantities of calcium mixed with a substance apparently metallic, not at all a later formation which would, in any case, be incompatible with the oil bed.

—Had they ingested sand, sediment or even stone?

—There is also a different kind of gas associated, but with high metal content; a type found in very old stars.

—Another time scale altogether. Something that shouldn't even be here; or else we've been deeply mistaken all along.

—Here's a garment fragment that resists decay.

—Only a cuff, maybe a collar.

—Less than 0.01 micron, one molecule thick.

—Like an oil slick.

—Is that intaglio on it?

—You see? It's an illusion, physically speaking, but we all sense it. Indecipherable to most of us. All but for some who believe it to be an introduction, a summary. Possibly a warning or a message that envelopes the rest like wrapping. Those who have studied the meaning claim that it goes something like this: "Look beyond within."

—And the content?

—A mystery which defies comprehension. Like trying to quantify the gravitational force of the universe. It makes you feel as if you were on the brink of revelation, yet very stupid. The dog looking at its master, being on the threshold of knowledge yet forever limited. So are we.

—Deeper than anyone had ever imagined, geologically speaking, long before Chicxulub. No one had ever thought of looking here.

—Makes you wonder what's deeper down.

—Only fire.

—Beyond that, the core I'm speaking of.

—Or?

—Can you interpret smell, temperature or vibration?

Roog is no longer our host.

To us he shall no more boast.

I am alone again with she who folds the land.

They were old, throve on trove. The couple in the suburban shuttle train.

Here they were! So far from Cyana, perfectly integrated and speaking fluently that most difficult of languages to master.

Saw there my banker too; had become an outcast living in discarded packing material, broad leaves and vines that stank of the putrefied products they had served to protect. His suit was thread bare, eyeglasses split and taped back together. He had become bald with only sparse pilosity remaining around the ears.

In big glass cases there are stuffed humans on malachite bases. Exhibited just as Bengal tigers once were in Indian places, temples and palaces.

In the main street hyenas are taking on an aging lion. It roars remembering what its paws once were, their jaws taking out pieces of his fur. Respectively waiting at a safe distance are jackals and vultures of several types.

We shop endlessly in an immense store. The smell of the powders in the perfumery department, the colors of the lipsticks, the touch of the lingerie.

—Observe people passing. Look at their shoes, gait, their eyes and coats. It's instant concentrated winter; snow is falling heavily in the store.

A man with a strange goatee that wraps entirely around his face nibbles on bread, trying to remember something he once said.

Others run engulfing food as they pass. Some are smaller than Pygmies.

We sit in the street. We had observed them feeding; they now watch us eat.

There is nothing tidy about this repast. Huge mouthfuls, luminous splatters. We have no platters, eat from the palms of our hands.

They have all stopped, parked their vessels and are now peering intently through windows; some move their jaws as if masticating with us.

Zanda stops chewing, proposes three situations:

1. a man smashes a fly against a white wall
2. catches and eats a fly
3. chokes while eating, flies lay eggs in his eyes

— They can provide sustenance when food becomes scarce. When emerging from hibernation the arctic fox trots along the beach, mouth agape, engulfing the clouds of flies rising from rotting seaweed thrown up by winter storms. Someday you'll do the same. There's no shame in playing this game.

A crowd has formed.

—They all hate.

—Why for then do they flatter?

I am eating with both hands, thinking of the sooty mangabey female, how she ate using her feet too. If only I had four hands constantly bringing food to the mouth.

The sauce drips oily from my beard.

A man sits next to me, too close, watches as I swallow.

Perception of unknown colors. It is another type of sun here. I kill him. As-sas-sin-ate.

She kisses me, sucking the oil from my beard.

—I'll weep, she teared, —I you...Depart, you.

Depart.

—Thank you so much for... thank you. I hope you, the dying man says.

Gathering God's broken body. The debris. Together we scour the street for remaining bits. Shall we dig deep pits?

—Do you remember Strobo, he who said to himself, "If I eat what the birds eat, I shall grow wings." Which he immediately set out to do. Quantities of grains, slices of fruit and saucers of water. This fare disgusted him but he persevered in the hope of one-day being able to fly with his own wings. For his effort he was gratified with a beak, long and pointed.

—Where has he gone?

—Stalking the shallows, he stabs for fat carp. They make sucking noises with their barbed mouths when caught.

A tired engine, Heaven leaks oil. Iridescent pools well up in the streets. Strike a match to light interminable fires.

We have descended some to lower limbs still a good distance above the jungle floor.

Here I find strong crossing branches and build a great nest of leaf and vine as I often do when hair hangs long, limp and orange from my back. But this is not Sumatra; it is Congo.

—We shall bed here the night.

Beneath pass Pygmies, real ones these, bearing torches. One kneels upon the narrow path they tread, passing humus between his fingers. He finds the wings of a drone cast down after having fulfilled its final task; deduces that straight high above there is dark forest honey which in these zones is almost black and flows sluggish like molten liquorice.

Climbing the trunk with a vine passed around the waist, carrying aloft smoldering embers wrapped in leaves to ward off the bees, certainly they would have discovered us had it not been for the sudden call of the judas bird farther off, betraying the presence of colobes monkeys as it fed upon their dejection dropping from tree tops.

We'll awake to a twilight within the night. The tree with the nest that I had built shall still exist, nothing else. Around, all will be desert land. Then I shall notice that, strangely, there are wooden docks planted in the sand with travelers awaiting the passage of some vehicle that is long in coming. Mostly Bororo women, one giving birth beautifully. We'll climb down and sit next to them on one of the wooden platforms above the sea of sand. Zanda will have made bundles of our personal belongings, I shall see that Urulu is tied to her back, African fashion, held there by a magnificent bolt of fabric, knotted about the waist upon which is represented the portrait of Carnu, unknown rebel hero from the

Lobaye forest area, murdered by French colonial authorities. Is it known by all today that Carnu's call came with the fall of a meteorite deep in the Ngoto forest, and that now, Aka tribesmen come to sharpen their spearheads and knife blades on this dark metallic stone fallen from the heavens? Surprisingly, instead of diminishing over the years from the constant abrasion, this stone grows.

An interminable caravan of elephants appears, because then will be now, and passes at a distance of not more than forty paces from the waiting crowd. These elephants are huge with deep purple brown skin; their tusks are cinnabar as if they had been turning soil rich in laterite, seeking salt or other vital minerals. Astride the largest elephant which is white, is a giant of a man, hands bound firmly behind his back with coils of rope. The only sound is that of the elephants passing wind, the growl of their intestines, some urine splattering. Guards ride other elephants to precede and follow the prisoner in an endless column.

The travelers are uneasy. No one hails the passing cortege, although certainly there's room enough atop the caravan for them, baggage and all. As it reaches the horizon, I see the prisoner slowly raise his arms, which weren't bound at all, and stretch as if he were just waking up.

—No prison will hold him, only the mobile one, mumbles an old man to his son.

—Is he?

—Yes, the meanest man in the world, perhaps even, the very cruelest in this part of the Universe.

The sunsets and this night fold into the first one.

She's in the shower. I hear water spatter pour. It's dangerous in there. No plumbing, mosquito larvae kicking in the H_2O of the stopped-up sink. The white of the sink is streaked with rust. The water has sulfur odor and taste. Serpents lie curled beneath the bathtub. Fluttering around the fractured mirror are huge moths with toxic powder on their wings. Through a little window high up comes the cluck of a turacoa stupidly strutting through the humid underbrush that surrounds the house.

There's a log pile near the bushes. I've stored a large turtle beneath the wood. First, I tied it with vines to form a suitcase handle on its back for easy transportation. It weighs at least thirty kilos and I've brought it all of the way from Brazzaville. The humidity under the logs will keep it fresh until I rip the shell from its body and chop it into pieces to throw into a stew that I will have prepared with special herbs, small smoked river fish and dried shrimp with lots of pepper. But that won't be all. There'll be smoked caterpillar, igname, manioc and fried plantain bananas. We'll drink champagne, served much too cold and dance to Kinshasa music. Shan't shog you.

The amber of her skin contrasts with the peeling turquoise paint on the wall, a color, they say here, that mosquitoes and flies fear. She has hair around the navel, nipples, and much beneath the arms. Cameroon.

We amble along the banks of lake Nyos, up from which occasionally belch pockets of lethal gas, killing everything for miles around.

—Why is it you were so long in finding me?

—Scientists have had a history of searching for ETI in the wrong places at the wrong time.

—Now you know we exist largely where conditions are too extreme, hostile for higher life forms as you conceive of them.

—Had we been capable of detection we would have been incapable of communication, unable to correctly interpret what was in front of us.

—Crossing paths.

She rummages through drawers, the pockets of the coats and jackets she's been wearing for the past few days, searching more and more desperately for something of lost.

—What have I done with my cigarettes? I know I had some left.

—Be back in two minutes, the *Tabac* round the corner.

The street glistens, somber clouds tremble with flickering light that comes from within, casting shaky, shifting shadows beneath all that passes. The very buildings acquire a certain mobility. The sky growls.

I'm thinking of her, the cigarettes, will they have the ones I prefer, the package with imitation fur? Or the ones that she likes with spikes and shrikes?

Boom-blam-crack! A blinding flash and all goes black.

Lightning has struck me, the sound, surprisingly brittle and not really so loud, comes with the bolt which doesn't actually come down on me but rather erupts from my head and feet simultaneously, blowing off my shoes, melting my eye-glasses, and projecting me into the air as if I were to follow the trajectory of this immense tongue of green fire that ascends into the heavens ever so slowly. My clothes afire, I land in the upper branches of a tree.

AKA

Have I told you? In this city, there's no solidarity in the face of danger, no spontaneous coming to the aid of victims of accident or disaster. Like a great herd on the move, there's no time to waste with those fallen by the wayside. Wounded, aged or ill, your chances are virtually nil.

I'm in my tree all blazing, when happens something of amazing. Heaven dumps an icy pond down on me. I'm all broken, still smoking, the water streaking cinder – what's left of my hair – down my face, when Zanda passes beneath me, probably thinking that I've forgotten the smokes after having run into Oloman, honing rationale gone off tomba him, and that she would finally have to buy the cigarettes herself. She brushes the dripping ashes from her shoulders as she passes under my tree, and without even looking up, continues her way.

I'm incapable of uttering a word, not even a grunt. My heart fails.

Eventually the branches give way under my weight and I return to the street. I smell of boiling urine, charred excrement, burned flesh and that strange, somewhat acidic odor, that heralds the birth of apartment fires when the flames begin to lick old wall paper and dirty clothes all the while melting the rubber coating of electric wires and household appliances, pushing forth a yellow smoke that comes in puffs from beneath door stoops and window sashes as if the building itself were breathing. These perfumes of the small hell I bear. Now I shall bawl'n yell, I swear.

People avoid me, fearing that I be a car bomber surprised in the act by his own infernal device, or a protester attempting self immolation for some lost cause, without the necessary quantity of fuel, leaving the job half done.

The burns are superficial, the shock of the fall has started my blood circulator going. I'm on my feet again.

Resume where I had been interrupted by the bolt. Into the *Tabac* after her cigarettes, several people gather round me forming compact group, paw at the smoldering jacket and tattered pants. I can hardly make it to the counter. Choose three packs, a beautiful blue with *trompe l'œil* ruby red heart and lung design on the label, the second one represents man fighting with grizzly bear, both on rock fragment which is separating from mountainside. This brand is called US (or Ultimate Struggle), and finally a brilliant green one named Photosynthesis.

—Saw him conversing with God, light coming from his mouth. Leapt into the tree with such agility! they say of me.

As I leave the bar, my jacket ignites once again, the fresh air having rekindled the smoldering fabric. Night is falling. I carry my own light now, though it be a wavering one. I have missed the afternoon prayers. Something flies past, so silent, so big. It's gone in a blink. I suspect a new species of bird, or rather, a mammal akin to the flying fox but much more voluminous. A flying man, one of the first ones to actually take wing? First they developed hollow skeletons, keel shaped breastbones which facilitated the anchorage of strong pectoral muscles for sustained wing action. Legs have atrophied to reduce weight. These are all subtle modifications that could go either way, but it's reasonable to say that I too shall soon be airborne.

Did not penguins, after having been birds, return to the sea and become fish, only to emerge again. We too have returned to the sea several times. Now we are taking to the airs. There is no sea. It has boiled away. Only fire. We communicate with a syntax of combustion.

Some days I'm a psychotherapist, but then I'm not quite sure whether my own analysis is terminated yet or not. Am I ready for these patients that come my way seeking in turn some sort of relief? Nothing is less certain.

This one's a Caucasian with an African leg that's clearly been grafted onto his white body. He brings a file on himself from a former doctor. Diagnosed as suffering from dysmorphophobia. Want's me to amputate him. Would this then be the "Miracle de la Jambe Noire" depicted in a splendid painting originating from the convent of San Francisco de Guadalajara, a scene purported to have been invented solely for the striking tonal contrast which the legend offered to Spanish artists. Central to the scene is a smiling monk admiring the healthy jet-black limb which has been fitted to his body; his own white gangrened leg having been placed on the body of the donator, an African who lies dead across the foreground, threshold which one must step over before entering the scene. Most contemplators hardly even wipe their feet on this mental doormat. In another rare version, the African survives, though agonizing in the foreground, without even the pale gangrenous leftover to compensate his mutilation. My colleague had made a serious mistake. This is no alien limb, unless of course you condone the CIA's treatment of the BPP question, wherein Afro-Americans were alienated, treated as an external problem. But didn't this treatment usually reserved to foreign entities, confer upon them by the same right, an autonomous status and unequivocal sovereignty? Then, indeed this would qualify as being an alien limb.

But for now I'm crossing the street with three cigarette packages held in one hand. A massive limousine is making a U-turn in the middle of the lane when suddenly a motorcycle erupts at a tremendous speed. Inevitable. It cuts the car in half. The motorcycle rider's head continues over the automobile roof, while his body passes through the interior of the vehicle decapitating the driver and passenger. Blood bursts in fan shaped patterns from the necks as three heads roll down the street together. A girl emerges from the gathering crowd, crawls through the window of the car and comfortably installs herself in the smoking wreck, next to the three headless bodies still spurting blood from open necks. She's very slender, tall, dark perhaps Jewish Argentinean. Wearing small white ped socks with high heels. Seems very fashion-oriented.

—Wonderful, she says, passing her hands through the three ebbing fountains and washing her face with the thick hot syrup.

This accident tout, crash-chaser, would be my next patient? Could prove to be perilous. She's most certainly the off-stage woman.

The street is extremely slippery from leaking fuel.

Refrain from smoking!

I'm wearing turquoise colored pants, red sweater, a woolly gray jacket and purple tennis shoes made in China. One can't pick his cloths when they're handed down to him.

All of my jackets tend to ignite and lightning seems to seek me out as if there now existed some sort of secret pact between I and the heavens, whether it be a simple connivance or a deep rooted bond remains to be verified. Wearing a straw hat is out of the question.

Advantages: I now dispose of abundant electrical supply, can even dispense it to others, no longer need to dodge overhead tramway cables, am capable of illuminating even the biggest Christmas trees by merely brushing by, can converse with Aba Abas and other electric fishes such as the Congo eel, capture even the faintest incoming radio signals including those emitted by the most remote galaxies in unexpected wavelengths. Engage in safe sex only, using thick rubber condoms, which must remain dry in the interior. This chafes the dermal surface of the penis which surprisingly enhances the pleasure, reminds me of when Zanda would introduce powders into her vagina (perhaps pulverized rhinoceros horn mixed with pollen scraped from blossoms at the crown of the highest jungle tree), reducing the opening and creating friction which would make penetration a challenge.

Disadvantages: constantly attract dust, cat and dog hairs, pinfeathers, fluffy seeds, blown ash, or anything that's charged with static electricity, shock people with uncontrollable leaping sparks that can arc through the air at surprising distances, especially in fog or high humidity. Am obiliged to wear rubber-soled shoes and gloves. Must avoid no-smoking zones.

Zanda's furious with me, arrives just as I'm wiping down the blood-bath girl and giving her my cabinet address. She attempts to wrench me by the shoulder to spin me about, (as with the scene in the cane fields, but this time there's been no prior penetration). Both of us being negatively charged, we're blown apart in a blinding blue flash that sparks the spilled fuel covering the street.

Fires like this can rage for days, entire sections of the city being dry like tinder, continually blaze. A misunderstanding, she assuming that I should have long ago returned with the cigarettes, not having realized that I had been struck by lightning. This she regrets. We settle our quarrel, cry together in the cinder. At the other end of the fire we discover planters busy preparing to burn this patch of forest. They've just slaughtered a handful of Indians. The last ones? No matter, mouths must be fed and there's gold underfoot. Better make sure they're all dead. Much work ahead. I help them, fanning these new flames with my straw hat.

She's positive again. We smoke, make love in the embers. Feed on baked armadillo. Using charred timber, blistered sheet iron and the hot remains of bicycle frames, I fashion a hut just before it really rains hard. Snug, we listen to the downpour drum on the roof, imagine we're riding in a purple Rolls Corniche convertible. She exposes her project to me: Found an Institute for the survivors of the African Diaspora, a prestigious sort of palace that would be guardian of memory, bringing to light what had been forgotten, just how Europe and America had become so wealthy, one going after and furnishing slaves to the other, the other roundly using this free labor to establish the foundations of its civilization. But this project is to be so much more: not only a lieu of memory but a place that brings to light what Africa and its Diaspora have contributed to humanity. So much more than that which had been recorded by Whites, ever struggling to preserve their precarious position at the peak of the economical pyramid upon which they had so ignominiously hoisted themselves.

We eat parboiled eggs.

We're in an un-definable zone where what seems to be a wall is in reality the edge of a very dense fog bank, impenetrable by its humid nature which would lead to complete short circuit. What appears to be a fog is instead a very solid gray wall which we can certainly traverse in some manner. Smiling handsome young people are in fact sadistic assassins while evil-looking, often deformed ones, prove to be surprisingly good. Here the venom of serpents, the most toxic mushrooms, massive nuclear irradiation and virulent chemical pollution are in fact the very best prescriptions for healing and general well being, while health-food tends to bunch in the esophagus and bore holes through the intestines.

This is where I become a highly specialized historian. My particular field of interest? The *commissure* of 20th/21st centuries, right around 1426 of the Hejir, retrospectively known, not for techno achievements, higher concepts of civilization, human rights, but rather for the doctrine of full-blown eco-warfare, the perfection of genocide, the development of an archaic form of super patriotism that robs an entire nation of clairvoyance.

An archeology of light, and recall that luminosity is associated with what is morally questionable, darkness being soothing, all healing and fundamentally good.

Junk the convertible Rolls Corniche that we were driving. Stripped down Mitsubishi's much better. Be exceedingly scrupulous with respect to the notion of passing time, which you should be in the process of acquiring by now. Don't waste a second of it. If you're taken by the urge to defecate while walking in the street, don't hesitate to throw your trench coat up around the shoulders, drop your pants, squat down making sure that the anus is well behind your shoes and pants that should be tightly bunched round the ankles. Let yourself go. If you haven't anything to wipe with, no Kleenex or silk handkerchief, snatch a lose clothing item from a passerby, even a wig will do when in this kind of a pinch. It's a cinch.

Difficult now to avoid time travel blowback, aliens sucked into the wake of returning human temporal trespassers. They're everywhere. We should have been more perspicacious, have realized that there was good reason for being so well camouflaged, our world being perfectly hidden, hugging close to a very banal little star of the most common type, one amongst millions nestled in the arm of a very common type galaxy, itself an unobtrusive element of a very ordinary cluster. This had all been planned, there was purpose here, just like the mottled feathers of a hatchling bird, or the stripes of a zebra in a fast moving herd. We had done everything that we shouldn't have, making ourselves the most conspicuous life form in the entire sector. It's as if we had painted ourselves a violent orange, screamed "Here we are!" and taunted "Come and get us!"

It so rankles me. Once again, mankind has proven its affinity with moths, flies, mosquitoes and other nocturnal insects drawn to light be it a raging blaze that'll burn the wings, predisposed to revere whatever is luminous or simply very white. A very peculiar conception of immaculate which ultimately leads away from miracles and straight into brilliant oblivion. You think this to be an ordinary flash, reflection of sunlight bouncing off of a car fender? That glint that caught you unawares in the dead of night would be simple spark illuminating the dark, this angelic little figure that could have alighted in front of you after having flown out of some decor where it was hovering over newborn Christ's manger. You're in great danger. Better eat ginger goat while sitting cross-legged in New York snow with Jamaican girlfriend. Cazabat recommends this as best remedy for forgetting smoking rubble stench from collapsed tower type disaster. He knows, bought my thorn socks didn't he?

Comfort comes from knowing that we too are aliens in our own right, can reap death beyond imaginable horizons, that conquest and genocide down here, have been invaluable practice for what's out there. Go, but bear no peace. Wear phosphorescence. Ultimately we are to be the victors.

Period of constant shifting, traveling. No nomadism is this. Great mental instability. The areas covered represent confined territories. Pilgrimage is an inner one. Can't claim that we're headed for three rivers or seven hills. Eclairs should provide sufficient illumination. If this doesn't work, burn numerous Christians on crude crosses along the way. Butterfly wings have all become transparent. The air seems to flutter with innumerable glass flakes. They can serve to reflect and amplify the light.

Halt. Prepare enormous quantities of food for limited company. Gorge ourselves. Fish pose no problem. We're from the river tribe. Can fill our mouths full of this fare. Spit out fish bones (wicked Y-shaped ones here) with surprising ease. Tricky tongue work. Don't try to do it! Could end up like our friend Oreste who gulped down a big bone that lodged in his throat. Got up from dinner table (in Paris), drove all night in small Fiat with big stinky dog while gulping mucilaginous matter such as snails, slugs and snot. Think not? Arrived in Naples at dawn where neighborhood doctor extracted with long tweezers and a little local analgesic. He fears fish now. When last in the jungle, performing pseudo-cultural acts, could only ingest slippery foods. Manioc mush, *igname fou fou* (cassava puree), and certain immense, rubbery mushrooms. Small mounds of fish bones betray our passage. Could be misinterpreted as indicating presence of raccoon or other clever piscivorous animal.

Indian summer. A soaring wind from the Southwest sends high altitude clouds racing. All's still on the ground. Thin lines similar to jet trails but circular with bounce patterns are higher up. Crickets sing final late fall song. The girl desperately needs to play with other children of her age. Impossible to have friends when constantly changing *lieux*. We find public park on low hill overlooking artificial lake near small midwestern town. Called Nevada like the western state, but it's in Missouri which my unknowing Eastern seaboard friends used to call "misery," before taking direct double-tower hits and becoming suddenly much less snotty. She mingles with other children. Blue jays are calling.

This is only a brief halt. Later she comes down with a fever. Is this the price to pay every time she wants to play? Can't keep her in a life of confinement. She needs to be with kids. Childhood sicknesses are a part of growing up. She needs to see her grandparents too. Becomes attached to whatever elderly we come across. This is painfully disorienting.

The real ones: Live in an old wooden house filled with books. Mostly on biology and linguistics. Completely hidden by surrounding vegetation. Between Coon Creek and Bear River, somewhere in the Ozarks.

I go into the woodland. Prolonged period of eating berries and roots. When emerging much later, admire high clouds that look like thunderheads, crowns catching the sunset. Rows of them across the landscape.

—Marvelous! gasp I, taking them to be storm front.

—This is war!, says she.

Return to New York. Live in an inflated tent shaped like a giant rat, covering sewer opening. Poison no longer works. Send down quantities of rat snakes captured in the midwest. What did you think we were doing there? Make small fortune in this serpent trade.

I walk a bear. Finish unfinished mural paintings.

How to sublimate life's end? Discern between tragedy and miserable death. Can we attribute a value scale to suffering? What's the commercial value of collective suffering?

Our remote control devices have been partially destroyed, chewed down by chrono-viral action. We turn in endless circles, looping action, lose direction, can't change channels, provide only limited entertainment. Obliged to operate manually.

Shovel tar from La Brea pits. Make an immense baby. Lay in wait for Uncle Remus.

Among Super-Giants

I am a shoeshine. They all wear immaculate white shoes. It is the fashion here. They slam their feet down on the box and growl "Shine!" The polish is white, penetrates the leather, skins of different beasts they have fashioned into footwear. Some shoes still bear the heads, the claws of the animals from which they were made. Penetrates my skin, this white polish.

—Whites are perfect for this job, mutters one as I apply a strong smelling wan paste to fierce small head with stiff grin and three rows of teeth. —Doesn't show on your skin, he's huge, translucent, almost transparent. The perfect specimen of those whom my ancestors had heralded as spirits, higher beings, gods on the walk.

A closer look reveals excrement transiting through an intestine and some sort of pale cloudy liquid pumping through a vascular system. Pernod with ice.

—Don't look up at me, boy! he snarls, shoving the other shoe beneath my face. An ammonia odor arises. Other feet pass, incessantly grinding the crystals upon which they stride. Malachite giving off a green powder that I must wipe down with a moist cloth before applying the wax.

There is no night here. It is the heart of an immense globular cluster, an exceptionally over dense region, cluttered with binaries and higher-order systems, fiercely competing to sweep up ambient, diffuse gas. Stars, mostly super-giants, so tightly packed that night is brighter than the brightest day on Cyana; morning brings the most blinding brilliance. I wear Eskimo glasses fashioned from walrus ivory with a fine slit across the eyes through which I wince. What truth to accredit to the theory that this compact gathering of stars be the pith of a dwarf galaxy nibbled away by a passing giant? These suns constantly interact, so near are they to one another. It is a zone of turbulent coronal fields and x-winds.

No mistake had there been as to the metallic content of these stars. They are without a doubt the most ancient in this part of the Universe, life having sprung up and remitted countless times here. Civilizations have had the opportunity to age just as the stars about which they revolve, many of them are beginning to swell having burned off their hydrogen. They take great pride, these peoples, in being of ancient lineage. They are oblivious to impending doom, having no science, they are unaware that they shall soon be devoured by their own suns; become blown foul vapors that will form evil nebulae through which it be best not to pass and if perchance they drift your way, it is wise not to linger.

Zanda's in some other part of this blinding metropolis, forced to perform dances and other services for them, during that period which corresponds to night but which is hardly less intense in luminosity. I shall set out to seek her later; for now, they have sundered our bond, at least the physical one.

The days seem endless, probably the equivalent of seventy to eighty hours, during which time there is no solace. Some diurnal periods seem even longer. Then suddenly there comes a day that is a mere blink, no more. I haven't yet any explanation. There are no time devices here. It seems to be of no importance to them. For me, it's exceedingly frustrating. What can be the reason for these blink-days? Perhaps the regular intrusion of a brown dwarf cutting through the planet's orbital plane, provoking a sudden rapid spin, slower rhythm resuming with the departure of the proto-sun. In any event, it would be invisible, a dull glow in the blinding heavens.

Are there no night creatures here? No moths, no owls. I miss them so.

They call me an "opaque," akin to their cloudy excrements. A rare specimen. Not one reserved for adulation conferred upon certain pets, but rather destined to servility. This is progress. When we first arrived, she and I were classified as domestic companions, animals, ill-kept ones at that. What peripeteia. We who had come here to conquer, to gather specimens even, purveyors of exotic exo-biology for great menageries, now specimens in our own right. The most absurd scenario. One that harks back to classical science fiction which I abhor. Humans in zoos, humans enslaved by other, more advanced civilizations.

Yet, this is an altogether different situation. The connotation in the context is fundamentally perverted. We find our own level here, no one, at least not at first, obliges us to bend down, to prostrate ourselves before these radiant entities. Believe we, these creatures to be superior beings? So shall they be unto us! Wish we to rebel against, evade oppression from or even conquer these self-imposed masters, the Evanescent ones, it is possible, theoretically at least, for rebellion is much longer in coming than one might suspect. Insurrection isn't the gratuitous, speedy act which one would have thought it to be. Why think you that Gueveras, Lumumbas or Xs were so revered on Cyana? Well merited adulation! Anti-heroes have been fashionable before, but I'm well under any such individual. By now you must know me well, treacherous, spineless, egotistical but in none of these, to the highest degree, which could, by the effect of role reversal, bring me to be the protagonist of some sort of dystopic saga of which I'll have no part. No. I prefer to be a frequenter of interzones, a small individual whose life has no significant effect on the *déferlement* of events. A regular, modest salary, security, a small office from which I can contemplate the world with total detachment, these are my aspirations. I'm so weary of being a jack of all trades, forced to improvise, share my bedding with moribund monsters, wrestle with angels from whose shoulders withered wings have long fallen. Would I be an ablator, the one who proceeds to removal? So ill equipped am I!

With respect to time and space, I wish that I could tell you that I'm looking back over my shoulder from beyond the observational horizon, at such a distance from Cyana that all information, including light, which might have eventually filtered your way in say, fifteen billion years, would have no chance of ever making it back to you for the simple reason that this neighborhood of the Universe would be receding with such velocity that it would take along with it, everything, including time itself. That it exists, this section of the Universe where I could now find myself to be, is totally irrefutable, but only by the phenomena of simultaneity can you begin to even remotely accept the existence of such a place. Remoteness of the most abyssal kind.

And yet all of this may not be true, for I could, in reality, be only a short stroll away from you, nestled in the heart of the nearest globular cluster. Not M13 in Hercules, nor Omega Centauri as you might have guessed, but Tucana 47. The Great Magellanic cloud has fallen in on the Milky Way, bringing along with it a host of gas clouds and clusters of great density. But so now then have many other such structures of compact star formation penetrated the Galaxy with the coming of Andromeda. What was heralded as an aberration in Hubble's law, the mating of the Milky Way Galaxy with M31, has resulted in an immense new elliptical galaxy (had I promised a compact dwarf spheroidal?), the undisputed heavy weight of the local group, not to mention the offspring, galactic whelp in the form of protogalaxies that have already acquired their proper rotational movement and are departing from the extremities of tidal tails which have proven to be veritable umbilical chords, nourishing the infant galaxies with outgoing H1 gas.

But why tell you I this? The context. Had not I defined the rules beforehand? Made it perfectly clear that we are beyond this preliminary encounter; that in fact, the entire local group has now joined the Great Attractor, and that this incommensurable structure which we have become a part of, is in its own turn, hurtling towards an ineluctable encounter with a Super Attractor, the character of which has yet to be understood.

As for the connotation: We are not pets. Or so we had first thought. We were not confined in cages, nor any form of prison for that matter. Would these have been kennels, perfectly equipped to receive dogs, we might have landed there by some most unfortunate miscalculation or perhaps; a sudden gust of cosmic wind which can reach speeds superior to anything known in normal planetary systems, could have blown us astray. With bowls, small shelters having low openings and thatch bedding, these refuges would have been as accommodating as any dog pound could have been. A gas chamber even, for euthanasia of those who didn't find a keeper within a specified time limit. This is hell for persons of Islamic upbringing as ourselves, the dog being considered, along with the pig, as being unfit for human company or even for any kind of consumption.

All of this, I have no memory of. It is Urulu who told me that she learned it in the elementary school here. Yes, they have here, an educational system which is very familiar.

Perhaps it would have been better to have been gassed right from the start. Instead, we performed tricks, tossing one another bones, fetching them. The Lumens (so I'll refer to these luminous creatures), came looming, eager to adopt. Afterward, we began to live out our lives in brilliant but miserable suburban gardens, endlessly pacing the limits of enclosures of another type, but no less confining, the ground littered with gnarled bones, tattered rags, our own excrements and perforated toys. We had parasites, lost teeth and skin, suffered from hip displasia and were headed directly towards being put to sleep anyway, after having endured too many severe beatings. A dog's life. Unexpected liberation came with action of the Lumane society whose members pointed out the fact that, on Cyana, there had been confusion between we and our own pets, that indeed presidents were often seen being preceded by a dog who had, in all appearance, an ascending power over the chiefs of state. That, given a chance, we too could be quadrupeds. At first, I thought that they so desired that we be dogs, these most brilliant of creatures, that they voluntarily referred to us as such.

But then the truth is that Lumens have great difficulty in discerning between cyanic species. For them dogs, humans, fishes, birds and even certain insects, present similar morphology: limbs, eyes, a brain, internal organs, stomach, liver and so on. What be the difference if the spider has book lungs and a combed fifth leg? These are minor details, insignificant. As for longevity, what difference is there between the life span of the midge fly and that of giant Galapagos tortoise? Identical temporal windows when compared with the smallest measure of time here, the blink, which encompasses a full million of our solar years. How then to differentiate? There is no science of evolution here, speciation isn't a preoccupation. Civilization is no criteria for intelligence. They never displace themselves, are thoroughly sedentary types. With less experience, we would certainly have mistaken them for rocks, giant radiant crystals, taken them to be inert gas or strata of immobile petrified fire. By peeking, I have acquired the capability of discerning morphology, beyond the intestinal transit, I have seen structure, skulls even, enormous diaphanous ones. Resembling juvenile neanderthalis with smooth sweptback cheeks, before the brow ridge becomes prominent and just as in these long-gone humans, the nasal cavity presents extraordinary development. I have at least this in common with them. Perhaps this, more than anything else, contributes to the cavernous quality of their speech which sounds as if the bowels of there planet itself were venting thought in an articulate manner that must first pass through abyssal wells and chambers the size of volcanic calderae before becoming a form of expression. Respiration is also a solely nasal operation, and here is the reason for the howling sound, the noise of wind whipping through the lanyards of a vessel at sea, or a giant bagpipe cast down and deflating itself, that fills the air at any hour. They take in scalding gas, flame even through their nostrils, and to them it is the coolest of breaths, a crisp autumn breeze. I have seen them taking in fire, blowing it down through this many chambered nose of theirs as if it were merely mild drug substance procuring ephemeral high.

—Why wander seeking to discover? say they. We knew that you and others like yourselves, would eventually come to us. Time, patience? We have so much of it. Here there are no coercive armies, no police states, no oppressive dictatorships. No one will ever force you to perform acts which are not of your choice. You're the ones who wanted to be dogs. Social structure? There's employment for everyone, free medical care, eternal retirements for gilded after years, and our years are so ample compared to yours. Here you are free, go were you desire, do as you please. Don't complain, you're in Heaven!

Seemingly all knowing, had they not suspected the reason of our mission? Hadn't they sensed that we were seasoned hunters? Have we come down amidst gods, at least a gathering of angels, whom in their bountifulness have forgiven us before even we have acted? Magnanimous, all forgiving spiritual wonders.

It took so long, even by their standards, to get accustomed to the brilliance. At first, no manner of eye protection would do and we feared to become blind. Impossible in these conditions to discern what was going on here. I had considered the eventuality of emitting ultra sounds by performing contortions with my larynx, bouncing these signals off of surrounding objects and then analyzing the feedback to determine shape, distance, movement even; but then my ears just weren't big enough and the squeaks hadn't the necessary high pitch. Rule out echolocation.

Compounded with the time factor, it was an almost insurmountable obstacle this brilliance, a veritable barrier which prohibited passing any sort of judgement upon these higher beings. They were as unapproachable as they were irreproachable. We were as early mammals, scurrying between the immense feet of dinosaurs who with each step, could have snuffed us out, compressed us into oblivion. Slowly we became accustomed to the intense radiance, began to take our marks, insert ourselves into this society of light.

True, no one forced us to take up the broom, sweep the streets clean of their shining expectorations which we first took to be heaps of gold, wipe down their dishes laden with the remains of repasts, which again, we thought to be debris from some giant jeweler's shop, so brilliantly did they glittered, nor even perform erotic dances when we thought to be alone, she and I. So it was that we came into their service, becoming attendants, unwitting performers of the most intimate acts.

—Frequenter of bogs, keeper of hogs, little man who once thought to have a plan, cleanse well this platter, scour that pan. With your dull eyes adapted to cavern life, with your slow spirit accustomed to the company of slimy things, robber toad, whistler frog, grunting one who emerges from unfrozen mud to rut quickly before returning again to fen, feel with your under-equipped, five fingered hands, the remains of what we consume. Today's the Epiphany feast, fare from other lands, the bones are for you, will bring refreshment to your parched heart.

Throaty moan, this windy groan blasting between mountain peaks, was the first revelation that we were dealing here with creatures less than noble. I had been a dishwasher in this palatial residence for some time, convinced that I was performing an elevated task, one which at least permitted me to bring home daily sustenance, for the little one who had somehow landed here with us, the pup as they had called her, was in need of care, and I was slowly discovering that here too there was a social structure which, if we were to survive, I must at some point integrate, even if it meant beginning at the bottom most level. Given enough time, could not we also become gods in our own right? Those on Cyana await the visit, so long overdue, of deities whom once came and whose return becomes ever more hypothetical as time passes on. While here now, we rub shoulders with them!

And so it was that, plunging my hands into the soapy warm liquid, I felt the remains of the repast passing between my fingers. Other fingers these ones, no less human than my own! Had they killed Zanda, feasted upon her like Frenchmen gobbling bobolink, towels thrown over their heads to inhale the vapor before the savor, while I most stupidly wiped down the very plates upon which she had been served up to these sparkling monsters? In which case I must, before turning upon the assassins, clean the bones, wrap them religiously and place them against my lower abdomen, held tightly against the skin by the serpent vertabrae belt, which I still wore. Fool, had I been! Slowly drowning in this pool of light where we had sought to capture gods, even small ones.

Frantically I sounded the greasy dishwater, diving in deep, perhaps thirty meters down, trying to find the Santa-Maria aquamarine ring that she always wore.

The Lumens pulled me up from the depths, by the feet and threw me into the street.

It's midday, the most blinding moment. All is white. Here now, comes upon me with the force of an avalanche, the revelation that clarity, whiteness and illumination can be evil; that solace, relief and profound blessing would indeed be the coming of darkness. No manicheanistic reversal is this. Beneath most brilliant of light, my skin ordinarily a very pale pink verging on albinism, appears black, indeed under this torch there is no difference between my de-pigmentation and Zanda's melanism. We are the same. Were, rather, the bones beneath my belt being all that's left of her.

There's no time to weep, to prostrate myself upon her tomb. Besides, I carry her sepulcher with me.

Erect shadow, I arise beneath this sky full of suns. Red giants mostly, which I exhort to go off speedily, cleansing this portion of the Universe. I can see again, cast away shoe shine kit, stride forward and explore these lanes above which blaze great arches of flame.

—Has this world suddenly surpassed the critical mass limit for deuterium burning? By theorist's definition, I would now be striding on the surface of a sun.

—Har, har! So you've come from far?

—Who speaks? Hath fire found tongue, teeth, to form words? reply I.

—I'll be tutor to your daughter, the schoolmaster to whom you shall entrust her, belches the blazing wan one who waves before me. —There are fundamental verities you should know, things that our children assimilate from day one. See how they feast on snacks which are nothing more than your higher abstract notions: politics, philosophy, law and history skewered and served up hot. Your gods? Parenthetically, please note that we simply let out our pets to relieve themselves on your world. Their excrements formed the foundations of your great religions. Aside from the fact that their bladders are full again, there's no real reason to hope for repetition of the event. You must console yourselves with relics or massively mythopoetize. However, it is certain that this fertilizer brought on the richest growth and that just as you would fondly evoke your vineyards soaking in the late autumn sun, musing over what quality wine the casks might yield several years hence, so we admire you evolving, ripening in your own way, awaiting the day that we shall harvest you, press your ideals and thoughts into an elixir that we shall quaff centuries hence. Your spirituality is like the noble rot that clings to certain grapes.

See our children, how they wear the Bible as a bauble, the Constitution is a comic strip.

I take Urulu by the hand, draw her in by my side. It is time we returned to our lair, an ancient termite hill with cool, dark interior. She will revise her grammar; we'll talk together of dark heavens, typhoons, waterspouts, heavy rain, a drizzle or a fog even.

She wants that we make a flag, a white one.

—Why white? Has this land taken hold of your spirit? Is it all that you can see anymore?

—White for snow. Then we can draw a polar bear on it as our emblem.

—So right, my little hoyden! This shall be our standard. Embroider the bear. They'll think "Truce," seeing only white on white, or an homage to their light. If only your mother were here, together we could capture one. Abduction of light. It's almost feasible now.

—When will she return?

—Soon now. I reply, caressing the bones tucked beneath my belt. They're polished ivory from rubbing constantly against my skin.

But I have said it, upheaval is no facile undertaking in these climes. Awaiting revolution I must undertake one more of those menial chores.

Firmly gripping what resembles a broom, I sweep the lanes, piling rubbish into symmetrical cones with broad graceful strokes. To think that this was to have been the most glorious of expeditions. Catching gods, had we thought.

I have method, clearing surprisingly vast sectors of the flaming city with relative *aisance*. The tool I ploy over the gold cobbles resembles not the bundled twigs strapped to haft, brooms of yore; this one's more of a toy. Made of green plastic, synthetic stems scratch the street, sometimes squealing with the shrill voices of swifts circling low in the sky. A gilden glint, lights my chin and throat from beneath. See these patterns I make with each sweep, broad strokes of ineffable purity. I imagine that I'm playing golf, the smooth twisting action of the hips and upper torso, propelling an immaculate small ball over faraway greens.

Take a break, drink coffee from a cuttle fish, eat an octopus pizza. The city smells of vomit, wet dogs, antiseptic.

—Art?

—Raise your head. See this immense piece passing over just now, a sculpture as large as a minor planet, being moved across the universe. It has taken millions of years to make. Other artwork is highly prized contraband.

—Is there no psychology in these parts?

—Yes, but upon a much vaster scale than anything ever conceived elsewhere. Here, an entire civilization psychoanalyses another. The immense sculpture is part of an on-going therapy program while skeletons perform remarkable acts in an amateur theatre.

—But, ah, to find a bench to lay upon, shade even, be it but a slightly dimmer blaze. There! Is this not passing shadow? Cloud high in this cloudless sky, even small vapor passing with swiftness upon burning winds would procure some manner of solace.

—Stagger not! Remember how when covered with glittering sand you contemplated the jaw fragment with teeth and attached dried ear of camel in the heart of the desert of deserts? Then you knew as now you could, that you weren't doing what you should. Hold up these arms. See how they become transparent. You too shall soon become light. If not a great god, at least a minor one. Creature to contend with.

Subject observed building large fires in abandoned lots of low-income residential zone of the Detroit area. Proceeds by methodically gathering rubbish, heaping to considerable proportions before igniting. Spends great deal of time contemplating the flames. Backs away before charging. Leaps over the flames with surprising agility. Talks incessantly and acts as if he were carrying on conversation with someone of invisible. This comportment may last for days until apparent exhaustion sets in. Followed by periods of remission, characterized by excessive consumption of fortified beer to which subject adds codeine. Sleeps in cinder heaps. Following surprise blizzard, subject has disappeared from metropolitan area.

I warn you: I'm emotive, impulsive and irrational; I have no self-control and fear almost everything. I attach more importance to conversations overheard between a madman and a cathedral, a prostitute and her poodle, a purveyor of substances and a junky, than to the information contained in the newspaper wedged beneath my head which serves for a pillow as I recline on the bench which I've finally found. You say you hear nothing? Monologues at best? Yet these dialogues are full blown. Pity you who can't read a poodle's mind. Knew you not that colored glass in stone rosette speaks too if properly stimulated.

Poe and Melville were dangerous. Taken by the style, the theme, we passed over the most important thing that each one had to offer; Records of bedlam to be searched, for the former, white dethroning black as the symbol of evil, for the latter. Not that evil be necessarily white. But it very often is. Don't speak to me of gray zones, the erosion of manicheism whereby there would be a blend. Only full-blown reversal.

—Reversibility then? suggests a small man with very large feet who's been hesitating for some time to approach me. Introduces himself as a cousin from Katanga, one who would have followed me all of this way to complete some sort of a family tree. He's holding a very small pair of sunglasses in his hand. Always. Perhaps he has a child. He informs me that he is licensed to carry a very archaic, metal-projecting device called a hand gun and that this would be the reason for his suit jacket fitting so awkwardly with an enormous bulge just left of the heart. I suspect a tumor or some other sort of massive physical malformation.

—It is no mirror image. We're not dealing here with reversibility as you may conceive it. Merely opposite points of view? No. Reversibility would be looking at yourself in a mirror, smiling and seeing yourself unsmile at the same instant. Being able to shoot yourself in the head and watching the bullet go back into the gun; in other words, it would also mean counteraction or rather anialation of any action unless... Chen Sing Wu, Wolfgang Pauli both thought they knew.

—Come with me to equinoctial zones.

—I know this to be untrue, your identity I mean. A lure at best, appealing to my borealic sense of what is thought to be exotic: the South. All being that there is no direction, no height, no depth, time nor even distance. At best, one could advance the concept of remoteness, in perspective then, with – and only this – a familiar point.

—Could this be a micro-pocket of irreversibility? Itself fraught with reversibility?

—It's not as if you were driving down a road and simply turned around to apprehend all that you had passed from the opposite point of view, giving an altogether different feel to the same landscape.

—I am increasingly attracted to remoteness.

—Ecology, concern for deforestation, preservation of species; aren't these mere manifestations of deeply rooted nostalgia anchored in man's spirit? A savory sort of "saving the elephants, the rain forest" and so on? Thoroughly archaic notions. I would call all of this "impeding progress." How I see the world? Pollution, yes! In praise of desertification.

—Can we place this conversation in the upper reaches of a jungle canopy?

—Not even a necessary evil as Alexander Humboldt would have had it.

—Sitting at a table, drinking tranquilly while all about burns and explodes?

—You have this longing for forlorn places.

—Survivors will be most successful. Look closer at viruses, ants, rats, hyenas and wild weeds, especially brambles, nettles and poison ivy as well as all sorts of strangling vines.

When I walk down the street, I don't deambulate in an ordinary manner. Disarticulated arms strike rear-view mirrors of parked vehicles with their stubby vestigial wings folded back that line the street. This makes for trouble, the owners being very touchy. I trip, run into signposts and very often fall flat. It isn't due to any sort of intoxication. I'm simply extremely awkward. I've been going this way for so long that my path's a junkyard traced straight through the city. Accumulated destruction.

When I sleep, it is as often as not upon my head or slanted at a perilous angle as if slumbering on the slopes of the Himalayas.

Rid myself of, shake off, these debts. Yearn to be a reptile; shed my skin and parasites along with it. An example to follow? A bad one at that? Not in the least. But don't forget they can wedge themselves in the lungs. Pentastomids are good at this. Especially favoring snake lung habitat.

Lying in the street sleeping, the skin came off clean. Blown into delicate ball.

I wear a red wool bonnet. My nose is also red. Beard too. One pant leg is rolled up exposing leg. You think I forgot? Have I told you that I had suffered amputation? Well, no. It comes back, the leg, sometimes; but only when I'm asleep. Like the most brilliant arguments that come only after the debate has ended.

Individuals have been observing me. They left pale blue powdery footprints, spreading long and delicate all around the bench. Similar in appearance to the tracks of an immense heron bird. But even here, there would be reasonable doubt. Any ornithologist would hesitate. Big prints do not necessarily indicate a big bird. There's the example of the small jacana spreading wide its weight in order to stride across water lilies. Here, we could be dealing with a very heavy individual spreading weight so as not to traverse the Earth's crust.

My mouth is separate. It hangs across the street, talking in mid air. I'm jealous of what it says.

It's much cooler now, gloom has come, or rather, it was I who went looking for it. Yes, there are caverns here, and though the light from the million and some suns, penetrates ever down deep, giving the very rock through which it passes the sheen of an iceberg's belly, glimmering blueness, a soothing newness.

At first we had wriggled into an abandoned termite mound, the young one and I. By and by, serpents come up, some glass snakes but especially cobras. I tell her of the Niobrara, the river that flows from Wyoming, across Nebraska to join the Missouri, how the banks were once lined with cavern openings, mostly filled-in now. We speak Niger-Kordofanian, she being much quicker than I in seizing the inflections which give nuance. Tells me that in the Orig language of southern Kordofan, nasals are to be pronounced very weakly in final position. She explains to me the difference between snake: *wín/yínét*, type of snake: *wàm/yàmát* and type of monkey: *wús/yúsén*, tells me that Shinkolobwe in the Congo, mined from 1921 onward, gave the highest-grade uranium ore which was eventually used in the Hiroshima/Nagasaki experiments. And then, was not the fiercest struggle centered upon whom would gain full control of the tantalizing mineral, colombo tantalite, better known as coltan, essential ingredient for microprocessors, portable telephones and secret alloys for the fabrication of atmospheric vehicles, rare ore, again to be found in the heart of the Congo Democratic Republic, formerly Zaire, once Belgian Congo, before becoming, and irrevocably so, Zaire again? Perhaps this was the hidden secret underlying the entire Rwanda episode. Would it be irresponsible and unpatriotic to doggedly cling to one's ideas, pin the responsibility to the world power of the time. Merely the logical continuity of methods having proven most effective. The footprints are deep, cutting through bedrock, such is the weight; formation of paramilitary troops upstream, a clean sweep of economic downstream, slaughter in between, preferably of a genocidiary nature to make sure the deck is clear.

How can I analyze? Astray you say? Maybe it's the fact that I'm one of the rare survivors of cryogenisation. Long ago I was frozen alive. Contrarily to our desires, most of us were used for spare parts, following strict legislation prohibiting genetic cloning. Many went to rot when the refrigeration failed. When genetically produced replacement organs, even entire new bodies finally became available, only the super-wealthy could afford them. Reanimated by accident, I was provided with hyena's heart, a pig's private parts, the liver of a baboon and the brain of a brigand thane. These alien organs secrete contradictory signals into my system. Is it clear that I fear death, suffering from acute thanatophobia?

Permit me to open a parenthesis. What if? We weren't at all in the heart of a globular cluster teaming with dense geriatric star population! These are hard times. We live in deep canyons left behind after the sea evaporated. The Marianna Trench or the Tasman Abyssal Plain, (see, I'm not lying to you when I tell you in *Zag*, that the final port of call is Zamboanga, somewhere between the two). How did this come about? Scientists totally miscalculated the life cycle of our star. In spite of being relatively modest in proportion, the sun began devouring its helium reserve with sudden ferocious appetite. A sort of bulimia nervosa upon a cosmic scale. If it can happen to humans, why not to stars? Haven't I indulged myself in similar unbridled splurges, engulfing all forms of feculents and sweets, taking on hundreds of kilos, my body swelling to the point of posing a potential threat to my immediate surroundings, a lobe of fat smothering the pet dog or crushing the serpents with which I keep company? At one point, I was even obliged to live on the floor of a mobile home (unable to stand or even crawl) which served the function of container, an exoskeleton keeping my body mass within certain limits. So it was with the sun which rapidly swoll. These zones, once deep ocean where throve eelpout, seapens, tubeworms and snakelock suddenly became shallows harboring cup coral, oarweed, knotted wrack, bootlace weed and ragworms. The sun, enormous now, has swallowed Mercury and Venus. Man hasn't yet been blown away like butterflies, nor have the mountains been dispersed like woolen flakes as Allah announced in the one hundred and first sourat, but that time is very soon upon us. Surprisingly, we are adapting, breathing in flame. When the swelling star reaches us, we will colonize it, live around the rims of sunspots, become nomads of fire, following the migration of the very hottest spicules and bursts. No need to place this chapter in some far off star cluster. I can be a historian specialized in the remote past, what were then called the twentieth, the twenty first centuries and surrounding, tightly bound, millenniums.

When Verdun was fought, when Triblenka and Katyn were wrought, naught was said nor done so that others would be taught. Certainly, heaps of dead were stacked, photographed, unearthed and unentwined to be properly buried, often steles and other commemorative monuments were erected but never was a better solution found than in the immediate aftermath of the Rwanda genocide where it was decided that no grave would do. Why do I so obsessively return to this episode? Indeed I could speak to you of the siege of Antioch wherein the Christians roasted Arab prisoners beneath the walls of the embattled citadel, feasting upon them while those besieged within, awaited to be conquered and served up. Rwanda! At Murambi, the bodies of those slaughtered were piled and exhibited (in various stages of decomposition) on planks where they continued to rot. Shocking barbarism, unsustainable spectacle, looking death in the face! And hadn't they already given proof that here now were the roots of barbarism, anchored deep within this frightening dark continent where thousands were brought down, bludgeoned to death or hacked to pieces with cudgels, machetes, sticks and stones even? Neighbors going at each others throats, transformed overnight, into the most savage killers. Recoil before this barbarity! Designate it as the most primal of all, a thing to appall, beyond anything that could ever befall us all! This is the surest, the purest cure. We can forget. Yet, herein lies veritable genius, offering up to behold what work had been done.

—Tribal warfare once again?

—No. These be the tailings of tantalite mining, just as uranium and copper mining left traces of blood in the Congo.

—But how much time must go by before a descent burial can be considered, for how much longer must these decaying corpses be exhibited?

—All of eternity wouldn't suffice! It must be shown what price was here paid, the sacrifice. Writings, words and images won't do.

Carrion feeders have had their fill and then more, had we thought, all the while neglecting the most potent of all, the long whiskered ones, with immense antennae deployed in the sky, soaring at altitudes where only a glimmer at sunset, a luminous trace in the dead of the night, would reveal that here were no stars nor passing planes but the most sophisticated listening devices of the time. Echelon, Intelsat, Carnivore. Establishing markets. Mobile asterisms of death.

Moralizer? Hardly can I, being that I myself have drawn strength from devouring my enemy's liver, have worn necklaces strung with the teeth of those I have vanquished and have, throughout long nights, vigorously beaten drums made from the skulls of those felled by my hand.

But then again, I'm not the only one intervening here. Perhaps the punctuation is confusing, a negligent and inappropriate usage of quotation marks, or their absence. It's my fault. Urulu has been speaking as well. Too young, you think? So thought I. Until I discovered her unnatural independence at a very young age. When strolling upon deserted beaches together, the three of us, Zanda, Urulu and I, the girl would leave us, going straight ahead into the pounding immense breakers, always emerging on the other side where the ocean appeared to boil, or down the shore alone she would go, to explore those cliffs far from sight, where the wind would howl, seeking the roost of the rare ocean owl, she would tell us when we would finally find her. Withdrawing to the attic or hiding in the basement of our numerous dwellings was a favorite pastime. She's no first timer to this world.

Caverns, I'm convinced, are at the heart of hominid diversification. Not the classical cave man scenario. We didn't live deep in, but rather in the wide open rim areas, cave lips I shall call these. We had in our service Neanderthals who kept clean the cave entrances, performed guard duty and other servilities. Paleontohistorians are fond of saying that viable intermarriage would have been impossible seeing what great difference there was in the genomic make-up. Don't believe them! We were able to procreate. I assure you that I had a Neanderthal mate. Or instead, wasn't it she the modern one? Was the prehistory of love, or rather will be, for this is the veritable future, we being much more in harmony with the universe at that time, and time is a reversible thing, like light getting caught in an absolute zero substance, compressed and thrown out again, not a mere reflection but an altogether new interpretation. We will have had a child that will have lived very long by prehistoric standards, fostering in turn a veritable tribe. No genetic ghost of Neanderthal to be found in our DNA today? Bone structure has its own memory, independent of DNA or any sort of genetic tractability. Retains memory of the diffuse medium from which we arose.

—Look here, at my brow, (thumping it). See how it juts forward; and these cheeks drawn back smooth, are they not Neanderthal in form? How do you think it is that I can interpret Lumen language, make sense of their howling? In what other manner could I have known the acoustic effect of the unusual nasal cavities?

The pure-blood Neanderthal were pushed back into the cavern depths, to clear these zones of giant bears and super-massive hyenas, just to make sure we weren't taken from behind by these formidable predators. We ended up by sharing the same bedding, heaps of dry grass, leaves and vines. Brambles even, our skin being thicker than yours. A smell of autumn leaves and hemp permeated these recesses. Mold too, a sweet scented one.

Darkness so pure! Even the concept of time changed down here. How is this possible? Have you ever held a blind man's watch, smooth brass shell with a disk that turns? Around the radius are little bumps and welts that refer to time. Had I been deprived of sight early on, and living in the perpendicular manner that I now do, it's sure that I would have conferred to this smooth mechanism of brass with its simple functions that so perfectly fit into the hand, an altogether different interpretation. Perhaps would it have been the origin of a sort of super-Coriolis effect based on spinning motion. Then again, I'm known to run in circles.

It is they, the Neanderthal, who brought down with them the images they had long produced with skin, bone and wood, now taking possession of the cavern walls, ever deeper, going down, down, down. Strike from your mind any notion of sapiens-sapiens having initiated art! The Cavern King and his retinue, living today at depths unimaginable, are of this lineage. A splinter group. An imploded civilization. No stooped swarthy creatures with drooped ugly features. I tell you there is great beauty to be found down here, but you must go deeper than deep. There you'll find blacker than black within which it is so well to be. A womb of sorts. Become inextricable!

Why do you suppose that we bury our dead? An unconscious effort to return there. Surface civilizations have no haven. They will erode.

—I told you I was cousin to these gods. No matter how luminous they be, I shall be accepted by them.

—The labor of deities you think? I tell you, something out there has been raising us, in the manner that we raised beef, jerking our spirits out at will. Of no use to these gods, the bodies are discarded. Somewhere, there must be an enormous collection of spirits.

—This has nothing to do with religion. I think it's more of a question of economics. Trade. The spirits are overhauled refitted with new physical parts and they go on. This is not reincarnation nor recycling. Cyana is nothing more than a feed lot, a place for fattening spirits.

Keep to caverns. Even when dwelling in other worlds.

Eat the orts left behind on tabletops. Become a cannibal in turn.

We wear huge, very soft-shoes, clothing with enormous logos.

I'm invited to a banquet. A woman is dancing patterns of earthen color that devour the light, her body cuts deep slashes of night into this blazing palace of flame where she performs.

K2! She here, intact? Her hand, it too? Be fear, in act!

Pull the polished bone hand from beneath belt of serpent vertebrae. Whose then be this?

—Your own! Keep it as souvenir of this land where pardon comes before crime, replies my host who isn't Roog, nor Oloman, but a creature with blazing blue head, arc welder's torch, once impossible to look upon.

Fellow felon, think I, if your candles be the proper measure of time, darkness is sure to come sooner your way than mine. In this event, I shall be prepared, eager even. Extinguished, snuffed out, you'll be, while I thrive again in some somber hive.

I drop to my knees but this is no prayer. With face to the ground I rub secretions from pre-orbital glands, an olfactory signature, into the glowing moss that covers the floor.

—Most flattering reverence, chuckles my host, —Ascending demi-god, you have well learned your position.

Indelible trace. K2 will pick it up. For the moment, she's impervious to it. Her own hangs heavy in the fiery air, exacerbated by the heat. Lumens have an extraordinarily well-developed sense of smell due to their habit of passing great quantities of hot air over the olfactory sensors lining the walls of their nasal caverns. Perhaps they'll pick up the message. Correct interpretation is an altogether different matter.

Bunsana Bua

That it would be modest and unpretentious to name all of the known universe *the immediate neighborhood*. To say that one can stride across the universe or cross the hallway with the same *aisance*. These are no notions of proximity, merely the realization that what we are able to perceive, however vast it may appear to be, certainly constitutes the most infinitesimal portion of that which lies within those very bounds, undetectable to us; what to say of existence outside of those limits? Just beyond our horizon is the general neighborhood, stretching a good deal further than anyone is yet prepared to imagine. After that comes the distant universe and finally, remoteness, a zone unconceivable to the astro-physician's mind, for lying in an area wherefrom no parcel of information could ever reach us, the time that it would take light to traverse this distance being longer than the life span of the galaxies existing simultaneously in these two separate zones, were they to remain immobile with respect to one another, the problem being compounded by the fact that they are perhaps indeed departing from one another at speeds which guarantee that each one takes along with it, its own light, or any other information which it has emitted. To be capable of one day saying, "willingly I went," there, of course, and "no regret any have I."

Bunsana Bua is my *nom de guerre* which means tribulations of the evening, for which it is best to prepare well before dawn. I am a mere auxiliary god, working clandestinely amongst veritable deities, trying only to provide for my family to whom I regularly send my monthly wages, though these wages most certainly never arrive, the distance being too great. The gods, the real ones, consider me to be a usurper. They wish not to be seen in my company, fearing that I might in this manner benefit from their aura. And so, unwittingly, they confer upon me a level of respect which I had never before, even remotely considered; in no way am I an outsider, but one who is beyond. The unobtainable.

If ever they were to come to me after having formed a committee for example – even though no single one of them shall ever confront me alone, not that I represent a formidable opponent but rather that they comport themselves as certain predators that perform best when in packs – I know exactly what it is that I would say to them, cutting them short before they even could have the chance to formulate a salutation. I have rehearsed it a thousand times, muttering it continuously to myself. Just to be prepared. Be it I'm young, born nearby the youngest star of an open cluster of blue giants, I shall blurt out, —I'm old! Too old! What do you want of me?

And being themselves older than old, the last generation of countless others having evolved over a time span immeasurable, with the smoothest regularity, never subjected to war or the hazards of impending doom, bolids falling from the sky or mountains welling up from the land, nor viruses that cull, they will inevitably reply with voices dull, muted by the thick hull of the heavy vessel with bending boom they ride, — Indeed, no communication is possible, we being so young.

Upon which we shall part, going our ways separately, they convinced that I am indeed ancient, I smelling the air in their wake, taking in the scent of the gas and metals which only the very eldest stellar populations ever release. The whiff of time. Soon there will be supernovae in great quantities. Stochastic bursts of star formation will sweep through this ancient cluster. Where's the necessary HI gas?

On Cyana there is nothing comparable to this, so peculiar, scent of age. Perhaps in the far reaches of Western Sahara when a gust raises the finely ground dust we call sand, a mineral presence invades the bucal cavity. It's more of a taste than an odor, one of copper, zinc, mercury even.

How had I acquired the taste for these things, you might ask? Forget not that as a child I was confined to engine compartments where the heat generated by the machinery would raise clouds of metallic substances. This, my oxygen, was an atmosphere propitious to the development of hooves and horns. There, between scalding piping, vibrating manifolds and shaved wiring that illuminated small hell with sparks, I would lie by the canister of oily fuel that it was my task to administer hourly. When ill, the high fevers which were mine, would shatter thermometers, releasing the mercury. These gleaming beads were my marbles, elusive quicksilver companions that I was sure were alive, as too, I could be. Only, they were free. To slake my thirst, I would draw water from deep artesian wells. Rust colored from the high ferrous quality which rendered it unfit for human consumption. Accounts of polar exploration were my bedside books. Perhaps this is the reason I so fancy the white flag with embroidered ursides, thalarctuos maritimus, (polar bear). The origin of my penchant for super-refrigerated huts.

But so dependant upon these polluted airs have I become, that without fire to produce blackening fumes, I am done. Ever must I smoke most voluminous pipes fashioned from clay by tribesman from Yakadouma in eastern Cameroon; pipes with bowels capable of containing immense quantities of pollutants. And if this suffice not, I'll empty libraries and heap books, setting them ablaze to foul the air. No *autodafe*, only billowing clouds seek I. This literary tinder will not hinder the formation of fine cinder. Contrarily, when written matter bakes, there are fatter flakes that when falling, spatter. Spare "Good Morning Revolution" and "Negro Rivers." If they're not bedside companions, it's that I carry them in a small backpack.

A chosen tempest you could have thought.

Naught. This isn't even Eden's twilight.

Incidentally, it was in this manner that I had first detected the presence of the Cavern King, all the while associating *metallicity* with my hourly rhythm. And a sense of confinement, being "inside of things," I being the one "within," neither organ nor parasite, but rather a passing spirit that makes here its home, there its bed chamber. I have learned to look beyond "within." Having attended this university of fouler education, my diplomas are charred ones. They cannot be displayed above mahogany *bureaux*, framed in gold for all to behold. Mine are ash that float nearby, black butterfly and somber petal that arise with the slightest breath. Accompany me, soot. Eternal certification that no Pacific typhoon, no Atlantic hurricane, can drench from my shoulders. External medication that no specific monsoon, no small panic can, again, ever wrench sky boulders. Small wings of night that most often are mistaken for surrounding shadow. It is of comfort to me that these clouds follow, especially here where light is such a merciless thing. No intention have I of shaking them off.

A blessing shadow. I have said it before; this is a world of most intense radiance. There is no shade here. Gloom isn't doom but blessing.

Send to me delegation, —Fabricator of small cloud, can you make bigger ones for us, systems even, perhaps? they inquire.

—I shall make for you storm cells of modest dimension but intense, I vow.

We hold our hands together like children, their eleven fingers on each clutching my five like leech. The phalanges are completely transparent, no bone, no tubing. Scalding. Have I grasped the glass blower's spit? This is no innocent pact. I'll bury them in a shallow pit! Prive their sun of its chore? Kill them before.

Be ye helium? Fuel to legion stars.

Have they now, for the first time, taken in consideration things less than blinding?

Just as certain passerines surprisingly wear poisoned feathers beneath the belly, so I bear the quills of the stone fish.

How has this come about?

In resume:

Our ship is an immense golden fist. Get the gist? Hiding within, I'm the cyst. We are kicking up a wake now, much against my wish. A long luminous plume resembling the tail of a comet. Sublimation, some call it. I play with the girl, asking her questions about creatures, pointing at their images; her mouth azure, hands are very small, resembling those of a porcelain doll. Curled locks, the stunning beauty of her eyes ablaze with hues of forest honey. I sleep.

While this: Late for an appointment, I'm running across rue de Rivoli. The *garçon* from the café where I was just gulping a quick coffee, runs after me yelling, —Monsieur! You forgot your attaché case!

Am I losing my wits? Brimming with vital documents for the trial I'm about to plead at the Palais de Justice, this negligence could have proven disastrous. I search my pockets for a tip to give this helpful fellow. It's an old suit I'm wearing. Though elegant, the sleeves are worn at the elbows (you don't sew on leather patches; it's just not acceptable here in France), the collar's threadbare. Sweat stains darken the cuffs. In my palm are the contents of the pocket: strikingly handsome coins of no value, tickets for the dog races at Pozzuoli (what's left of Naples), some seashells and sand. I give the waiter a pinch of it.

Xoma sleeps in a car.

Judges wear the most magnificent purple satin robes with collars of spotted white ermine; no wigs though. This isn't GB, or any part of its former empire! But even in this dream, Paris has already dramatically changed. Around the Place de la Concorde, there are dry docks, high thin viaducts soaring over chemical pools across which it's risky to pass for two reasons: the structure being unsound you could fall in or the rising toxic fumes might overwhelm you, even if driving at full speed.

Win this court case! I convince myself. My client is terrified as the French often are when staring the justice of his or her own country in the face. Are not these magistrates, descendants of inquisitioners known for putting suspects to "la Question"? Pre-revolutionary trace.

Realize that I've just been to see a sci-fi movie. That it bears the indelible trace of western 21st century thinking. The future alien worlds are largely set in desert environments. Cultural elements such as music and hairdressing are Arabo-African inspired. More than exoticism, or a more common type of orientalism, it confirms the prevailing alienation of Arab and African peoples by Westerners during this small temporal window within which I'm practicing law.

Quickly convince myself that I'm really here. Go to the cleaners; recognize Zanda's clothes. Buy medicine for the child at the pharmacy. Yes! I have the prescription.

No matter that when passing before storefront mirrors, I perceive an altogether different person. Charity wardrobe attire: green bell bottom pants made of very thick velvet that's completely tattered at the ankles, over the ugliest gray socks and black rubber shoes. Awkward stance from legs slanting outward. Pattern baldness.

No matter that I've abandoned all ambition, settled for working an old bistro where I refuse to serve any thing other than black coffee and red wine. Sign discourages using cell phones. "Inconvenience for the clientele." Wait on myself sitting at a table in the corner cluttered with medicine and the stray cats that I've taken in over the years. Zanda's here, muttering and coughing after years of smoking, or perhaps she's just allergic to the cats. Once every ten years we receive a postcard from Urulu. We talk about her a lot. Hangs, framed on the wall, the *"Declaration des Droits de L'Homme et du Citoyen, 1789."*

Just what would this tend to prove? Can we start trapping bubbles from here on in? Entrain! Doesn't this behoove? Measure the frequency with which these events occur within their respective systems. No need for extrapolation. Nothing vain. No need either to proceed by syllogisms. It's simple entropy.

Is there then hope? We might actually come from Merope! Carefully examine our entourage. Some are truly holier than the Pope. But they can't cope without their dope. Nope!

Keep your eyes open. Even if life's just a big grope, don't mope. Wash sins away with soap. Think I'm a misanthrope? When the devil sets up shop, interlope. You'll need no license. His very name's a trope.

Reach down in your pocket again. What's there now? A length of rope? Understand that at this early stage of the game, venomous snakes have already become necessity. Whether for personal use or simply to fling in someone's face.

Had enough, my Darling?

Let's elope!

Awaken suddenly. The child's gone! fallen overboard while I was sleeping; somewhere out in that immensity behind me.

Xoma was in the dream.

Spin about, operate the difficult maneuver that few pilots have ever even practiced, much less performed. More difficult than bringing a ship into the wind, changing the sails to go back after a w.o.b. Obliged to back into swift current, stall her at just the right point, let the pull swing the bow round and re-engage an altogether different mode before she's come back on herself.

Where can she be? I had traversed this area in such a rush. Now I'm forced to admit that it wasn't just space but time as well. Hell! There are no standard candles in view, no RR Lyrae, no Cepheid variables, and even if there had been, it would have been virtually impossible to get a magnitude/metallicity relation. The brilliant bouquet beyond the dog-vane could very well be close sub-dwarfs as distant blue giants. For now, they're mere iceblink.

Gods are with us! We recuperate her, floating frozen, just as I had left her. Playing with a luminous arachnid of the most venomous type. While I slept, she had piled three chairs atop each other (as little children often surprisingly will) to reach the upper drawers where the spiders were stored. From there, tumbled and went overboard.

Brittle sargassum heaves with the wind. There's a faint tinkling sound here in the utter emptiness. Oriental fire-bellied.

We're off again. A concentration of old stars like none known. Most are binary, too massive, too concentrated to have separated.

Adjust my monocle. Carefully study them. Seek out the most intense.

Behold! There lay they! All of fire made. Alive at temperatures incalculable! Breathing more than fire. Pure heat. Excreting light. Striding upon limbs of searing turbulence. Engulfing sun storms. Wearing plumes of stellar incandescence that vault into space to span half a galaxy. We must penetrate, ply between the islands of fire. In comparison, our own sun is mere smut.

Xoma joins me for flaming safari.

Walk nimbly on these fire carpets. Cartography of shifting bursts. Cycles of strong seismicity. Repetitive hybrid quakes, merge into continuous volcanic tremor. Pyroclastic flow. Mounting pyretic activity. Surface swells to form dome. Lateral blasts, dome collapses bringing down hastily painted flaming frescoes.

Followed by period of seismic quiescence.

We're on one another's thresh hold. They sense our presence as being a super-refrigerated intrusion. Perhaps similar to comet penetration. Particles of refreshment lapped up by the great fiery maws. They've succeeded in separating us.

Silence. The one who has ears left, hears a roar composed of no single note. I camp between great columns of fire. Blazing bivouac. I too am now made of flame. Though it be of lesser dimension, my combustion is even more intense than theirs. A star within a star. But my fire blazes only for her.

They have an exceedingly slow ascension rate. Escape beneath the mantle. Aggregate around spicule formations. Erupt, twenty-two year life cycle. Thrust deep my lance, pull Xoma from core captivity.

Postcard says: "I'm writing to you from a land where there is no land. Only fire." No stamp, but a hole burned through the top right corner.

Episodically, I still return to the bench beneath the small passing cloud, the copper colored one. Yesterday, for example, I lay there all day, an arm dangling with hand resting on the ground, palm open to the sky, an empty alcohol container at the fingertips, cigarette behind the wrist in the shadow. I took in the shine from these million suns. When came night no less bright, I squatted between two parked vehicles. This was my toilette, the place where I copiously relieved myself. A careless Lumen slipped on and fell into this unctuous diarrhea brimming with parasites brought in from other worlds. Would this be the beginning of an epidemic? Those walking the streets were disgusted. They have large private toilettes, very comfortable and lined with pink flame fluff. Strong perfumes are dispensed to cover the odor of their excrements.

I have acquired a motorcycle. It's made of glassy substance but flexible. Makes a gentle gurgling noise when at full tilt. I believe that it functions on Brownian movement.

Recent news from Cyana: The air is full of poisonous gas, hissing noises from steam and there are many reptiles. Mammals come with timid grunts and growls like bear cubs. Fur is now a new thing as are feathers along with higher body temperatures. Milk too. Stars are shifting are they not?

Of course there have been invasions, rebellions, slaughter. All of the worst-case scenarios have occurred. And then again what? People haul about garbage bags full of their own lives. This is why, if explanation there must be: War is a beautiful thing. It has become an art. Ship's prows bear again golden figureheads and cannon mouths are sculpted in the form of dragon's maws with jagged baroque flames jutting from the rims. Bronze is again employed by the fabricators of arms. All manner of statues and monuments made of this substance have been toppled and melted down. And this is well, for I so despised the heroes whose images throned upon public places, gathering streaks of pigeon droppings down their faces, (very ordinary jealousy).

Given to the most primal impulses, the population devours its own children, feasting upon one another when there is no offspring at hand. These banquets are accompanied by the intake of the strangest plants, flora of which they would never have partaken before. Women out of their wits, vainly attempt to recover their children. A vicious bite to the face and all is over. Broken bloody puppets, the half-devoured children's bodies litter the ground. Horrified by the fact that we were once like they, I bury my face in my hands and pray. Knowing that we'll do it again.

In Kinshasa, September is black. It is a good season. Xoma is talking to me from a very long ways away; in the background I hear children playing, birds whistling through long beaks, but also the noise of something with huge claws, approaching, that make the sound of an ice-pick scraping a hard floor.

What is this sticky black substance oozing up from the street? Not oil.

We live in a beached cargo off the coast of Angola. It is the same ship we used to live in, anchored in Algiers bay, at the height of the most intense terrorism, when the country was awash with slaughter. The name proves it: *KISS OF FIRE*. But the final *IRE* has weathered away leaving quite abruptly: *KISS OFF*. Famished lions, real ones, flank the entrance. Their manes are tattered round the maws, human remains scattered under paws. Incoming rollers break and thunder along the hull, sending geysers high over the forecastle. The ship shudders with each wave; like living on *Old Faithful*'s rim in Yellowstone. The captain's quarters have been splendidly decorated. A late Titian, *The Sacrifice of Marsyas*, hangs from the wall. The painting in which the tortioneers go about their work with delicacy, peeling flesh from their prisoner faun with a very small knife, the kind of artists in their own right, who could conceivably extract the hypo-thalamus without leaving a trace and even introduce an alien organ in its place. Exquisitely performed acts that raise the art of torture to cultural summits that far surpass the refinement of butchers employed by inquisitor generals such as Tomas de Torquemada. The cabin is paneled with freshly cut mukulungu planks that exude a sticky white latex to which cling struggling flies.

Heaped on the floor are science-fiction books. Ordinary encyclopedias, history books even, you might incorrectly judge the piled volumes to be? Indeed, they appear at first glance to constitute a mere library of non-fiction. Yet, for those who compiled this collection, the content represented the most hallucinating form of science fiction imaginable. These works, however familiar they may appear, are of most remote provenance, a very well camouflaged planet, nestled in the hinterland of one of the innumerable blue compact galaxies which lie at such a distance from our own that it has no clearly definable position, only general direction, somewhere beyond the Super Attractor, at least double again the distance separating us from the Great Attractor.

When gorged on this literature, I wander inland, but never too far. Bloody bandages litter the ground and landmines abound, all of clever, undetectable, late occidental fabrication. Some resemble seedpods, others, pebbles or even twigs and grains of sand. There isn't an able-bodied man left in this land. A kingdom of amputees. Here I'll finally be at home. Without doubt, the most beautiful music ever it has been given me to hear, rises from the bush land at night, reaches my ear. Songs about Sabla Wangel and Bati del Wanbara, Nzinga of Angola and Dona Beatrice of Kongo, Yaaq Asantewa; women all, the founders of African history for sure. Oh, but to have been a member of Nzinga's harem, young men dressed as women at the service of this queen disguised as a king! Even at eighty she continued to rule, having defied the Portuguese with her invention and gift to mankind: guerilla warfare.

My astrolabe collection? When Europe fell, I engaged in the most opportunistic looting. Should I have undertaken more humanitarian action? There's nothing of human about me! I'm indifferent to the sufferings of these fabricators of suffering, purveyors of arms, exporters of wars fought on battle grounds other than their own, always at a safe distance from home. A moralist you think, no better than they, would I be then? You yourself moralize in this peremptory judgement that you cast upon me so instinctively!

I had no plan, didn't even need a crow-bar, the doors were all open, so suddenly had come the demise; no apocalyptic event as often imagined, just an abrupt and overwhelming disinterest in all that had ever been accomplished. Straight to the Bibliotheque Nationale where I made away with an astrolabe attributed to Ahmed ibn Khilaf of Baghdad. You know the one? Most magnificent! Then directly to l'Institut du Monde Arabe for the one by Mahmud ibn Shawqa al-Baghdadi. Baghdad again, the capital of studies. No scholarship here, only inconclusive occidental experimentation concerning the effects of low-grade uranium inhalation by civilian population. Abd al-Aimm, Isfahan at the Louvre, much more ornate with vegetal curves and a beautifully wrought double circle over the spider's web engraving, as I'm fond of calling the lines which represent the declinations as seen from Mecca, totally my point of view. A *maghrebin* one from the Musée National des Arts d'Afrique et de l'Océanie. I spent weeks plundering for astrolabes without even leaving Paris; the Observatoire de Paris and

Muhammad Kbalil decorated by Baqir al-Isfahani; took here also one by Ibn al-Shattir.

How to thwart this fiery passage, leave these flaming fields before I in turn erupt with bi-polar outflow jets, develop the Wark-Lovering rim of chondrites too often subjected to rapid heating and cooling episodes. Return to zones of accommodating surface inventory, CO_2, H_2O and N_2. Oxygen fugacity and tidal torque have left me in a near mineral state. Seek thermally pulsing asymptotic giant branch star and world nestled within its young glare.

—Stay you yet?

—These fires are my bed.

Just to the north, the Cabinda enclave has become a prosperous coastal zone. The remains of a most complex road system links it to Huambo and Kinshasa. We have developed other solutions for transportation. Bolids covered with vegetal matter, spiny thorn fringed vehicles that function on wind tear. What's left of the cloverleaves, the vast bridges and elevated roadways that soar over endless urban development where jungle once thrived, serve as parking facilities. Shops and commerce have been set up all along the freeway spans. These are free trade zones with immense antennae covering all. No parabolic dishes nor towering spires but tattered bunching that resembles the sloppy webbing of hunting spiders.

We have brought with us a juvenile igneous-like formed creature. She is delighted by the robotic wildlife, stumbling mechanical giraffes that hardly hold up even though covered with remarkably well rendered skin patterns. Here's the reticulated variety. Splendid. But the way it collapses to drink isn't at all convincing.

—What creature comes calling?

—Come flitting, little white fire beast. Light me with your bright white flame!

The final phonemes of these phrases underwent reduction in their original version before translation. The words are affected differentially in utterance-final and utterance-medial. Also the morpheme sequences are to be studied. Pay particular attention to the primary glottal stop of stems which is deleted following certain prefixes. Or lengthening of the last vowels, like the call of a certain owls.

I communicate by yelps, grunts, barks, sniffs, coughs, snorts, clicks and growls. I can also utter obscenities, violently blink my eyes, thrust out my tongue with the greatest vulgarity, clear my throat and stutter. I twirl upon myself while walking, do deep knee bends, squat and often retrace my footsteps. Sometimes I'll scramble up a small tree or methodically peel the bark off of a predetermined zone. Banging my head against walls and striking myself is a favorite pass time. On the verge of retina detachment, I rarely make myself understood.

Brief instructions must be given on how to cross these prairies.

The kidnapped flamelette, so intense at first, wanes to a flicker and is finally snuffed out by a light breeze. As all beautiful things taken from their natural milieu, deep sea fish that lose the sparkling iridescence of their scales when hauled from ocean depths or certain butterflies that, when captured, eject their chromatic magic in a magnificent small cloud of brilliantly colored powder before dying, and rare plants whose roots, simply will not take hold in soil other than that from which their seeds originally germinated, she had very little chance of surviving and I myself mustn't linger here any longer, immersed in this mounting sentiment of guilt which will soon overwhelm me if I do not depart again with the greatest speed from this forlorn zone where hope now, so rapidly dwindles.

Observations: Subject is obviously suffering from Tourette's Disorder. Constantly utters obscenities associated with complex motor and vocal tics. Cutaneous problems. Picking skin and nail biting.

Amidst flames again, I'm forced to admit that improbability disappears with time. That most anything can become a certainty, even that which first appears most unlikely to occur. Physically: I'm completely covered with ridges like an air-cooled engine. A walking manifold. Must keep moving so that the air can circulate, ventilate my body. My home is a flaming hearth. Shelves upon which are placed skulls, line the walls. No macabre souvenirs are these, rather the remains of ancestors, polished and venerated by me. Rightly so, you'll wonder how it is that I who had lost the small urn containing my own mother's ashes while travelling to the sea upon which waters she had asked they be scattered, ever succeeded in gathering these glorious remains, preserving and so piously conversing with them. Each bears the appropriate inscription painted upon the bone. "Tear" which can be interpreted as lachrymal throw off or the present tense of ripping or shredding action, although with an altogether different pronunciation. My family, you might think. Incorrect, at least biologically speaking! Aliens with whom at first you'd naturally assume that I had no ties, had become my family. Develop here the question of feeling greater affinity with total aliens rather than with a specimen of humanity arriving suddenly in midst of this alien world in which I now live. Especially physical. Go ahead, you do it! The bonds are deeper than those linking me with my very own family, my race or even those of humanity at large, I insist.

The planet became subject to large obliquity fluctuations before finally flipping over into synchronous rotation. We have now entered a phase of radioactive-convective equilibrium. At first, we thought to be doomed, trapped in the night hemisphere, the cold so intense that the major atmospheric constituent, condensed out of the surface just as C.F. Chyba et al. had speculated. How then to deglaciate? Rekindle an oxic environment or adapt to toxic retirement? This is atmospheric collapse! If only there were a large stabilizing moon. But we wouldn't survive the stochastic glancing collision with the embryonic planet size object necessary to form another moon.

Temporary solutions must be found. We dig vertical shafts down to deep subsurface biosphere. Inverted skyscrapers, core-scratchers we'll call them. It's hot down here. We've achieved temporary quiescence.

Begins a very difficult period for me. I've been fingered as a traitor by the real traitors, the ones that the immense civilian population looks up to as being perfect examples of democracy and justice on a universal scale. But democracy has become a tool of conquest, and in certain cases, a very effective method of obliteration. Take a classical tribal structure upon which would suddenly be imposed a democratic government. Only purebloods would qualify as candidates and of course their lineage would be determined by excavating early records established by missionaries or even the BIA (Bureau of Indian Affairs) which, itself would have based records on the Dawes Register. Would be ineligible, half-breeds or other *metis*, in other words, fully eighty percent of the tribe, being that early on in, there were many mixed marriages between the *coureurs des bois* and tribal members. Repressive regimes are to be scrupulously avoided.

It is during these hard times that I run across my leg. After having been traded here, advertised as being the limb of an authentic rationalist, a relic cult had sprung up around it. "The foot of clear thinking," they call it. It is true that, in these climes, their brains are usually located in the feet. This then, would be Dendroxa. The place so feared by the ferret-featured girl in *Tigers of Glass*.

Hungry again during one of those recurrent famines which seem to regularly befall any population which I'm visiting, I roam far from my home. Naturally, the large-scale mushroom agricultural program, once considered to be the only viable solution to the food shortage, has miserably failed. No bats = no guano = no mushrooms. I'm exploring some of the lower chambers lining the abyssal structure of the core-scratcher when I discover my leg, presented outstretched, like the leg of a ballet dancer extended full length upon the toes, suspended in mid air and mysteriously illuminated from within. Small replicas, evidently some sort of foot-shaped light bulbs, are sold as souvenirs to visitors. The vendor is absent, the merchandise, finding its true value, is abandoned.

After admiring the remarkable state of preservation of the missing limb, I gulp it down whole. How's this physically possible? I haven't told you what I look like for a long time. In appearance, nothing has changed since the living manifold description. No sudden and monstrous metamorphosis, but I have become a carnivore for some time now, and in so doing, have developed a capacity for suddenly ingesting enormous quantities of meat which greatly facilitates this act of autocannibalism. I have to admit that it's not bad, but I should have taken the time to crack open the long bones to extract marrow.

This first taste of human flesh, be it my own, leads to endocannibalism in which I eat members of my own tribe and finally to exocannibalism whereby I discover the real gastronomical refinement of roasting the head to process the brain case, opening it at just the right moment when the brain is boiling hot but still tender and uncooked.

Disgusting? Barbaric? That's just the way it is. Be it said that these practices save the population from starvation and I'm heralded as the person with solutions. Osteologists will have a hard time determining who ate who and macrobotanical clues will be scarce. The bones, as always, go to the bone merchant, the one I'll kill in *Cobras Coiled*, just before hunting elephant. I'm already a poacher of sorts.

Now is 4.5Gyr from lecture. It's a short time from the now, you know. Consider the span to be a mere parenthesis, beyond which real history shall begin. Before which, between your now and my now, which we'll refer to as then, many things will come to pass. Some sublime, others less so. Parenthetical purgatory.

Understanding means standing under something, rather than comprehending. We're all illiterate and it's only upon returning from then that I'll learn to read again. There'll be confusion, misinterpretation and hidden meaning.

I know that I'm alive. I'm capable of motion and procreation. Smaller manifolds are running free, invading available living space.

It's time to return to Samaracand where the word is written in blue tile applied to tall thin towers from which tumble prayers four times a day and during the night as well. I'll live atop one of these spires no matter what transpires. With song, I'll kindle fires that'll burn beneath biers.

I have with me a baby Cyclopes who's no monster but a very sensitive being endowed with superior intelligence all of his own, owing nothing to tomba, the brain drug responsible for boosting the I.Q. of the very few super-rich who, along with some lucky thieves, can afford it. This little creature seems to have an innate cleverness, a cunning beyond anything imaginable, a wisdom that embraces the knowledge of scholars gone and philosophers yet to come, all of this allied with the joy and unparalleled humor of a child. Standing no more than a foot and a half high, his one-eyed heavy head is just beneath my kneecap. It is he who steeps me in the art of finding "le Savoir," seeking out the where, tapping it like a keg by using a peg, or as one would place a straw into a thick milkshake and vigorously suck. Knowledge, you by now must know, is a living thing in its own right, an entity that doesn't need humanity nor any other living thing to survive. It is always present, there, but you must have flare, dare and draw from it deeply. Be a pig about it, leave nothing behind for others to profit from.

—These things that have been bothering you? The debt collectors, the flame creatures, his voice is ominous, the sound that one would expect to come from the mouth of an enormous cavern, home to a howling tribe. —The disappearance of Zanda?

Create a debt between them, one must owe the other some money, a game will do, derivative of poker, a betting game, one can loan the other one something, even a small sum.

True, you've managed to temporarily shake off some of them, others have been eliminated in situations that usually resembled accidents, and this is all to your credit, but don't forget that you're dealing here with the most dogged pursuers.

Fire needs oxygen.

Have no fear of God. The children of Rwanda and Bangladesh proved his non-existence.

I want Zanda to return. Desperately. Descend to the lowest level of this underground world. Down by the core where things are really hot. There's a small bar here where they serve coffee, next to an Asian fast food with imitation rice and egg rolls. The waitress looks vaguely Chinese. Close to core transportation system where commuters pass, their clothing on fire.

A question of perception:

I have two drinks served, constantly. After the twelfth glass, the waitress seems perplexed.

—Yes, I tell her, there are indeed two of us sitting here. The problem being that you only see what isn't really here, and that which is actually present isn't perceived by you. Remains totally invisible.

Refuse to step into absolute nothingness.

Even if it's God's will?

I'll contest any authority, won't stand in line; will disobey all orders, even little ones like the sign on the toilet wall "please leave this latrine as clean as you found it." Invariably, I'll smear excrement on the walls and urinate on the floor. If I'm told to chose sides, even by the Chief of State, rest assured that I'll not chose the one you're expecting me to. Am I a traitor for as much? Perhaps not. It is certain that nazi Germany couldn't have built its power on the shoulders of individuals such as myself.

Where does this rebellious spirit come from? Don't forget, I'm half-French. Contestation's an art.

I take my daughter to school in the auto, the weather being too foul. High acid content of the rain burns holes into the trunk lid, only remaining metal part of the body. Should have covered it with plastic bags. She's eight now. Explains to me the fundamental importance of Nasserist ideology, situates it in the world context of that period, stressing the effect on the subsequent Algerian revolution, the lessons to be drawn from concomitant weakening of colonial authority in sub-

Saharan Africa. We argue about whether any true Arab philosophy ever came from the new Egyptian doctrine which eager university professors were in a hurry to define and teach.

—Did you lose your gloves? I ask holding her cold hand.

—But Dad, you know they didn't fit.

—What manner of hand be this? I ask, turning the appendage in the dim light.

—You know that I have flippers, wings, four legs and a very long tail. I'm a mixture of everything that ever existed here on Earth, thrown together by some crazy computer. Can swim, fly, dive for days, even survive in anoxious environments.

—All the better for survival my dear.

She meows.

—Are you a cat now?

—Of course! A wild one who lives in trees and under bushes. I'm capable of killing a cobra, but lizard eggs will do. See the feathers hanging from my mouth. I just caught my morning bird. Only a sparrow though. My favorite's the magpie. Use its long tail feathers as camouflage. Dazzling.

Automobile: the body's been burned twice, once by lightning, the second time by housing-project youths just for fun. It's extremely brittle, holds together thanks to flexible plastic coatings. Rebuilt engine. Tell you how we feel inside. It's a choppy ride. Cube shaped wheels. Hacks up the conversation. Can't really confide. When you open the fuel tank, smells like something died. Stay off the streets, go under them or use the rooftops, even if you're obliged to leap. We've developed loose skin under the armpits, rather disgraceful when arms are held akimbo. Becomes striking wing structure when spread out. Permits graceful gliding, not only from rooftop to rooftop but even sustained flight. Just last week I leapt from the top ledge of my home only to alight on the dome of Napoleon's tomb. Rising hot air currents from many fires burning in the city (don't worry, no disaster, only hunters smoking game) lifted me over the metropolis. From high, the surrounding jungle hedging in on, and penetrating the city, seemed almost black. So dark is the foliage! The air carried the calls of tropical birds, men's singing, monkey howl, (I carry gingered monkey fingers in Tupperware).

I warble. Haven't I told you that our communication is basically a musical one? We hum, sing and whistle to each other, individually or in chorus. Some of us even have musical devices in our throats. Harmonicas that render our breathing melodious. Snoring has rhythm. Invective, formulas of hate, expression of violence, all have a musical beauty. Where I to decapitate you, the swing of the sword, I assure you, would be controlled to incorporate voluptuous curves, bringing the blade to sing while coming down. Pleasure for the ear even if it's the last thing you hear.

Nitroanthraquinone

Trimoborane she spews in a fine mist coming straight from a vein. I know her anatomy, have studied specimens, rather well kept, and full color cross section diagrams. Behavioral theorists had it all wrong though. I can tell you that, straight away now. If I hadn't surprised her following an asphalt truck, inhaling the fumes, she could have passed unnoticed.

Would a burst of benzofluorine be considered blunt, an uncouth introduction?

Try triazine!

Fluoborate it shall be; and with that I hesitate no longer, mixing generously with thalium to give warp and woof, a grain like the richest *tapisserie* woven on the noble upright *metiers* of the Gobelin Manufacture Royale.

Away hyena woman! Furl your spots! It is clear that she's too near. Beyond the chemical syntax, I "hear" fear. My own which must not trespass.

Anthracene is the reply, immediate, unequivocal. I am awash with it and she appears to have no intention of shoaling off.

Should I have recourse to nuance? A trickle of benzo...benzo what now?

Tetrahydrobenzaldehyde.

Nothing betrays this walking toxin encyclopedia. No protruding mechanisms, hanging hoses, nozzles nor control valves. She is natural in exterior appearance; you would readily trust her, ask for directions, engage a conversation even.

You had best revise your list of hazardous chemicals and pollutants, have at hand a good provision of the most lethal samples from which a provisory vocabulary may be hastily constituted. Practice your rhetoric! Save you.

How to interpret?

The forced confessions of a political prisoner. Several levels of interpretation:
1. he admits to just get it over with
2. he lies to save his skin
3. confesses and embraces new ideals contrary to his own

I cannot better be prepared, three opposable thumbs on each hand, a fur thick enough to repulse the most torrential rain, be it lethal.

But once again, Gog has lied to me. For this I shall break his arm. It will be an open fracture, the bone protruding like a jagged ivory spearhead. I'll disengage it from the shoulder joint; primitive surgery but most effective like the first trepanations. With this weapon I'll excavate his heart.

It is sworn. A new assassin is born. There'll be no solace before this traitor's heart is torn, cast to the feral bitch's new born.

All about, innocent diners have fallen dead. People who should never have been subjected to this deadly conversation. The poisonous spray has formed a mist which disperses the light from a most voluminous young star that trembles on the horizon casting its slanted shafts into the feeding lounge. There is no blue nor red or green. All is in tones of brown, burnt sienna, raw umber and shades of ochre as if here lay the preliminary cartoon, the earthen hued bozetto for a grand Renaissance damnation scene. Just a tinge of ultra violet about the edges, a halo.

Victuals remain hovering in the air, motionlessly awaiting to be devoured. No hand rises to pluck them.

The lethal one and I carry our conversation on into the night, the toxic cloud all aglow.

I remember the technical drawings showing the position of the venom gland and the communicating reservoirs dispersed throughout the body. To what torero's patron saint must I pray? Perforate with a spiral thrust after having shuffled to one side? Impossible in this situation.

But then, it is not her death I seek, but rather how to acquire this living, very healthy, specimen.

Dioxane, bipyridilium and butylphenol constitute the romantic lexicology of the five civilized tribes which she is employing. All depends on the manner in which you compose with them. She has put them together magnificently. Never could I master such a complex conjugation.

Methenocyclopentalene is the only possible reply. I haven't any! Nitroanthraquinone will have to do. Will she understand? I hardly do.

If only I had an osphoradium scent organ like that of whelks and winkles.

We are awash with a brown syrupy liquid that clings to our bodies and runs down slowly to form a sticky layer about twelve centimeters deep. Biohazardous, this mess. I suspect she has been throwing in anthrax, botulism and new strains of tularemia, just for good measure.

How to interpret this most lethal mixture? Is it merely the residue of overabundant toxic emanation? Maybe not as lethal as first thought. Certain elements must surely cancel each other out. Rather precious information, the memory of our conversation spanning much more than just time. Can I live with this long enough to interpret correctly? Deciphering of no other code hath ever been so perilous. There is language here and surdity will not impede its interpretation.

—Couldst thee accept, I say —we dive into the Fontaine de Mars in the Luxembourg gardens.

—If you're going to go on with this, it's time we made for you a glass suit.

Together, we gather the necessary fine sand, build a small furnace for producing glass, make the molds for the different pieces: chest plate, helmet, arm tubes, leg sections. Jointing and intermediary pieces will be made from flexible material. We slit the bark of a heveas tree (they grow here in the wild state now), and collect the milky sap to make rubber which we fashion to fit. The suit has many imperfections. The glass isn't all that pure, presenting cloudy areas, bubbles and trapped impurities, the rubber has blisters and strange pale brown color, but the suit is perfectly impermeable, and the general appearance is one of beauty, quite as if ancient Roman artisans had fabricated a costume for combat in the arenas, the unexpected imperfections of the primitive glass bringing on the strangest beauty, irisations along the surfaces and constellations of captured pearls of air deep within the translucid mass.

—Learning Arab or even Chinese is easier and much safer for a Westerner like yourself, she says, washing away the sticky syrup.

—The shear weight! Never will I be able to wear the imposing mass of this carapace of glass.

—It's an immobile combat. No physical agility is required. You can lay in a heap. Besides, this armor will serve again. You'll see in *Cortez*.

And if ever you find yourself to be utterly alone, take it off and place it in front of you in a sitting position. You'll find that it can make excellent conversation.

In the meantime, it's best I returned to the school of toxicology.

I'm seated in the last row. The teacher is explaining the notion of time. She asks for my wristwatch, which I lend her without making a fuss. She says that the concept of time, history and all related conditions are things of the future which we are all heading away from.

—Many things have already occurred in the far reaches of the future, while others have yet to happen in the distant past. What you consider to be the future is in reality the past, and what you think of as being the past, is the real future. We are unfortunately heading away from it.

—A doubly backwards world then?

—To bubbly outward curled when?

—Express yourself by using acidic substances with characteristic odor and enhance by modulating the heat. I'll not permit in this class, the help of phonetic footnotes; they are of no use, there being no sound in the language you're to learn, nor shall anyone be allowed to adjoin written explanation. From here on in, we'll work from memory alone.

The other students all have deformed craniums. They appear to be humanoid but just barely so. It's a mixed group, going from children through adolescents, to adults and even aged individuals. Most of them already have a good notion of the toxic language, being from lethal lineage and having at least one family member who's fluent with fluids and aerosols. Mine is a severe handicap, which I can only overcome by putting out maximum effort. I'll be obliged to constantly revise, homework that I'll have to do in the basement, the attic or the backyard. If you're a student in night classes, better be prudent and wear the right glasses.

—Better to go to vacant lots, abandoned zones near heavy industrial sites. Slice viral genome with restricates, blend with alien genes. You'll have recombinant DNA. It's as simple as that.

—How to preserve virulence?

—Employ a regulatory peptide. Beta-endorphin will do well.

But all of this is merely mild poison.

We have often spoken of death. If you're the sort who's in need of sympathy when dying, make sure that your death is a public one; even if this means reverting to heinous crime and submitting to injurious court procedure in order to accede to a public execution. No matter how evil you've become in the process, someone out there will feel for you.

I now dwell in an ancient pump house that was constructed over a well. The pump draws up splendidly blended chemical pollution from aquifers that lie deep beneath the city. I'm not sure that part of Los Angeles hasn't slipped beneath Paris; sometimes traces of the cinema industry emerge, in the form of a frothy scum riding toxic crest. Tap water. Not far from here, rings a great bell.

I awaken in the very early hours of the morning, that time when it's easy to see incoming meteorites, the Earth spinning straight into them. Xoma's lying on her side next to me. Her shoulders are broader than mine, much more so. There's abundant hair around the thighs, almost a fur. This excites me greatly. She asks if she can suck me. It's not unusual that men ask women to suck them, but the reverse is unexpected. Simple things like this can be disorienting. I think of all that she has done for me. Publication of the journals, the manifestos, even the most virulent ones that put our lives in danger. She had built a house for us, given me a daughter.

In the apartment: the sudden apparition of passing emissaries, bearing messages, some desperate. "Send shoes, money, medicine, weapons, combat cloths. Prepare a putch," invariably interrupt our planned activities.

The giant cook is already afoot, yelling in the kitchen, filling the entire building with the odors of his cooking. He's from Cameroon. Name's Michael Nkede. The dish he prepares is a mixture of rare weeds and smoked fish. There's jungle odor and deep pounding noise while he grinds tubers with a wooden mallet. Our girl loves his loud voice. She first heard it while still in her mother's stomach when he would bring forest fare to her bedside.

Distant family members fill the house, bearing packages to entrust to those of us leaving on long journeys to remote destinations from which we may not return. Others wait patiently, filling the courtyard in front of the house, lining up in the street. All claim to be family members, going from third cousins to distant relatives. They expect gifts. Must decide at what point they cease to be real blood relatives, create a dividing line somewhere. This human chain can go on, developing at an exponential rate if not somewhere bridled.

A man with a crest on his head is smoking in the living room while reading the results of rhino-races. On the wall, an oil painting depicting a slaver's ship. She's in trouble. Masts have fallen, and she's riding rough waters amidst rocks from which there'll be no escaping. Ironically she's dubbed "Esperenza," though hope seems to play no role in the final voyage here portrayed. There's no mutiny on deck, seems as if they're doomed to go under all. Knaves and slaves together beneath the waves. Also, an old print framed under glass which first appears to depict an oblong geometric pattern, perhaps inspired from a seed pod cut open to reveal what's within. And in a way, it's just that: a diagram of a slaver's hold, the black bodies perfectly aligned, distributed to make the best of the smallest space. At the prow and poop, they're arranged in a half moon, radiating outward so as to occupy to the fullest the curved space at the ship's extremities. These seeds are the key to America's economic success, how the nation got off to a head start; free land stolen from the Indians and free labor stolen from Africa. Overly simplistic? You bet! But then so were tricks devised to keep black power out of the political arena. The parceling of Macon County for example, to make sure that Tuskegee Blacks wouldn't form a majority. And lots of other simplistic manipulations which went unnoticed over the centuries. Altogether very effective.

We have a conversation, Zanda and I, the girl having gone off to school.

—What is the value of life? Is there a scale upon which can be balanced the value of one life as compared to another? Would the life of an infant hacked to death in Rwanda, weigh less than the roundly fulfilled career of a leading economist, say one who had saved countless lives by instauring an agrarian revolution to avoid a famine that would have decimated millions?

—Potentiality must be thrown into this balance, the African baby could have become a Kabila, a Julius Nyere or another person of power. No different than infants slaughtered in Europe during the first techno war, buried beneath rubble of bombs while still at their mother's nipple or gassed in chambers.

—I'm persuaded that cruelty is at the base of survival.

—You're advancing the antithesis of Christianity. Dangerously condoning dictators and the likes.

—They didn't have it all wrong you know! See how democracy itself leads to destruction, is incompatible with tribal structure, destroys perfectly functional ancestral systems.

Study lions and cheetahs. You'll see that competitive behavior brings them to kill the young of their own kind, even wipe out entire rival prides. It's a merciless comportment that we would qualify as cruelty if applied to humanity, vile by comparison with other species. Even the hyena.

—My children will receive no such indoctrination! You'll not find them rehearsing the Talmud or sourats on the way to school, nor screaming slogans of hate before puberty has taken the cutting edge from their voice.

—Ah, but they should, these things are formative, can lead to great cycles of war. And without regular full-scale war, the parasitic community we call humanity will overpopulate and devour the host planet.

She's wearing a blonde wig again. This one is cut short, bringing out a certain cruelty in her face. Elephants come out in the humidity, sensitive feet, softer terrain. We track them through the city.

After thirty, maybe forty kilometers, we find the place where they leaned up against a termite castle. Here the bull lay to rest the weight of his massive head, first to the left, then to the right, leaving the trace of a peculiarly curled tusk in the clay. Another thirty kilometers farther, it's the imprint of the same tusk against another mound. We extract large fan shaped mushroom from termite hill, eat it with a little rock salt.

Hippos come out with the rising moon, smash through small lettuce patch planted with great pains by starving colonist after clearing the land.

Riding rapids smelling of fish slime, we go down river in a pirogue to get milk for the little girl.

My teeth are in deplorable condition after forty years in the colonies. Only five left. Poorly fabricated dentures have left me with abscesses and cysts, the beginning of cancer of the gums. This infection will certainly affect my heart.

Have you ever noticed things disappearing around you? Even your own body parts. I'm convinced they've been taken without my permission, for useless experiments.

After the removal of one leg, I'm well again, but only briefly. Is it before or after? Perhaps just a different place, nothing to do with time. Why are you making that face? The choice was mine. I pawned my body parts to several agents. They fought with each other before coming after me. Winning time.

1) My bones would be gathered, ground and sold for animal meal. (But first, and according to signed agreement, —and only if I hadn't paid mortgage in time— they'd collect the remaining leg, my arms, vital organs including heart and brain, leaving the turquoise testicles. It's like jumping bail; there's always a bondsman coming after you. One was carrying a bagful of eyeballs.)

2)The hypothesis that my skeleton would be cleaned and carved into magnificent sculptures has proven ill-founded. Instead it is probable that very small individuals will utilize the longer bones to make scaffolding, permitting them to attain the upper reaches of the miniature skyscrapers that they are constructing. The skull will be used as a temple or some sort of sanctuary.

3) She will have burned me, leaving only the five teeth. Medical records are nonexistent due to nomadic life. My remains will never be correctly identified.

The last option is unlikely, being that she has just fashioned for me a new penile sheath, this one from semi-porous materials. I pack it with dirt to keep my private parts filthy. I've also learned to always keep a little urine in my bladder, never completely relieve myself. This maintains a permanent state of excitation which can enhance erections, delay ejaculation. Always think of her pleasure which must pass before my own.

At first you think that you've just misplaced your keys, a pair of shoes, gloves, eyeglasses. Then you realize that they're not lost, but have truly vanished. One of the shoes was on the foot that was on the leg that was cut off; the wrist-watch, which you're only now missing, was, after being returned by the professor, on the wrist that was the extension of one of the arms that separated from your body at the shoulders. It's just as well this way, you didn't really need to keep this false notion of time so near at hand. These are sure signs that they're out to get you.

Relax. Listen to Oum Kalthoum. Pick and chew bastard speedwell. This could be Eurasia.

Astrophysicians had grossly miscalculated the age of the sun. Helium depleted sun swells precociously, throwing off burning gas shells. The prospect of imminent doom has deeply transformed humanity. Society cleaves, divided between last chance Epicureans and those hastily seeking spiritual purification. Some of us physically adapt to the coming inferno. We are rare.

Just yesterday, a young man was sitting on the riverbank fishing. An immense serpent emerged down river and slithered along the bank behind him. Striking the youth square between the shoulders with its massive head, it fractured his vertebrae bringing instant death. Bystanders watched, hypnotized by the spectacle, as the snake slowly worked its wide-open mouth with dislocated jaw round the boy which it swallowed headfirst. The snake should have returned to the waters without leaving a ripple. Instead, it furiously splashed and fled the river, returning to the bank. It was evidently too heavy with the unusual feast. There had been legends of giant serpents eating humans but it had never been proven. Muffled cracking noises came from within the serpent's belly, as it applied pressure to the boy's body to crush the bones before beginning digestion.

A Frenchman wanted to intervene. A German prevented him from doing so, —Let nature have its way! he said. This is why Europe never really was viable. But it's also why Europeans always had greater political maturity than Americans.

Finally someone reacted and killed the giant snake, which was more of a small dragon. It is said that its name was George. I arrived at this point finding the snake cut open lengthways, the broken boy covered with digestive slime, lying in the middle. Predator and prey had been put onto the flatbed of a pickup truck, the serpent's head hanging over the cab, with its tail trailing a good ways behind the rear bumper.

Here I discovered three things: the boy was an Indian, probably a Yanomani from the upper reaches of the Amazon, and the serpent was an anaconda. Neither should have been here, Indians vanished completely from the face of the Earth long ago and anacondas, just like howler monkeys, were riding a tectonic plate that plowed over Los Angeles, not Paris. Finally, the boy and snake were both boiled, which explains why the serpent hadn't remained in the water but also proving to what degree the river has heated up from the prevailing cosmological conditions.

It is more correct to interpret time through smell and feel rather than by applying calculation.

I'm on crutches. Zanda catches my face between her hands, gently brushes cinder from my eye. Many things are afire and ashes ride the winds. We get into a car, a Volvo 244L with poorly applied reflective adhesive that forms shining blisters over the windows. Don't lose from sight the fact that ordinary looking vehicles have mostly been converted into time machines. A Mazda convertible with torn top that's held together with safety pins, a Corvette Stingray, body parts assembled with silver ducting tape; automobiles of course, but also buses (preferably of the standard Gray Hound variety), motorcycles and even bobsleds will do. Basically all one needs is a little inertia, entropy does the rest.

Time machines are really, really common, coming and going like wind born seeds. This has led to enormous gaps in our knowledge of the present universe, exploration of space having been abandoned to the benefit of investigation of remote temporal zones.

But it is also profitable to skip into recent history. Just now I'm returning from Sutton Hoo with Beowulf's harp, purse and sword. All eyes are on me as I ride the suburban shuttle train. Less for the loot which I can hardly carry, than for the severe face wound which I incurred back there, I know not how.

Debt collectors have proven to be doggedly tenacious, not hesitating to plunge into time, hot on the tracks of an evading debtor, sometimes just for a dime. Merely for practice they say. When heavy debts are at stake, the life/death barrier proves no obstacle for them either.

This situation obliges me to constantly invent new jobs, ones that can take me over a great distance, for instance purveyor to menageries. It's imperative to bring back unusual life forms in good health, no fragile specimens that might perish, all the while keeping an eye out for the pursuants. And then again, might not it be best to lay low? Assume an innocuous function, street sweeper, dishwasher, let them pass over with out a second thought? If you're not my princess, be my bag lady! Blow me in the bathhouse.

Let's blast away at each other with bastard culverins. Eight pound shot will do. Catch and eat batfish.

The disguises, the constant morphological changes? I've told you before, at first it was only meant to bring about loathing, make her forget, see in me the vilest poltroon; now it seems to please her. It's no substitute for polyandry.

On the radio there's a talk show concerning couples of widely differing ages, about the process of aging and the effect it has on the couples' sexual lives. Perception, phobias, plastic surgery, the incapability of having children, physical attraction.

Are these comedians reading from a script? Is it improvisation?

We eat a bird together. Her fingers shine, greasy, as she dismembers the fowl. Pieces of flesh remain around her mouth, cling to the oily lips. She wipes her mouth with her hand, runs fingers through hair.

—There are no lower classes, no poor. In a perfect reversal of the Russian Revolution, they've all been eliminated.

—See, I told you communism wasn't so bad after all.

We have English, Chesterfield style furniture covered with green plastic imitation leather. In an aquarium, we keep torpedo fish with a 500 volt potential, harnessed with copper wiring to provide glimmering flashes of light, spurts of music, intermittent air conditioning. It's difficult to keep frozen foods, but then our intestines have become resistant to bacteria that develop from the constant thawing/freezing process. Though run-down, our home is vast enough to play hide-and-seek in, for weeks on end. An Okapi runs free but usually keeps to the central zones where there's dense tropical vegetation similar to its original habitat. But there are also Chinaberry trees, wartle and hortle berry varieties, in memory of more temperate zones. She binds my wrists with braided stars.

Our daughter confides in me, tells me about Yongawi and Yongawa; two humanoids who share the house with us but are known only to her, standing about a foot and a half tall, covered with green fur verging on blue, they feed on earthworms and occasionally hunt. Y and Y smell like dogs when wet.

Performing complicated diving patterns, we exit from high openings in the building. Why use the stairs when there are windows? This is the Louvre and we're living in it. We listen to Chinese music, songs from Mauritania, very faint and trembling. There are four hundred and three rooms. This is factual. No grooms, only two wee brooms. Filth. Actual.

Organize races down the great hallways, pitting politicians against businessmen, clergymen against nobles. The pet hyena bitch often interferes, mistaking them for ordinary prey. She mauls them when they slip and fall at the end of the hallway. Otherwise, she's becoming a bit of a problem, impossible to domesticate. She regurgitates her food in stinking piles, urinates on the sixteenth century carpeting, strips embroidered satin from the furniture and chews the feet from the chairs, making stubby stools of elegant high fauteuils. Can I do without the high protein milk, the richest milk of the mammalian world, which she so generously provides?

Prepare for cavern warfare. It's best to be on the inside. Use the looping technique whereby you draw in aggressors, double back through a loop and wall-up the intruder, before going on, down other shafts. If the access is too narrow, partially or totally blocked by rubble or bars, grow thin till you can go in. Don't worry for a minute about robust nuclear earth penetrators. No matter what the yield, there'll be cratering allowing for release of hot plasma and much radioactive material: the now famous "Roman candle" effect. Surface dose rates soar to well over 300 rads, while deep down under, all's cool. Adieu topside fool!

One of the concepts of Islam: Though no imam, I can tell you that Earth is a foul place. Only prophets have set foot here. It is world unfit for God, (the real one, not the open-mouthed one from whose head I yank teeth). This sets Islam apart from other religions wherein God and other divinities have trod down here. Give more credence to the calendar that begins with the Hejir. Believe not in sanctity gratuitously inherited from birth.

He taught prior prophets and will teach all of those yet to come. This is no breach of faith. Never shall I be pure enough. Beware, I'm one of the worst sinners. This has been clear right from the start. The devil can become a pollard, rid of his horns, fill pock to acquire smooth skin, shed pluvial tears to show compassion, lull your worst fears and even condemn pogrom, but only to better prepare future fare. If he endears you with his ploy, keep in mind that he's Hell's plenipotentiary envoy, that those plimsole shoes he wears are adapted to hiding hooves rather than made for sport. Behind the smile, the mind is all a plash with fire and blood. With wet flash all can turn to mire and flood. It's best not to expire in this mud.

Think for awhile before you plaudit he who wears vest of plush with purl stitch. Yet don't listen to the final piffle of those about to go phut after having fed on thin domenical wafers served out from gilded pyx.

Call me Phospho.

If you're impressed by his pelth, question in which door's lock will fit the passkey he offers. Sign no promissory notes. Stay with the proletariat, flee plutocrats.

Pure pukka. I'll whisper when caressing her pudendum. Live in purlieu, one foot in the forest. And if she's in danger, don't hesitate to seclude her, revert to purdah. Settle not for the quango offered by this quisling. Full liberty is at hand.

Never drop kick severed heads. Place kicks are much more precise.

Now, as for Gog, he's no god but the patron for the menagerie, the ever so vast one, to which she and I are purveyors. The creatures we hunt are no Barbary lions.

How be it our bed's still warm, yet we've been gone for so long?

She prepares for me two dishes from Cameroon: "Congress" which is truly a royal feast destined to honor in the highest manner he whose stomach it is to fill. The base is chicken, but almost anything imaginable is heaped upon it. As in most American dishes, quantity counts here too. Throw in bacon for the pork loving palate of Whites. Vegetables, but not only those gleaned from surrounding forest. Small yams, pale peanuts rid of their shells and ground down into purée, coca leaf again and an odd powder obtained from grinding black stones together, all of this with much pimento of the bulbous variety that burns the mouth like nitric acid if pure while giving an intoxicating perfume to the stew. Its aroma hangs heavy in the hot air along with the smoke from wood fires. Indispensable miando, sticks of manioc that glisten when the leaves are peeled back, offer respite to the burning mouth.

Accompanied, or rather preceded by Pepe soup with smoked zebu and porcupine, much spice too. The porcupine's fine, but beware for sharp little bones and buckshot. Better have plenty beer. Keep at hand small green mangos that you can suck on after having bitten off the tip.

We speak Arabic in these zones now, but it isn't as simple as you might think. Berber, French and even Spanish fused to form a dialect. Hardly any one understands literary Arab.

Push over this palm tree, tap the trunk and let the sap ferment in a plastic jug. Makes the very best palm wine that bubbles in the mouth.

Don't leave your car in this street. They'll set up shop on the hood or the trunk, sell rotten things that'll leak, stain and eat through the body. Won't even be able to chase them off before they've finished their business. It's their street. They own it. They'd rather kill you than break shop.

I asked a woman once to take up her shop, told her I was in a big hurry, needed my vehicle fast.

—Tired of life? she asked. —Just step out of it, like shedding a skin or undressing. Don't tell me now that you feel naked!

We have adopted patterns that belie the so-called unpredictability of humans, a north-south disjunct distribution, moving poleward in the summer, carrying along near-term embryos. Should I tell you that polar zones are tropical, that all in between is fire? Travelling through deep valleys and canyons where only boiling ponds remain of the oceans, where many creatures have adapted, become part flame rather than dying off, is most perilous. Will the few of us who have survived succeed in this perilous conversion to combustion?

—Why remain when you can go anywhere?

—Remain faithful to those who can't!

The Sun's organized a *battue*. We jump like beach fleas. Avoid being bemauled.

—Bawcock, you've been cast in a beast epic. To find the real "*you*," submit yourself to shroff. Feed on beadeye, (stone cat). Don't confuse smallage with cigue. Fimbriate. Take your bebeerine. Sun's your bedlamp. Or witch ball beneath which it is well to waltz. Times for beer and skittles! Brush beggar's lice from sleeves. Sing me a *berceuse*.

Cortez

I can live with it. They haven't souls, nothing worth saving, I tell myself. Between me and them, there's a universe of difference. I'm the civilized one. They're hardly more than animals. No remorse have I. It isn't slaughter nor even conquest, albeit of the most violent sort, that I wreak upon them. Call it appropriation. No more than fanning flies from an apple, digging worms from the flesh before taking a bite.

No animosity had I towards them when first contact was made. They were sitting on such wealth; riches that were totally unexploited by them. I knew right from the start that I would have to get around them somehow in order to take possession of the treasure.

Me finally here, nothing should get in my way.

Contempt for them wasn't long in coming. If I had been momentarily dazzled by their golden skin, the way it caught light, reflecting the entire spectrum of their dim sun, it wasn't long before I perceived the smell that each one bore. An odor of over-ripe fruit fallen to the ground and worm ridden. Fruit that had lingered on the limb too long, awaiting the never coming plucking hand.

They hadn't any manner of civilization; no laws, no religion, no culture, no technological achievement and certainly no commerce. Didn't even qualify as a Type I civilization according to Nicolai Kardashev's classical scale.

What would have been the point of preaching, attempting to inculcate democracy or even trying to do trade with them? Evangilization, colonization, the rudiments of civilization? Would they be worth teaching? To what avail? Who could want to live here? Their sun, though it be a distant one, sends in slanting caustic rays in a color that I'll call vouge, close to rouge, almost violet and subdued, this ill-hued glimmer draws warts from human skin and eventually brings on hyper-pilosity. Teeth appear yellow, the white of the eye too.

Core-helium consumption is underway in this star. Comparison with solar-metallicity Padova isochrones has proven beyond doubt that we're in the 30 Myr range. But this is no infallible caveat. It would be wise to use a variety of methods and tracer objects.

The wealth which lay beneath their feet, over which they daily trod, sat or bred upon, obviously wasn't theirs. It had been waiting for me over periods unimaginable. They weren't even nomads tending flocks. Mere migratory species were they, temporarily occupying space without detaining any manner of title or property rights. True, they did come to meet me in fashion which could have been interpreted as being a reception with primitive protocol. Drink came in my direction, not upon platters nor in pitchers or goblets, but in the form of oblate bubbles of sticky fluids floating in the atmosphere that would run down my arms stinging when I would attempt to grasp them. These were accompanied by bundles of wrapped small creatures that resembled struggling insects.

I'm certain now, that this was no offering; rather poison flung my way, meant to keep the intruder that I was at bay. But now then, was not this in itself, the manifestation of a form of intelligence?

Hate for them set in quickly. At first I had sought to distinguish family structure. Male adults, females and young. Maybe this was an attempt on my behalf to seek some sort of affinity. They procreated and love did seem to exist. There were even families with offspring.

But as with vermin, this was merely an extension to what had to be eliminated.

Time to collect.

I was alert, needing some slight pretext to initiate the self-appropriation process. A threat or an aggressive action coming from their quarter? But they were so totally inoffensive, peaceful to the highest degree, living together in the purest harmony. It would have to do, this purity of theirs which could be interpreted as being a manner of threat in itself, an extremely contagious thing, contrary to humanity, which if permitted to pass on, could very well wipe out entire sections of the Universe. Together, they already appeared to have a rolling action. In time it could become an impenetrable structure, this putative rolling motion, apparently non-Keplerian, composed of complex vortex lines, permitting distortion while offering virtual immunity to destruction. Simultaneous poloidal and toroidal rotation.

I've made fine soft gloves and delicate fans from the tender skins of their underbellies. My light, my touch are in turn gilded. I wear their teeth in heavy necklaces. Most sparkling collar. Bejeweled, starchains about my neck, I drink their blood, which has the property of never coagulating. I've even bottled and sold it in Naples on the occasion of the annual feast of San Genaio. How many earthquakes have these small miracle-bearing vials warded off? Not to speak of countless snuffed volcanic eruptions.

Finally, I found that buried with the treasure there were traces of civilization. An infinite quantity of signs in suspension. It was like wading through alphabet soup, all the while trying to interpret the meaning. Though I came across patterns and alignments, I obliged myself to believe that it was probably just chance association devoid of any sense. These symbols clung to me, sticking to my clothing like autumn burr bearing seed, impossible to brush away.

What I perpetrate here is beyond genocide. Weary of killing, I set up camp. They gather round. Are they mustering for battle or simply lining up to be slain? If I'm to come to the end of them, I'll need method. But being from a world with such rich genocidiary history, I'll have no trouble with method.

Haven't I already employed timeless formulae?

Lessons in hate:

1) Consider yourself as one of a very special chosen people. Selected by the only God, superior to all other deities. This God will have given you command to spread veneration by all means appropriate, conquer lands occupied by mecreants or believers in false deities, reclaim territories where you were purported to have lived during pre-prophetic times. Deportation of other races by progressive or massive colonization of the lands which they occupied, the assassination of political leaders. Dismantle any tribal hierarchy, pitilessly eliminate kings, queens, their heirs and their court; even slaves, dwarves and jesters, for they too can accede to thrones; but especially spiritual leaders. If your race has suffered in the past, lessons can be drawn and applied. You can show the way by inventing the car bomb for example, provoking the targeted ones to adopt the same methods and then over-retaliate, wiping them out as a preventive measure. Deportation is always useful. Stonewall Jackson and Hitler, in just that order, had both

understood this. And hadn't Hertzl himself toyed with the idea of freeing unexploited lands of their unproductive occupants by simply "displacing" them? Carefully reread his journals.

But if time is short or if you are alone and under-equipped, it is best to skip the preliminaries and go directly to basic butchering. Use anything handy, clubs, mechanical tools, or even writing material.

2) Consider them as being different from yourself. Focus on what can be interpreted as being inferiority. Exacerbate all elements that can make them appear to pose a potential threat.

3) Have no guilt, and if remorse begins to make its way, brandish the suffering that your own people experienced in the past. This is the perfect shield, cutting short criticism; in itself, a splendid protective garment.

—The above are time-tested, developed by great researchers over the past, (never forgetting that this "past" will be the future): Cortez and Pizzaro against the Aztecs and Incas, Hitler against the Jews, Sharon against the Palestinians. Does the degree of barbarity vary?

But especially, slavers holds were filled and nations were built upon these precepts.

—I'm not asking that you squeal with glee each time you kill one of them. But you can at least smile.

You may be shocked, trying to convince yourself by saying, "I had nothing to do with any of these sinister happenings. Neither did my father nor my grandfather" Or maybe you're one of those who reduces the impact of these events, refers to Rwanda (forgetting even Cambodia) as the true measure of barbarity, denying that war in the West was ever anything else than chivalrous engagement, sparing women and children, devoid of any manner of barbarity, while men maneuvered upon well defined battlefields. Would you be of those who sanctify the term genocide, declaring that only one people ever suffered such fate? And that they in turn are now sacred and incapable of perpetrating their own kind of hate? It's not something you can simply appropriate.

Climb back down far enough along the family tree, and if mankind really did spring from a single pair of small, timid mammals, chances are that one of your ancestors participated in some type of wanton slaughter somewhere along the way, and if they didn't, then at least they knew of it and could have acted in some manner to avoid what was to come.

Be your family tree clean, unearth it and shake the roots. You'll most certainly find clinging there, ugly things that the soil had so well hidden. No need to go all of the way back to reptile ancestry.

What is this crude time reversal? Simply a question of fecal matter going back up into the anal cavity, working its way up the colon, being undigested so as to climb the esophagus and exit the mouth, landing intact in one's plate? A menu of pig for example. From there, re-entering the oven, going back to the butcher's stall, the slaughter house, the pig farm where as healthy adults, swine contaminate the soil with their urine, run-off water filling rivers and ocean bays with nitrates that render emerald green the sea where fish, already loaded with mercury and chromium, can no longer breath.

They wear wrist watches here. If only I can examine one of these, note the time, hope that the date and maybe even the year will be in some manner indicated.

The pig is a suckling being fed anti-biotics developed by a major pharmaceutical laboratory that also produces the fertilizer necessary to grow the corn to feed the pork as well as the nitrate that ends up in the pig piss, eventually running out to sea. This company is a big shareholder in Vitality (the water purification company) that treats the great quantities that you daily drink and wash your car with. It has been said that you wear only couture clothing, that an important part of your modest budget goes to vacation in Morocco. You fly there on an airplane constructed by Space Dynamics.

Does this sound like some sort of a children's riddle?

Would it be altogether confusing to introduce here Simon Nzapa ti gongo, (the god of palaber)? He announces to French and Belgian colonizers, imposing their law along the banks of the Uèlé river, that the day will come when Africans will order Whites to climb up the palm trees, power will be inversed, things will be set straight. —Whites will be at our service, he says. This is 1953.

Glib eco-political discourse, this? Portent of things to come?

Let's reconsider the Moroccan scenario: World press moguls are all friends of the king's and have there, their own private palaces. Journalists are offered free exotic vacations here, movie stars too. Writers, nostalgic of the beat era, also live here. Would this be the reason you've never heard about this conflict? The Western Sahara one, where Occidental citizens so unwittingly contributed to the oppression of the exiled Sahrawi people. Of course these good democratic people of France and America were politically manipulated, uninformed or misinformed by media, while their governments gave themselves carte blanche.

But then, there's always been the possibility that we thought ourselves to be so well informed that verity couldn't pass behind our backs while indeed, it might have slipped beneath our very noses.

I unwrap broad dark leaves protecting a kanda paté made from crushed squash seeds mixed with smoked river fish and jungle herbs. This fare has kept well, unspoiled during my entire trip. Think of how Awa had caught these fish, pulling them with her hands from under rocks during low water of the dry season, the herbs she had gathered at dawn, entering the forest when it was still hidden by the morning fog, the fire she had made at sunset to cure the fish, the smoke blowing back into the jungle. Lightning had started brush fires.

Realize that we're in a city, on the edge, hardly more than a suburb. In no way are we in the surrounding jungle, the hinterlands.

While continuing this campaign of ethnical purification, ethical validation, I'm constantly discovering new things about them, things I hadn't perceived at first. For instance there are manholes here, but all of the covers have been removed. Why? What were they used for? Primitive traps. (Earlier, I will have fallen into one).

My only weapon is a defensive one, the most magnificent glass armor, upon which inoffensively slipped the teeth of the neighbor's pit-bull when I jumped the fence while testing. True, it's a burden to wear, weighing some seventy kilos. Being totally naked within, my skin sticks to the inner surface when I begin to sweat. Fortunately, heavy perspiration brings on a natural lubrication and all is slippery and well thereafter.

They go down without resistance. No more innocent were baby seals, clubbed to death for their white fur on ice banks gone red.

A semblance of morning arrives with a whisky flavored pale copper fog. It's time that I take practical measures if I'm to come to the end of them. Alone, could I set up a carceral system here, in order to facilitate industrialized killing? Hardly! Finally, there may be time for the installation of a semblance of democracy after all, passport for the universe of the wildest long-term repression of emerging worlds.

Or yes! Swiftly scatter the seeds for the foundation of several religions, they can even have the same common source which will save considerable time, separate into clans, each one convinced they are a chosen people.

—They're all alike?

—Look closer. Some have whiskers, others are slightly paler than the majority. Complexion is a vital tool. Here's a minority!

Return to democracy. Only the pure bloods will be eligible to run for office.

—They're all purebloods?

—I forgot to tell you that during the brief time before I became disgusted with them, we interbred. And even afterwards, while engaged in full-blown slaughter, I was raping mother and daughter. Many *metis* were born from these beds of fire, all the while cutting off heads. Require that I, the sire, don't inquire about the souls of those who expire? They simply haven't any!

Sacrifice my very own offspring? Will there be no help for this ill-born whelp?

Many are spared. Though forbidden to hold political position, they bear the genes of violence, my gift to them. This ensures that they'll rebel, overthrow and so on.

By now, I have serious doubts. While further exploring, I find more traces of civilization, one much more advanced than ours ever will have been. Had they already gone this route, only to turn their backs on it? Simply a question of memory? Or was it a civilization that they themselves, had long ago conquered with their overwhelming peace?

Dusk here is green, they day went by so quickly, providing the most striking contrast with their purple hemoglobin that floats in the atmosphere in long strands. I can't even wash it from my hands. It sticks like tar, (my palms are excoriated from trying to rub away their blood). In certain places it undulates upward, real far. I imagine myself to be a nonchalant sea lion playing in giant Pacific coast seaweed, while hunting immature octopae. Just this sort of light, the same tranquility.

If I had been apprehensive the first few nights, expecting some kind of reprisal, I have now learned to relax, remove my protective attire and cleanse my wounds; mainly blisters from wielding primitive weapons. I've placed the glass armor beneath the tent, in a sitting posture,

(I should also inform you before it's too late, that it's the glass suit of armor that's been carrying on the conversation with me in this section of the *Book of Fever*). No doubt, I needn't protection from any aggressive action coming from their quarter, but more from the effect of my own deathblows dealt with such ferocity. Heads bounce back when improperly decapitated, the biggest danger being when the act is incomplete, the wind pipe or whatever strands of flesh might be left, acting like giant rubber bands, confer to the heads a whiplash action. Also, any severed limbs flying around in the thin atmosphere, can become dangerous projectiles.

I speak to this semblance of company, the seated glistening armor.

—We must plan the coming night, say our prayers together.

Having had nothing else at hand, the tent is made from their skins, roughly sewn together.

Ejaculation is deep blue. What misses the orifices (the females have two mouths and several sexual cavities), floats in the air.

Change my mind. Form warlords. Leave behind wealthy warring factions. Will become consumers of arms, soft drinks, in exchange for crude fuel and ore.

A caricature?

All before was just rehearsal. I'll oblige them to pay taxes; if they don't, I won't hesitate to cut off their hands with axes!

The fact that they're humanoid only increases the pleasure of whacking off a limb or severing a head.

Provide for them, a primary education. If they want to learn more, they'll be obliged to travel very far, beyond the most distant star.

Guilt?

An additional layer to the thick skin I already have.

Becoming very interesting here. Could spend several eternities just contemplating. They're developing a full-blown technological civilization. I'll withdraw, satisfy myself with being considered as their god. I must leave before the chosen ones discover that they've been abandoned. The *metis* will be demi-gods.

Roll dice without pip. This could all be a pipe dream. Plague-bearing insects. Prepare pesticides! Without piperonyl butoxide, there'll be no smooth mix.

What's this twitter? Be it the song of some pipit? If it's true, that'll do. Pish! Perform pirouettes. No need for *pissoir*. I'm no *pitier*. The very best *plastiqeur*. And I can honestly say, *"mon heure est venue!"* (plaudits). The pleasure principle guides my action.

Think you, me, to be on some sort of mission, sent out by a powerful government whose doctrine would be that of Manifest Destiny, revised to recognize no limits? No need to subtilize in order to realize that it's *unwize* to theorize about the size of the prize I'll ravish from these creatures I terrorize. Rise! Have you no intuition? Your mind's like a vitrine, transparent, leaving secret thought out in the open. Yet nothing could be less apparent. Are these not words of verity I have spoken? Some foul liquid flowing from a latrine that's been broken? Spirit bearing these criminal thoughts should be put in quarantine like an ill voyager harboring deathly virus. Take not this new strain to a laboratory. Rare token. Build a research center up around it. No more fever than I, had Pyrus! Plundering is my substantive right. You'll put no snaffle bit in my mouth. Archangels have no fear of soiling their hands. You'll never find us to be near, but off toiling in distant lands. Roll up your sleeves and join in!

Hair springs from my face, cascades down the cheeks in long silken curls. No werewolf appearance, but rather the look of a noble lord wearing his wig down over the face in the manner of a veil. It so well conceals the warts welling up. Tusks shall emerge too.

I'm tired from the killing. Raise the square yellow flag!

—Oh Hernando! And you, Gonzales! How swung yee double-edged swords with such ease? It is said that with a single blow, you could divide Indians cleanly down the middle, that you had mastiffs bigger than horses and horses that were even meaner than these ill-tempered dogs.

Ariel! So clever were you, wielding fallen Gemayal's phalangists in Sabra and Chatila, mere gloves protecting your hands from the taint. Thistle! But this'll not prevent me from taking Levi's prayers to the wailing wall, he too old and without other family than myself, I'll insert them along with my own. His for those herded and turned to ash, mine to bridle he who wars on fellow Semites. Useless sneck, these prayers folded and introduced between four-ton stones that hold alone? In a strictly spacio-temporal context, Sadr, Harb, Jarradi, and Musawi lie not far from Rabin. Lodged in humanity's windpipe.

Left of right, which really isn't right at all.

Scimble-scamble? Political considerations bubble in the blood when emerging from abyssal time. I've said it before, it's a recurring constant. They can bring on the bends just like nitrogen, best to filter, insert in stonework. It's clearly explained above.

Sell raw peanuts in small bottles. Lay out your wash along the road. Passing tanks will press patterns into the fabric.

I've decided to settle down, reside for a while. I'm dressed in camouflage, not the leopard pattern worn by the elite Kamanyola division under Mobutu's orders in ex-Zaire, but long shreds torn from the vegetal motifs of the Dame à la Licorne *tapisserie*, woven during the Middle Ages. Over my shoulders, I've thrown a purple shawl; I wear golden slippers and carry a bright red woman's handbag of considerable size.

Just when was it that I crossed the border that I had vowed never to trespass?

Our conversation becomes slurvian. Ride a sloat to the next act.

I force the glass suit to swallow fermented drink. It's full of brew.

Are not the monuments here more impressive than anywhere else? These giant viaducts over which no vehicles pass. Those canals that hold no water, vaster and more intricate than anything Schiaperelli had ever thought to see on Mars. Here, statues float in the air. Any sculptor's dream, to behold his own work aloft in this manner, the question of the cumbersome pedestal forever resolved. Here's an immense hand with three missing fingers, half a face blown from a giant stone Buddha's head and slowly spinning with its very own rotational movement, two mouths brimming with crystallized blue sperm. There's a woman's portrait hanging in low geo-stationary orbit. The size of a small hill, she's smoking a cigarette, real smoke coming in perfectly formed circles from her half-open double lips. Anyone here would give anything, even suffer amputation, just for a puff.

I decide to import a continent, ship here immense quantities of red African soil. Build a palace which will only serve as a kitchen, with rust colored wallpaper and thin gray felt on the floor. There's a skylight. I still live in a tent just off to the side. Someone has tried to cheat me. Mixed in with the African soil are readily identifiable sloth claws, remains of howler monkeys and Yanomami Indian artifacts.

What music is this I hear? The sands vibrate with deep rhythm. It's the voice of the dunes, so rarely heard elsewhere, that circle this planet and collide with one another, taking on new beat. Not only percussion. Birds and insects of varieties unknown, sing together, complex melodies they have learned.

Vehicles exist. They are parked in garages without exits. They can traverse walls, roofs, floors.

Temporarily, I'm a mechanic, disassembling the engines.

The wing that I sand down while kneeling over it is too stubby to permit flight. It tricks the air into believing that it can do so.

Such weapons have I made available here! Have you ever heard of delayed assassination? Deal the blow, you'll have plenty of time to flee. Like the ingestion of certain alpine mushrooms, the effect will only make itself felt a year or ten from then. It's called "mountain climbing" or the "clean sweep," where death enters the victim, taking him back through time, to efface his life at an early stage.

They in turn, have become arms merchants.

Now the land is awash with their treasure, a lubricant that permits super-conductivity at any temperature, facilitates travel at supraliminal speeds, simultaneous communication over the longest distances, obliteration of horizons.

Great amounts of re-radiation occurring, with high concentration of small particles, mostly thread-like whiskers of carbon and iron. They are incapable of retaining heat and re-emit almost immediately absorbed energy on a totally different wavelength. Does this reflect the conditions from which this star emerged from interstellar gas?

Finally, from this point of view, it has become evident that there is widespread anomalous redshift in surrounding galactic field, resulting in great confusion in the Hubble diagram. Should Arp have been removed from telescopes? Narlikar, Burbridge and Hoyle been so bridled?

Had not cosmology, astro-physics, become fields wherein theory served only to validate theory?

Don't expect any kurana from me. A kurbash at the hip, a kukri beneath the belt, sitting beneath a kurrajong, I delicately pick the petals of the yellowish bellflowers that shower down with the wind. The sky is yellow with dust. No need to revise my koniology to know that germs are flying today. I've made good use of knots, tying a Mathew Walker at the tip of the whip (almost turning it into a knout), and running a Black-wall hitch over a hanging hook to suspend the glass armor. Tired of it always being seated when we speak.

—A little respect! No more kyoodling or I'll kick your kyte!

—Leprotic Leninist! it replies, a sudden lensing effect, glinting off the shiny gut plate.

—Looby! What am I doing in this lorn place with you? Lucent losel!

Things are going wrong between the two of us. We have lobscouse for dinner. The meat's gone bad. Need to lunt the fire several times. Coff a blood snake. Never cloy of this fare. Cloots! Where's my clinah?

I'm in love with one of them. Deeply so. No letch. Abyssal romance. Were we oceanic, we would be frequenters of marine trenches, canyons, cold and black where water pressure would compress our bodies, making separation impossible. Liquid loe. Eternal penetration.

She has no nose, just two holes with slime flowing out. I'm obliged to incessantly wipe down this area with silken handkerchiefs in order to remove the fine sand that adheres there. The sparkling effect is beautiful but the resulting abrasion irritates her skin in this most sensitive place where are concentrated her thermal sensory organs. She's ablepharus. How does she perceive me? Immense, ruddy image which fluctuates in her mind? A type of lethal mirage with which it is amusing to play? Or on the other hand, does she sense me to be a crystalline thing, cold immobile, posing no manner of threat? She's surely aware of the slaughter that I've wrought. When I approach, there seems to be an instant of hesitation, recoil even, before we enlace. She's beautiful, crumpled fingers and all. Let's embrace! No need to knot her salpinx. Put on the sallet and squint through the vision slit.

—You think me to be some sort of pervert? We'll have a show of hands.

—No, no, says the smooth transparent one who makes conversation with me in this silent place.

—Don't be a schnook!

Scrape sinter from geyser vents. Wish for silver storm. Drink syllabub.

(Skyward) —Think you to shrive me, fawning parasite? Easier than shooting shoat. I'm no schnorrer.

Together, we live beneath the tent. It's been greatly expanded, covers well over an acre. Sections have been closed off with heavy curtains. Very theatrical. She installs vast aquariums, home to newts, olms, mud-puppies and hellbenders, all imported with great difficulty and hardly ever visible due to the murky water in which they thrive. The prize is a diplocaulus from Coal Age swamps. Most beautiful slimy anvil shaped head with soft swept-back horns. An occasional ripple on the surface, an odor of swamp are the only signs of life. She did it for me, knowing that instead of pets which might appear sophisticated at first sight, futuristic even, I prefer these creatures that are so close to primal perfection. A leap into the unexpected direction of the backwards world, the future being, I insist, beneath the past.

Yet, I must leave all of this, retire to become their god. Leave before the chosen ones realize that they're about to be orphaned. If not, they'll soon attain a level of technological achievement which will permit them to see me as I am. The *metis* are already demi-gods in their own right, just as I shall have been in *Bunsana Bua*.

Where's my aide-de-camp?

Is this not remorse that I'm experiencing? A desire for pardon. As if I wanted them to kill me. Sacrifice which, this time, would permit me to properly come down in their midst. Attempt to endear them to me, return their love, just when they haven't any left. They'll even prove that I never existed.

—Was it worth it? says the glass suit.

—In this I admire the spider merchant. Such simplicity. Effortless. She knew what to introduce, that which would produce. Spiders have eight eyes. Pesticides are the best buys.

The soil is too hard to dig up and when there are dunes, they prove to be extremely mobile, unfit for covering the quantity of bodies which have slowly fallen to the ground. They are remarkably well preserved by the hot, dry climate.

—What will you do with all of them? asks the suit of armor.

—Do you think we're dummies? We'll line them up for shipping. I know just the place to sell these golden mummies!

—I'm all athrill. Waiting atiptoe! Want some atropine?

—If I succumb to atropism, you'll remain forever empty. Stay here. Fill with sand.

—Atweel! *Au fond*, I'd be an hourglass.

—Audacious aumbry tinted auld carapace. Observer of birds. Awless one. We'll come to some manner of Ausgleich.

—Unsheik your coal scuttle blonde, you spagingy-spagade! Do it down in bam. Monkey-hip eater mon.

—Fagingy-fagade. Enough of this bookooing.

—Axiomatic! You've performed here a veritable tour de force, moralizing while terrorizing.

A thick sand mist sets in, yellow of course, like China bai. Must maintain baculine discipline with this insolent armor. Perhaps the fact that it's made mainly of reflective glass explains mounting impertinence. Badb! Better play a quick hand of Bolito, haven't the time for more than two digits anyway.

I make a scientific chart of my cranium parts. The tongue goes all the way around the tent wall, the perimeter of a measured acre. To properly reproduce certain details I'm obliged to open up my own head. It's the most delicate of dissections. Once again, I discover reptile structure. Whose cousin am I? Varanus Komoensis. Not a water monitor, nor even the high-mountain lizard.

A feast is organized in my honor. A long table constructed on the model of medieval chateau-fort furniture, massive wooden, feet sculpted to form the paws of griffins, with matching chairs. The table cloth is the original Bayeux *tapisserie*. No need for silverware or plates, the food floats in the air; no glasses either, fluids being more like gases. I'm eating on the portrayal of a knight hacking off his own sex with an axe. Yet there is a sauceboat. Brimming with samp.

Claqeurs applaud here!

Change decor. Have hack-leg furniture. Smoke hookah.

To catch our fare, we play games, leaping and twisting in the air like trained seals. The noseless woman, SWW (for South Wind Woman; she always turns in that direction when going to sleep), has installed a large landscape oil painting of high mountain peaks, that contrasts strikingly with the flat surface of this planet where all is low and hugs the ground in spite of the thin atmosphere and the want of erosion. I weep. She brings cups to the cantle corners of my eyes, catching tears, which she chugs. Chimborazo Mompox. Pleinairisme. Toothed birds have come to perch. There's a risk of smallpox.

—Bear me bairn.

The skulls of the felled ones are of many different shapes and sizes. Beaten with batons, they produce a surprising variety of notes. Plenary indulgence.

Water comes strangely, yellow, pushing its way over the land. It doesn't fall from clouds. There are none. The spearhead of some great river of unknown source. There must be a monumental spring somewhere, opening up like a great wound in the land, and this liquid would be its blood.

—Better analyze this ooze! says the suit.

—Have you had too much booze?

—Baith of us, full of barley-bree. Could pose for a quickly painted bambochade.

—Continue in this vein. I'll cut T-shaped face slit in your headpiece!

—Canst accept sub-villain role?

I listen for the buzz of flies, look for vultures. These things I miss. They could help with the bodies lying all about. Hyenas, jackals, even wild dogs would be welcome.

Sudden *éclaircissement*. All's aglow with bastard amber. Proof again that this might be a stage. Secret side-act.

The surviving golden ones plunge into the water. There are even cataracts now where the flat land has given under the weight of freshly formed lakes. Returning from their swim, which they perform in swift spirals like puppy dogs going for their own tails, they appear to be rapidly changing. The head structure thickens, jaws swell, speech evolves, coming from deeper down. Suddenly they seem aggressive.

—*Sauve qui peut*! There'll be no scramble. There are only two of us. Better put on your sandshoes.

—Take along sandwiches?

—Enough chutzpa.

—Fill the pyx with sacred wafers!

Deliquesce.

Colcothar

Middle world isn't the place you'd think it to be. If it shifts, the entire context will shift along with it. Middle thinking, middle art and middle civilizations are in reality situated to the outside of anything central. You must understand that this holds true even if they first appear to be right on target. Exo-culture, slips between God's squeezing grip like jelly, taking along with it, the gravest forms of pathogenic genesis; slip through fingers the size of quarter universe. Squirt. This is median. The outside's inside. Like pork gut, vermiculated to better retain savor. Our edifices are also vermiculated, even when built of the hardest stone. Mineral substances that make marble, basalt and granite seem like tender sponge or a plate of over cooked noodles that no engineer could ever manage to construct with. They'll not fall in soft heaps. We dig coils into this building material, fit blocks of it together. Have a serious revolutionary history. Underground galleries are full of it.

What then would be middle art? Immense battle scenes and insurrectional portraits; posing with AK-47s or hand-held RPGs over the shoulder. Long-eared companions can appear at edge of frame. Mules have always been better than jeeps, especially in mountainous terrain.

Dwellings? Hard materials are limited to public buildings. Mud palaces can be built ten stories high. Haven't any metal available here? Use bamboo scaffolding. Can go plenty high. Prepare white patches on facade to accommodate small mural paintings. Blue hyena near the skyline, just beneath torn up tin roofing. Some sculptures on rain gnarled columns. Man playing pipe. Draw brilliant blankets across courtyards and passageways. Motifs illustrate war between Yoruba and Fon factions. Interference comes from White slavers. Lion mauls hapless upside down Black man. Panther divinity with horns supervises scene. It is estimated that Fons had upwards of 2000 casualties, mostly

Amazons, when French conquered Dahomey in 1892. French lost 10 officers and 67 soldiers.

Use immense musket to shoot monkeys from small trees. Each man will have his own throne. Sit on army hiding beneath. Each queen will have her king. Every princess will have her red doll full of pins. Play Azande harp that's shaped like little standing man with strings drawn between belly and brow. Use your many bladed NZakara throwing knife. Can't miss! Throw Mangbetu shawl, made of bark crushed by ivory club, over cold shoulders.

Direct a play where comedians wear space suits. Story set in Kinshasa.

Carry heavy white crates overhead at arm's length. Bon voyage to Hell! Wear yellow shirt and white tie with upward-pointing red chevron pattern while engaging in this exercise.

Set up Ochomma street corner barber saloon. Make a poster showing different hair styles. Sit on giant dead cow's head while attending flock of guinea hens. With white nipple milk black child. Fuck devil's bride from behind. Make sure her tits are pierced with small golden coconut clusters that tinkle when you bang her. Never perform this act outside of the city. Can insert index finger in rectum. Dress up like a cowboy and charge through Somalia firing at anything that moves. Withdraw, shocked after suffering a few casualties. Call this Act I. Implying we'll soon be back for part II. Stand at attention while receiving posthumous military decorations. True, you're already stiff!

Pick cotton, prepare manioc in a tub. Teach Kung fu to neighborhood kids. Equip everyone with rubber boots. Keep a picture-album of classic time machines. Make your own from a kit. Organize a protest march. Brandish big photo of Ho Chi Minh. Wear Chinese straw hat in African jungle. Hang a map of the black quarter of Stanleyville on the wall. Make a very crude painting of the "discolobus thrower." Dress up in western suits. Don't forget cane and cigarette. Buy magnificent white wedding dress. Peek from behind big tropical leaf while wearing sunglasses. Walk through busy city streets wearing only a cape, thrusting beautiful full breasts forward. Dance all night beneath purple lights in small bars. Drink great quantities of ice cold beer. Continue wearing the cape. Conceals scarification patterns on back.

Review the battle of Adowa. But first, study the two differing versions of the Treaty of Wuchale between Menelik II and Italian king.

Ask for Middle Art. Salute the manager in charge. Commission a sculptor from Ghana to make a coffin for you. Provide a good photo of melted porcelain cup from Hiroshima nuclear bombing for the model. Wear a pith helmet. Make sure it's white.

Publish a review entitled "Walking on Eggs" with two stylized elephants on the cover.

Build giant mausoleum resembling seated woman. Cover it with square patches of white plastic. Leave round opening at the base. Illuminate interior with lamps. Entire edifice must be at least fifty feet high. Provide perches in upper reaches for native birds. Carefully follow Pume's design while constructing this monument.

Carry out important military maneuvers on vast perfectly flat plain. Keep kneeling camels out of sight behind row of low trees to the side. Pretend to ignore satellite surveillance. Never spear mating antelope. Speak to fish, scratch their backs.

Don't dance to just any music you hear. Reconstruct shattered young nations by hanging flags on clotheslines.

Dress like an American Indian. Attack a tank with a sword. Put on a French casquette. Grab a microphone and make a political speech.

Join miners deep in mine shafts in Belgian Congo and South Africa. Car wreck.

A head opened up like a food tin. Who's been feeding here? Interrogators.

The sack of Benin City. Treasure (carved tusks etc.) taken off to Germany, burned during WW II bombing. Plaster models still exist in Paris museum reserve.

Exile of Jaja of MPopo.

Set sail. Go gunkholing. Niggle with everyone.

I have chills. Don't think that we never catch cold here in sub-tropics. But then again, the desert isn't the place it's said to be. If the temperatures fall somewhat with nightfall, never do they plunge. The cooling is only relative. From three million gauss down to 45 for example.

Steven Biko's death, the assassination of Dulcie September, can best be illustrated with artwork, even if I'm certain that some thick-browed,

Dutch-speaking, southern white man's gotten away with amateur film footage of torture sessions of the former. Tortioneer pardoned by the Truth and Reconciliation Commission. As for the latter, the French secret service most probably had direct role in the Paris killing. Exaggerate *à outrance* the size of the head in your drawings.

Is it only now that the French are discovering the widespread use of torture by army and police? Their very own war crimes? (mainly against Algerians).

Middle world. From here we guide (often very awkwardly), miniature replicas of ourselves, or immense ones. Is it they that control, to either side, we who think to be the middle lords? Wear heart in head position, bury head in poitrine cavity and then, like the pelican in Christian lore, tear into your own chest with immense beak to reveal real countenance: smile that will defile, offering for thirsty children. Richer than any blood. Extract the middle and inner ear mechanisms. Stapes and Incus, Cochlea and internal auditory meatus. Carefully clean and examine to make sure no foreign devices have been introduced while sleeping.

Be an *agent provocateur*. Constantly prowl. Eat agouti.

Avoid scraping with finger nails or sharp objects.

Cup hands together to hold shotgun shells. Understand that if birth rate soars, it's only because God's parsimonious about peace and happiness; not so with cruelty which he most generously melds with ambition to obtain war.

Go to Mozambique, Angola. Dig for land mines. Bumper crop. Thinking oblique?

Check points and Roadblocks again. How to cope with them. South Africa/Israel. Don't aggrieve me.

Something's agly. Again, I'm all aguish.

Prone political assassinations in order to prevent future terrorism, bulldoze houses of innocent citizens to retaliate for suicide bombings, (Ahmad Qassir often considered to be the very first, was preceded by members of Irgoun and Stern). Rip up landing strips at airports etc. Chills, swallow pills. Write final wills. Hide in ateliers amongst rubber sculptures, make sure the artist is a mannerist so that you can blend with the highly distorted bodies. Avoid high mountains. Climb over low hills. Don't ever pay your bills. They're what kills!

The city's full of children resembling Jane Alexander's Bom Boys. Blindfolded, wearing masks with beaks and rabbit ears. I wear high, conical, dark felt hat. Bright blue tongs. Pose sitting with my daughter in front of me. The wallpaper's made of fashion magazine covers and advertisements. Can glimpse downtown area through tear in the wall. U, Y, O and T-shaped buildings. One with giant ears. Another sports pink plastic tongue that thrusts laterally from building facade, most insolently defying the law of gravity. Tramway erupts from, or penetrates, tunnel entrance set square in the middle of immense glass ass. Passengers waiting on the quay are warned of imminent penetration/defecation. They enter smooth turd-shaped trolley that rides carpet of gas. Good transit.

God speaking: —Come to me my thirsty little gnu. Bring your dry snout to the surface of my waterhole. Let me seize you by the nostrils, pull you under. Sure, there'll be terrific splash when you fight back. I'll draw you in. Strangulate ungulate. Pull you apart piece by piece. See I haven't incisors. All fangs, my maw. Jam divided quarters beneath underwater roots where I'll let them rot. Fight off aquatic scavengers, (can name them after fallen angels). Go soft. Be my tapioca. When immature, how many stork's beaks had I escaped. Jaws of bigger crocs too. Deity survival. Hag! You'll make no bag from my hide.

Reinterpret this information.

Observe other gnus. This one's severely mutilated, hind foot missing. Will certainly fall prey to hyenas further along. Others, in too big haste, piled up and drowned. Such waste. Nourish riverine biotope, no less so than floating human corpses. Not only in the Zambeze river, but in the Yangtze, the Seine, the Hudson and the Mississippi. Don't think so? Patience!

A woman listens, wrapped in cashmere shawl. Isse Myake pleats. Very dark face, shoes surprisingly big (like sculptures worn on her feet), though very streamlined and terminating in fine pointed tips. Big feet. If headlights go out due to some kind of fuse problem, tie torches to the front fenders, avoid smoke blowback by driving slowly. It's a good set-up for night poaching, but also discover the path by watching top of the grass twelve feet over head. Head into jungle enclave. Along the way, converse with big pistol-wielding man (pearl-handled grip) who slams down his fist on the heads of fellow swimmers in friendly race across private pool. Kampala. Palace with frescoes of running impala. Don't write him off so fast. Didn't he evict MOSSAD from embassy and replace with PLO, way back in the seventies? Everyone thought him to be mad.

Quickly write a play about very special survivors of Hiroshima. After blast, half-broiled cobbler's children in smoking wreck of home ask dad, "Where are we going to go now?" without hesitating, he replies, "Nagasaki!" Yes they actually existed, cobbler and family, but also a kite-maker, and a few other individuals who all made the extraordinarily sinister choice of going to Nagasaki when fleeing from Hiroshima. Very unfortunate folks. Who else has twice been to Hell? These are the so-called "double-survivors." It is not known if others followed the same path, only to disappear in the second nuclear experiment. Introduce side acts with U.S. aviator POWs and Korean prostitutes caught up in Hiroshima nuclear debacle. POW can survive too by jumping into big clay jar filled with damp burlap bags while heading for forced labor task. Japanese guards are baked. POW eventually makes it back to the States, has numerous cancers over thirty-year period. Government refuses to pay bills. Demands he provide concrete proof of having been present during Hiroshima bombing. Evidently all Japanese military records concerning US POWs present in Hiroshima City went up in mushroom cloud along with a lot of other things. The Korean prostitute is kidnapped by Japanese kamikaze pilot who takes her away just before early morning nuclear blast. Can use kite-makers daughter gone blind for off-stage narration to fill gaps and provide factual information. Somehow succeed in introducing a cricket, a pearl diver, a giant mola fish (and why not a witch?) as ancillary characters. Did you know Navajo was used as impenetrable secret code, which the Japanese never were able to crack? All of this is factual.

Take her advice, avoid politics just as she had warned me. Rid myself of the Haitian head if I'm to go after my own which has been taken by presidential candidate who's now in office. Whose head shall I appropriate? Permit that I borrow yours? Let's see what's in it. Bet there's lots of entertainment, low alpha ray out-put from much passive viewing. Useful material: answers to witty game show quiz situations. A human encyclopedia you are! This is perhaps the real reason for being in the middle. Promise, just temporarily, I'll give it back, (your head). You protest? Shouldn't have gotten involved with *aka*. It's difficult to distinguish just where the *Book of Fever* kicks in.

This could get really complicated if I don't succeed.

Remember that wherever there's beauty, there must always be something of slightly flawed about it.

Details of living conditions: walls are paper-thin. Can hear the neighbors whispering to each other about us, scratching their asses, discretely passing wind. The entire city has been organized along the lines of this principle.

The classical cemetery scene takes place in an animal cemetery where people cry more over the death of their pets than they do for the passing away of fellow humans, (they might be right about this). This funeral is for Wob's rhino. Many pallbearers are necessary. Horns protrude from coffin. Wob has become huge from stress and anxiety since I last saw him. I admit, he's had very little part in the development of this work. Shouldn't have left him out. Could even have played the role of an enemy. Was always too over emotional. If the distant cousin of recent acquaintance passed away, he would break down in tears. Promise Wob'll have a bigger role in next volume.

Go to the body parts storage building. Handsome listing tower with fin-shaped projections protruding from upper structure. Architectural allusion to the fact that this might be some unexploded primitive device dropped from passing aircraft. There's nothing of sanitary about this place. Human pieces are strung up on clotheslines in an immense basement. Dried, stinking like ingredients of Chinese apothecary or the storage for a decrepit natural history museum. Some have been smoked. Many are missing. Suspect that night watchmen (only Whites are willing to work nights for such low wages) have been snacking.

Zanda accompanies me. Her nipples are showing through the fabric of her blouse. She isn't even wet. It's simply that there's so much contrast between the thin white cotton and the dark rings of flesh pushing up from beneath.

Spend several days in the archives room. Third floor is the clinic. The Chief of State is to undergo a benign intervention. The Surgeon General transplants my brain into his head. They've had the whole head for some time. This coup d'état will be a medical one. No need to travel, this all happens right next door.

Zanda's uncomfortable speaking to the new head which I'm wearing, apparently yours.

Praise noble medical team, —Your feet (paws I'm thinking with your borrowed mind) are truly beautiful.

They're actually wolf-like, broad, blunt phalanges that curl under, fat stubby knuckles covered with gray fur. Smell of fen and gnarled bones. Once again, the mind being down in the foot, they simply can't resist this sort of flattery. Offer them soft airy sandals.

Severely distorting surface mirages due to the heat coming up from the cityscape, prohibit me from giving much detail on just how it is we recuperate my head, put it back in place. Mostly by groping.

Swap. Left yours (sorry) with the President. Make off with my own. What can I offer you in exchange? Aren't you better off than you were? It'll send you friendly mail when it travels, especially when national security is threatened and the President is flown around from city to city on Airforce One. You'll receive postcards from Omaha, Waco and other such places. Didn't you always want to be a Chief of State anyway? Can hold your arms out to the sides as if ready to draw a gun whenever the nation's under attack, stride decisively across the White House lawn, declare world-scale "Crusades" and print up "wanted dead or alive" posters. Be a living time machine, capable of bringing back, single-handedly, a macro version of the Far West. Better than the rest of us who are reduced to actually going there, with a chance of landing smack in the middle of Wounded Knee and risking being shot on the spot for vaguely resembling an Indian. Repeat to the public, "Don't make any mistake about it!" when promising revenge.

Replace with what? See, I knew you'd be happy. No grudge? Haven't any regrets? Keep the pot on your shoulders; renew the water every three days, change the flowers every week. Bouquets of Jack-in-the-pulpit are the best. You're doing fine. Feeling lonely? Watch more TV.

On the return journey, I shoot a fine big bison specimen just to celebrate. The Indians (Minatree, recently freed from federal prison) laugh at me, say that it's an old female, cow too tough to eat. Should have aimed at a younger one; perhaps less impressive but much more tender under tooth. I lose my mount. Wanders off from the campsite during the night. *Coureurs des bois* feast on it. Frenchmen have always loved horsemeat.

Major arterial tension problem. Blood rushing through carotid makes gushing noise. Keeps me awake at night. Hinders my hearing during the day. Like living next to busy airport.

The ubiquity of humanoids? Due to the vulgarization of ttds they're scattered throughout the Universe. Expected to encounter only the strangest of creatures? Cosmic exoticism? Don't be so crestfallen. It's hardly more disconcerting than running across Pygmies wearing cut-off jeans and Tu-Pack Shakur tee shirts. Shave your head and grow a Fu-Manchu.

Utter void? Would tend to prove I've been fooling you all along. That we're indeed alone in the Universe. Don't feel so forlorn. At least this would mean that we're definitely the smartest things around, no?

Just fooling anyway. We did have some visitors from deep time. They incarnated everything previously feared by the most fertile human imagination and even more. Getting up enough courage, we tried communicating with them. They remained completely oblivious to our presence no matter what we did to attract their attention, even setting off nuclear devices. Finally they left. Only then did we realize that they were simply engaged in some kind of competition, an off-road race of sorts across the Universe. The brief halt amongst mankind was merely a form of technical pit stop. We appeared to them as being nothing more than part of the landscape in spite of frantic efforts to make our presence known.

I live Boulevard Odo in Marseilles. The air smells of near-by soap factory. I'm a frequenter of the Perroquet Bleu, (this is a long time before it becomes known as a fashionable address). Prostitutes, consumers and purveyors of drugs, alcoholics, dockers and lost sailors whose ships lie at anchor in the bay, tethered with glass chains, frequent this place. It's hot. The music is much too loud, thumping in my chest. A girl named Geraldine says she never kisses on the mouth, is sweating. Another, Marcelline, is laughing. Her mouth's wide open, the tongue hugging the bottom. A carpet of wet pink velvet. I imagine her voice being the most marvelous soprano, but no sound comes. How much sperm has gone in? (this is pre-AIDS, when they used to swallow enormous quantities of it). They're having real fun, not the feigned divertissement that others will seek in there wake some thirty years hence. It'll be a fashionable discotheque, a place with no memory. Only the blue ceramic parrot on the facade will be preserved. To make himself heard, a little man with welts on his head, cups his hands and yells in my ear. Something about a bird. Then on Hamburg and how when there's a tempest, the Elbe stands on edge and leans over the city. Music and screams again. This is the third.

—She digs a hole in the ground..., he yells, squatting on the floor and going through the motions. The floor around him is littered with broken glass, syringes and cigarette butts. —and gives birth there in the dirt! Scoops up the newborn, ties it to her back with vines and goes right on hunting...

His lips continue moving. With an exaggerated sweeping movement of the arm, he pretends to throw a lance, seems to be in a trance.

Somewhere above, there's already that great arch of fire, thrusting outward before coming back in an immense loop. I find it more convenient to keep my research papers on scrolls that I unroll in hallways and down stairwells. Neighbors think me to be some sort of an archaic accountant. Specimens are kept in steel barrels or on makeshift shelves. My favorite: a little mesoskeleton from Magellanic Cloud expedition. How different it looks now with the amethyst flesh gone.

I have no luck with house pets. Birds are too fragile, I lose my dogs and fish go belly-up.

Still have a hard time ridding myself of certain nervous tics apparently acquired from promiscuity with the President's person: the habit of thrusting chin forward when speaking, waiting until it's completely safe before visiting disaster sites, quite unlike Winston Churchill who wouldn't have hesitated for a second to don helmet and plunge into flaming debris.

Other Hotels and bars. More knowledge here than in the archives of great institutions.

Bar de Templiers, rue de Rivoli, (same bar used to be in lower Sevres, down by the river before being transferred here). Only women present are my two year-old daughter and many effigies of Joan of Arc, sculptures, medallions, paintings. Joan's image has been most unfortunately appropriated by FN, French neo-fascist party. They hold their annual rally at the foot of equestrian golden statue Place des

Pyramides just down the street. Happily, there's another one on a street that still bears her name. She's afoot this one, perhaps nearer to the final blaze, but certainly free of any doubtful political appropriation.

In preparation for her Afro-Diasporic Institute project, Zanda and I work together in the office. She's perched on a ladder going through books from top shelf. I go under her dress, press her to my mouth, (she's wearing no underwear, or yes, loose fitting Prada again; yellow with white lace this time, that I have no trouble pulling to the side permitting me to push my tongue deep) then she goes beneath desk while I try to write outline of future program. Watch her through the glass desktop. Let's do this *à fond*.

We're children again. Adolescents, mature adults, geriatrics one more time. Mix, there's no order. She's terribly old but still extremely beautiful. Her hair's white, contrasting strikingly with dark skin. Few good nurses are left. Most do this work against their will. Only for the salary. Weren't even born yet when we were already prowling the streets with other geriatrics, violently attacking techno-youths to rob their expensive gadgets. This nurse has no patience with you? Fling your bedpan in her face! Broke your rib last night did she? Bite her arm and hang on. Haven't any teeth left? Gums will do, arms are covered with soft tissue. Infection will surely ensue. They'll throw us out into the streets. Aiblins we should abscond. Find better abri.

Would rather fend off feral dogs than suffer indignity. Even if they attack from behind when you're on all fours. Protect your vital parts with bedpan taped across the buttocks. Don't let them abscind your balls. Blow plenty smoke in their snouts; they'll leave you alone.

I'm in a disphoric mood. Neither depressive nor anxious; something altogether different. Absolutely no will power. Abulia? But then, am I afflicted by ascolia just because my shit's gone white? Was convinced that I was the doctor, dentist, psycotherapist. Discovering now that we've been considered all along as being patients, at least the subjects of a study. Can't even whistle or hiss without being diagnosed as having acouasma!

Everything is subject to analysis. Decisions are almost impossible to take. This fellow who's been standing curbside for three days, trying to analyze why he wants to cross the street. Finally, yes, the whole world's now run by a team of psychiatrists. Entire nations are considered as patients. Search early history to understand just where things went wrong. What nation suffered childhood traumatism which it will, in turn, perpetrate?

Fire seems to fulfill the metabolic properties which define life. Eukaryotic organisms present very similar chemical reactions to those of combining organics with molecular oxygen which sustain fire. To a certain degree, fire is self-replicating.

Trap gases in clathrate.

Where's my gun moll? Using pearl-handled revolver, I draw from the hip and shoot a big black-bellied bustard. No vagrant resident, but thoroughly indigenous which shows you just how accommodating the Paris area has become to this warm weather fowl. Stomach full of termites; count 13 scorpions and 210 beetles. When approaching I hear aggressive voice and growling call. Advertisement is short wheezy rising whistle, hiccup and cork-popping "quok." Has come north with the rains. Find nest near anthill with handsome clutch of brown blotching eggs. Two females take wing. Dispersed lek system likely. No omelet. Break and suck dry as would any opportunist. Excellent flesh, this *outarde*. A feast for ten of us. Oily meat quite like fat goose.

We go deep for many reasons, not the least of which is the capture of giant squid. Quantities of ink for brewing the most sought after black alcohol. "Abyss/Kiss." Jet-black lips on the label. Avoid arctic smoke. If I'm hounded, grant me grith.

I'm contemplating returning to America, but am put off by my Nigerian Consular Advisory Warning to Travelers:

Violent crime committed by persons in police and military uniforms, as well as by ordinary criminals, is an acute problem. Use of public transportation throughout the United States, including taxis, is dangerous and should be avoided. American airlines have aging fleets and our Nigerian Embassy in New York is concerned that maintenance and operational procedures may be inadequate to ensure passenger safety.

Business, charity and other scams target foreigners worldwide and pose danger of financial loss. Recipients pursuing such fraudulent offers risk physical harm if they come to America. Persons contemplating business deals are strongly urged to check with the Nigerian department of Commerce or the Nigerian

Department of State before providing any information, making any financial commitments or travelling to America. "Sting" targets foreigners, including Nigerian citizens. Scams usually involve phony offers of either outright money transfers or lucrative sales or contracts with promises of large commissions or up-front payments. Alleged deals frequently invoke the authority of one or more ministries or offices of American government and may even cite by name the support of American government official. The apparent use in some scams of actual government stationery, seals, and offices is grounds for concern that individual American officials may be involved in these activities.

Due to security concerns with major cities and while travelling inland, the Nigerian Embassy advises against visiting in downtown areas or in the American hinterlands after dark. Crime affecting foreigners is a serious problem. Visitors and Nigerians residing in America report armed muggings, assaults, burglary, kidnappings, carjackings and extortion, usually involving violence. Carjackings, roadblock robberies and armed break-ins are pandemic. Assailants often shoot victims for no apparent reason. Law enforcement authorities usually respond to crimes slowly, if at all, and provide little or no investigative support to victims.

When driving it is unwise to bring assistance to roadside accident victims. If the vehicle you are driving should be struck or rammed by another vehicle, do not stop. Proceed to nearest Police station, (making sure it's a real one).

When going to and from George W. Bush Airport, embassy employees must notify the Embassy in advance. In addition, the Embassy discourages travelling after dark. Embassy employees are required to travel in armored vehicles between Manhattan Island and the International airport. There is high risk of pickpockets and con artists inside George W. Bush Airport, outside the terminal building and in parking lot.

Didn't America once issue the very same Consular Information Sheet to its citizens heading for Nigeria? And with that, former France is still all a shambles. Started when the French opposed destruction and reappropriation of Mesopotamian civilization by the U.S. only to suffer debilitating eco-punishment at the hands of the latter. How dare this little country slow our momentum! had said she. The results have been more devastating than anything ever imagined. Total pauperization. Back to the days of doing the wash in a communal *lavoire* with Marseilles soap, wiping your ass with old newspaper or a handful of weeds and being stone drunk on *vinasse*. Now we only eat dandelions, sometimes with snails. Save the Camembert and *baguette* for *fête champêtre*. Pull down your old worn out beret over your bulbous red nose. And keep it out of politics!

Comfort myself by acquiring three black virgins: "Vierge en Majesté" form La Chapelle-Geneste, Haute-Loire, "La Sarassine" from Sarance in the Pyrenées Atlantiques, "La Negrette" from Espallion, Aveyron.

Onset of epilepsy. The usual cycle of taenia solium, the pork tapeworm, goes much like this: eggs are shed in gravid proglottids, ingested by hogs where oncoshperes penetrate the gut, heart and other muscles. The tapeworm is benign to humans who've carelessly consumed undercooked pork causing nothing more than indisposition. Adult worms remain in intestinal tract where they can attain the respectable length of 10 meters. However, and such seems to be the case with me, it's an altogether different situation if humans swallow the eggs directly due to poor socioeconomic conditions. Emerging oncospheres migrate directly to the brain, leaving behind distinctive Swiss cheese pattern. Is this any worse than human skin bot, dermatobia hominis, which can provoke myiasis in the brain? How's this possible, you ask? Larvae can enter simple 4-mm hole bored through anterior fontanel. Hardly likely to be the case with me! Pronounced acrocephaly confirms premature closure of my skull sutures. High pointed skull proves advantageous when going against strong currents are even while engaged in anticonsensual thinking. Back to the bot fly, my mama hated all form of flying insects and certainly wouldn't have permitted even a gnat to land anywhere near me. This incessant struggle to keep flying things away from me is the main reason it took her so long to earn her Ph.D.

Patiently plug holes with rejuvenated gray matter, even if it takes so long to perform that Alzheimer's sets in. Plenty *amour propre*.

Watch for cinnabar patches appearing along edges of cerebral vermiculation.

Love my colcothar queen!

Steal a bike. Authentic Enduro type. Sitting on a motor. Accessories? Need several helmets of different sizes and shapes. Head's subject to great change. Tires? Should be adapted to climbing vertical walls several miles high (many infinity buildings exist, thrusting upward into low orbit zone), and going across ceilings of territorial dimension. Custom exhaust, permitting musical notes, foot pegs for comfort of large clawed feet, oversized saddlebags for carrying whatever contraband I'm dealing in, a quick-fill fuel derrick. Wrap-around jelly windshield.

Paint the motorcycle with panther pattern. Drive at full tilt beneath anticrepuscular arch.

Simply cross the Seine to go down the Nile. Go up the Congo by wading the Nile. Abstruse? Easy. They're braided together.

Generally speaking, near is far. Going to your neighbor's door may take an eternity. On the other hand, venturing to the most remote places, beyond the known horizon of the Universe, can be accomplished in an instant.

Want me to leave this carceral environment, vacate the overcrowded cell? Give me my gate money!

Suffering from brain fag. While abed, listen for the moho.

In addition to the mating of Andromeda with our own Galaxy, it has been discovered that the Sun is part of a very wide binary system on an eccentric orbit with separation distance being well over 1000 AU. Orbital decay due to gravitational torques may be responsible for subfragmentation in the abiatec phase of fragments formed in the isothermal phase. Broken sister star approaches with her own cortege of planets. Nothing permits to believe they're inhabited.

Intramandibular Hinge

We are in the treetops again. The little one is sleeping in the crook of my arm. She has a fever. It's time for me to feed her. I must gorge myself if I'm to properly nourish her upon returning. I brace her between three branches at the fork of a trunk several dozen meters above the ground.

Dropping to the jungle floor I slip my long yellow tongue into the air sweeping my head from side to side. Drawing it back into the mouth, I feel upon the left portion, a concentration of carrion molecules; assessing the distance of the carcass of whatever it is, to be under four kilometers away, I set off silently slipping through the underbrush. Fortune has it that I encounter an antelope of the little forest variety. I give it no chance, charging and smashing it down with my massive head. Immediately tearing into it with my accreted teeth, I rip its belly open, slinging the intestines to either side so as to empty them of all fecal matter. Knowing that I disdain this offal, other natural prey rushes to roll in the excrement. Indeed, this newly acquired perfume which envelopes them offends me. I shall not partake of them.

Had the antelope escaped me, the skeptic concentration of residual flesh from previous victims jammed between my teeth would have proven as fatal as the most potent venom. Only I would have been obliged to make patience, perhaps four to six days while the bacterial toxins did their work. Then keep alert for this walking larder to fall. Find it again before others made their repast of it.

But now I'm filling up on this fallen catch, eating viscera, flesh, broad sheets of pelt, hooves even. Such large mouthfuls make I, that I'm forced to dislocate my jaw by operating several moveable joints; the intramandibular hinge permits my bottom jaw to open wide enough to accept this bulky fare.

Putra Sastrawan of Udayana University and Donald Gilespie of the El Paso Zoo were the first to realize the full potential of my highly infectious saliva. Bacterial venom was the new classification that they created especially for me.

Quickly I must return now to the little one in her treetop perch; avoid ritual combat with rival males which might delay my protection of the little female.

I have two openings in the temporal region of the skull.

My claws are not long enough making ventral scales a necessity for climbing. The child is as I had left her, still sleeping. The fever has abated and this is well for I had feared to leave her. I regurgitate some of the antelope. My mate has returned. High in the crook of the tree we sleep in a heap together with the offspring. Small flies hover, attracted by the scent. Other gnats gather around our eye and nostril openings, seeking what sticky suppurations they can find. Far beneath a pair of paradoxa paradoxa float over the jungle floor, born upon transparent wings; petals of glass flickering in the falling patches of sunshine. They alight upon a dark stain, panther piss absorbed by the humus, and remain sucking sustenance before flying off into the depths of the jungle. A flight composed of flickers and festoons as if they were now intoxicated by the rare nectar they have just absorbed. Immediately they are replaced by a cyclone of color, other butterflies rushing in to partake of the potent feast.

You may wonder how it is that we, massive reptiles, are capable of such contemplation and sensitivity, be they primitive. Be it known as of now that there never was mass extinction, no KT limit. Earth was never struck by huge bolids, no enormous volcanoes erupted. Glaciation is mere conjecture.

—But the traces are there to prove the contrary! you'll surely retort —What about mammoth remains preserved in permafrost with the heavy fur? Morains strewn with debris left behind by receding glaciers in zones now temperate?

My reply is that heavy fur functions as insulation. It can preserve internal freshness in a tropical climate just as it can maintain body temperature in the cold. Mammoths, woolly rhinoceros and even cavemen reveled in their own sweat. They loved it. Like your friend Kakugee who lives in the heart of the Sangha Mbaéré jungle, wears seal skin coats and smokes from pipes with oversized bowls, keeping fire close. As for the rubble attributed to the passage of icecaps, these are merely the traces of large lithophagic creatures that would gorge themselves upon stones, churning them in enormous digestive pouches before vomiting them upon the land. So you see, the evidence of abrasion, the smoothness from friction has nothing to do with any sort of glaciation.

Indeed mammals did appear, but long before what has been generally accepted. They were minor life forms, furry snacks at best. If they at all exist today — you are the living proof of this — it's thanks to the purely reptilian concept of conservation.

Reptiles have evolved, unimpeded. You might as well accept the fact that mammals are an exception, unadapted quirks.

Don't be so sullen. It's not your fault, all this imagined civilization of yours.

Our civilization? I'll take you there, to one of the major citadels; well maybe. You'll see there for yourself other mammals, a few humanoids, mostly in pet shops; none in the streets though. Too fragile! We keep you indoors. This could pose a problem. Even in my company, you'll be immediately noticed. Perhaps I should throw you in a sack, sling you across my back, at least bind you in some manner.

What am I doing in the jungle you ask?

—I'm a throwback! (this is screamed with such force that irreparable damage to vocal chords is sustained. Marvelous singing may no longer be possible).

Observations, File third card: Rumination disorder. Patient was relatively calm today, following period of massive regurgitation. Esophageal reflux is apparently uncontrollable. Has lost much weight; claims to be a Komodo Dragon. Extremely irritable between sequences of massive vomiting. Hunger leads to chewing newspapers, plastic bags. On one occasion, we observed that the subject ripped the sleeve from his own shirt, hasty mastication and swallowed whole. Also seen to climb trees in urban zones. Numerous complaints filed by residents. Subject was joined by woman and child. Arboreal comportment. These three individuals spent a total of five days in treetop. Tends to confirm suspicion that this might be a clinical case of "folie à deux."

Very gently, she places me in a sack, and we penetrate the serpent city. Wrongly you would assume it to be a slithery place filled with hissing sounds. Nothing could be less true. Immobility is the first impression. Like stones, they all lay about, basking or lying in wait for some prey to come their way. There are sudden spurts of action, the flick of a tongue, a tail whipping about.

Thermal pollution is important.

—Being cold-blooded, staying warm is of the utmost importance to us.

And so the city is immersed in water vapor, steam blowing down from complicated tubular structures that appear to provide habitat as well.

Forbidden things hang in bundles, suspended from vegetation which is quite dense in places. Can be found bales of mammal tails, primate scalps, including those of humans. Am I to become indurate, capable of watching without wincing?

No innocuous innuendo.

Collisions are called impingements.

Vehicles are soft, adapted to their body form, appear to be made of latex or some form of second skin with pitting like golf-ball surface. Exhaust fumes have an almond odor. Make several levels of buzzing noises, from the flutter of butterfly wings to the sound of mosquito, fly, bumblebee.

Libraries contain thermal/olfactory literature, must be able to interpret the subtle syntax of temperatures and odors in order to acquire knowledge here. Tone too. Best not to suffer Purkinje shift.

Molted skins fly about in the air, riding ascending currents. They often float for miles before coming back down, slowly falling veils that catch in the thorns of cacti and acacias.

True, they do have high buildings, great bridges, formidable arches, but all are dangerously listing. They apparently haven't mastered the art of solid foundations or perhaps tunneling activities haven't been properly regulated.

Humanoid artisans and artists have been employed for the decoration. An anaconda swallowing a man, sculpted from the finest travertine marble, the Laocoon group reinterpreted in a darker hued stone, both adorn city squares. The streets are paved with mosaics depicting encyclopedia images of reptiles.

Their claws delicately clink.

Inevitably, the theme of Saint George and the dragon has been revised to give the dragon the lead role, the knight thrown from his horse and lying at the dragon's feet. Most paintings are awkward as if the artists had been hobbyists painting by numbers, but here are some magnificent oil paintings adorning the interior walls of vast hallways and palace entrances. Splendidly painted. Had managed to bring back Vitor Carpaccio. And when the scene hasn't been reversed, they'll simply tell you that the knight represents evil and that if indeed he's spearing the dragon, it's nothing less than a scene of martyrdom, the dragon being the good one.

—What about the remains of his meals, these skulls and dismembered human bodies that lie all about the dragon? Is this not proof enough of his forfeiture?

—Look again. Those are reptile skulls and remains. You see, the knight had been killing serpent maidens for some time, devouring lizards with immoderate appetite, before the dragon came along to challenge him.

I'm uneasy in the sack. Want to climb out onto her back.

From here the view is better. I was getting tired of the "hidden-camera" vision that I had from inside of the bag.

The city is immense, sprawling over low hills to the horizon in every direction that I look. They're crawling after fresh kills, the entire landscape is moving now. The buildings are pitted too, the surfaces being drilled with countless openings. Building facades are covered with the mouths of grottos for denning, perches for napping, vines for slithering along. Most have perfected the art of gliding to the highest degree and leap from high, soaring from building to building. Thundering torrents flush the city and provide perfect habitat for aquatic reptiles, descendants of crocodiles.

What will be expected of me? Will I be asked to perform oral surgery, treat, fangs and vomerin teeth? Or will they insist that I put my artistic talents to their service? I could take mannerism to new heights. Create friezes of writhing intertwined elongated bodies, immense organic puzzles on cupola ceilings, where one would pass hours trying to mentally unravel, guess to which serpent belongs this tail, what coil so well rendered in oil. Should it spoil, boil, wrap in foil, avoid hard toil. I don't mean to embroil, simply haven't the time for words of turmoil.

Concerning the Big Bang, correct interpretation came from Fred Hoyle.

She grasps me tightly and takes me up into one of the many small caverns dotting the building facade. Surprise. Up until now I didn't know that she could fly, thought her wings to be merely decorative. She puts me down on the edge of a ledge. Looking out from this level I can clearly see that the city has no end, peering down brings beta wave rhythm to a halt. How could she have taken me so high with only a few wing beats?

Here I realize the strangeness of their building construction. Solid cement monoliths are erected and from these masses they gouge out individual chambers none of which interconnect. There are no interior hallways, no corridors, stairwells or any means of communicating from one cavity to another. Truly independent, no social structure whatever; highly individualistic. Here, she examines my flews, measures the height at the withers, runs her claws over my croup, down the breech and hock, over the stifle, scratches the pastern and brisket. She summons friends; each arrives by his own means, all seem perfectly humanoid but they're deeply reptilian. Plan they to be my duressors?

One is suffering from severe abdominal pains. With quick palping, I diagnose the need for duodena jewjunostomy. Use a small silver flute to create artificial passage. Digestion will be musical from here on in.

She rearranges the Duncan Phyfe furniture, mainly early pieces in Sheraton and Directoire style. I'm seated in a chair with lyre motif. Looking at me from right profile view, very close in, she declares that I haven't ears at all, but small ports that seem to radiate an ultraviolet, verging on red, light around the rims which are dimpled.

—When perfectly lined up, I can see all of the way through your head, she says. There's a very fine canal that seems to traverse your skull.

—Don't believe a word.

—Want me to run a long fine needle through and through to prove it?

This panics me. I remember how young slave mothers would have recourse to the services of an old woman who'd pass a rusted needle through the brain of newborns. Death leaving no trace which would spare the newborn a life of slavery while depriving the owner of his property. Is it only because she's black, I'm thinking this?

—Do it! I say.

Finally it's painless and I don't feel a thing. Indeed there must be a narrow duct that goes clean through my skull. Like certain Afghan lizards.

Cousin to the mangoust, thick fur protects me from bites, I can be very swift, dodge and go for the throat.

It would be to easy to continue saying that this is an entirely reptile world, that we're situated across the universe at a great distance beyond any notion of remoteness that you could hold; places so much colder.

I'm older than my father and my daughter is older than me. That's the real order of things. Just as it may be overly simplistic to say that I'm a lone mammal irreversibly caught in a reptile world. In fact, I develop reptilian features just as quickly as these reptiles begin to evolve into mammals. The cycle is extremely rapid. There's no synchronization, or rather there is one which guarantees that we'll always be opposites. It's an inextricable situation, one I must make the best of while here, go on with life, all the while alternatively molting fur and scales.

Nevertheless, there appear to be a few poles from which I can deduce that not all is without reason. I'm often in the presence of my mate and our offspring. And whether they sweat from beneath the arms wetting their fur or perspire from the mouth, there's an indubitable genetic tie. Also there is the wreckage of a ttd which much resembles the family model I once had with a baby seat in the back. This could invalidate the lizard-jungle introduction, discredit the bag version whereby I was introduced here riding in a sack slung across Awa's back. The time device has suffered irreparable damage making this a classical dead-end situation. However, it is most uncertain that any great distance in either space or time has been traversed to arrive here. Certain things would tend to confirm propinquity. Maybe I can simply walk out of here.

For example, I come across the remains of humans who have evidently been used as ammunition. Powder burns on the feet, heads imbedded in walls, tree trunks and other targets which they've been fired into. Only humanity is capable of delving out this sort of treatment unto itself. Employing real "live ordnance."

Lacking wings now, we're obliged to live low. Down by the river, though a perilous location, is where we reside.

The temptress is here again. To attempt seduction she employs deceit in three ways:

1) I receive a call, young woman's voice, desperate; —George! Save me, I'm sequestered by a violent lizard. He tortures me. Has just gone

out. Come quickly! This call is repeated two times. The instructions are precise. I must go a considerable distance, hardly have the time to get there before it returns if I'm to save her and avoid being devoured myself. At this point, I myself am an immature individual, hardly capable of defense against an adult reptile. The circumstances make for there being no time to make a decision. On the last call, I race to the lieu of rendezvous but become lost in a dense fog.

2) We cross paths in the street. Her eyes are green, slight converging strabism in the gaze makes me realize that she's looking at me from very close. "I'm leaving for South America, tomorrow, Venezuela or Honduras. Won't be back for many years. Realize that you're very important to me, probably the most important thing in my life. Come with me tonight. My husband is already gone. I have an apartment that we can go to. It's on the Ile Saint Louis. We'll be together, just the two of us."

3) A fourth call, much later, the voice has matured, full female in prime. It's Zanda who answers but I can perfectly hear what's being said on the other end: "I'm an art dealer in Italy," comes the voice from Venezuela. "Yes we have very important cultural structure here in Caracas. Want to purchase all of your husband's latest work. So sensual, especially the intertwined serpents." Zanda passes me the call. The tone changes immediately "I miss you so terribly. Dream of you every night. It's urgent that we meet. I'm here now. Look out your window." Again, there's a dense fog. Stupidly, I go down into the street.

Counter this pressing attempt to interfere, to disrupt my sexual characteristics. I've consistently been a monogamous creature; the eagle, the albatross are no different. No Bonobo am I. This has nothing to do with pondering upon the validity of fidelity or infidelity. Neither is it a mere question of speciation. K2, Zanda and Xoma, together being the one daughter of Awa, revealed unto me this bond that I share with noble birds of prey.

Do not serpents breed in wriggling heaps? Don't attempt herpetological interpretation.

A cold snap is setting in. Must resolve the reptile/mammal dilemma quickly. Be in the right phase when things freeze over.

I discover that this isn't at all Paris, but New York. Armored doors that once protected the entrances to the greatest vaults, remain standing, the buildings, the treasures which they once protected, not only bullion but a certain form of democracy gone sour, have disappeared. Time has found its path round and behind, broken and entered the strongest of fortifications, confirmed all things worse feared. It is as with the most powerful, highly developed military nation, being brought down by ill-equipped terrorists armed only with patience and a surprising way of operating which like the wind or time itself, penetrate deeply, trespassing with ease the most complex defense systems, ones anchored in the stars and relayed to the most sophisticated structures of artificial thinking, intended to defend against an attack conceived by technological theoreticians; incapable of anticipating what devastation can be wrought with the spirit alone when no arms other than what lies at hand, are readily available. Of what use was it to have levied unbridled deluge of fire upon those who took refuge in grottos, communicating with falcons.

These serpents then? Are they descendants of this nation's most staunch defendants? Patriots weaned on hate'n riots? Mammals I mean, it now being me the scale-skinned one, nevertheless capable of assessing the situation from a post-political point of view.

Could cave crickets be valid witnesses? I repeat: many things happened in caverns. Jesus and Mohamed both withdrew to caverns. Cavernicol creatures would be the only ones to have known that something was transpiring, even if they apprehended what was happening in a totally different manner than might have done some scribe or faithful follower had they accompanied the prophets into underground reclusion. Don't cavil with me. There's no caveat emptor. I never guaranteed quality when this story began. Ask cavers.

Once again, I reverse the situation. Using my weak energy field, I provide for them electricity. Hence the new appellation they confer upon me: Megawatti.

I propose that barbecued dog be added to their daily diet. Balconies must be overextended to get the smoke away from the buildings. Realize that the West was deeply mistaken on almost every count. African culture should never have been interpreted solely on an ethnical basis, nor as a separate, isolated element; in a context of alienation, so to speak. Couldn't we have understood that this was no good. Better to look outward from the core of humanity where all that is African, of the

Black Diaspora, or even remotely related, including quarteroons and even octoroons, is nothing less than the heart of mankind and its vascular system.

I briefly engage in smuggling: cigarettes, alcohol, firearms, perfume even. I obtain a supply of counterfeit passports in Bangkok, go to Port Said, return to Algiers. Very clever work, the image changes, taking on whatever form is desired by the holder. During a dog bake, one of the overextended balconies collapses when overloaded with too many guests. Several prove to have been recently arrived debt collectors who had wasted no time in finding my trace here. Having no wings, they plunged to death while feasting on Jack Russel hock basted with French bouldogue saliva. Eliminate yappers and snorers. Couthie fellows.

Surprisingly, no one is angry with me over the structural failure, no law suits, no prison. Quite to the contrary, they want me to build more of these precarious structures that can come down at any moment, providing an unexpected thrill to guests. Must do this for them, *coûte que coûte*.

Here too, there's much pollution. Lethal clouds put out by some sort of heavy industry nestled within the heart of residential zone, blow down low over the city. The sun is very near the horizon, sending slanting rays through the vapors. Citizens run in this decor. This city is girt with jungle. In the morning, hunters leak from the forest, carrying the night's catch. I live beneath a waterfall. No Victoria Falls but a simple cascade where, once again, I catch salamanders by torchlight come nightfall. During the day I hide away behind the curtain of falling water. The farthest reaches of this luminous cavern are filled with printed matter, all that remains of another civilization, awaiting rediscovery. I study pornography. A sort of Qumran of the twenty first to third centuries. Revelation. My path is traced, reptile comportment erased. Bid adieu to the scaled slender ones and return to Paris just in time to witness an aging lion attacking a gnu on the Boulevard Saint Germain. Many new buildings are made of soft shiny foil that swells and shrinks with a breathing action. Most older structures have disappeared. The Roman baths of Cluny are still standing. This is where my family has been living, subsisting on the benefits of contraband which I had regularly sent to them. They use the, still famous, Unicorn *tapisserie* as a tablecloth. Livestock roams the city during the day and is herded into little dome shaped enclaves with the coming of night. These structures are made of scrap material, time machine carcasses, barbed wire and sheet metal, sometimes covered with the hides of former occupants.

Alone, I wander at night through the city and out into the surrounding dunes that hedge the southern suburbs. The wind makes strange music when blowing through the protective enclosures within which ungulates ruminate, their bellies growling. Ewes cry with trembling bleat, seeking lambs that have been taken away; camels grunt, donkeys bray. From the shining tents come coughing and snoring. All else is silence. The sky is brilliant with the shine of untold new stars that have joined the Milky Way from merging with giant Andromeda galaxy. Many are more brilliant than Venus or Jupiter. Constellations have been dispersed, reshaped and distributed anew just as this land which some great hand has taken up, broken and thrown down again in heaps. From atop the dunes I view the three moons that are now ours. The old one and two new ones, both angular, one of them almost a perfect cube, the other seems the sperm whale's snout and even blows steam forward just as does the great creature at an angle slanting low to the sea and always from the left side.

Cataclysms have been collective and mental. Men's minds awash and bubbling with the finest lubricant. Blood. We're very different now. It's not so much a physical modification as a functional one, taking possession of what was already there, though lying dormant within the protective shell of each one's skull, the immense unused portion of the brain. Mainly the realization and the acceptance that we have been and are to be so many things, not only those remotely related to us by the way of some obscure evolutionary process. Alien things, concepts and chemistry are all now a vital part of each one of us. Linked together, a formidable experience begins to make its way, a knowledge that is without limits, a torrent that sweeps away all along its passage. After having been uprooted, cast down, left to drown, it is now time to emerge, ride along with this swiftest of currents and draw from it.

Push back intramandibular hinge, draw down long jaw and take in entire pieces of the land or the ocean. Digest tranquilly. Be at peace with yourself. Understand that even if there has been unacceptable slaughter, it was all in preparation for what is yet to come and that the doing must often pass by the undoing.

This concept can be applied to the ecosystem of the planet: collective human experience from the most distant past to beyond the future, reuniting immense morphological diversity over time but also within it. Race, civilizations. See how even within a race, itself situated within a time capsule, there is tribalism. In like manner, inside of a city there are neighborhood micropockets where different tongues are spoken. Different religions and political interests bring social cleavage. Some are married to the land, living with it as husband and wife, intimate with it while others are tied to the sea, perhaps freshly emerged from it or ready to return. 50M yrs is a flash, time enough for legs to become flippers, for the nose to slide up the face towards the top of the head and become a blow hole. Or contrarily, for the fish's fins to become legs permitting land incursions; not only primates and monkeys which seem so close but apparently headed elsewhere. Ramifications, come round through porosity. Even the most remote of paths must be trod. That of an ant, a mollusk, or a plant.

This is the beginning of consciousness, not that acquired by learning from books. It's not a question of establishing valid cladograms. Wreck all. Experience permanent perpendicularity.

Take this reticulated crynoid, hold it in your hand. Repeat after me: I have been this, shall be again, it is an immense respiration. The claws of the lion, the stench of its maw are yours, but not only this. The virus within your gut that kill, but with time shape certain body parts, even these stones held in my open hand, the grains of sand that now blow up over the slip face of this dune, fanning out at the cleanly cut ridge to shower down over some distant bay, this mountain that has risen up before your eyes in the time it took for you to foster a mere one hundred and thirty generations, most of which have proven to be the most dirty of offspring; that fold of the land which curls up like paper to guide down its fresh channel, armies pursuing refugees before funneling the blow-back of civilizations, you too are part of these and they are all a part of you. It is more than physical interpenetration or temporal integration. It is unicity. Why is it you're so fond of certain landscapes, of cloud formations of weather, rain drizzle, arctic conditions, volcano rims, ocean floors, the surface of meteorites, Europa's fractured husk of ice through which pass incoming bolids that send up geysers of life bearing liquid upon impact with the regularity of heartbeat and respiration? All of this forms a smooth vegetative function which even the most primitive brain could command!

Think no longer as most of you usually have: "It is frightening to be so small, insignificant in an infinite Universe" but rather, " It is so beautiful to be an element of infinity, certainly one that is tied in with All in the manner that the so sought after, but most elusive Grand Unified Theory (better known as "gut") meant to reunite even the most disparate elements." How deep goes your experience with alterity? Must begin by contemplating the opposite sex, then take age into consideration but not as usually conceived. Consider a child and a geriatric to be just like you are, simply occupying slightly different time spaces than your own, or rather sharing it but being further along or behind. Take into consideration the apelike ones along with those so formidably different at the other end, the ones yet to come who'll view you as having been very primitive, so evolved will they think themselves to be. Never forgetting that it hasn't been established with any degree of certainty which way we're heading, and what is really advancing, like being seated in a train, next to another one, both of them waiting to depart. You think you're taking off when you begin to slip away from the other train, before you realize that you're not going anywhere at all. It's the other train that's moving.

Accept that everything fits together, the entire Universe, and in all directions, like an infinite pythagorus theorem where all equates. I'm not alone in these dunes as I had thought to be. Over the sands come two figures, conversing in low voices while holding hands beneath several new moons.

Just as distances in space are often incalculable, there being no reference point, here too now, it is almost impossible for me to estimate at what distance the approaching couple can be from me, or even if they are indeed coming near or drawing away. I rise, walk towards them. Ought to see. Each dune resembling the next one, the one behind those to either side. They form troughs from the bottoms of which only the sky is visible, each new crest brings the question, —Where are they?

Traces disappear almost as quickly as they have been lain down. Of what use are the stars to me? No guidance provide they. Must I explain to you why they don't?

I'm drawing closer now. I'm certain that I'll be abreast just over the next crest. The conversation is no longer a murmur. I can detect fervor. Smell a perfume. Almost feel her fur.

Can I hear what they say? Naturally, it's a tongue that I don't even speak, not from the past, but one from the future. It resembles the sound of broken glass. The dunes answer, speaking back with a deep rumble that wells up from the heart, where they grind down dinosaur skulls, taking debris along over great distances, some five thousand yards every ten thousand years. This is blinding swiftness for which I'm unprepared. But don't let yourself be despaired, run along now and catch up again with these speedy sand mountains. Climb over them.

Ah, but they play tricks with your feet when you attempt to ascend, making three steps only one? Not so long ago you were a lizard. Cut sideways, ride lightly on your toes, feel the ridges and how they are more solid, paved almost. Follow them till they go down and then slip up along the next one. No straight path?

There's a tent here but it's been taken down. Furled like some sail. At anchor or preparing for a coming storm? Fine sand coming down coats all and glistens beneath the starlight. The two are making tea.

—Come, we'll be three, they say to me.

They raise their veils. It's my Xoma and our daughter. Have they been submitted to the strictest form of Islam?

—Thought we'd get away before the slaughter.

In praise of females: I can assure you that protection of the head is of imperative necessity in these parts.

The tea has strong liquorice flavor, burns in the throat. Often I've come across the two of them, just like this. It's being in the inside of things, the zone of germination from which things can emerge, the deepest recess of life.

If they were reciting poetry together, fables, counting, reviewing the table of multiplication, performing equations, drawing in the sand with sticks, talking about the next day's fare, it's that there's a school somewhere. No matter how distant, I'll take her there.

Migratory birds, disoriented by the shifting magnetic fields, the strange star patterns, the triple lunar pull, circle aimlessly, momentarily lost, before striking out again. An exhausted fledgling falls by the folded tent.

Hadn't she seen it coming? While I had thought to be meditating out here alone, they had broken camp. No philosophical quest. Women know best.

Reconsider my looks. Yes, do imagine that we're very different physically than anything before even though I swore that I wouldn't portray myself anymore. I'll do it in a roundabout sort of way. I've rested my head on a tripod. Zanda tells me that momentarily it has a metallic appearance, color gray verging on blue during the day with welts resembling welds running down along the sides. She says that I now have a profusion of small pointed ears that act together like one giant pair and eight eyes grouped on the forehead as with hunting spiders. It is she who speaks, describes these small flesh peaks and other attributes more often associated with cunning providers. I shine with the coming of nightfall, no blinding brilliance but the crisp radiance of a crescent moon set in twilight winter sky. Contrarily to moonlight, this is no reflection but an inner glow. Eyes deep green like darkest jade. My thinking is muddled, certainly due to tomba abuse and cumulation of unsuccessful attempts at acquiring eternity. Don't be afraid. No longer are all of those people after me for debts unpaid.

I've spoken to you of having wings, but these wings are like none others, mere vestiges, buried in the flesh of my back, souvenirs of flight. You missed the passage, somewhere between here and *Wovoko*, where I flew incessantly, actually quite incapable of landing, staying out at sea for several years and was completely monogamous, though no eagle nor albatross.

A leaf is following me, blown by a breeze, it scutters along the stones behind. Softly crackling. Must beware of even the most insignificant objects. No ordinary leaf is this. It follows me every way I turn, even against the wind. Same with the dust falling, clinging to my clothes.

With two goats, we strike out, going over the first dune. It's high noon. Rarely do I give in to technical considerations, but the vehicle we ride is simply too dazzling. Refracting light into its countless chromatic constituents (rainbow here is composed of unknown colors), it throws back the burning rays with twice the flash. All of this with the repetitive fingertip pattern of the panther pelt. We ourselves give off more heat than the burning sands over which we travel. We are fire, fully prepared to assume a tranquil, most ordinary life within the sun's atmosphere. So it is that inferno is cool to us. We take precautions to avoid catching cold.

Ndatou

In this land of fire it is best to seek shade. If you find none, make your own. Wear it as eclipse plumage.

Ndatou means the moment of dawn. Seems it's her name too. It is also where we are, although I'm not certain which side of dawn we're really on, nor which way we're headed. It is best to re-enter the night, coming from the morning. A distant friend has just told me of an ice storm and this is refreshing. Only momentarily though.

Singing comes from within the night. Now I know that we shall re-enter her. Night is feminine. At first it is difficult to locate where the music is coming from. So purely does it rise towards the stars, in one straight column. We hold hands advancing. I want to kiss her. My lips have severely blistered. Ecthyma; wasn't I just now with goats? We have time before reaching the preceding sunset. Many people are about in the streets, animals too. Edgewise is the only way to advance through dense crowds. Beware of frotteurs. Venging Echidna, mother of Chimera, Hydra and the Sphinx may prove to be an echinated problem.

Dyslogia. Enter night by doing full twist through half-open Dutch door. When writing lengthy political manifesto disguised as novel, proceed like frost work. All over at once. Be all ears.

Walls were built around sacred city by those who believed to be the only chosen ones, living in a Promised Land. Earth for them. They kept at bay others who wished to pray in a different way. Finally, didn't these walls prove eft to be prison rather than fortress?

Dig up and chew earth peas. Find the grass table and drink to satiation. No ordinary *eau*. Deep water has fermented. Cup hands to catch efflux.

Leading industrial nation stands trial for ecocide. Not only. Elinguation of media permitted massive oppression of peoples beyond horizons while re-kindling domestic patriotic fervor. Intellectual implosion ensued. This country hasn't yet cut its eyeteeth. Administer emetic truth to land of ill-gotten wealth. Enema too. Even if only by way of clandestine revues, hand-printed posters, and secret pamphlets. Display idiot card.

—Look now! pulling lengthy spotted tail from shadow pants. —Thought me to be ecaudite? Hell, it measures all of twelve ell!

—Ebullient companion, effulgent fellow, eche your horizon. End your effrontery. Rather listen. Is this not an escape tune we now hear? The purest *échappée*.

—Elfen nymph, I'll carry you in crook of arm. Wear crystal elbow-cops.

—Eloign further from suns.

Kneeling women elutriate manioc tubers in marigots. The waters are of strikingly different colors; grenadine and black, one is white as if the earth were giving milk, and this is perhaps the case. Girls seek elver beneath rocks in riverbed.

—Could we have understood that the concept of emancipation bestowed to mankind by those of African descent would prove to be the key to overthrowing Gog? This one for whom we have so long played purveyor while performing incessant prayer. Spiritual fog! Is your spirit so emarginated?

Recumbent. Offer you blue glass bear in bronze cage. Embosk before the coming of light. Have I wounded you? Let me embrocate your heart.

How to regulate blood that roars through carotid? Freeze reason to form embacle. Lie together on this Empire meridienne. I'll gently introduce my empurpled prick into your tiny offered orifice. Enamoured with you. Do become enceinte. What child will emerge from love's embouchure? Come *Enfant terrible*! Frorward daughter, capture frosh by hand. Make a frottage of frowzy techno-civilization. Declare wisdom ignotus. We'll be ilk.

I'm the end man. Player of bones. Know why nothing goes? The world's been set endways to fix its broken feet. Melt frost feathers from windward side of your face.

Frogmouths are awing. Take a 3 Myr catnap. Have discovered that there are many highly advanced civilizations that have no economical structure, no technology. Realize that ichnite will prove to be our footprints put down in remote future.

Drive mule-train beneath splendid night sky. Beach boat high on foggy shore. Wrap net round rocks, pretend this to be my miraculous catch. Squint from window with white eyes. Imagine you can see things. Wade along banks of shallow lake. Watch for edge-ice. Set tires afire in streets. Yell. Wave muskets, put your jeans to dry on cinder block pile of some house that hasn't yet been built. Heap. Wash hands in full filthy drum. Within strong cage, sleep.

Hold in your palm small cylindrical quantity of water which you contemplate. Pose with your mother for a portrait. Squint intently at the camera. Laugh. Lean on an elegant cane. Hitch a ride along a desert road. Wear a striped coat in a furnace. Disappear beneath an Islamic arch in strong *contre-jour*. Siphon gasoline from a Honda. Two aboard a red motorcycle, slowly drive by the charred corpse of a man lying beneath burned tire. Smile, (sadly). Do thriving business beneath bridges. Participate in a lynching, even if you're only a distant spectator. Wear a yellow shirt wide open down the middle. Chose between para-military boots and thongs. Put on a red wool bonnet and sunglasses.

Write on a green blackboard, "RULES" and "REGULATIONS." Apply these to yourself. Break them. Arrest yourself. Force yourself to strip, (keep your glasses and necklace on). For identification purposes, make yourself wear a big letter printed on cardboard square placed over the groin area. Can read A or T. Still nude, squat and beg for money. Hold the coins in your mouth. When it's full, fill the anus. Women have extra storage area in vagina. Wrestle with a friend in dusty courtyard. Pose before a publicity advertising "The Pearl of Banking," (do this in New York). While sitting in fine sand, spread your legs and make patterns with fingers. Write your name. Live in flooded areas. Race toy cars that you've made yourself from discarded tins. Three of you, lay down with heads touching and your feet stretching outward like the rays of a star. Think together. We're three. One's in the shade, two in the sun. The older one pouts, somehow guessing what's ahead. Adults now, look mean. Dance cheek to cheek with a girl from Mozambique. Thin scars on the face, perfect lips. They were put there by her mother to ward off snakes when she was four. Drink a lot. Howl. Wear a fish-net tee shirt. Fight over worthless currency.

Mal de ojo? Beware of this. Children are especially at risk.

Buy the girl you love a golden plastic dress. Brush her hair straight out like an explosion. Explode in her. Walk barefoot in garbage. Take broken glass from your foot and lick it. Sell small quantities of gasoline in whiskey bottles. While in prison, teach a cockroach to do stunts. It will show the rat; the rat in turn will educate the guard, who'll pass the word to the Director. Permit him to join the act if he's sincere, but only in exchange for the keys. Throw your shadow against a wall and leave it there. Drop the padlock in the dirt and leave it there as well. Find your wristwatch. Cross salt flats. Fill buckets. Curl up and go to sleep on an ugly cement dock in front of dirty sea. Mombassa. Listen to dockers working cranes that swing cargo held in strong nets over your head. Now apply all of this to a State situation, to international politics, to cosmology.

Return to Paris. Admire a thunderhead forming over the jungle. Drop your wristwatch. Red earth eats it, snarling. Ride your motorcycle into the river. Wash it there. Then wash yourself, taking plenty of time and lots of lather to clean penis.

—Ndatou! Is that you?

Offer the woman you love a light green bikini made of spongy synthetic fabric. See how she's a little plump, how beautifully her dark brown skin drinks in the light of three suns. Now do her hair up in thin long spikes thrusting outward like sputnik antennae. Now make her blonde; back to brown, give her a brushing. Draw in deep the odor of her sweat. Place a pink towel beneath her. Pull down her bottom. Fuck her right there on the blistering hot stairs leading up to no where, maybe out over the river. Dive into the water. Swim together for long time beneath the surface. Admire her body as she passes through underwater patches of light. Emerge. Often dance together. Persuade her to smoke less. To remain a little fat. Have a child.

Use the cinder block pile to build your house atop a wooded knoll. Resist when urbanists try to apply the theory of tabula rasa. Fight them off. Cling to your diminishing cime. Finally live atop a tower of dirt. When evicted, occupy empty shopping mall in Houston. Fully assume Dissociative Fugue on a universal scale. Then move to abandoned gas station before going much farther. Try penetrating her navel, her ear. Place penis beneath armpit slippery with sweat. Insist she doesn't ever shave silky hair there. Beg her not to cut thick curls spreading wide around crotch either.

To avenge Echidna, must I slay Argus?

Briefly become inane. Kick giant cave hyenas like curs, making them go beneath furniture. When they refuse to come out, go after them on all fours or simply overturn furniture. Repeat until immotile. Throw a rope over "obstacles." Too light? Tie monkey paw and try again. Odzooks! They'll not keep me out. No wall will prevent me from admiring the splendid golden dome of Al Aqsah. Proudly wear a tee shirt representing this magnificent mosque.

While setting traps for yourself, drink hot rubaboo.

Flatter your therapist. Bring her gifts. Invent intriguing symptoms for each new session. The second time you see her, call her by her first name. While keeping your emotional expression deep, baffle her by avoiding romantic flights of fancy. Don't have a fit when you discover an unflattering photograph of yourself.

What paradox that we poor are the sky's keepers, not just what's immediately overhead but for vast portions beyond what you can immediately detect; while kings and wealthy business barons haven't the simplest constellation, the closest star to behold. They don't ever look up, only ahead and sometimes behind, but rarely. Be it that we're so often afoot at night, worries rendering sleep impossible for us? Worms slipping over wet sand leave patterns that you would do well to interpret. Serpents form knots that needn't be undone. On the surface of quiet ponds, mosquito larvae rise and listen. Microscopic creatures deliver epic warfare in labyrinths of slime. It is sometimes difficult to ascertain exactly to which world they pertain. Frogs expel chordes of eggs in serpentine patterns. When seen from beneath, they flame.

Move through freshly seeded bacterial lawn. My eyes deviate up, down and sideward. Slurred speech and tongue protrusion.

I brood, worry and feel I do not deserve to have fun.

Snap out of it. Start pulling patches of hair from my own head. Conceal resulting alopecia. Ambush passerbys. Seize handfuls of their hair.

Attack dogs, cats, mohair sweaters, shaggy carpets. Anything fluffy will do. Engage in serious bouts of excoriation, gnawing and nail biting. My hair follicles present distinct signs of trauma: catagen hairs and wrinkling of outer root sheaths.

Discover my very own rose garden. Smell the heavy perfume of these unknown varieties which don't yet exist. Bury nose in them. My great, great grand daughter planted them long before I was born.

I make considerable advance preparation for starting a major fire. Anticipation is keen. I'm in an acute state of arousal. Carefully prepare arson paraphernalia.

Terrified by the periodic dreams of office work, I have great difficulty finding my sleep. Some nights, I have several successive nightmares. They're becoming sequential. I realize that it's here, in this dream world of rational thinking and business entrepreneurship, that I've incurred the heaviest debts. My pursuants actually originate from there. Just how it is they manage to follow me back here is a mystery to me. After awakening I have lingering feeling of fear and stress.

Go to the big mirror resting on the bathroom floor. Must hang it on the wall. It's important that Ndatou can see herself while dressing. Kneel. Confrontation with positive frontal release sign and saccadic eye movements. Possible destruction of subcortical structures.

Too easy to target Church. True intrinsic valor of missionaries unfolds much later.

Perform protracted shadow dance. Hold a rooster to your chest. Sit back to back meditating. Perform Xala by posing on stairs covered with red carpet, wearing white suits and talking to paternal white man who's momentarily pretending to lend an ear to your troubles of an "emerging African nation" type. Play Gillo Pontecorvo's "La Battaglia di Algeri" several times. Give a brother his last drink. Wear colonial militia uniform. Ride a motorcycle with zebu horns strapped to the handlebars. Foam at the mouth. Run a clandestine radio station from a closet. Paint your saxophone yellow, black and red. Listen to Caboverdiana music. Jump with joy. Design a building that won't hold up. Re-urbanize America by instilling the principal of tropical architecture. Apply "the colonial city" layout. Inspire yourself from District Six, Capetown before its destruction under Group Areas Act. Redesign port of Dakar to accommodate ships of another kind. Form dense crowd and hold aloft posters of Gamal Abdel Nasser. Demand and refuse a referendum. Commemorate Nana Prempeh. Lay on a dirty mattress in the middle of busy street. Cut out the shape of your reclining body from the mattress. Extricate your vital organs and suspend them along the walls in transparent plastic sacs. Nonchalantly stride through a streetful of corpses following brutally repressed riot. Effortlessly cut someone's throat. Wearing pajamas, take refuge on a public bench. Dress up in combat fatigues and paint "last Supper" scene using portable easel on the sidewalk. Live in a library. Eat books. Relax in rocking chair covered with splendid tropical flower motif. Cradle saxophone. Put saxophone down in chair and leave. Will continue rocking alone. Stand under blue neon light in Lapa neighborhood of Rio. Smoke from pipe with extremely long stem. Hold the rooster up against yourself again, just in front of your eyes this time. Its look will partially eclipse yours. Massage sore ankle after having taken off shoe and sock. Fight over rubbish with vultures, rats and hyenas. Refuse altogether to wear shoes. Don't accept chairs either; sit on the ground. Catch Devil and cut off hooves. Sell these. Try to reanimate aborted 6 month-old child abandoned dead in ditch. Strain under weight of the coffin you make for her. With muscles bulging, pose for poolside photo. Frequent disreputable bars. Leave there much money, time and health. Adopt highly threatening attitude. Exhibit deep scar across forehead that almost folds your face in half. Be dignified whatever the circumstances. Accede to the nobility of which you've been systematically deprived over the past 500 years. Remember how rich and diversified your economy was before the imposition of monoculture by colonial power. How inter-ethnic marriage prevented tribal warfare. Tired of wearing guerilla attire? Try on this splendid armor. Blue steel early eleventh century, beautifully swelling chest plate with intricate golden inlay design flowing down into spider-work apron. Smooth leggings over high red velvet stockings. Protective collar forming small fortress around neck. Studded with pearls, rubies and other gems. In addition to long double-handed sword you have radiant halo over your head. Wear white silk gloves that contrast strikingly with your black skin. Caucasian Pope that you're conversing with is stunned by your appearance. Pretends to look elsewhere, but he can't get his eyes off you. Call yourself Saint Maurice for the occasion. Thebian legionnaire. Assure yourself the company of Candid, Victor and Innocent. Realize that transrhenanian cult devoted to you and your companions sprang up as early as the seventh century.

Always manage to maintain at least a minimum degree of cruelty in your relations.

Briefly wear chain mail. Then go completely nude, swimming streams wearing nothing more than white turban, curved knife clenched between teeth. Advance with such grace that ducks and fish continue feeding as you brush past. Along the way, cast handful of pagans to Hell. Fight with a lion for the control of a woman's soul. Disguise yourself as an elephant to go unnoticed amongst large boulders. Definitively deprive Solomon of the Queen of Sheba by eloping with her. Don't linger by the decapitated heads of the prisoners you summarily execute. Bound hand and foot, spend eternity in big blazing fire that some can interpret as being true inferno. Emerge, unscathed.

Time? See, we're really going ahead. The proper direction.

Work a bone. Extract marrow and consume. Make perforations. Can be possible mouthpiece for flute or whistle. Make a throwing stick with cut marks on the proximal end to help give firmer grip when using. Make a convergent scraper, a spatulate tool (by using split ivory), a spheroid. Highly sharpen distal extremity of pointed tools (employ bone, limonite, quartz, or ivory), a denticular side-scraper and a bifacial lancelate.

Leave clear traces of *debitage* around pile of seventy spheroids. Make cairn of offerings to spirits of a spring by using stone and bone fragments. Feed on wart hog, jackal, gazelle and ostrich. Barbary sheep, buffalo. Keep in mind that rivers can dramatically change; erode deposits which they had once formed. Land uplift can be accompanied by marginal downwarping, especially in areas of monoclinal flexure.

Eventually blend with other animal groups, mainly broad range of primates mixed with proboscideans and hyracoids.

Limited orogeny makes for striking latitudinal zonation with remarkably symmetrical vegetation pattern.

When trying to determine correct stratigraphy of cave remains, provide for surface soil attrition and gradual infilling of cavities.

Would that this be attributed to Ian Tattersall or colleague, incursion into the temporal window has proven it to be fallacious. Actually, we lived on high perch, from which we would lurch to join primitive church. Food gathering consisted of sweeping the air with immense nets to catch small birds which we ate whole. We engaged in highly sophisticated communication by booming with blasts of infra sounds. Armies of woolly rhinoceros and cave hyenas were under our orders.

Resolutely break with tradition by posing for profile portrait while giving to see the side where you lost an eye during chevalresque jout. Kneel in manger scene and re-kindle little fire by blowing. Along with dirt and gnarled small bones of rare birds, sweep all of the above considerations beneath convenient rug. Sleep in immense bed covered with deep blue sheets bearing golden fleur-de-lis design. Listen carefully to Salmon, whom upon your request, has rushed to your bedside at this early hour to make middle-of-the-night conversation. At the foot of the bed, Barbary ape preens white dog while dame dressed in pink crushed velvet paints her own image using small hand-held mirror in adjacent room. Stars glimmer through open high windows. The very next night, awaken to an angel holding your heart out to you. Scene is illuminated by torchlight. A servant wears white silk with flame pattern on short pleated skirt. Long pointed white satin slippers on his feet. Take up the dog and pretend to eat it, beginning by the tail. Disregard monkey's vigorous protests. Duck beneath rain of falling scythes that fell every living thing surrounding you; pigs, horses, deer and fellow humans. Assume sitting position and read a book among the dead. Stand alone in dark garden pathed with sleeping men dimly lit by the torches they bore, stars and two faint comet tails. Put on long dark *cagoule* with embroidered golden swans. The inside is lined with light colored fur. Generously sow seeds beneath scarecrow of an archer. Carefully listen to the peacock's vow. Serve couples platters of red berries while they dine nude in wooden tubs full of wine. Surprise the secret conversation of richly dressed women gathered in royal bedchambers. Pretend to be deaf if they discover your presence. Remember for all of time what it was they were saying. Pretend to be Joseph guiding the ass upon which ride Mary and the infant Jesus during the flight to Egypt. Permit yourself a swig from small keg. Pose for two very rigid portraits executed in ancient Rome, one in the painted wax technique, the other in mosaic. Be the woolly dog in bottom left corner of the Duke of Gonzague's family portrait painted by Andrea Mategna in Mantua.

Engage in outright masochistic activities: Tell the woman you love that you love her beyond life itself. Follow her like a dog behind a bitch in heat. Try climbing on her when she has her period or a splitting headache. Have heated arguments about how to raise your children. Systematically oppose yourself to her point of view even when it's the same as yours. Take to looking at other women, even if they're really ugly compared to the one you love. Fight about money. Avoid responsibilities. Pick up severe drug habit. Become alcoholic. Beat her. Become obese. Never take a bath. Let your teeth get really rotten and constantly force kisses on her. Watch plenty TV, especially sports. Belch and pass wind. Become really obese.

Include in a film script that you're trying to sell, lines whereby protagonist openly professes to recognize the validity of Hizbollah doctrine. Do this in the first person. Address yourself to major studio owned by Jewish person. In another manuscript, let transpire admiration for Ariel Sharon. Try to publish this work in Iran. If that doesn't work, try East Jerusalem or Gaza strip with small Palestinian editor. Make sure you don't inadvertently confuse the texts when submitting them.

When disserting on racial equality, indulge in non-assertiveness. Miscegenation must be avoided at all costs, or only used to introduce confusion.

Move to New York. Let your neighbors, mainly firemen and policemen, know you loved watching WTC coming down. Convince them that you're an Arab by wearing turbans and carrying paperback Koran under arm. Have big Semitic nose to confirm Arab origin and infuriate them by ostentatiously entertaining only 100% blonde American women at your home. Drive a white Hummer with smoked windows and store crude oil in backyard heap of barrels higher than any house in vicinity. Boast to neighbors that your son's enrolled in flight training academy from which he'll be graduating in no time. Explain that unusually quick progress is due to the fact that he skipped take-off and landing instruction. Declare that Afghanistan never really ever was riddled with caverns and tunnels filled with terrorists. Just beautiful mountain landscape inhabited by clean- model citizens. Constantly vaunt the superiority of Mesopotamian civilization over that of America.

Now let your Armenian neighbor know that you're actually a Turk and that you believe the Armenian genocide never really happened.

Visit an Indian reservation during tribal pow wow. Get intoxicated and admit that you secretly admire the United States for having pitted rival Indian tribes against one another during the war of Independence before wiping them out and putting the leftovers on reservations. Obviously chew Red Man tobacco. Shoulder a Savage Arms rifle. Flip an Indian-head nickel. Just before falling into an ethilic coma, claim that Indians have a problem with alcohol; can't hold their liquor.

While White, give a speech to a Nation of Islam meeting. Introduce yourself by declaring that you have recurrent dreams in which you're whipping your way through cotton fields full of dying slaves. That these were originally captured and sold by Muslim brothers on the African continent. Returning from the fields to your ante-bellum mansion, you force your house Negroes to wipe the blood from the flanks of your stallion (white of course) using silk handkerchiefs with which you'll tie them come nightfall, before raping them until dawn comes.

Now be Black. Go down South, deeply so, and with big GM motor purring (you put it together on Detroit chain line), slowly drive giant pink convertible Cadillac through a KKK gathering while swigging cheap sweet Bali-hi wine and fondling with your long gold-covered black fingers, the pussy of a pulpy White blonde who's sitting next to you with her pants pulled down. The deeper you go, the more she giggles.

"Miscegenation!" yell you, laying on the horn.

Scrupulously delete all sardonic material.

When unconscious, fish for buffalo near fort Lewis while barging down the Missouri. Make pencil sketches of the Ponca and Vermilion rivers. Slip past Medicine Butte. Halt at an Arikara village at the junction of the Grand and Missouri rivers. Stay with Mandans. Note that Indians make regular pilgrimages to stag antler pyramid. White eagle is known as a nun. Pass the Milk River. Discover giant catfish. Corner and kill more bison. Indians call the Rockies the Wolf Mountains referring to the abundance of these creatures. Medicine man. Bear skinner. Calumet bearer. High priest of Mad Dog ritual. Escape from captivity by singing your enemies to sleep. Women warriors. Hungry dogs attack an immense male moose. Invoke manitous. Believe in signs and portents. Striking blue flowers of the camas cover large areas of prairie giving illusion of lake surface. Avoid chance encounter with sworn enemies. Drag your personal belongings behind horse on a travois. Can serve as ladder for erecting teepees. Write message incorporating the use of ideograms. Faithfully reproduce exact patterns of depicted pinto pony. Featherless eagles, dogs with hands and empty cages. Stockades, American flags and mules. Juvenile moose. Shoot deer in the autumn just before mating season. Receiving a sign from a green ram or a monster is considered strong medicine. Hold red-hot coals between your teeth. Ascribe joyous hidden meaning to the darkest storm. Adopt ghost dance ecology. Thank Wovoka for this, (not to be confused with Wovoko who I often am). Bison will go underground.

Analyze historic and migrant trails across western North America: Butterfield Overland, Good-night Loving, Chihuahua, Cimarron Cutoff, Honeymoon, Gila, Oregon and Santa Fe Trails.

Go on to following position which is a summit, though not a very high one.

Be dove couple oblivious to heavily armed hunting party. When finally alerted, set off by flying low between the hunters who'll invariably shoot each other while trying to down you. Avoid all manner of unnecessary stress; dogs, ferrets and falcons. Coo. At sunrise drink 'dew.

Explain to gathered crowd that we've entered the domain of untestable theory, more metaphysical than physical. Bolster theory with unobservable elements.

We've passed through another day going the wrong way. This is only to say that when night is found we should stay. Quickly enter. We're forced to duck when going in this time. Shoot down the panther that's lurking over night's entrance. The owner is furious, tells us it's only a skin put up for decoration. Calls us trigger-happy. Wants us to pay. Yet there's blood here.

Carry each other on the back or over the shoulder for undetermined periods. Transfer what knowledge we have to parrots and remain perfectly stupid while they manage our affairs. Make ourselves armors of very thin beaten gold embossed with comical motifs of bats, butterflies, frogs scorpions. Convince ourselves that this is sufficient protection. Grow blue corn in small quantities on high mesas. Be as unpredictable as the wind and in this manner become naturally associated with Ehecatl-Quetzalcoatl. Once again I admire myself in the reflection of a tezcatl. Replace your eyes with convex pyrite mirrors. We make a colossal statue of Coatlicue. Briefly inhabit a cliffside pagoda over a tormented sea where shipwrecks occur frequently. Light fires to lure ships onto rocks, finish off survivors with clubs and axes. Plunder the shipwrecks. Return to pagoda to meditate in all serenity. This capacity of adaptation is a fundamental quality of being human. Learn it well if you are to go on. Now head inland over the cliffs. Be Zhong Kui accompanied by subservient demons. No matter what your attire or general appearance, the eyes must be cruel. Travel through fantastic mountainscape with much mist, bamboo forests. Always take time to halt and meditate. Drink tea from finely *craqeulured* porcelain bowls. Play jade flute and sniff concubine Yang Guifei's purple scent bag while still digesting small demon from whom you confiscated these stolen objects before devouring him. Smell the odor of ancient paper and inks that permeates these scenes. Unpack portable shrine. Again, live behind a waterfall. Through the water curtain, admire herons, willows and prunes in the snow. Seduce Willow-and-Moon Kannon. Stroll beneath spearhead style cloud bands. Vitiate intensity of final suffering and paradisiacal rewards by rendering in archaistic fashion. Accompanied by trained monkey, engage in poetry competition. Step into a world where only foreshortened perspective is permitted. Advance among palaces of great geometrical purity. Wear high bomb shaped silk turban and beautiful white talismanic shirt with gold chinoiserie calligraphy on blue reserve. Blow a finely sculpted oliphant. Use ivory tableware of sapi-Portuguese style when dining. Gather bouquets of Lords-and-Ladies. Refuse to call them cuckoopint.

I'm no cunctator.

Now let's sit and converse together of our adventures, surrounded with the severed heads of six avowed enemies. Sacrifice Isaac. Don't hold back. Go all the way. Organize a descent of the cross scene, knowing full well it's no Christ you're lowering. Go to the desert. You do the tempting during a forty-day period. Use Afro-Portuguese salver. Draw splinter of real cross from your foot. Storm a castle with fellow wild men. Harvest pepper in Coilum. Descend in primitive diving bell to observe dark ichthyophagis in lake bottom situation. See how they are accompanied by dogs and all manner of mammals having also adapted to underwater conditions. Riding camels in inverted position, cross the ceiling of this world. Preside at an auto da Fe. Construct an immense lodge on high thin poles directly over large fallen tree that forms high arch sweeping from beneath your home like a giant tongue. Do this in Irian Jaya. Wear kite like structure over your head. Liberal use of nose and ear plugs (use CDs again), many bracelets on both arms and legs. Fashion big double bodied pirogues for high sea fishing expeditions. Wear plume mask ten times as high as yourself, making neck reinforcement and use of crutches obligatory. Make massive thatched ceremonial hall with numerous small windows for presenting head trophies. Do not create the type of artwork that would be expected of you. Wear an owl mask. Make a very complicated headrest with surprising number of feet. Lacquer it black and inlay with star and moon symbols made from mother of pearl. Always carry an enemy's head ready to brandish at arms length.

Now let's assume that there has been none of this interpenetration, no braiding of the universe. First signs were to have been entire sections of Africa erupting in Europe; parts of Lagos and Kinshasa jamming into Paris or Berlin, physically so, with red dirt, riverine fauna and all. Yet the river's clogged with crocodiles; tropical storms dumping lakes of warm water onto the cities while snowstorms and arctic creatures come down on equatorial zones. We've made it perfectly clear that New York is tropical, no longer has high edifices without elaborate usage of flying buttresses and that the South is generally much richer than the North, northerners willing to do most anything to go down there. None of this would be true? The Sun hasn't an approaching distant sister star as was earlier announced, that contrarily to what had been considered as being a certainty, Andromeda and our own Galaxy have had a near miss, brushing past one another in mere flirtation? There has been no galactic mating? They continue their ways, separating as Hubbell's Law would want?
Do not worship the snake. She is cold, too calculating. She knows.
Will tell you that there is no jungle left. Not anywhere on Earth. That all is now an immense urban zone, even the southern, most hostile tip of Cape Horn, Terra del Fuego where there are now huge brooding cities dominating remote foggy bays where orcas once fed on penguin and sea lion. That even across the still roaring forties, all of Antarctica has been urbanized and that it's really not so cold there either. There haven't been any time machines, nor has space travel advanced anymore. Who here would even dream of going to the moon? It's not even known whether or not this has already been done. In fact all of these notions are only distant memories, part of a remote past when flights of the imagination where vectorial in the sense of carrier of disease producing microorganisms from one host to another. The World has become an immense super-populated fortress, perilous enclave where the inhabitants only think about how best to devour one another. A mostly

White world. Very little trace of genetic diversity. Certainly no manner of written record concerning defanged rebel's spawn. Only Smoothtongue is spoken. Beware she doesn't slip a refrigerated coil round your head as you read from the *Book of Fever*.

White Citadel

We inhabit a skull. It's an ivory city, vast as the brain that was once in it. Echoes resonate within.

I'm not a scientist
I'm not an astronaut
Nor am I a researcher

Only a contemplator am I. Knowing where to look, realizing that there are codes. The patterns on the sides of certain fishes, the toxic chemistry of the death frog, the design on an *azulejos* plate painted by an insane Portuguese girl that you will have met by now, she dismissed for "insult" before being interned in the most barbaric mental institution. Women of all ages left to wander within the confines of an old courtyard open only to the sky, obliged to accept whatever might fall upon them: sunlight, rain, lightning and even moonlight, for they hardly ever returned to their rooms, the director having opted for the concept of freedom to roam. One woman gnarled the roots of the big plane trees and with her nails she pulled patches of bark from the trunks, baring them to the height of two meters which was the maximum of her reach. Another woman built herself a hut of leaves, which she maintained in all seasons. As for Maria Magdalene, she forever gazed at the sky. To do so she was obliged to remain prone or suffer horrible neck pains from constantly turning her head heavenwards. Beyond the walls of this prison for the demented, only a short flight away for even the slowest of birds, lies a glittering pile of broken ceramic tiles, fiercely reflecting the sun, sending up its own hue of blue much stronger than that of the sky.

Other elements have their importance. A mirror from Angola. It is covered with tar through which has been scratched a pattern. This

AKA

mirror is a small circular one that was planted, by coincidence, in the belly of a Lunda sculpture on the very day that Maria Magdalene was interned in faraway Portugal. The design, however, was not incised until just after her death, which was about the time that mercenaries and colonial troops were warring through the jungles in a final effort to retain this gem for Salazar.

Had there ever been any sort of link between the mad girl and the African colony? Only one, in the manner of a migratory bird, that in passing would halt, a day or a week, often longer, bringing along songs that it had learned from species indigenous only to the African continent. Purveyor of messages, songs that could only be recognized by those who had sojourned in sub-Saharan zones. It is said that in much the same manner that the aging Henry Mortimer Stanley, retired in his beloved English Devon and listening to the song of the marsh warbler freshly returned from its annual African migration, could therein detect the call of those indigenous species which it would so adroitly mimic, so could Maria-Magdalene decipher wing born messages, however different they may have been from the form of song which might have been expected, and deduce what manner of magnetic carpet, what heliotic currents had been ridden and how they in turn reflected the greater order of things for which no one had, at that time, even the slightest interest.

The number of hairs covering the head, legs and abdomen of the tarantula spider, highly variable, divided by the number of eyes that it possessed, always the same.

An olfactory vocabulary. One of taste too. That of a woman comparable to the strongest black coffee, the most violent alcohol or yet the urine of a lioness. All of this mingled with her beauty, one that doesn't exclude wrinkles, loose skin under the arms or dropping breasts. It is a language, not one for the young nor even for adolescents.

This isn't the beginning of pain but the birth of bliss.

Only one thing compares, the most violent drug I have ever taken. Head wrenched from this body, stars entering through the new orifice. The comprehension of time is to be obtained only through suffering.

There are cold drafts in this skull, even upon the most clement day, and when the wind rises a howling is to be heard.

—Draw thick curtains before the eyeholes, plug the nasal cavities with tangled vegetal matter, hemp or jute. If we're not careful, we'll all fall down, scuff our knees and catch our death in this breeze.

Ngoubekpa.

In another month I shall be gone, departed, exploring other *lieux*. Places where there shall be no traces. Memories of the Ordovician, not the flora nor the fauna, but rather a question of light. Shadows had then an altogether different appearance, more of an aura about them and they were never black, hardly even somber, as if light from the sun were in some manner capable of penetrating matter, whatever it might be, tree trunks, the huge fern like fronds and then of course even rocks and the geological structures they constituted. Or perhaps it was just that the light had a way of wrapping around obstacles.

It is a good place from which to ponder upon suffering, this skull. Its smooth surface accommodates pain. To touch it, be it merely with one's eyes, is soothing. How I wish for others to discover in what manner they may crawl in. Not through the orifices, mind you!

Explore solace, quietude and relief.

Here are canals along the vault, the skull top. No need to portray upon this lofty ceiling, Sistine scenes, nor even the more mannered images with exaggerated foreshortening of testicles and vaginas seen from beneath. Frescoes of Corregio or the Carache brothers. These channels seem carved into the bone, gouged out or molded when the skull was yet soft and malleable. Perhaps oversized veins through which coursed torrents of umber hued blood. Had this creature seminal ducts traversing the cortex? This pit, suprainic depression? And this extraordinary zigzag where join the parietal bone and the occipital is more lightning bolt than suture. The lunate sulcus is well down. This was no ape! Yet there is an extraordinary sagittal crest to which formidable jaw muscles must have been attached.

Look through the eye openings. Only empty fields with no galaxies.

—There! Intrinsically faint, a dwarf flare star. You thought this radio emission source to be remote? It's quite close, I assure you.

Hoard loot here? Keep it bare and uncluttered! A place to purify one's body upon returning from slaughter. Cleanse the spirit as well. Sweep sweet grass smoke over your chest. Wash your face with it. Inhale deeply. There's nothing of shamanic about this.

You with your warring ways, wish to heap booty here! Are not the stables full enough? The fires we build when the skull turns chill with the call of the whippoorwill, darken brown the bone.

For that matter, I am dark matter myself, immense and all devouring. The revelation is that I am the one who engulfed the content of this cranial cavity with ferocious parasitic appetite. That repast consumed, I polished the bone with my three tongues, one rather raspy for the rough work, the other two, much finer for the finish.

I am inside of within, underneath below, over above, beyond away.

Just as Gavroche lived in the belly of a giant plaster elephant, Place de la Bastille, I now inhabit this disproportionate skull that dominates the Seine from a high bank where some tidal surge left it marooned. Of human origin there's no doubt, but so monumental. I suppose that just as small lizards developed into dinosaurs, so shall we become enormous with time. More than giants, or perhaps will it have been only the head which so enlarged, other body parts remaining the same or even atrophied? Homo Megacephalus. But this home of bone definitely comes from the future.

Time travel has of course become a common thing but much more risky than ever expected. If you wish to decorate your table with a bouquet from the Precambrian, bring back from the remote future just such a surprising trophy as this skull which will surely reek havoc with any paleontologist's wildest predictions, or simply enjoy a Carboniferous landscape during your lunch-break picnic, it's possible. Returning intact isn't a sinecure though. The side effects being that your genetic makeup, may very well break up, or that you may lose pieces of your own anatomy along the way.

Missing body parts: usually small, falling in the category of larynx, spleen, prostate which can be an advantage if suffering from prostate cancer but deadly if loss of larger vital parts occurs. Unless blessed with reptilian regenerative capabilities.

A seasoned time traveler, I can assure you that it's possible to even acquire elements that are totally unrelated to your metabolism. Whether discreet or cumbersome these usually prove to be pathogenic. More rarely, they can avail to be beneficial.

Stochastic sweeping bursts of star formation are the surest sign that much time has gone by and that most probably, our own galaxy is now mating with Andromeda. Stars are not colliding as one might naively assume. It is important to remember that individual stars within a galaxy are proportionately farther apart from each other than are the galaxies themselves which constitute the general neighborhood cluster. Other worlds are however, just at hand, only a stone's throw away at the most. It has been a passive form of intergalactic travel.

I'm tired of polishing this bone to give it an ivory luster. Can I muster the energy to exit?

I emerge. Surprisingly the sky is very dark. My favorite constellation? Some prefer to behold the bold graphism of Crux or Ursa, much flattened now. Camelopardalis is my favorite. Hardly an asterism, still very dim, most arbitrary.

The river is belching geysers of gas, pockets of long forgotten toxic waste. This for me is an ill omen. Avoid the night bullet. I must from this moment on, keep my eyes open while taking a shower, open mail, even small envelopes, at arm's length, never let anyone, not even a child, approach me from behind. Things I learned while living in Senatobia, not the minor planet but the small town in Mississippi.

Removing my shoes, I discover that I now have semipalmated feet. Simple syndactyle anomaly rather than evolutionary modification, this will help in crossing the river, the bridges being all down.

This crinkling sound? A furtive figure is stooping over my dustbin, rummaging through the refuse, trying to discover carelessly discarded confidential information. Perhaps IMG is seeking my trace again. Debt collectors are the most versatile time travelers, hugging to the host like tenacious parasites. I'm prepared to suffer another amputation if it comes to that. I have reptilian capacity for hibernation and the healing of wounds, even deep ones. I'm sure that I'm on the verge of limb regeneration.

Then again, this could be purely political.

Halfway across the river I gulp down bubbling froth boiling upon the surface. It's warm, stings the throat like a carbonated soft drink. Quench.

Ichtyofauna: several kinds of African freshwater fish now live in the Seine. They are best adapted to the swift currents. Dwarf and pygmy species such as Kribia nana, small enough to take refuge in the tiniest cavities or brace themselves against rocks with their stiff spines, are the most common. Larger and swifter anguilliform fishes feed on allochthonous material dropping to the surface in areas where thundering torrents develop during the rainy season. These fish are profiled for the most violent straights with bomb-shaped heads to fight the flux and a variety of suckers or other clasping devices to cling to the bottom when at rest. Estuarine conditions prevailing towards the mouth of the river have lured species with high salinity tolerance far out into the ocean while bringing the marauding bulldog shark deep inland. As the dry season advances, pools of slack water form and the dissolved oxygen content of the water drops. Those fish incapable of developing resistance to anoxia die off in great quantities. It is a time of feasting for the crocodiles. With jaws agape, they glide silently along the surface taking their fill of gasping fish that have come up, desperately seeking air. Within the city there are diverse faunistic zones created by the seasonal changes.

Deluge creates flooding which permits the proliferation of a lacustrine fauna, distinct from the riverine species. Rate of speciation is extremely rapid.

The mainstream turbulence spins me about at a dizzying speed. Several times I'm sucked under scraping the bottom, where I take in epilithic organisms, only to be spit out again further downstream. Plunge again to the river bottom, bring up enormous quantity of aufwuchs, juveniles and sub-adults. This is only wistful. I surface with a fistful.

Oloman wears sickeningly sweet jasmine perfume. He sips coffee mixed with clove and vanilla, smokes highly flavored tobaccos laced with hazelnut and cinnamon aroma in a small porcelain pipe from Palestine.

—I wish you luck; hope that you can get your bearings and find your way before you get yourself irremediably lost in your inextricable mystecology, he says gasping between drinks as he gulps down the water of a *narghile* instead of smoking through it. Yesterday he ate the protective leaves wrapped around a miando manioc stick. Just as I'm beginning to question whether he's even from here at all, he rises and attempts to walk through a wall.

He's not lost and even if he were suddenly blind, he should know his way around. After all, we're in his home. Perhaps he's dead.

I could have told you that this has become an extremely sophisticated world, at least from a technological point of view. So advanced that the simplest mechanical procedure, say shifting gears in a transportation device or properly entering a lavatory, requires a higher education. For me it would be an extremely complex operation requiring the translation of a twenty four-page manual, to simply accomplish the act of passing from one gear to another or gaining access to the latrine. Everything in this world, acquiring information, obtaining currency, making oneself understood, stems from the accumulated knowledge of a million years gone by, over which I have vaulted with one bound, landing totally ignorant, beast-like in their smooth world where I stand out like a jagged spike, rusted and all covered with the scum of time which I have so suddenly traversed. Brushing temporal sediment from my sleeves, I discover that it just simply isn't so. It is I who possess the knowledge. It came along with me, though of what use it could possibly be here now, I'm not certain. Each one here is a god unto himself, erecting small altars in his own home. The central element is a mirror of considerable size. They engage in long hours of self adulation. Those who are the most fortunate possess pools of still oil over which they lean. The reflected image has greater depth and the background is less obtrusive. If I'm to succeed here, I must obtain an Aztec mirror of polished obsidian. A tezcatl with gilden wooden frame. I could pass eternity admiring myself. Permanent dwaal.

None will do. From the greatest core I shall strike my own stone. Alone I will undertake the chore of polishing the surface, but before, though I be the patron of no sorcerers, consider the fact that I'll need no dwarves nor servants. Keep in mind that my Aka tribesmen are forever with me. The women make for me shirts of ntchamé moss taken from the highest treetops. This fiber is all aglow with captured fireflies. The tribesmen guide me. Wherever they, go I follow. Whatever they suggest, I undertake. *Prive* me not of their guidance lest there be no survival. These six points would be Solomon's seal? Two taken away, the four cardinal points you think? Hardly! A firm believer would suggest crosses or Xs with medullar circles. Neither! Nor stylized birds either.

Wouldn't it be much simpler to self-appropriate Montezuma's divinatory mirror which Cortez had planned to offer to Charles Quint before the French corsair, Jean-Fleury of Honfleur, made off with it in 1522? True, it has important pale striations, but the image is almost perfect.

Other mirrors have been fashioned, brass ones, jade ones.

Are there peaks here that I can ascend to discover myself, as did Ernesto Guevara climbing the Popcatépetl? Frequenter of caverns and grottos within which I can stash arms and supplies, gullies and ravines where I can withdraw when surrounded. Although this proved to be a fatal habit in the Che's case, permitting a numerically superior enemy to fire down upon dwindling guerilla handful.

Clad with this winking vest which I'm sure you wish you had, I venture out. The fit's not bad. Hardly have I gone five strides that I've been given yet another name. Zebulon which isn't to my pleasing, unless of course it be in memory of the one who ascended Pike's Peak. But then, am I as he, to later lose my life in some obscure conflict like the one concerning independence from King George and incorporating suppletory native Indian forces in which rival tribes have been pitted against one another? This technique is always valid, whether it be Iroquois against Hurons, Ouzbecs against Pachtouns or simply Sunnis against Shiites.

Involve the natives! Put them on the front line of fire. Look at how Europe put a good two million Africans on the front during the World Wars, testing machine gun fire, land mines and poisonous gases. Really brave soldiers, never cringing nor looking back. Heavy smokers, many would be picked off by sniper fire while standing nocturnal vigil, the flaming cigarette or glowing pipe bowel making the perfect target for the night bullet.

Like Allah, I have ninety-nine names, though mine be much less divine. Would this be some sort of "Hydra project"? Complex polycephalic plot involving conflicting minds attached to a single body, from which they haven't sprung but have rather been grafted onto. Impure for sure, "The Creator" becoming "He who Destroys," "The Donator" is now the "Taker"(I prefer "The Grand Confiscator"), life not necessarily being that which I take, nor material things obligatorily those destroyed by me.

"All-Hearing" and "All-seeing" would be bluntly simplified to become "Deaf and Dumb." Each name has a deeper meaning, an underlying story, be it a children's rhyme, a riddle, a simple mathematical formula or even a cryptic secret code such as "Y2.Q2.B2.C1" which simply translates to "covered 2/10ths at low and medium altitudes and 2/10ths at 5000 meters," confirmation of visibility for the 8 to 9 o'clock period on august the 6th, 1945 over Hiroshima city. If there are only ten ants living under a stone, God will see them. He'll provide for them.

The brain is a vestigial organ. Highest state of development at birth, regresses with age. Comes to resemble gut-associated tissues, the Peyer's patches in small intestine. Has the brain been swallowed?

Rwanda's reason enough to overthrow God. It's time to strike! Seek him out in his warren of light.

Why then didn't you rebel earlier? Holocaust should have proven to you his evil trait. Were you cowarded by Lucifer's fate?

He's much burlier than Satan, fur's even curlier.

Don't merely treat the teeth. Make no fuss. Draw your knife from its sheath. Swim through the puss.

Dig up what's beneath. You'll save all of us.

End pyorrhea! Evacuate these theological considerations! Flush heaven's latrine.

The fine mirror that I employ, permits the detection of the reflection of numerous other heads. Surprisingly, they don't spring from my shoulders but hang in heavy necklace around a single neck. Are they spent? Don't discard! They're the ones that will have permitted me to say, "I went!" referring to incommensurable remoteness to which, habitually, no one ever goes and from which it is certain that there's no return.

Wearing only green plastic thongs, I have a *matinal* semi-erection. She's dressed in pink mohair bikini.

—Let's go to church. We'll draw holy water with a *shadoof*.

—Why do you speak to me of such things?

—It's an occasion to use a double affricative.

—Other words, more acceptable, could permit you to exercise occlusion, plosion as well as frication.

Very, very pale hominids, certainly not extinct ones, nor specimens from our fold, sweep through urban zones. They go by twos or threes. They seem to require no sleep and when they do rest, it is more often than not, atop a crest or other high perch that these ones momentarily halt. With out a doubt, they are much more evolved than we, this is plain to see.

There's much evisceration going on. Assassination is common place. It's mainly a question of getting the vital parts, organs or even limbs, that are in great demand on the black market. It's the only way to obtain replacement elements to go on. Here in the North, we simply can't afford the price of clone livers and hearts available in Africa or Asia, (sometimes just across the street). The rich have been going on like this, replacing whatever wears out, for hundreds of years. Some individuals have survived, —what say I? —thrived in unimaginable luxury for a full millennium, sometimes even two. Mohamed VI of Morocco is the best known example. In this manner he truly incarnates the divine descendant he is purported to be. His empire spreads from where Senegal used to be, up through parts of northern Europe and all of the way across to former Libya. Algeria is a mere memory. The French, holding an eternal grudge against Algeria, crushed the rebellious Polisario to the benefit of Morocco. Harboring deep nostalgia for monarchies, they naturally encouraged the ensuing exponential spread of empire with which the image of their own glorious past was associated. A Renaissance of sorts, which ultimately devoured the last vestiges of democracy which had become just another lost cause. Many things had occurred in very rapid succession when viewed from here. A nuclear waste, train convey had derailed on its way from the Cap de la Hague treatment plant, a mobile Chernobyl that spilled 400-degree plutonium over the French countryside.

Pakistan and India finally wiped each other out in a three-minute war that provoked severe mutations among Tibetan monks. China was saved from contamination by the Himalayas, only to succumb to the influence of western economical war. A billion starved. Mongols have returned riding swarthy ponies, they sweep through what's left of Europe. Cyclical! Expatiation, a reservoir awaiting awakening, killing and massive slaughter which reveals what really happened to Neanderthal. Major genocide had indeed only been a form of practice, permanent rehearsal.

—I don't get the picture! Need coherence! Why would IMG be after you? Why would they want your body parts more than any other?

—Haven't really thought about it.

—You're a living reservoir, only surviving example of an extinct branch, possessing certain vital traits.

—I suppose that I am a little different.

—True, just as certain sapiens had low prominent brow, hyper developed nasal cavity, short pharynx permitting rudimentary speech while protecting against accidental choking, you present unusual particularities. But don't assume that these be priceless advantages. No. I think it's akin to the question of keeping alive the last specimen of a lethal virus, smallpox or anthrax, for example.

Cloning's expensive. Homeless and third world (Occidental) organs are much cheaper and more readily available. Wealthy can be heavy smokers, alcoholics, don't worry, it's no more complicated than replacing a blown out tire or changing your underwear.

Spare brains even, though only a certified "clone origin" can guarantee that one remains herself or himself, permitting smooth transition into a *moi*, assuring continuity. Imagine the results if black market brains were implanted!

Keep fridge full of lungs, livers and hearts. Extra prostates, ovaries (know of a man who changed penises every three weeks), ensure fuller sexual life with these spare parts.

Customs have evolved: no longer are there business lunches, but relieving sessions, where affairs are discussed while shitting together in a tight circle.

Never lose face. If you slip in shit, pretend to surf.

From here on in I won't let you see my visage anymore. I'll give no description. Not even a glimpse. You can see me seated naked in the red dirt, hands crossed over my knees pulled up to the chest, the feet are bare. The ground's clear except for a few peanut shells and a cigarette. This would prove that food is abundant. Or it could be no more than my daily fare. My head blends with shadow that falls across it. Don't complain. I could give you another version, where I'd only permit you to see my feet, planted slightly askance on a dirt road. I don't wish to be redundant. Plenty shade here too.

New fauna, flora, not from mutations due to massive pollution, nor evolution. No ready explanation. Yes we had fitted many life forms with atomic parts for preservation; even flies, mosquitoes and certain viruses. I have mentioned the tiger-sized alley cats, no mere growth factor. They're different in many ways including genetic make-up. Botany: Carnivorous plants have adapted to colder climates. Some can survive in permafrost, others emerge during arctic winter, gobbling polar bear and small white fox, tempting seal by giving off strong fish scent. Scientists too are sometimes sucked down core drillings while seeking fossil records. The tubular form that their bodies acquire from violent aspiration facilitates ingestion by permafrost flora. Others have gone to the ocean where they seize sperm whales and sometimes, ships, tangling the screws before engulfing the entire vessel, digesting the crews and spitting up the hull like some mere nutshell. "T'isn't heaven but hell," say the sailors when they encounter these shifting sargassum seas that'll raise up like some monster's flews.

As for me, my pharynx is even more elongated now, permits other levels of speech, can sing, whisper and yell all together, emit words that you couldn't even begin to spell, instantly learn concepts that no one could possibly teach, invent riddles too complex for any sphinx; drink, eat and converse all at the same time with no risk of choking; kill as I preach, cry while joking. Deal with phrases said to be of flight, not derived from the verb fly but rather from the action of fleeing. Realize that there exists a higher level of communication and that access is often situated just between two words such as illegible and ineligible. There are many openings, but they constantly shift.

This hill above the beach? No dune. Something thrown up on the shore. I've told you, we've returned to the sea several times before. Monkey's muzzle is another name for a blowhole. This is no lore. Why do you think I always wore a hat (all of straw to facilitate breathing) in that chapter? There's nothing worse than bird droppings or pollution down this type of respiratory system. Await the neap. Develop clasping device for submarine sex. Atlantis? We built no cities down there. Not ever! Abate 'n go deep. Expensive shame, cheap pride. Wave your flag, don't hide.

I'm scouring the area for driftwood. You know, women judge men on how they build fires. "Betrays how they make love," they say.

Desperate to prove excellent fire builder.

—Take your time. I want no furnace, she says.

I've made it perfectly clear that there's nothing of elitist about time travel, that it has become a very common thing with public transportation going in and out of temporal windows all of the time. There are cheap shuttles, providing little if any comfort, destinations are never fully guaranteed and there's no manner of recourse should you be displeased with the results. Most of all, it's very likely that you may never return to your lieu of departure. Also baggage claims are only approximate; best to travel lightly or with nothing at all though household pets can make the trip. Assuming that you do return from abyssal time zones, sufficient time should be allowed for decompression; just as the diver coming up from the deep is subject to the bubbling of nitrogen that affects the brain and the joints, you too will be riddled with small pockets of alien substances and even strange knowledge, unwittingly acquired along the way, that can cause irreparable damage.

Seek ever larger abandoned cranial cavities. Like the hermit crab, it is time you changed shells. Place an ancient television on the wall (this one's a Zenith) with vintage entertainment constantly playing, it has taken on the value of the Bellini painting that is placed on the opposite wall, next to a rather naive portrait of Benito Mussolini. Also a fresco by Annibale Carraci "Jason and the Argonauts, transporting the ship through the Libyan desert," formerly in the Palazzo Fava at Bologna. In this painting, Hercules unceremoniously kicks the lion and clubs it across the head, a very inoffensive small panther with sliced open belly cowers before a splendid Jason wearing wrinkled ruby tunic gone rust colored with time, a pair of hovering harpies darken the sky and a bulky Argo rides the backs of an Argonaut horde in the background. As is often the case with these chef-d'œuvres, light seems to enter the painting with the viewer, never quite making it to the far reaches of the distant landscape where there is little more than a glimmer. The head of some gigantic wolf-like creature lies across the foreground. The type of scene that would flatter Chiefs of State and Entrepreneurs. Would not the protagonists and the real action be in the background, the laborers carrying the Argo upon their shoulders, traversing the desert which is reputed to be one of the most extreme, while the hero figures in the foreground who engage in divertissement, would be in reality playing mere second roles or only minor figuration? Just as in real life.

All are masterpieces (including the Zenith TV) from their common time period, the early Renaissance. The curve of the inner surface of the skull makes hanging a difficult affair, just as it was once almost impossible to hang ordinary paintings in the Guggenheim Museum, (a problem certainly foreseen by the architect).

Reconsider the condition of labor, analyze the feudal residue that survived for so long in agricultural enterprise throughout the West during the 20/21st centuries, big banks having replaced medieval landlords. Why was Trotsky mistaken about the potential of communism in Africa? Why did Guevara so miserably fail in the Congo, while all three Kabilas brilliantly succeeded there? Undertake empirical study of social codes, relations between workers and their patrons; found an Academy of Moral, Science and Politics. Hold face to face encounters between enemies. View terrorism from within rather than from the exterior. Summary understanding of Abou Hamza's doctrine is imperative. Recognize Dr. Abdelaziz Rantissi, Hamas cofounder, as being essential to the balance of the Middle East. Freshly reinterpret Antonio Gramsci's analysis of Machiavelli's writings with respect to the development of European power: Elisabeth of England, Ferdinand of Spain, Ivan the Terrible in Russia and Louis XI in France. Can we truly speak of an elliptic paragon?

Scour down the inside of this other skull, even if it is to become the primary siphon of the spirit's sewer, destined to accommodate all that is too filthy for an ordinary cloaca. True history rarely comes to the surface.

Distress, no joy, deepest depression. Of what use is it to resist, to fight for lost causes? Palestine, Western Sahara and democracy itself. Purest effort is crushed, ground down to a purée.

Defy the will of most powerful economy? Only minor ruction. Rubricate your destiny. This new skull is tubiform. A very long hallway.

Ninka Nanka

We spend much time making love by the light of Bandulu, the morning star which can also be the evening star though bearing a different name when in this phase: Kossi si ekoro. These are names given by the riverine peoples who forbid their women to partake of dog meat being that it so closely resembles the flesh of man and that we are just now beginning to consume human fare with a semblance of moderation and that a good substitute would, to the contrary, be welcome in order to permit human population to normally develop. This may seem contradictory but it isn't meant to be so.

When our sleds are heavy with severed heads we halt in dry riverbeds. There are many parliaments, congresses and embassies in this land. Diplomatic and government vehicles seem prestigious and well kept. They're mostly third-hand. The World has become a game, a talk show, people are given to enjoying entertainment or providing it, even if this only means watching them as they watch you. There are many hyper-obese that ride flat-bellied in low carts if they ever venture out at all. Their blood looks like fresh cream. It's an oily substance that's a much sought after lubricant. It is for this reason that they are often harpooned when abroad. As with cachalot, their numbers are dwindling.

In fluttering cyclones of color, butterflies fiercely compete for the strong urine of enormous primitive cats that mark the limits of their territories with spurts of pestilential piss that run down lamp poles and building corners in dark sticky streams. Erratic wing movement makes it almost impossible to distinguish individuals but I have become quite good at it. This updraft carries little budama along with ula, mera mera, cobaltina, kayonza, usambara, somalina, bansana, moyambina, dubiosa, azurea, bwamba, unyoro, caerulea, chala and niobe. These are all quite small, no larger than a dime. All of them are blue.

That wind beaten downblow of brown is exclusively composed of the pterou pterou variety.

White winged tsomo, notoba and hintza hintza spiral while broken-winged boma drop to the ground.

Erupt red pyroptera, ngoko, juba and sangaris.

Have you recognized African taxa? The hills of Kenya, the hollows of Uganda, the forest trails of oriental Cameroon and the Njawarongo Valleys have intertwined with Ile de France.

Bigger: zalmoxis, porthos, xiphares, andina, zampa zampa, phaetusa and phosphor, makala and antambolou.

All have sworn to be our companions, even if the world's to freeze over three times or burn in a thermal burst. We share rotten prawn and over-ripe prune along with other very smelly things.

Jabone, eupompe and ione have dipped their wings in blood.

Eat African green pigeon and Namaqua dove. Crab plover have come this far inland. Purple swamphen are afoot.

Carmine bee-eaters nest colonially in cliffside river burrows. They're opportunistic runners of brush fires, seizing fleeing insects very near advancing flames, in and out of smoke they go. Sometimes their feathers burst into flame and they drop into the advancing brush fire. Given to the burning, these are the Tuileries gardens just off of the Place de la Concorde in the heart of Paris.

If there's no fire, use oryx, gerenuk, topi, people or vehicles as beaters to flush out flying insects.

While attending grass fires, halt for a bout of bill wrestling, pursue own image through high business tower windows. Perform hooting duet with companion. May sound rather loud and mellow or soft and tinny depending if heard from afar or close by. Chicks utter incessant soft peeping.

A "golden age" during which time we briefly but very intensely trade for sophisticated exotic weaponry, superior transportation devices and new substances, especially tomba the brain drug, all of which have been introduced by higher beings visiting our sector. Arms are ecology friendly and very practical for preparing game. Will sort out the organs and put them aside even before the victim drops. The vehicles will take you anywhere at virtually any speed and in desired style. As for tomba, you've been experiencing it all along without knowing what it really was. Now you know.

We ululate amid the high buildings, echo giving a sense of ubiquity.

—Ugsome friend, avoid further uglification by pasting down your hair. Conceal ulotrichy. Don't take umbrage! We haven't yet reached our ultima Thule, unco umbrose place.

—What's this underhand? Dipped your arrow tips in upas, have you? More potent than urari? Go over Urd's breasts and slip beneath her uterus to enter the underworld. Fill urn full of her urine when passing down. Wear ursine pelt to protect from urticants.

They've ordered that I submit myself to an uroscopy. Writhe while passing spiny urolith.

Who's this heading usward?

—Let's warsle till we're all wat from sweat. Pass through water smoke while watching for water witch.

Imagine I'm a whiffler whigging along with whiffets.

—Whisht! Listen to whinchat and whippoorwill.

White ants have eaten our wigwam. Given me a bad case of the whim-whams. Console myself by whaming whale suckers from host and eating whole. Winze, they're good! Lap from diminishing plash.

I live utterly alone, squatting in midst of ever-passing indifferent crowd. Wearing a dirty sarong, my back is pressed up against a red wall. Just over my head is giant painting of a woman's hand gently plucking one tealeaf at a time from bush, rendered in exact fine detail. Can guess Orange Pekoe quality. Live in tent made of discarded plastic and burlap bags, covered with large hand-painted movie poster of big woman's face. Soap down and bathe naked in street. Live under a bed. Cook there too. Nipple feed baby. Live on doorstep of abandoned palace or in dirty gully by train tracks with lots of crows all about. Keep personal belongings in big wicker baskets. Sleep in junked cars with stomped down roofs to provide bird baths for migrant species.

I have the ability to climb high barbed-wire fences (even electrified ones), as if they were simple ladders. Can shout political slogans from top position. Repair watches using small aquarium type structure over head to keep fragile mechanisms dry from monsoon.

Celebrate this wedding under big suspended steel bridge over which much traffic passes. We wear bright clothing, walk barefoot in slippery mud. Know that it will someday collapse into the bay and that I'll then have great difficulty crossing with single leg.

Lots of drones and low satellites. Knock them out with crossbows before they can locate you. Especially if you appear to be "a tall individual revered by those accompanying him" or are firing in the air to celebrate a wedding. Finally set the fire you've been so thoroughly preparing. Wring your hands. Very vigorously kick yourself into another world while screaming "Happy journey!" Carefully examine the contents of big urban garbage bins. Don't hesitate to plunge in headfirst. Put your fingers down into opened tins. Withdraw and lick sticky substances from tips. Wear thick layers of rags. Lay barefoot in front of a luxury shoe store. Attempt to de-louse yourself. Haggle over the price of freshly flensed skins that lie in bloody pile. Hold back your tie while drinking from big, generously juicy, sticky green fruit. Walk through dense traffic entirely nude. Heave stones at passing automobiles. If you're blind again, listen for them.

While walking in dusky alley, be a thirteen year old girl wearing brilliant red dress and pulling back black hair over perfectly smooth dark forehead decorated with single red dot pasted in the middle. Behind is glittering statue of unknown goddess in a big glass case carried by men. Fly high on makeshift swing over busy city street. Catch a glimpse of bookshop called "Knowledge Stream." Realize that if you're the seven tenths of humanity, this may be as close as you'll ever get to acquiring an education. Especially if you're the little girl living in India. Nevertheless, watch that the men carrying the glass case with goddess don't trip while looking at you.

Observe a passing street dog in Calcutta. Realize it resembles pygmy dog and Amazon variety. Advertise big cure for private diseases and sex-weaknesses. Mox-all. Become wealthy. Pretend to be a painter. Pretend to be a poet. Pretend incredulity concerning the reasons Khmer Rouge massacred intellectuals under Pol Pot's orders. Settle a jillion problems.

Sell used jackets, hats, records in the street. Be one of thirty-five carrying immense fishing net. Nude, help slide a heavy wooden ship seaward over flat wet sand. Proudly pose next to early model time machine body part you're polishing on an assembly line along with other factory workers in Japan. Give a friend a haircut on a park bench near Hiroshima City nuclear epicenter. Make sure the date's correct! Out of respect for Little Boy, bow, but not too low. Sell soup, apples, cabbage on the sidewalk. Hang onto the backend of an overloaded tramway. Cut out the entire trunk area of an older automobile and install portable nuclear reactor. Make sure wheels are spherical and made of high quality steel to support the weight. (Now we're getting somewhere!) Be extremely disciplined in all things you undertake. Pose among fresh war ruins. Scour the countryside for firewood. Watch reflections in ebb tide passing under bridge over estuary. Ride barge train shipping garbage out to sea. Count the gulls following you. Tend children under belching industrial smokestacks. Join picnickers in sunny park by tall pagoda with several tiers of flying eves. Sip soda. Give baby the bottle. Discard bottle, paw open mother's blouse and shove nipple into baby's mouth. When baby's finished, suckle on it some yourself.

We're together again, riding transportation devices that appear to be entirely organic or solely mineral. In near-death skeletal condition, we pose for a family portrait. Three of us manage to remain seated. The inferior limbs of a dead infant lying between us, hang limply over the edge of the bench. Two of us have already collapsed on the ground. A child's sitting between the fallen ones. Only the top of his head, the tip of his nose, and a swollen knee emerge from the dark zone he occupies. The photographer has placed our bodies in restful positions to give impression of peace. They are horribly emaciated. Wolves run the banks. (This is all happening somewhere deep within our concept of Asia).

Proceed counter-intuitively.

Make yourself a ninja mask from an old stocking cap. Wear a shawl with portable telephone pattern. Put on a tee shirt with big pistol printed on the front. Walk endlessly these wide red trails where refugees from genocide await for a volcano to erupt beneath their feet. Call this place Goma. It comes. Haven't they proven beyond any doubt that there's no god? Fall into a coma.

Children make footballs from discarded surgical gloves, condoms and other malleable plastic and rubber debris littering the compound area. One boy fashions a bicycle from fragments of wood that he whittles down to size using an awkward blunt axe head.

Turn widdershins round serpent deity you worship. Observe how water bears go tun during draught. In this light, humans represent a most risky evolution experiment.

Make special umbrellas to protect from black rains. Daily clip chéloïdes from your skin. Must become a habit no different than shaving chin or legs. Realize that no more than a single of the thirty some kilos of uranium 235 carried by Little Boy, actually reached fission. The rest came down as highly radioactive dust. About the same percentage of plutonium 239 achieved fission in the Nagasaki Fat Man experiment. America has paternity of the "dirty bomb" concept wrongfully attributed to Saddam Hussein.

Wear a cowl, carry burning cresset overhead with plenty pitch; steep thick rope in rosin. *Scream cri de guerre* from crenel. Harbor deep criminal contempt for all authority even if ultimate result *is crime d'etat*. Become cynosure of all contestation. Name Ndatou Czarina. Have a *czarevna* with her. Assume snarling facial expression even when happy or at rest. Watch for unusual atmospheric effects: blood afterglows, Bishop's ring (a broad opalescent corona around the sun), extraordinarily long and brilliant sunsets, skies that become progressively more brilliant after the cessation of twilight, amber afterglow with radiant spokes, anomalous sunsets with development of crepuscular rays, leopard-skin effect of deep purple patches in midday skies. Green freckling. Equatorial smoke streams. Blue sunshine. Remote wide conflagrations; but more of this hereafter.

When all life disappears, spiders are pioneers of renovation. Remember that Sumatra and Java once formed one single land. Thin clouds resembling smoke pass before the sun at quite a distance from the surface of the Earth. I incline then to the opinion that when sea suddenly withdraws, you should swiftly capture stranded mermaids and run for crest of hills measuring at least twice the height of sea withdrawal depth.

Generously feed orphaned cygnets that gather round small floating island of chemical waste you now live on. Chug cutch while sailing a catboat from island to island. Degauss your hull. Scratch your back with catbriar when stung by cow killers. Cosh yourself in the back of the head using left arm with sweeping upward motion to stay awake during protracted night journeys. Store whatever fish you catch in corves hanging overboard. Watch out for unusual rise in water temperature, formation of water domes and spouts. Throw anchor and clubhaul to quickly change helm if necessary. Converse with corbies flying low near single forward mast. Keep cool, don't make a coof of yourself when off-stage woman boldly enters scene to dance cootch for you. Refuse to be commoved. Share no spelt cakes with her. Confabulate when memory falls short. Have frequent recourse to conflation. Confute. Keep plenty pretty fossorial specimens in your pockets. Engage in delict. Delight in dementia. Dehort demirep. Avoid unavoidable coition.

All this notwithstanding, run ashore and hastily harvest squirrel corn when passing remaining fertile zones. Not that this would be the clou. Clobber approaching clinical analyst. Hang her on convenient cleek. Occupy catbird seat and from here attempt to correctly control your destiny.

In the hurry of leaving the house, we had left behind certain essential things including the child's toys. Obliged to go back for them. Approach and enter cautiously. The dwelling may already be occupied. At first sight, this doesn't seem to be the case. During the brief absence, the lot upon which the house is built has already become separated and is adrift in the river.

Burning petrol refineries along the banks illuminate scenes of sleepy gnus being drawn nose-first by crocodiles into the murky waters. Armies of homeless slumber fitfully beneath the bridges. Further along a geriatric gang has set up a roadblock. They force automobilists to strip at gunpoint.

The stairs creak. The old wooden floor in the child's bedroom too. Someone's here? No use being sneaky about it. Charge up the stairs and jump across the room in order to land directly on top of her toy chest. Just which one is it she most wanted? No matter! Stuff as many as I can into baggy Fila brand sweatshirt with drawstring hood that I'm wearing. Down the legs of my matching pants I dump plastic parrots and elephants, lots of dinosaurs, including Xenacanthus and Dunkleosteus (the real ones might very well be swimming the river that we're drifting down), all sorts of miniature vehicles, some of which function on real fuel including archaic plutonium tablets; stuffed mole, bear and panther; fossil techno-gadgets that we had dug up together in shale banks.

Am suddenly confronted by creature from which emanates intense light.

Beware of this one. She has seven toes very neatly fit into tip of couture shoe. Tries to talk with me in eleven different ways. Frightening ability with tongue. House begins to list, spin.

I leap out through the window. Wing failure. I climb onto a dangling steel cable upon which groggy cormorants roost digesting crawfuls of contaminated gizzard shad.

The house goes over low waterfall and disintegrates. An intense radiance goes under water with non-floating debris. River glows for some time. I take three cormorants to the bank and force them to regurgitate. On all fours, I dine on half digested fish. I'm still in this position when the radiant female rises from water. Much steam blowing off her. Sense she has something of severely flawed deep inside. Recently lost a child or perhaps was beaten and raped by family member when young? It's often like this with gods. This is the fundamental reason that they so thoroughly enjoy developing such sadistic scenarios while planning out human destiny. Nothing can please them more than snuffing innocence.

—Slimy man brimming with toys. Aquatic Saint Nic?

—Let's play the master trick!

I sleep for weeks in a hammock following severe malaria attack. Wear an alarm clock as an earplug. Become fascinated by the shadow of my aircraft slipping over rough terrain. Remain beneath shade tree with friends. Walk a long rope bridge between two distant planets. Blow immaculate powder over Zanda's dark skin. Inhale this substance through nostrils. Illuminated by a tallow torch clenched in her maw, follow the hyena bitch through dismal worlds. Dress as an Indian and entertain a conquistador. Heat fresh scalps over fires to dry quickly. Torture a prisoner by introducing arrows into his penis, up the anus all of the way to the liver. Amputate arms, legs. Hang these up to smoke slowly like ham. Will have nearly the same taste. Hold a fête chinoise.

Become all-seeing. Let eyes erupt all over your body. Do away with cloths forever. Trace directional arrows across your back pointing up to the head area. Ride Napoleon's stuffed horse until it collapses. Wear a penile sheath with the rising price of fuel printed on it. Read aloud Amadou Hampâté Bâ. Shred Africa like sisal fiber. Harvest cocoa. Watch a woman wash her sex using a teakettle full of cool water, she very bluntly declaring she wants you. Drink dark brown beer. Carouse.

Bridging of the Seine is simple. Where old stone, cement and iron bridges have fallen, use the rubble heaps to span the river by placing long branches, slender trunks and bamboo end to end over these. Tie all together with vines. Cover with transversal shorter spans of wooden debris. Today there are many more bridges than there ever were before. Changing banks requires no thinking.

Indiscriminately shoot lots of South Africans. Whites for having applied apartheid, Blacks for having forgiven the Whites. Firmly refuse any psychiatric help. Try to remember what you don't know. Hunt the world's last gorilla. Enjoy the meat. Catch the crescent moon by the use of a noose. Introduce it into your nose. When lying on your deathbed in geriatric ward, pose holding a portrait of yourself when you were young. Keep creeping servants at your feet. Speaking of feet, when chilly, tattoo sock design on them right up the ankles and to the knees if necessary. This will bring some warmth. Hang photo of Nerhu, Tito and Nasser sitting together on your bedroom wall. Visit Mitsuaki Ohwada in his Yokohama studio for full-body job. Contemplate having something really dark done. If necessary, can be removed and mounted on a presentation dummy.

Carefully analyze series of last drawings made by Urulu where remote future technology is labeled "prehistory." Realize that she somehow knows. Reinterpret microwave background to refute Hubble law. Carefully analyze the contents of small leather pouch in which you used to keep your koranic prayer beads. She's put inside of it a small clawed paw with well rendered articulations, tiny red shoe, trident, spiked collar, an empty jewel box and an ear made of velour and apparently ripped from stuffed animal. Claims they will protect me from here on in. Take time out to fight a duel with plastic swords.

She poses for portrait holding pet fawn in arms. An immaculate long-eared African sheep is in the foreground.

Knowing that few animals are so silent, keep pet skunks. Also nurture woolly bears with polished black heads that give fine Isabella tiger moths. Look a wasp in the face. Classify aquatic insects: stone fly, electric light, backswimmer, water scorpion, riffle beetle and dobson. To enhance your night vision, lay in thick bracken, sleep in center of ferry rings. Colonize, expropriate and slaughter Indians, bust sod and build pioneer legend. Carefully, very carefully, study the effects of nuclear war. Determine best HOB, (optimization of energy yield to produce certain desired effect over maximum surface area). Peak overpressure. Study footprint coverage. First hour immediate effects, crisis relocation. (It is said that US government permanently relocated in Midwest). Reaction, recovery and long-term effects, realizing that some can be globally positive. For example: increased exercise for survivors (fewer automobiles would make bicycling or even roller skating a necessary practice), abrupt and permanent termination of TV addiction (television stations were first targets), reduced intake of fatty products, (raising livestock is much more energy consuming than growing crops). Sorry Cain!

It's a glum day. Heavy low clouds make for little light. Somewhere off in the bush birds emit sinister twittering noises that simply cannot pass for song. Zanda's wearing very ordinary jeans which I pull down gently. I lay her to rest on a conveniently placed *Directoire*-style Recamier covered with old purple velvet torn open in several places. I who have fashioned bronze feet for this piece, begin to lick her while caressing the soft belly, the back of the legs and around where my mouth is placed. She's very furry. Pause to drink burning hot coffee and immediately place my mouth back again where it was. Push up her tee shirt which has many big holes in it, faded out Polisario flag printed on back, to expose big breasts and budding nipples. The fact that this is due to silicone implants further excites me. I ask that she smoke a cigarette, look indifferent or preoccupied, read a newspaper.

This would be no classical Soviet vs. U.S. type scenario but rather a question of rogue utilization of nuclear technology. Not by States but by some of the numerous populations now capable of making nuclear devices from inexpensive kits. Chemical warfare? Rather than letting hazardous chemicals go to waste, properly mix alcohol, sodium fluoride, dimethyl methylphosphonate with phosphorus trichloride and you've got yourself a good potent batch of nerve gas.

—Little laboratory worker, third rate scientific researcher, don't just sit there stupidly looking at me through your oversized protective glasses! Agree with me!

Want another rebuttal to the Fermi Paradox? Consider then that ETI have indeed visited Earth on at least two other occasions. Both times we had already perfectly adapted to high radioactivity levels and toxic atmosphere. Not so with them.

Have I told you yet about Zanda's inner chapter that fits somewhere into the *Book of Fever*? In it I'm called Camano and am largely absent. She goes by the appellation of Naïna. We've just been fighting with the Razor People living on the brink. Those on the very edge of the ledge get pulled off.

It begins with a cryptic conversation.

—Back then, who knew?

—No one of new.

—Not even a few?

—You!

Make of it what you will. She says we were both very ill. Her story goes something like this: Goneness and a kiss of leprosy, (she received a call from her sister and went). When she returns Camano is no longer there. Blown away by sudden war that erupted in her absence. Many animals bask in empty valleys. She recognizes the howl of his favorite hunting dog coming from a distant crest. It hunts well she thinks. Alone now, can she be like this predator? The king has died. The throne and some gilded plates remain. Tobacco too, in great heaps. There are a few survivors scattered about smoking and begging for water which lies all around, oil-covered and iridescent. Other animals bark including birds and certain fishes that raise their heads from the waters. Winds sooth or drive mad. The intensity of the fighting drew the water up from caverns, flooding the land and attracting small marsh birds. Unmasked bandits. They bring alien repertoire; know of other seasons in distant galaxies. Frogs trilling in several octaves. She goes up into the hills seeking Camano's dog. It's silent now, hiding and feeding on the dead. Only meat. Naïna finally finds the animal beneath a rose laurel stripped of its flowers. She's struck by the strange pearlescence of the flesh. Only meat. High clouds form sky-lace. She screams seeing the reflection, (not hers but its).

—I'll be Diane and this my lance. You, my hound! We'll chase what game can be found.

—Felwen went.

—Noria and gone.

A voyagers log in the remote confines of the future, expected to be luminous, is dark.

—No know.

A green honey leaking from the corner of her mouth (she sees this when wiping it off on her sleeve), and freezing at the *comissure* of her lips.

Enter Camano. He's crystalline, made of brittle long spines scintillating as he speaks. Alive in methane at -300°.

Aliens are on display. They're not alive nor are they in cages, but naturalized and arranged in the painted landscapes of their respective worlds.

The shore of the methane beach. The sun is now a red giant. We have withdrawn to Triton, (the moon of Neptune). From here we watch Earth rise and set near to the sun. It is the morning and the evening star, Mercury and Venus having been swallowed up. For Venus, it was a question of gas drag bringing about orbital decay. Thermal pulses continue to sweep over Earth with unexpected regularity as the Sun's outer shell seems to adopt a breathing rhythm.

Watch is only a way of speaking, for we no longer see as you might think we do. We communicate by heat waves. For us, temperature has become a tactile thing and it is in this manner that we apprehend one another. If I were to describe to you the appearance of Zanda or Urulu for example, it would be a flame portrait. We are beautiful, self-sustaining fires that require no explanation. This isn't to say that we consume ourselves. Rather we had temporarily adapted to living within the sun's outer shell before withdrawing to Europa, Titan and Oberon (the moons of Jupiter, Saturn and Uranus respectively), before finally coming here in 12.274-12.276 of the 10^9 year range of ages. Once one has known a "never" zone, adapting to another, be it the extreme opposite, poses no difficulty. Certain aspects of our culture remain the same. For example we still enjoy water and utilize copper piping as always we have. Only the shape has changed. Our plumbing is spiral shaped, like interminable koudou horns, rendering to water its natural energy. It has been generous with us, offering hydrogen or oxygen separately and whenever desired. Inversely these elements spontaneously give water. There is no complicated technology, no Tideworks to achieve these transformations. It's a simple question of *bonne entente*, a sort of natural agreement which arises in a quasi-intuitive manner between elements sharing the Great Unifying Theory as experienced from within where it's not a theory at all but something which has been naturally lived out from all directions at once.

Never attempt to model stellar mass-loss in a canonical manner. Even the study of well-observed K supergiants is misleading.

What's this new death coming our way? Would it be that we've simply worn out? Depleted all options. No borrowed beggar's body available? An end to lizards and other winged creatures! Thought you we to be speaking of reincarnation? This was evolution! Fires dim. Remember ember? We'll be cold things then. Mineral and immobile for great lengths of time.

The hyena bitch is ill, regurgitating bones she once was capable of digesting. I shouldn't have taken her in. The matriarchal pack leader had become my companion. Friend to man, would she some day take in two suckling babes as with the Tiber she wolf? If so, she would certainly kill one straightforward as hyena maternal instinct dictates. It's the law of survival for this mottled kind.

Time I turned her out, time she return to her fold before mankind's frailties fully take hold.

—Strong shaggy one, begone with the night air. You who so taught me the ways of the hunter, (in this she surpasses the lioness). Blink your eyes in the black. I'll think of you. Don't look back.

We color our flags with water-soluble felt-tip pens. Blue's the color. They run when we fight in the rain. Go purple when mixed with flowing blood.

Poseur, stand out front and hold high limp wet blue.

We've nothing to do with you! There's no resemblance what so ever. Remain with the apes from which you sprang. Keeping household pets is not the impossible task you would think it to be.

The above are micro-environmental considerations. Valid only for individuals in sedentary mode.

Solar winds blowing through the galaxy are comparable to tides washing through mangrove. Straddle broken surfboard. Paddle between the roots. Fish crab, gulp abalone and chew on mandrax. Seek toxicity refuge. Anent? Observe the clown fish hiding within the venomous sea anemone.

Most of all, are you prepared to correctly answer Munkir and Nakir? Death's two angels accept no lies.

There's rumor of a new ruthless dictator having taken power. A female ayatollah who decrees fatwahs as effortlessly as she breaths. All debt collectors are to be eliminated. IMG members are chased down and executed several times in a row to make sure they're really dead. Once again, geriatrics are cared for. Never shows her face. It is said she is most beautiful. Her own flag is a snake, cut in three segments with rain coming down. I remember a little girl who did the very same with worms that she would slice and save.

Firmly believe that there is never "no solution."

Zag

Zachary is a town of central Louisiana, but that's not where I am. Zamboanga, named after a seaport southwest of Mindanao, will be my final anchorage though it isn't really in that place either that I now find myself to be, just as zag usually follows zig and should also be the final chapter although it may well find its way back to other parts of the story.

What if I were to suggest to you here, that we should reconsider communism? Would you immediately imagine me squatting in the middle of the street, a copious diarrhea running from my rear in a red long streak? Think me to be an immigrant from Zelenograd or Zhitomir? Most shameful spectacle, one that one should turn away from.

Look up! I'm perched right above you. Bloody red stools come down on unexpecting fools. If we were to remain in the twenty first century, this body of thought would be tagged "political science fiction," a rare classification experimented by the French with mitigated success, before being pitilessly banned from publication in English, the official tongue of commerce, thereby assuring that no cinematographical version would ever be elaborated from it. And this is just as well, the entire movie industry having sundered to magmatic zones in *Bunsana Bua*.

Communism?

Have I been politically manipulated?

No brainwashing have I undergone. No violent sodomy have I suffered. This is mere evacuation. It is a natural function, which with aging, presents certain unpleasant aspects. This is no agitprop.

Were it a simple question of economical equality, couldn't we just go for the Islamic zakah, whereby a clean fortieth of annual income be given to the poor?

If you find this political parenthesis to be disagreeable, you can associate it with the other ailments which I mention, lump it together with the problems of aging, although I personally would refer to it as the beginning of maturity. I'm much older now, certain body parts have been spared others have been reclaimed long before I was prepared to relinquish them. Many no longer function. My heart has been fitted with a very primitive pacemaker acquired at the flea market. I picked it up just in time. A young couple shopping for kitsch gadgets, proposed double the price as I was paying for the device. An artificial anus that I had commissioned a neighborhood artisan to make for me, arrived just yesterday for a final fitting. Today I can control the flow which ran freely before. Just this morning a man insulted me, called me a traitor just because he overheard me speaking in French. I detached the collector pouch from the anal device and squeezed hard the rubber bladder, spraying him with fresh warm excrement. Had I been vigorous, young and intact, this would have been impossible, yet it certainly was the merited reply. Aging has its advantages. And with that, I still smoke, drink heavily and immoderately consume the most dangerous drugs to say nothing of the venoms and radiation which I must have daily.

Disadvantages? I'm obliged to live alone in a home filled with toxic animals. The ever more potent doses required demand a strict discipline: keep vivariums full of Dendrobates, raise crickets for them and maintain the humidity with mist-making machine. There are other tanks containing mambas, boomslangs and gaboon vipers. Ocean-water aquariums for the keel-bellied sea serpents.

Let's reconsider communism. I insist. It isn't a subject of disgrace to be transferred out to another place, along with amputations, severe mutilations or the onset of poverty as has so often been the case with the painful preparation of the *Book of Fever* that in reality is nothing more than a hidden chapter of *aka* wherein is relegated the sum of suffering which I would rather not confront directly. An elusive chapter which breaks down like quicksilver to return to its place of origin. A free, rebellious group of thought which will lurk in the folds, hide in the deeper sulcates.

Can it be rewritten to be more accommodating, as was the case with *Pawn Shop?*

Why adhere to this doctrine of fear now that it's finished, a thing of the past, an evil one at that, you say?

I'm a free electron, unimpeachable, having never run for office, and totally untenable, having no economical ties with fabricators of lies. Too long have I lain prone, so utterly alone. I can advance directly now, look boldly in your eyes, say coldly as I arise: Realize that fully nine tenths of the world population has nothing to lose, everything to gain, and those who fear most the return of such a host will never do more for the poor than to propose a toast at some charity, rather than confront the verity.

Have no fear of spoiling the social dinners of those who do not want to hear. Philosophy has become simple zymurgy seated within smallish cranial cavities. When the pressure of fermentation becomes too great, zygomatic arches and temporal bones detach, the entire skull structure will unweld and permit swell. I'll not be bought, though there will be no subvention nor advertisement to help finance the reanalysis of the thought which so implacably fought against fascists before even the West cared to know about the camps of death they brought. True, gulags also existed. But then, haven't other peoples, the very ones who had the most suffered at fascist hands, in turn, adopted deportation as a means to reclaim coveted lands, sending former inhabitants into desert zones and sucking the water table from beneath their feet? No apology, no ill-founded comparison is this; merely a reminder that evil can be a sticky contagious thing, one which you simply can't wash away with a good antiseptic soap. It jumps from one host to another, gaining strength with each leap, as any good virus would do.

Do I hear a wawl, some newborn infant's first call? Or be this some witch's cry coming stifled, from the heart of a squall. Both faint, so similar in sound, one pure the other a taint. Weak whiff, what waugh be this? An odor sweet, yet of death.

Hark! The whistle of the water ouzel and the grunt of the yapok on the edge of this fen, blend with odors for which I have no yen.

To call this, perfume of Ebliss, would be to pardon man's self-born evilness, that one which regularly wells up within him. Never is there remiss.

Vehicle of flesh, my body, which for so long has born primitive blundering spirit, mine. Dow or lugger, this rogue pirogue, yawl or sampan, bears the marks of passing time. The sails have shredded, become decorative tassels. The helmsman, the captain I, below decks, ill with final fever.

A hull that no longer holds water. No saline gush pushes in. Pollutants pour out, poisoning all about.

Beach this wreck upon some forgotten sand bar before it sinks in fathomless water. If none is to be found then the Skeleton Coast will do.

What form of vessel be it? A composite ship like those of the tea trade, neither wholly wooden nor entirely of metal made. As for the wooden portions, it's a mixed-timber vessel. Banaba, Blue Gum, Cuba Sabicu, Hackmatack, Mangachapuy, Rock Maple, Huon Pine, Puhutukawa, Tallow-wood, Thingham, Yacal and even Yew were all employed. Knuckle-timber was of harder sort. Through many a forest roamed I, to find the right shapes for the knees, choosing the forks of certain trees. Spriketting too, was of stronger timber, thus avoiding the traditional additional thickness of the tween-decks ceiling, just above the waterway.

All of those structures which had been so well reinforced in prevision of the roughest seas, finally rent, shattered, rotted through and splintered. The foaming of the forecastle-bulkhead beneath the poop, and twixt the bridges, has all come undone. So it is with the gussets, those angular plates that go between the strong-hold-beams and the hold-beam-stringer-plates. The monkey-forecastle has been beaten down by some pounding mountain of water, hardly having the height now to accommodate a crew of the smallest stature. Even my Babinga team (some members actually from the neighboring Aka Pygmy tribe) would be cramped. Should be renamed: forward crawling quarters or slithering space. The zigzag bulkhead is now aligned in the most unnatural manner, passing straight through the decks rather than being spaced off at intervals as should be. The weight of upper decking has brought to bear on the lower orlog deck, which in turn has no height. Side-intercoastal-keelson-angle-bars are bent. Strangely, there's a coalbunker athwartships, even though this vessel never ran on steam. It has collapsed, greatly reducing the breadth of ship, which is an advantage for slipping through narrow channels but severely jeopardizes sea-worthiness.

Roaming through and round about what's left of her, much can be deduced. A hard life was hers, plowing through the thick waters of the post-polluted seas. See how the hawse-chock is broken, the hole and piping obstructed with chafed cable. Maneuverability has been reduced. Even the helm-port or *jaumière*, that round aperture in the rudder-trunk, the *tambour* as the French call it, through which passes and turns the upper part of the rudder main piece, is choked with the solid chemical waste that drifts on sea currents where breeds a new type of eel. Scupper-pipes are condemned in like manner, being full with oil-cake mud. Warped is the keel. Surprisingly, the draught-marks on the stern and stem are still visible.

The cathead projecting beyond the bow is fitted with a carved piece representing something of round and yellow with black spots, a circular red opening in the middle of it. The sheave-holes and sheaves at the far tip await a cat-fall to be roved, an anchor brought up from under the hawse-pipe. It has the shape of a giant cat's paw, all claws out, and it goes without saying that the carved timber along the cat-head, though no figurehead, represents a cheetah's wide open maw, the beauty of which is only surpassed by those sculptures aft, on the escutcheon at the stern, where are also engraved her name and the arm's of the owner. The name is misspelled, giving *Cheat'ah*, most probably, voluntarily altered to bring an altogether new meaning, casting some light upon the missions which she carried out and even partially revealing the intentions of its captain and owners. Black mackled felines share the stern area with the proprietor's blazon upon which are set what appears to be the representation of spore or viral structures, greatly enlarged, beneath the inscription, *Here be Dragons*, meaning, as all know, that this is the realm of utter nothingness where astronomers in want of some reference, place fabulous monsters.

Dimenhydrinate would have been of no help to ward off seasickness when crossing the seas which this ship rode. The shade-deck is no more, hoods or *tambuchi* ripped from over hatchways. But then there is no more ingress or egress to protect from rain or the wash of the sea. No longer do I spend nights in the chart-house. Navigation's at its end. Gone too is the skiff we'd put down to harpoon Zygorhiza. Given to zar, we've beaten our heads bloody against the bulwarks.

But before leaving this wreck to the surf, descend to the engine room, explore the environs of the collapsed coalbunker if you can find your way. Forget not that this vessel never sailed on steam, no flue-boiler used she, you'll not find warping-engine-rod-top and keep-bolts here. Strain your eyes in this dim light given off by the few rays that pass through the bull's-eye port made of the thickest glass. Here on the engine room flooring, scattered across the *parquet de la chambre de chauffe*, lying on the *piso de la càmara calderas*, sprinkled on the *heizraum flurplatten*, are the remains of combustion. It's no ash-pit but you can nevertheless, guess what fuel it was that propelled her. She burned hope and now there isn't any of it left.

Perhaps some beachcomber shall come upon her and sense the beauty of the dream while viewing what's left of the beam.

Communism then? This insidious idea, recurrent unwanted theme. Bear with me now at this voyage's end. We've ploughed into a coraline reef. The shock was much more violent than if we had grounded her on an accommodating sandbar, but then there were none to be found. The ship has been christened many times, changing names and often form, over the centuries perhaps more than I myself have done. A lumbering thing in the beginning, too much ballast had been thrown overboard. Then she leaned, and it was with a dangerous list that she completed most of the pilgrimage.

Red. Is it the color that enrages, like bull charging cape in the arena, an entire nation furiously blind? Yet, the color of life it is. A hue from within, the slightest pinprick will prove this to be true. Flakes of paint on the hull attest that this was her color too.

I wear the most impeccable elegant gray suit, cut from the finest bolts of flannel. Polish my shoes, I have a pair of them now even though I still only wear one, to a lustrous brilliance, trim my beard and nails with great care. There are ventilators to evacuate all animal odors from my home. No filth here, none of the *laissez aller* so commonly associated with the elderly, those "on the way out."

I observe younger ones attentively as they devour time, feasting on clocks, watches and other time keeping devices as I once did. They haven't yet understood that time massively copulates, procreates, is a living thing.

Zosma is still in Leo! Vault then the lion's loins on your way out.

But I'm all sloppy within, a captured insect liquefied by the spider's venom which holds it in silken larder for repast to come. Only a purée inside of an exoskeleton awaiting consummation. I ask of you only one thing: That there be no burial. Fling my bones up into the crown of the loftiest jungle tree, plunge my remains into the deepest ocean abyss. No vault or confining coffin for me. Let me rot free.

A young student in zoology cares for the animals. She is blond and yet there is something of African about her. Most beautiful. We have long conversations. The form of her chin, her insolence, the sparkle in her eyes, I seem to recognize.

—All that is dangerous and wild isn't necessarily fearsome and proud in appearance, she says. —The hyena's high-pitched laugh, its ugly awkward look are not in keeping with its ferocious predatorial capacities.

Somewhere in the upper stories of the building, a woman is singing. Her voice is a slow flow, deep and low:

They shall never separate us
you and I
Never are we to part
me and you

It is Zanda's voice, but this is impossible. I know the upper floors of the building to be empty, nothing up there but confused memory.

With the coming of dawn, the elderly take up staffs and head out to form supra-violent gangs of geriatrics that roam the streets. They who have been abandoned by the very social systems which they once created. No pensions, no retirement or medical assistance. Predation then! Form the most violent of packs.

From the sky comes a deep mooing. This is no dove cooing. A distant horn or conch shell being blown in short bursts, warns of coming undoing.

—Rehearse: I shall depossess you, says the Shaggy One, their uncontested leader.

—What should the inflection be? they ask him.

Clutching a calumet, he replies —A whisper if you're far off, but scream when in close.

The steel tip forms a bowel for smoking, a spike for killing. He stole it long ago from the Smithsonian collection. Spiritual solicitation and life's end held in the same bony hand.

They possess evil looking weapons, but all have art. An anachronistic AK-47 with a head carved into the stock, bullets with ears that spread out to spin upon impact.

I can appreciate this violence, having just gone through a very difficult period of surviving on an arctic beach, the left bank of the Seine river in the industrial southern suburbs of Paris, running through rotting seaweed, my mouth hanging open to catch the clouds of flies that my passage would make rise. This fare provided protein, though difficult to digest. The arctic fox, so expert at flushing elusive borealic prey, operates no differently when emerging, half starved, from winter's end.

The Shaggy one yells, —The poet's language! and lets go a round, spraying the street with death. They catch and butcher a young man, taking what little he possesses. The calumet man brandishes the severed head, holding it aloft by a golden earring. The weight of the suspended head grossly distends the ear lobe.

—I have sacrificed Isaiah and God has naught to say!

The head separates from the ear.

Anthropophagic supermarket: Plastic presentation containers having the very shape of the human parts they hold. Choice pieces are covered with cellophane, attractive labels read "honey-cooked Indo-European thigh and calf" or "Tika-style buttock."

If we don bermudas, basketball shoes and baseball caps, can we converge by groups of twos and threes, go unnoticed, mingling with the civilian population and perpetrate a coup d'état during the tourist season? I pack a fat purple pistol filled with sky blue jelly. Looks like a child's toy, in truth, a powerful enzyme that will liquefy you. Developed it years ago while playing games with my daughter. Went something like this:

—Daddy, we are wild pigs! Big, shaggy with curled tusks on our snouts. We are stinky, sleep in mud, come out at nighttime. We knock down hunters, destroy their nets, break their guns. We eat everything, dig big holes in the ground with our muzzles, swallow roots, mushrooms, salamanders and frogs.

—But what then, my dear, shall we do if hunters return, well armed and in number?

—We'll turn them into mush, the same way that the spider does with its victims. Liquefy the insides!

There you have it. Add to this the fact that she was wearing a Robin Hood costume with a purple water gun under the belt and that I too am now liquid within, it all makes sense.

Magnolias are in bloom. Somewhere nearby a man sings, deep tenor or bass. Responding to the woman above, just before. Water is trickling and splattering on a flat hard surface. You've guessed it. I'm blind.

This is just when a young boy carrying a stick approaches me bringing along with him an odor that I've smelled before.

—I'll guide you where you left off guiding me, he says thrusting the stick hard into my ribs. —Take hold of the end, tied together we'll work the streets again, for small change.

—What's your name, boy?

—Ablook.

—Be gone. I've no need for your kind. You kook!

—You've been on my mind since you left me blind.

—Leave me. Don't drink my jook.

Zanda, her mother, what is it I so love about this woman? Dare I speak in the present tense, of one long devoured? Was it the way she would take my scrotal pouch whole into her mouth, the bright blue testicles being swallowed by the brown of her lips? How, there for an eternity she would hold them, wet warm clasp between tongue and palette, leaving the penis free to swell, she looking at me over the stiffened flesh, through half closed eye lids, sometimes releasing but never letting it go, like a cat with its prey.

The years gone by left traces around her mouth, small wrinkles at the edges, incisions of time. The texture of the skin of her hands was so unlike that of a girl's. Hands that had done so many things, been exposed to the coldest night air, to the flames of the hottest star. Hands that had taken life but had given it as well. Beyond, always farther than. I had imagined cutting the skin from her body, drawing it tight over an armature to make a lampshade through which all passing light would become amber. Light that I would be able to contemplate for an immense time span. Devour entire portions of her body. Once, she had lost two fingers during an altercation. Cut clean from the hand, I gathered them up and stripped the meat from the bone which I finally crushed between my teeth before swallowing all. To me, it was the revelation of something long forgotten. She told me that the fingers would grow back with time but this hasn't yet happened. It had been an appetizer. I contemplated consuming an entire thigh, the breasts, her ass, the cheeks and lips too. The missing flesh should expose part of the skull and the teeth. Like the bodies that large carnivores leave behind, to be discovered at dawn after a night of predacity, wounds large and well defined. Surrounding skin bears no trace of blood but retains the odor of the predator's maw where the whiskers had brushed the skin. Enormous wounds, these, like an anatomy lesson revealing innermost secret parts. Here was the home of the heart, the soul's cabin, the spirit's dome. How morning light sparkles, rainbow along the membrane covering exposed ribs where the lungs were. The mechanical perfection of this hip joint! Only the face removed or the abdominal cavity completely emptied leaving a small cavern lacquered with deep purple stains.

At other times I thought of her as being a living fetish from the far future or the distant past, beyond deep time, tutelary objects embedded within her organs. No stones were these. Things small and pure of form, senseless to me but certainly of capital importance to one more evolved than myself. I no longer had the taste for adolescent bodies, julep or mint, things sickeningly sweet or totally bland. Her's was a taste akin to that of strong tobacco, violent alcohol and certain powerful chemical drugs: "do˙=c`eh tixan" (it doesn't taste sweet to me), in Hupa, an Athapaskan language spoken in the Mad River area of California. You should know this, had you been less bent on developing the industry of entertainment with constellations of artifice, so massively bringing money to those who came after tribe snuffers.

Constantly she would whisper in my ear series of enclitic and proclitic word modifiers which contrarily to all established phonological rules, she would use independently of the forms to which they should have been attached.

With certainty, I know now that we descend from the killer lineage of mankind; Not children of Abel but those of Cain. Man has risen from this grain. Adam was mud, Eve his rib, but we come not from them. Only, these brothers are at the other end of time and we aren't heading the way you'd think.

Now say: Caprine shall I make thee, with eyes up front to either side of a small cone shaped skull, horns close in by the brain. Engage in butting. The tremors thereby produced will procure intense pleasure.

The configuration of man's skull is so close to that of the goat's, eyes well placed, horns never far away, and he draws such pleasure from waging warfare. To him, this is the very stuff from which civilizations arise. It is the grain of history, peace being the chaff. Would this be one of the gods whom the Lumens had let out to relieve themselves upon our world, that is now reminiscing on genesis? Stranded fish or small crab, abandoned in a tidal pool by the receding sea, to be captured and momentarily adulated by wading brime flecked children.

Woven in tassels like so many garlic bulbs, goat skulls hang from the eves by my oven. Snakes have changed, hunt in packs, tear their prey to shreds. This panther sized cat you see prowling, was once an alley cat. Look at his pelage, how it's striped. Soriano.

As for me, I'm one of those dangerous geriatrics who roam the streets alone or in gangs. I have an old machine gun equipped with a 45° mirror mounted on top to compensate for my bent-over posture. Seems I can see again when it's time to fire. My back is so deformed with age that it presents a small shelf in the upper reaches, upon which one could serve up drinks, read the Koran or write a scroll, and it very often serves one of these purposes for which I'm paid small sums. I can also recite for you chapters of African history while you drink upon my dorsal counter. It'll make you think. The fall of Abbot Fulbert Youlou or three decenies of political development in the Congo: power and revolutionary dreams, the founding of the Congolese Working Party, M22, the illusion of CMP, the advent, the departure and the surprising return of Sassou Nguesso. Not to forget the adventures of Claude-Ernest Ndalla who was sentenced to death after being associated with car-bombers before being finally acquitted, Marien Ngouabi who was assassinated in circumstances never elucidated and Dr. Seraphin Bakouma, leader of a splinter group of the CNOC-UAS.

Shall I tell you about the formation of the Istiqlal party in Morocco, the murder of Ferhat Hached, or, how about the story of the "cowardly fox?"

—Enough of this political dissertation! insolently sneers one without ears, slamming down hard his glass somewhere between my seven cervical and twelve dorsal vertebrae that have fused to form the platter upon which the drinks have been served up to he who now hears the voicing of his worst fears.

Over my shoulder I pass the very last natural sponge to be found, so that he may wipe the spilled drink from the luxurious fabric of my suit which I insist on keeping perfectly clean.

—Dig to the pith, the medulla, to find turmoil's fuel. Western petroleum companies pitting tribes against one another, fabricators of arms selling their wares. Knew you that Zag was also the name of a locality in Western Sahara? A lieu of particularly sinister appearance where wounded survivors of Moroccan armored infantry fleeing the blazing remains of their t-74 tanks that the Polisario Front had destroyed in the most brilliant guerilla action of Lebouirate, crawled up cliffsides and hid in small caverns. Many military mummies are to be found there today.

A new client is on my back. Claims to be a producer just arriving from the early twenty-first century.

—Why is it that politics and religion constantly make their way into your scenario?

—It's like caisson disease! When returning from deep time, there's a bubbling action, like the nitrogen that wells up from a diver's blood bringing on the bends, these themes invariably emerge from the recesses of memory where they've been shoved back to be forgotten. You see, disinformation and massive political manipulation, really served no purpose, the real history will always come to the surface however disagreeable it may be.

—Can't you rid yourself of this material? Most of it is contrary to the taste of our public, has no place in this type of work. Edit!

—Think you to extract it like some sort of vulgar parasite? Pull it from beneath the skin like a common guinea worm? Better employ the old-fashioned but effective method of seizing the worm's butt when it emerges from a blister, wrapping it round a stick and slowly winding, remembering that it's generally a full meter long, loaded with a million eggs. A good week's time is recommended for extraction in order to avoid rupture and ensuing excruciating pain.

Should I have used zaffer, resembling smalt and containing cobalt oxide, when fabricating the glass armor? This would have given the glass a blue color and certainly have contributed to giving me a better disposition, an appropriate humor, while making golden mummies in *Cortez.*

Ah, blue! You would think it to be beautiful. Ocean, sky? A source of tranquility. Only the purest blue will do, no half tones verging on gray or green.

Tired of its insolence, the endless jabbering, I've broken down the glass suit. Further usage: I've made window panes, vases and even marbles from the shattered remains. But contrarily to what I had expected, this has brought no rest. Each piece now speaks. All moralizing to constitute an infinite consciousness of which I'll have no part.

—You sank the slaver off Zanzibar! Told you not to. Slavers and slaves all drowned together didn't they? clamor the marbles as one.

The stairs.

Is it the souvenir of a childhood book, a passage from Robert Louis Stevenson? Read when lying in some hospital bed while other children were out playing. In any case, there were stairs, a very perilous set of stairs —those ones were broken— that rose through ruins of some abandoned castle. Mostly hanging in the airs, many steps were amiss, vertiginous deep void beneath, others teetered in precarious balance ready to tumble. Another type of danger, pirates or brigands, I remember not. A young boy with whom I naturally identified myself, undertook the ascension in a desperate attempt to evade capture.

Is this the reason for which I now make my home beneath the stairs I find? They are fabulously monumental, these stairs, leaving the ground and going off towards the sky at an oblique that defies the laws of physics. A giant lance planted perpendicularly into the ground, they lead to no where, unless of course you are coming down from the sky, and then they *do* lead to the earth.

There is no architectural element at the upper extremity, no top floors, no bridge, nothing for these stairs to hinge upon. Only the sky. How do these steps hold at such a slant without resting upon something of firm? Pillars, the upper reaches of an immense edifice or even a hilltop, the side of a mountain, not to say the crest could do. Without support why don't these stairs come crashing down?

It is the purest architectural element ever to have been raised. Or was it built from the sky, down? And by the hand of whom? Certainly one who had legs attached to feet needing these carefully measured steps for rising and descending. The architect of this structure must be praised. Surely one who believed in impossible dreams.

I sleep in the wedge shaped area beneath the first steps where the stairs meet the ground. Snug in the deepest recess of this purest of angles. From this geometrical sanctuary I can, lying in a prone position, flick out my long sticky tongue like a mammal of the order *Edentata*, an anteater, an armadillo or a sloth (like they, I have very few teeth left), not that I be fond of snacking on the ants that pass, even though they provide a welcome dietary supplement, but rather for the sport of targeting such minute mobile fare.

I failed to mention that I share this sanctuary with a small mummy that has golden skin. It isn't at all human.

Sometimes I hear footsteps, always going up, never going back down. Some are cautious, hesitant, while others are bold. Some even seem to charge up the stairs at full tilt. Where do they go? I do not know, but never, no never, do they ever come back down.

I drink coffee from a silver zarf.

Would life be a zero-sum game, the sum of the gains and losses of the players, always being equal to zero?

Briefly, I revert to highway robbery. Returning to Central Africa, the land I so love (I even wish to be buried there whenever I do really die; ah to be this red earth, beneath that sky!), I'm a Zaraguina, a true "road cutter," hopping from ambush to waylay travelers. I take everything, not only watches and jewelry, but even their shoes, pants and underwear. If they resist I don't hesitate to zap them, and some times even do so just to instill fear, further accredit my reputation. Finally there are no more travelers; I suppose that I've frightened them all away. Too much zeal! Return to one of my lairs, the one beneath the stairs.

My teeth are all gone; feed on zabaglione. Dream that Zanda has become zaftig from constantly licking creamy sweet foam from my whiskers. Look up at the moon, can plainly see Zagut in the fourth quadrant.

Just as zalambdalestes once fearfully crept between dinosaur feet, I too must adopt a circumspect attitude if I am to survive these heavy-footed humans that walk past.

And then, one night, or rather very early one morning, tightly wrapped in my zamarra, at the hour at which it is said that Allah comes to earth to listen to your problems, roughly between four and four thirty a.m., I heard footfall, ever so light, coming down. Impossible thought I, this is someone who ascended long ago, remained up there for an eternity, and is just now timidly returning. The last footsteps that I had heard climbing the stairs, were very heavy ones, a noisy shuffle that took interminably long to reach the top, and for once, I had heard a distinctive thud farther off as if the climber had thrown himself into the air from the last step, ending his life suddenly, without wings nor even faith to sustain him. I could have lent him or her a pair, rehearsed a prayer. It had been during the sunset, at the exact moment that the swollen star bites the horizon, the hour when the evil one displaces himself on the land, going from place to place unhindered and affecting in some manner all who cross his path and others who have never seen him or even suspected his existence. To counteract the danger of this encounter, it is recommended to pray at two-hour intervals all through the night. If this is properly done, you can obtain thirteen rhakas, which cumulated with the nineteen others gives a total of thirty-two. But if you are ill, a few will do. This is not a martyr's religion. Your well being is important to your God.

These steps have the particularity of being open-backed, you can see through them, and if I was lacking the desire to reach out and seize the descending foot from fear of grasping the hoof of the sunset wanderer, returning after several nights spent aloft, never would I have thought that this passing limb might be that of a more elevated being coming down for the first time. Have I not already lived amongst God's gods, those flaming ones who had claimed that our own were nothing else than their pets released on Cyana to relieve themselves, and in turn learned that they too were subjected to the will of even higher beings, somber ones these, and so on as my daughter had made it perfectly clear to me at age seven, four years before turning eleven, when she told me that we had had it all wrong. It's no game of *claire-obscure* had she then said. Have no dread of being dead. You'll actually be ahead. In any event, I most miserably missed the passing deity, certainly the prophet for whom these stairs had been designed, the problem being that the time separating visits of a higher order such as this one is longer than all of recorded history. How to console myself, perhaps invent an excuse? Hadn't I rolled a carpet of the finest red velvet down these stairs, in anticipation of rightfully honoring the one who was to come? Not realizing that all the while, I'd no longer be able to see from beneath who would be on the stairs, however silent the footfall might be.

Zanda. How can I so deify a simple woman? Through giving birth are not women closer to the cosmic forces which bring galaxies together, and certain ones among them even closer to divinities, than any man shall ever be? I'll surely be condemned for such impious analogy. But perhaps I'll be given the occasion to repent only moments before death, and then, will not God take me into his fold, a converted sinner being more precious to he than the most constant of faithful followers? The most perverted simony?

For this very reasoning, proof of premeditation, I'll surely lose my foothold in paradise.

Haven't you understood yet that we are two beggars, she and I, having taken refuge beneath the stairs and that this is merely the transcription of our conversation when we hit the bottle too hard? We drink only zinfandel. Our last ship was named Zinjanthropus. No one is going to be redeemed here, we'll both most surely be damned. Are not we already huddled beneath hell's footstep? Being cast, at once, into inferno and this most unfitting of roles. Together with her, no? Zeugma! She's Zande, originally from the region of Zemio, the geographical heart of Africa. I now know that that's where we should have gone instead of having stayed here, feeding on smoked zander. Taken refuge behind the thorns of a hastily constructed zareba. Butchered a zebu, roasted the hump and discarded the dewlap. Or off to Zipangu, but not here.

Could there be a third party involved? One that we can't see but with whom we form perfect equilibrium, as in the zeroth law of thermodynamics. Chances are zilch to a zillion. At least I'm no longer suffering from zoanthropy. Zoundz! No matter how this sounds, it isn't something done with the zip of a zipper. Life itself would be a formidable zollner illusion; impossible to zonate the universe. Avoid the clutch of zygo dactyl feet. I'm down with zoster.

What friends come calling upon us? Who sees us here? I know that in time it will collapse, this staircase like none other, the whole mile of it, dropping to pinch me. Healthy imago, no idealized parental figure but rather the sexually mature adult insect, crushed and rendering pulp. But for now I'm snug. It's a minor risk, being that I'm often out —other animals try to take my place when I leave — like living in Naples or Los Angeles but only for a couple of centuries and in addition, being mostly absent. You'll agree, living beneath these steps, now that the prophet has passed, has no real value, unless it be in penitence for having missed his passage. Life's end zone is often full of regret. What war shall I wage now? Zooks!

Surprisingly different contrails fill the sky. In the blue, none are straight like the ones we knew. They all form high zigzags, immense hoops. Craft clearly bounce across the upper atmosphere, using the technique of skipping stones across pond surface. I haven't seen or heard anything pass today, neither on the stairs nor in the airs. I've recovered my sight. Woman upon the top step, Zanda? Shall I, in turn, ascend? Not falling in, but rising to love. It could very well lead to a zugzwang situation. Would that it could have been so.

421